Anxious People

FREDRIK BACKMAN

Translated by Neil Smith

MICHAEL JOSEPH
an imprint of
PENGUIN BOOKS

MICHAEL JOSEPH

UK | USA | Canada | Ireland | Australia
India | New Zealand | South Africa

Michael Joseph is part of the Penguin Random House group of companies
whose addresses can be found at global.penguinrandomhouse.com

Published by arrangement with the Salomonsson Agency
Originally published in Sweden as *Folk med Angest* 2019
Published in USA as *Anxious People* by Atria Books 2020
Published in Great Britain by Michael Joseph 2020
001

Printed and bound in Great Britain by Clays Ltd, Elcograf S.p.A.

A CIP catalogue record for this book is available from the British Library

HARDBACK ISBN: 978–0–718–18661–6
OM PAPERBACK: 978–0–718–18662–3

www.greenpenguin.co.uk

Penguin Random House is committed to a
sustainable future for our business, our readers
and our planet. This book is made from Forest
Stewardship Council® certified paper.

Anxious People

*This book is dedicated to the voices in my head,
the most remarkable of my friends.*

And to my wife, who lives with us.

1

A bank robbery. A hostage drama. A stairwell full of police officers on their way to storm an apartment. It was easy to get to this point, much easier than you might think. All it took was one single really bad idea.

This story is about a lot of things, but mostly about idiots. So it needs saying from the outset that it's always very easy to declare that other people are idiots, but only if you forget how idiotically difficult being human is. Especially if you have other people you're trying to be a reasonably good human being for.

Because there's such an unbelievable amount that we're all supposed to be able to cope with these days. You're supposed to have a job, and somewhere to live, and a family, and you're supposed to pay taxes and have clean underwear and remember the password to your damn Wi-Fi. Some of us never manage to get the chaos under control, so our lives simply carry on, the world spinning through space at two million miles an hour while we bounce about on its surface like so many lost socks. Our hearts are bars of soap that we keep losing hold of; the moment we relax, they drift off and fall in love and get broken, all in the wink of an eye. We're not in control. So we learn to pretend, all the time, about our jobs and our marriages and our children and everything else. We pretend we're normal, that we're reasonably well educated, that we understand 'amortization levels' and 'inflation rates'. That we know how sex works. In truth, we know as much about sex as we do about USB leads, and it always takes us four tries to get those little buggers in. (Wrong way round, wrong way round, wrong way round, there! *In!*) We pretend to be good parents when all we really do is provide our kids with food and clothing and tell them off when they put chewing gum they find on the ground in their mouths. We tried keeping tropical fish once and they all died. And we really don't know more about children than tropical fish, so the responsibility frightens the life out of us each morning. We don't have a plan, we just do our best to get through the day, because there'll be another one coming along tomorrow.

Sometimes it hurts, it really hurts, for no other reason than the fact that our skin doesn't feel like it's ours. Sometimes we panic, because the bills need paying and we have to be grown-up and we don't know how, because it's so horribly, desperately easy to fail at being grown-up.

Because everyone loves someone, and anyone who loves someone has had those desperate nights where we lie awake trying to figure out how we can afford to carry on being human beings. Sometimes that makes us do things that seem ridiculous in hindsight, but which felt like the only way out at the time.

One single really bad idea. That's all it takes.

One morning, for instance, a thirty-nine-year-old resident of a not particularly large or noteworthy town left home clutching a pistol, and that was – in hindsight – a really stupid idea. Because this is a story about a hostage drama, but that wasn't the intention. That is to say, it was the intention that it should be a story, but it wasn't the intention that it should be about a hostage drama. It was supposed to be about a bank robbery. But everything got a bit messed up, because sometimes that happens with bank robberies. So the thirty-nine-year-old bank robber fled, but with no escape plan, and the thing about escape plans is just like what the bank robber's mum always said years ago, when the bank robber left the ice cubes and slices of lemon in the kitchen and had to run back: 'If your head isn't up to the job, your legs better be!' (It should be noted that when she died, the bank robber's mum consisted of so much gin and tonic that they didn't dare cremate her because of the risk of explosion, but that doesn't mean she didn't have good advice to offer.) So after the bank robbery that wasn't actually a bank robbery, the police showed up, of course, so the bank robber got scared and ran out, across the street and into the first door that presented itself. It's probably a bit harsh to label the bank robber an idiot simply because of that, but . . . well, it certainly wasn't an act of genius. Because the door led to a stairwell with no other exits, which meant the bank robber's only option was to run up the stairs.

It should be noted that this particular bank robber had the same level of fitness as the average thirty-nine-year-old. Not one of those big-city thirty-nine-year-olds who deal with their midlife crisis by buying ridiculously expensive cycling shorts and swimming caps because they have a black hole in their soul that devours Instagram pictures, more the sort of thirty-nine-year-old whose daily consumption of cheese and carbohydrates was more likely to be classified medically as a cry for help rather than a diet. So by the time the bank robber reached the top floor, all sorts of glands had opened up, causing breathing that sounded like something you usually associate with the sort of secret societies that demand a password through a hatch in the door before they let you in. By this point, any chance of evading the police had dwindled to pretty much nonexistent.

But by chance the robber turned and saw that the door to one of the apartments in the building was open, because that particular apartment happened to be up for sale and was full of prospective buyers looking around. So the bank robber stumbled in, panting and sweaty, holding the pistol in the air, and that was how this story ended up becoming a hostage drama.

And then things went the way they did: the police surrounded the building, reporters showed up, the story made it on to the television news. The whole thing went on for several hours, until the bank robber had to give up. There was no other choice. So all eight people who had been held hostage, seven prospective buyers and one estate agent, were released. A couple of minutes later the police stormed the apartment. But by then it was empty.

No one knew where the bank robber had gone.

That's really all you need to know at this point. Now the story can begin.

2

Ten years ago a man was standing on a bridge. This story isn't about that man, so you don't really need to think about him right now. Well, obviously you can't help thinking about him, it's like saying 'Don't think about biscuits,' and now you're thinking about biscuits.

Don't think about biscuits!

All you need to know is that a man was standing on a bridge ten years ago. Up on the railing, high above the water, at the end of his life. Don't think about that any more now. Think about something nicer. Think about biscuits.

3

It's the day before New Year's Eve in a not particularly large town. A police officer and an estate agent are sitting in an interview room in the police station. The policeman looks barely twenty but is probably older, and the estate agent looks more than forty but is probably younger. The police officer's uniform is too small, the estate agent's jacket slightly too large. The estate agent looks like she'd rather be somewhere else, and, after the past fifteen minutes of conversation, the policeman looks like he wishes the estate agent were somewhere else, too. When the estate agent smiles nervously and opens her mouth to say something, the policeman breathes in and out in a way that makes it hard to tell if he's sighing or trying to clear his nose.

'Just answer the question,' he pleads.

The estate agent nods quickly and blurts out:

'How's tricks?'

'I said, just answer the question!' the policeman repeats, with an expression common in grown men who were disappointed by life at some point in their childhood and have never quite managed to stop feeling that way.

'You asked me what my agency is called!' the estate agent insists, drumming her fingers on the tabletop in a way that makes the policeman feel like throwing objects with sharp corners at her.

'No, I didn't, I asked if the *perpetrator* who held you *hostage* together with –'

'It's called *House Tricks*! Get it? Because when you buy an apartment, you want to buy from someone who knows all the *tricks*, don't you? So when I answer the phone, I say: Hello, you've reached the House Tricks Estate Agency! HOW'S TRICKS?'

Obviously the estate agent has just been through a traumatic experience, has been threatened with a pistol and held hostage, and that sort of thing can make anyone babble. The policeman tries to be patient. He presses his thumbs hard against his eyebrows, as if he hopes they're two buttons and if he keeps them pressed at the same time for ten seconds he'll be able to restore life to its factory settings.

'Okaaay . . . But now I need to ask you a few questions about the apartment and the perpetrator,' he groans.

It has been a difficult day for him, too. The police station is small, resources are tight, but there's nothing wrong with their competence. He tried to explain that over the phone to some boss's boss's boss right after the hostage drama, but naturally it was hopeless. They're going to send some special investigative team from Stockholm to take charge of the whole case. The boss didn't place the emphasis on the words 'investigative team' when he said that, but on '*Stockholm*', as if coming from the capital was itself some sort of superpower. More like a medical condition, the policeman thinks. His thumbs are still pressed to his eyebrows, this is his last chance to show the bosses that he can handle this himself, but how on earth is that going to work if you've only got witnesses like this woman?

'Okeydokey!' the estate agent chirrups, as if that were a real Swedish word.

The policeman looks down at his notes.

'Isn't this an odd day to have a viewing? The day before New Year's Eve?'

The estate agent shakes her head and grins.

'There are no bad days for the HOUSE TRICKS Estate Agency!'

The policeman takes a deep breath, then several more.

'Right. Let's move on: when you saw the perpetrator, what was your first react —'

'Didn't you say you were going to ask about the apartment first? You said "the apartment and the perpetrator," so I thought the apartment would be first —'

'Okay!' the policeman growls.

'Okay!' the estate agent chirrups.

'The *apartment*, then: Are you familiar with its layout?'

'Of course, I'm the estate agent, after all!' the estate agent says, but manages to stop herself adding 'from the HOUSE TRICKS Estate Agency! HOW'S TRICKS?' seeing as the policeman already looks like he wishes the ammunition in his pistol wasn't so easy to trace.

'Can you describe it?'

The estate agent lights up.

'It's a dream! We're talking about a unique opportunity to acquire an exclusive apartment in a quiet area within easy reach of the throbbing heart of the big city. Open plan! Big windows that let in plenty of daylight – !'

The policeman cuts her off.

'I meant, are there closets, hidden storage spaces, anything of that sort?'

'You don't like open-plan apartments? You like walls? There's nothing wrong with walls!' the estate agent replies encouragingly, yet with an undertone that suggests that, in her experience, people who like walls are the same sort of people who like other types of barriers.

'For instance, are there any closets that aren't – ?'

'Did I mention the amount of daylight?'

'Yes.'

'There's scientific research to prove that daylight makes us feel better! Did you know that?'

The policeman looks like he doesn't really want to be forced to think about this. Some people want to decide for themselves how happy they are.

'Can we stick to the point?'

'Okeydokey!'

'Are there any spaces in the apartment that aren't marked on the plans?'

'It's also a really good location for children!'

'What does that have to do with anything?'

'I just wanted to point it out. The location, you know. Really good for children! Actually, well . . . apart from this whole hostage thing today. But apart from that: a brilliant area for kids! And of course you know that children just love police cars!'

The estate agent cheerily spins her arm in the air and imitates the sound of a siren.

'I think that's the sound of an ice-cream van,' the police officer says.

'But you know what I mean,' the estate agent persists.

'I'm going to have to ask you to just answer the question.'

'Sorry. What was the question, again?'

'Exactly how big is the apartment?'

The estate agent smiles in bemusement.

'Don't you want to talk about the bank robber? I thought we were going to talk about the robbery?'

The policeman clenches his teeth so hard that he looks like he's trying to breathe through his toenails.

'Sure. Okay. Tell me about the perpetrator. What was your first reaction when he —'

The estate agent interrupts eagerly. 'The bank robber? Yes! The bank robber ran straight into the apartment in the middle of the viewing, and pointed a pistol at us all! And do you know why?'

'No.'

'Because it's open plan! Otherwise the bank robber would never have been able to aim at all of us *at the same time*!'

The policeman massages his eyebrows.

'Okay, let's try this instead: Are there any good hiding places in the apartment?'

The estate agent blinks so slowly that it looks like she's only just learned how to do it.

'Hiding places?'

The policeman leans his head back and fixes his gaze on the ceiling. His mum always said that policemen are just boys who never bothered to find a new dream. All boys get asked 'What do you want to be when you grow up?' and at some point almost all of them answer 'A policeman!' but most of them grow out of that and come up with something better. For a moment he finds himself wishing he'd done that, too, because then his days might have been less complicated, and possibly also his dealings with his family. It's worth pointing out that his mum has always been proud of him, she was never the one who expressed disapproval at his choice of career. She was a priest, another job that's more than just a way of earning a living, so she understood. It was his dad who never wanted to see his son in uniform. That disappointment may still be weighing the young police officer down, because he looks exhausted when he focuses his gaze on the estate agent again.

'Yes. That's what I've been trying to explain to you: we believe the perpetrator is still in the apartment.'

4

The truth is that when the bank robber gave up, all the hostages – the estate agent and all the prospective buyers – were released at the same time. One police officer was standing guard in the stairwell outside the apartment when they emerged. They closed the door behind themselves, the latch clicked, and then they walked calmly down the stairs, out into the street, got into the waiting police cars, and were driven away. The policeman in the stairwell waited for his colleagues to come up the stairs. A negotiator phoned the bank robber. Shortly after that, the police stormed the apartment, only to discover that it was empty. The door to the balcony was locked, all the windows were closed, and there were no other exits.

You didn't have to be from Stockholm to realize pretty quickly that one of the hostages must have helped the bank robber to escape. Unless the bank robber hadn't escaped at all.

5

Okay. A man was standing on a bridge. Think about that now.

He had written a note and posted it, he had dropped his children off at school, he had climbed up on to the railing and was standing there looking down. Ten years later an unsuccessful bank robber took eight people hostage at a viewing of an apartment that was for sale. If you stand on that bridge, you can see all the way to the balcony of that apartment.

Obviously none of this has anything to do with you. Well, maybe just a little. Because presumably you're a normal, decent person. What would you have done if you'd seen someone standing on the railing of that bridge? There are no right or wrong things to say at a time like that, are there? You would simply have done whatever it took to stop the man from jumping. You don't even know him, but it's an innate instinct, the idea that we can't just let strangers kill themselves.

So you would have tried to talk to him, gain his trust, persuade him not to do it. Because you've probably been depressed yourself, you've had days when you've been in terrible pain in places that don't show up in X-rays, when you can't find the words to explain it even to the people who love you. Deep down, in memories that we might prefer to suppress even from ourselves, a lot of us know that the difference between us and that man on the bridge is smaller than we might wish. Most adults have had a number of really bad moments, and of course not even fairly happy people manage to be happy the whole darn time. So you would have tried to save him. Because it's possible to end your life by mistake, but you have to choose to jump. You have to climb on top of somewhere high and take a step forwards.

You're a decent person. You wouldn't have just watched.

6

The young policeman is feeling his forehead with his fingertips. He has a lump the size of a baby's fist there.

'How did you get that?' the estate agent asks, looking like she'd really prefer to ask *How's tricks?* again.

'I got hit on the head,' the policeman grunts, then looks at his notes and says, 'Did the perpetrator seem used to handling firearms?'

The estate agent smiles in surprise.

'You mean . . . the pistol?'

'Yes. Did he seem nervous, or did it look like he'd handled a pistol plenty of times before?'

The policeman hopes his question will reveal whether or not the estate agent thinks the bank robber might have a military background, for instance. But the estate agent replies breezily: 'Oh, no, I mean, the pistol wasn't real!'

The policeman squints at her, evidently trying to figure out if she's joking or just being naive.

'What makes you say that?'

'It was obviously a toy! I thought everyone had realized that.'

The policeman studies the estate agent for a long time. She's not joking. A hint of sympathy appears in his eyes.

'So you were never . . . frightened?'

The estate agent shakes her head.

'No, no, no. I realized we were never in any real danger, you know. That bank robber could never have harmed anyone!'

The policeman looks at his notes. He realizes that she hasn't understood.

'Would you like something to drink?' he asks kindly.

'No, thank you. You've already asked me that.'

The policeman decides to fetch her a glass of water anyway.

1

In truth, none of the people who were held hostage knows what happened in between the time they were released and the time the police stormed the apartment. The hostages had already got into the cars down in the street and were being driven to the police station as the officers gathered in the stairwell. Then the special negotiator (who had been dispatched from Stockholm by the boss's boss, seeing as people in Stockholm seem to think they're the only ones capable of talking on the phone) called the bank robber in the hope that a peaceful resolution could be reached. But the bank robber didn't answer. Instead a single pistol shot rang out. By the time the police smashed in the door to the apartment it was already too late. When they reached the living room they found themselves trampling through blood.

8

In the staffroom of the police station the young policeman bumps into an older officer. The young man is fetching water, the older man is drinking coffee. Their relationship is complicated, as is often the case between police officers of different generations. At the end of your career you're trying to find a point to it all, and at the start of it you're looking for a purpose.

'Morning!' the older man exclaims.

'Hi,' the younger man says, slightly dismissively.

'I'd offer you some coffee, but I suppose you're still not a coffee drinker?' the old officer says, as if it were some sort of disability.

'No,' the younger man replies, like someone turning down an offer of human flesh.

The older and younger men have little in common when it comes to food and drink, or anything else, for that matter, which is a cause of ongoing conflict whenever they're stuck in the same police car at lunchtime. The older officer's favourite food is a service station hot dog with instant mashed potato, and whenever the staff in the local restaurant try to take his plate away on buffet Fridays, he always snatches it back in horror and exclaims: 'Finished? This is a buffet! You'll know when I'm finished because I'll be lying curled up under the table!' The younger man's favourite food, if you were to ask the older officer, is 'that made-up stuff, algae and seaweed and raw fish, he thinks he's some sort of damn hermit crab'. One likes coffee, the other tea. One looks at his watch while they're working to see if it will soon be lunchtime, the other looks at his watch during lunch to see if he can get back to work soon. The older man thinks the most important thing is for a police officer to do the right thing, the younger thinks it's more important to do things correctly.

'Sure? You can have one of those Frappuccinos or whatever

they're called. I've even bought some of that soy milk, not that I want to know what the heck they milked to get hold of it!' the older man says, chuckling loudly, but glancing anxiously towards the younger man at the same time.

'Mmm,' the younger man murmurs, not bothering to listen.

'Getting on okay with interviewing that damn estate agent?' the older man asks, in a tone that suggests he's joking, to cover up the fact that he's asking out of consideration.

'Fine!' the younger man declares, finding it increasingly difficult to conceal his irritation now, and attempting to move towards the door.

'And you're okay?' the older officer asks.

'Yes, yes, I'm okay,' the younger man groans.

'I just mean after what happened, if you ever need to . . .'

'I'm fine,' the younger man insists.

'Sure?'

'Sure!'

'How's . . . ?' the older man asks, nodding towards the bump on the younger man's forehead.

'Fine, no problem. I've got to go now.'

'Okay. Well. Would you like a hand questioning the estate agent, then?' the older man asks, and tries to smile rather than just stare anxiously at the younger officer's shoes.

'I can manage on my own.'

'I'd be happy to help.'

'No — thanks!'

'Sure?' the older man calls, but gets nothing but a very sure silence in response.

When the younger officer has gone, the older man sits alone in the staffroom drinking his coffee. Older men rarely know what to say to younger men to let them know that they care. It's so hard to find the words when all you really want to say is: 'I can see you're hurting.'

There are red marks on the floor where the younger man was standing. He still has blood on his shoes, but he hasn't noticed yet. The older officer wets a cloth and carefully wipes the floor. His fingers are trembling. Maybe the younger man isn't lying, maybe he really is okay. But the older man definitely isn't, not yet.

9

The younger officer walks back into the interview room and puts the glass of water down on the table. The estate agent looks at him, and thinks he looks like a person who's had his sense of humour amputated. Not that there's anything wrong with that.

'Thanks,' she says hesitantly towards the glass of water she hadn't asked for.

'I need to ask you a few more questions,' the young officer says apologetically, and pulls out a crumpled sheet of paper. It looks like a child's drawing.

The estate agent nods, but doesn't have time to open her mouth before the door opens quietly and the older police officer slips into the room. The estate agent notes that his arms are slightly too long for his body, if he ever spilled his coffee he'd only burn himself below his knees.

'Hello! I just thought I'd see if there was anything I could do to help in here . . . ,' the older officer says.

The younger officer looks up at the ceiling.

'No! Thanks! Like I just told you, I've got everything under control.'

'Right. Okay. I just wanted to offer my help,' the older man tries.

'No, no, for God's . . . No! This is *incredibly* unprofessional! You can't just march in in the middle of an interview!' the younger man snaps.

'Okay, sorry, I just wanted to see how far you'd got,' the older man whispers, embarrassed now, unable to hide his concern.

'I was just about to ask about the drawing!' the younger man snarls, as if he'd been caught smelling of cigarette smoke and insisted that he was only holding it for a friend.

'Ask who?' the older officer wonders.

'The estate agent!' the younger man exclaims, pointing at her.

Sadly this prompts the estate agent to bounce up from her chair at once and thrust her hand out.

'I'm the estate agent! From the HOUSE TRICKS Estate Agency!'

The estate agent pauses and grins, unbelievably pleased with herself.

'Oh, dear God, not again,' the younger police officer mutters as the estate agent takes a deep breath.

'So, HOW'S TRICKS?'

The older officer looks questioningly at the younger officer.

'She's been carrying on like this the whole time,' the younger man says, pressing his thumbs against his eyebrows.

The older police officer squints at the estate agent. He's got into the habit of doing that when he encounters incomprehensible individuals, and a lifetime of almost constant squinting has given the skin under his eyes something of the quality of soft ice cream. The estate agent, who is evidently of the opinion that no one heard her the first time, offers an unwanted explanation: 'Get it? HOUSE TRICKS Estate Agency. HOW'S TRICKS? Get it? Because everyone wants an estate agent who knows the best . . .'

The older officer gets it, he even gives her an appreciative smile, but the younger one aims his forefinger at the estate agent and moves it up and down between her and the chair.

'Sit!' he says, in that tone you only use with children, dogs and estate agents.

The estate agent stops grinning. She sits down clumsily, and looks first at one of the officers, then the other.

'Sorry. This is the first time I've been interviewed by the police. You're not . . . you know . . . you're not going to do that good cop, bad cop thing they do in films, are you? One of you isn't going to go out to get more coffee while the other one assaults me with a phone book and screams "WHERE HAVE YOU HIDDEN THE BODY?"'

The estate agent lets out a nervous laugh. The older police officer smiles but the younger one most definitely doesn't, so the estate agent goes on, even more nervously: 'I mean, I was joking. They don't print phone books any more, do they, so what would you do? Assault me with an iPhone?'

She starts waving her arms about to illustrate assault by phone, and yelling in what the two officers can only assume is the estate agent's imitation of their accents: 'Oh, hell, no, I've ended up liking my ex on Instagram as well! Delete! Delete!'

The younger police officer doesn't look at all amused, which makes the estate agent look less amused. In the meantime, the older officer leans towards the younger officer's notes and asks, as if the estate agent weren't actually in the room: 'So what did she say about the drawing?'

'I didn't get that far before you came in and interrupted!' the younger man snaps.

'What drawing?' the estate agent asks.

'Well, as I was about to say before I was interrupted: we found this drawing in the stairwell, and we think the perpetrator may have dropped it. We'd like you to –,' the younger officer says, but the older officer interrupts him.

'Have you talked to her about the pistol, then?'

'Stop interfering!' the younger man hisses.

This makes the older officer throw his arms up and mutter: 'Okay, okay, sorry I'm here.'

'It wasn't real! The pistol! It was a toy!' the estate agent says quickly.

The older officer looks at her in surprise, then at the younger officer, before whispering in a way that only men of a certain age think is a whisper: 'You . . . you haven't told her?'

'Told me what?' the estate agent wonders.

The younger police officer sighs and folds the drawing, as carefully as if he were actually folding his older colleague's face. Then he looks up at the estate agent.

'Well, I was coming to that . . . You see, after the perpetrator re-leased you and the other hostages, and we'd brought you here to the station . . .'

The older officer interrupts helpfully: 'The perpetrator, the bank robber – he shot himself!'

The younger officer clasps his hands tightly together to stop him-self from strangling the older man. He says something the estate agent doesn't hear: her ears are already full of a monotonous buzzing sound that grows to a roar as shock takes hold of her nervous system. Long afterwards, she will swear that rain was pattering against the window of the room, even though the interview room had no windows. She stares at the policemen with her jaw hanging open.

'So . . . the pistol . . . it was . . . ?' she manages to say.

'It was a real pistol,' the older officer confirms.

'I . . . ,' the estate agent begins, but her mouth is too dry to speak.

'Here! Have some water!' the older officer offers, as if he'd just fetched it for her.

'Thanks . . . I . . . But, if the pistol was real, then we could all . . . we could all have *died*,' she whispers, then gulps at the water in a state of retroactive shock. The older officer nods authoritatively, takes the younger man's notes from him, and starts to make his own additions with a pen.

'Perhaps we should start this interview again?' he says helpfully, which prompts the younger officer to take a short break so he can go out into the corridor and bang his head against the wall.

When the door slams shut the older man jumps. This business with words is tricky when you're older and all you want to say to some-one younger is: 'I can see you're in pain, and that causes me pain.' The younger officer's shoes have left reddish brown marks of dried blood on the floor under his chair. The older man looks at them disconsolately. This was precisely why he didn't want his son to become a policeman.

10

The first person who saw the man on the bridge ten years ago was a teenage boy whose dad wished he would find a new dream. Perhaps the boy could have waited for help, but would you have done that? If your mum was a priest and your dad a policeman, if you'd grown up taking it for granted that you have to help people if you can, and not abandon anyone unless you really have to?

So the teenage boy ran out on to the bridge and shouted to the man, and the man stopped. The teenage boy didn't know what he should do, so he just started . . . talking. Tried to win the man's trust. Get him to take two steps back rather than forwards. The wind was tugging gently at their jackets, there was rain in the air and you could feel the start of winter on your skin, and the boy tried to find the words to say how much there must be to live for, even if it maybe didn't feel that way right now.

The man on the bridge had two children, he told the teenage boy that. Possibly because the boy reminded him of them. The boy pleaded with him, with panic weighing down each word: 'Please, don't jump!'

The man looked at him calmly, almost sympathetically, and replied, 'Do you know what the worst thing about being a parent is? That you're always judged by your worst moments. You can do a million things right, but if you do one single thing wrong you're for ever that parent who was checking his phone in the park when your child was hit in the head by a swing. We don't take our eyes off them for days at a time, but then you read just *one* text message and it's as if all your best moments never happened. No one goes to see a psychologist to talk about all the times they *weren't* hit in the head by a swing as a child. Parents are defined by their mistakes.'

The teenage boy probably didn't really understand what he meant. His hands were shaking as he glanced over the side of the bridge and saw death all the way down. The man smiled weakly at him and took half a step back. Just then, that felt like the whole world.

Then the man explained that he'd had a pretty good job, he'd set up his own relatively successful business, bought a fairly nice apartment. That he'd invested all his savings in shares in a property development company, so that his children could get even better jobs and even nicer apartments, so that they could have the freedom not to have to worry, not have to fall asleep exhausted every night with a pocket calculator in their hands. Because that was a parent's job: to provide shoulders. Shoulders for your children to sit on when they're little so they can see the world, then stand on when they get older so they can reach the clouds, and sometimes lean against whenever they stumble and feel unsure. They trust us, which is a crushing responsibility, because they haven't yet realized that we don't actually know what we're doing. So the man did what we all do: he pretended he knew. When his children started to ask why poo was brown, and what happens after you die, and why polar bears don't eat penguins. Then they got older. Sometimes he managed to forget that for a moment and found himself reaching to hold their hands. They were so embarrassed. Him too. It's hard to explain to a twelve-year-old that when you were little and I walked too fast, you would run to catch up with me and take hold of my hand, and that those were the best moments of my life. Your fingertips in the palm of my hand. Before you knew how many things I'd failed at.

The man pretended – about everything. All the financial experts promised him that shares in the property development company were a safe investment, because everyone knows that property values never go down. And then they did just that.

There was a financial crisis somewhere in the world and a bank in New York went bankrupt, and far away in a small town in a completely different country lived a man who lost everything. He saw the bridge from his study window when he hung up after the phone call with his lawyer. It was early in the morning, still unusually mild for the time of year, but there was rain in the air. The man drove his children to school as if nothing had happened. Pretending. He whispered in their ears that he loved them, and his heart broke when he saw them roll their eyes and sigh. Then he drove towards the water. Stopped the car where you weren't allowed to stop. Left the keys in it. Walked out on to the bridge and climbed up on to the railing.

He told the teenage boy all this, and then, of course, the teenage boy knew that everything was going to be all right. Because if a man standing on a railing takes the time to tell a stranger how much he loves his children, you know he doesn't really want to jump.

And then he jumped.

11

Ten years later, the young police officer is standing in the corridor outside the interview room. His dad is still in there with the estate agent. Of course his mum was right: they should never have worked together, he and his dad, there was bound to be trouble. He didn't listen, because of course he never does. Occasionally, when she was tired or she'd had a couple of glasses of wine, enough to make her forget to hide her emotions, his mum looked at her son and said: 'There are days when I can't help thinking you never really came back from that bridge, love. That you're still trying to save that man on the railing, even though it's as impossible now as it was back then.' Perhaps that's true, he doesn't feel like checking. He still has the same nightmares, ten years on. After Police College, exams, shift after shift, late nights, all his work at the station that's garnered so much praise from everyone but his dad, even more late nights, so much work that he's come to hate not working, unsteady walks home at dawn to the piles of bills in the hall and an empty bed, sleeping pills, alcohol. On nights when everything has been completely unbearable he's gone out running, mile after mile through darkness and cold and silence, his feet drumming against the pavement faster and faster, but never with the intention of getting anywhere, of accomplishing anything. Some men run like hunters, but he ran like their prey. Drained with exhaustion he would finally stagger home, then head off to work and start all over again. Sometimes a few whiskies were enough to get him to sleep, and on good mornings ice-cold showers were enough to wake him up, and in between he did whatever he could to take the edge off the hypersensitivity of his skin, stifle the tears when he felt them in his chest, long before they reached his throat and eyes. But all the while: still those same nightmares. The wind tugging at his jacket, the dull scraping sound as the man's shoes slid off the railing, the boy's scream across the water that neither sounded nor felt like it came from him. He barely heard it anyway, the shock was too great, too overwhelming. It still is.

Today he was the first police officer through the door after the hostages were released and the pistol shot rang out inside the apartment. He was the one who rushed through the living room, over the bloodstained carpet, tore the balcony door open, and stood there staring disconsolately over the railing, because no matter how illogical it might seem to everyone else, his first instinct and greatest fear was: 'He's jumped!' But there was nothing down there, just the reporters and curious locals who were all peering up at him from behind their mobile phones. The bank robber had vanished without a trace, and the policeman was alone up there on the balcony. He could see all the way to the bridge from there. Now he was standing in the corridor of the police station, unable even to make himself wipe the blood from his shoes.

12

The air passes through the older policeman's throat as roughly as a piece of heavy furniture being dragged across an uneven wooden floor. When he'd reached a certain age and weight, he'd noticed himself starting to sound like that, as if older breaths were heavier. He smiles awkwardly at the estate agent.

'My colleague, he . . . He's my son.'

'Ah!' The estate agent nods, as if to say that she's got children, too, or perhaps that she *hasn't* got children but that she'd read about them in a manual during her estate agent's training. Her favourites are the ones with toys in neutral colours, because they match everything.

'My wife said it was a bad idea for us to work together,' the policeman admits.

'I understand,' the estate agent lies.

'She said I'm overprotective. That I'm one of those penguins that squats on top of a stone because I don't want to accept that the egg has gone. She said you can't protect your kids from life, because life gets us all in the end.'

The estate agent considers pretending to understand, but replies honestly instead.

'What did she mean by that?'

The police officer blushes.

'I never wanted . . . Look, it's silly of me to sit here and go on about this to you, but I never wanted my son to join the police. He's too sensitive. He's too . . . good. Do you know what I mean? Ten years ago he ran on to a bridge and tried to talk some sense into a man who was going to jump. He did all he could, *all* he could! But the man jumped anyway. Can you imagine what that does to a person? My son . . . he always wants to rescue everyone. After that, I thought maybe he'd stop wanting to be a policeman, but the opposite happened. He suddenly wanted it more than ever. Because he wants to save people. Even the bad guys.'

The estate agent's breathing has slowed, her chest is rising and falling almost imperceptibly.

'You mean the bank robber?'

The older policeman nods.

'Yes. There was blood everywhere inside the apartment when we got in. My son says the bank robber's going to die unless we find him in time.'

The estate agent can see how much this means to him from the sadness in his eyes. Then he runs his fingers across the tabletop and adds with forced formality, 'I have to remind you that everything you say during this interview is being recorded.'

'Understood,' the estate agent assures him.

'It's important that you understand that. Everything we say here will be included in the file and can be read by any other police officer,' he insists.

'Everyone can read. Definitely understood.'

The older officer carefully unfolds the piece of paper the younger officer left on the table. It's a drawing, produced by a child who is either extremely talented or completely devoid of talent for their age, depending entirely on what that age is. It appears to show three animals.

'Do you recognize this? As I said before, we found it in the stairwell.'

'Sorry,' the estate agent says, looking genuinely sorry.

The policeman forces himself to smile.

'My colleagues reckon it looks like a monkey, a frog and a horse. I think that one looks more like a giraffe than a horse. I mean, it hasn't even got a tail! Giraffes don't have tails, do they? I'm sure it's a giraffe.'

The estate agent takes a deep breath and says what women usually say to men who never seem to think that their lack of knowledge should get in the way of a confident opinion.

'I'm sure you're right.'

In truth, it wasn't the man on the bridge that made the teenage boy want to be a policeman. It was the teenage girl who was standing on the same railing a week later that made him want it. The one who didn't jump.

13

The coffee cup is thrown in anger. Right across the two desks, but the unfathomable ways of centrifugal force mean that it retains most of its contents until it shatters against the henceforth cappuccino-coloured wall.

The two policemen stare at each other, one embarrassed, the other concerned. The older policeman's name is Jim. The younger officer, his son, is Jack. This police station is too small for these two men to be able to avoid each other, so as usual they've ended up on either side of their desks, only half hidden behind their respective computer screens, because these days police work consists of one-tenth actual police work, with the rest of the time devoted to making notes about exactly what you did during the course of that police work.

Jim was born in a generation that regarded computers as magic, Jack in one that has always taken them for granted. When Jim was young, children used to be punished by being sent to their rooms, but these days you have to force children to come out of them. One generation got told off for not being able to sit still, the next gets told off for never moving. So when Jim writes a report he hits every key all the way down very deliberately, then checks the screen at once to make sure it hasn't tricked him, and only then does he press the next key. Because Jim isn't the sort of man who lets himself be tricked. Jack, in turn, types the way young men who've never lived in a world without the Internet do, he can do it blindfolded, stroking the keys so gently that even a forensics expert wouldn't be able to prove that he'd touched them.

The two men drive each other crazy, of course, about the smallest things. When the son is looking for something on the Internet, he calls it 'googling,' but when his dad does the same thing he says: 'I'll look that up on Google.' When they disagree about something, the father says: 'Well, it must be right, because I read it on Google!' and the son exclaims: 'You don't actually read things *on* Google, Dad, you *search* for them there . . .'

It isn't really the fact that his dad doesn't understand how to use technology that drives his son mad, but the fact that he *almost* understands. For instance, Jim still doesn't know how to take a screenshot, so when he wants to take a picture of something on his computer screen, he takes a photograph of the screen with his mobile phone. When he wants to take a picture of something on his mobile, he uses the photocopier. The last really big row between Jim and Jack was when some boss's boss decided that the town's police force should become 'more accessible on social media' (because in Stockholm the police are evidently massively accessible the whole damn time), and asked them to take pictures of each other in the course of an ordinary day at work. So Jim took a photograph of Jack in the police car. While Jack was driving. With a flash.

Now they're seated opposite each other, typing, constantly out of sync with each other. Jim is slow, Jack efficient. Jim tells a story; Jack simply gives a report. Jim deletes and edits and starts again, Jack just types and types as if there were nothing on the planet that could be described in more than one way. In his youth Jim had dreams of becoming a writer. In fact he was still dreaming about that until long into Jack's childhood. Then he started to dream that Jack might become a writer instead. That's an impossible thing for sons to grasp, and a source of shame for fathers to have to admit: that we don't want our children to pursue their own dreams or walk in our footsteps. We want to walk in *their* footsteps while they pursue *our* dreams.

They have pictures of the same woman on their desks. The mother of one of them, the wife of the other. Jim's desk also has a photograph of a young woman, seven years older than Jack, but they don't often talk about her, and she only gets in touch when she needs money. At the start of each winter Jim says hopefully: 'Maybe your sister will come home for Christmas,' and Jack replies: 'Sure, Dad, we'll see.' The son never tells his dad he's being naive. It's an act of love. His dad's shoulders are weighed down with invisible boulders when he says, late each Christmas Eve: 'It's not her fault, Jack, she's . . . ,' and Jack always replies: 'She's ill. I know, Dad. Do you want another beer?'

There are so many things that stand between the older policeman and the younger one now, regardless of how close they live to each other. Because Jack eventually stopped running after his sister – that's the main difference between the brother and the father.

When his daughter was a teenager, Jim used to think that children were like kites, so he held on to the string as tightly as he could, but eventually the wind carried her off anyway. She pulled free and flew off into the sky. It's hard to tell exactly when a person's substance abuse begins, which is why everyone is lying when they say: 'I've got it under control.' Drugs are a sort of dusk that grant us the illusion that we're the ones who decide when the light goes out, but that power never belongs to us. The darkness takes us whenever it likes.

A few years ago Jim found out that Jack had withdrawn all his savings, which he was planning to use to buy an apartment, and used them to pay for his sister's treatment in an exclusive private clinic. Jack drove his sister there. She checked herself out two weeks later, too late for him to get his money back. She didn't get in touch for six months, then she suddenly phoned in the middle of the night as if nothing had happened, and asked if Jack could lend her 'a few thousand'. For a plane ticket home, she said. Jack sent the money, she never came. Her dad is still running about on the ground, trying not to lose sight of the kite way up in the sky, that's the difference between the father and the brother. Next Christmas one of them will say: 'She's . . . ,' and the other will whisper: 'I know, Dad,' then get him another beer.

* * *

Obviously they find ways to argue about beer, too. Jack is one of those young men who is curious about beers that taste of grapefruit and gingerbread and sweets and all sorts of other crap. Jim wants beer that tastes of beer. Sometimes he calls the complicated version 'Stockholm beer', but not too often, naturally, because then his son gets so angry that Jim has to buy his own damn beer for several weeks. He sometimes thinks it's impossible to know if children end up completely different despite the fact that they grew up together, or precisely because of that. He glances over the top of the computer screens and watches his son's fingertips on the keyboard. The little police station in their not especially large town is a fairly quiet place. Not much happens there, they're not used to hostage dramas, or any sort of drama at all, really. So Jim knows that this is Jack's big chance to show the bosses what he can do, what sort of police officer he can be. Before the experts from Stockholm show up.

Jack's frustration is dragging his eyebrows down and restlessness is blowing a gale inside him. He's been teetering on the verge of a furious outburst ever since he was the first officer into the apartment. He's been keeping a lid on it, but after the last interview he marched into the staffroom and exploded: 'One of these witnesses *knows* what happened! Someone knows and is lying to our faces! Don't they understand that a man could be lying hidden somewhere, bleeding to death right now? How the hell can anyone lie to the police while someone's *dying*?'

Jim didn't say a word when Jack sat down at his computer after his outburst. But when the coffee cup hit the wall, it wasn't Jack who threw it. Because even if his son was furious about not being able to save the perpetrator's life, and hated the fact that a group of damn Stockholmers were about to show up and take the investigation away from him, that came nowhere close to the frustration his father felt at not being able to help him.

A long silence follows. First they glare at each other, then down at their keyboards. Eventually Jim manages to say: 'Sorry. I'll clean it up. I just . . . I can understand that this is driving you crazy. I just want you to know that it's driving me crazy . . . too.'

He and Jack have both studied every last inch of the plan of the apartment. There are no hiding places in there, nowhere to go. Jack looks at his dad, then at the remains of the coffee cup behind him, and says quietly: 'He must have had help. We're missing something here.'

Jim stares at the notes from the interviews with the witnesses.

'We can only do our best, son.'

It's easier to talk about work when you haven't quite got the words to talk about the other things in life, but obviously those words apply to both things at the same time. Jack has been thinking about the bridge ever since the hostage drama started, because during his best nights he still dreams that the man didn't jump, that he, Jack, managed to save him. Jim thinks about the same bridge all the time, because during his worst nights he dreams that it was Jack who jumped instead.

'Either one of the witnesses is lying, or they all are. Someone must know where this man is hiding,' Jack repeats mechanically.

Jim sneaks a glance at Jack's two index fingers, tapping the desktop the same way as his mother after a heavy night at the hospital or prison. Too much time has passed for the father to ask his son how he's doing, too much time for the son to be able to explain. The distance between them is too great now.

But when Jim slowly gets up from his chair with the full symphony of a middle-aged man's groans, to wipe the wall and pick up the pieces of the cup he threw, Jack gets quickly to his feet and walks to the staffroom. He comes back with two more cups. Not that Jack drinks coffee, but he understands that it occasionally means something to his father not to have to drink alone.

'I shouldn't have got involved in your interview, son,' Jim says in a low voice.

'It's okay, Dad,' Jack replies.

Neither of them means it. We lie to those we love. They hunch over their keyboards again and type up the final transcripts of all the interviews with the witnesses, reading them through one more time in search of clues.

They're right, both of them. The witnesses aren't telling the truth, not all of it. Not all of them.

Witness Interview
Date: December 30
Name of witness: London

JACK: You'd probably be more comfortable if you sat on the chair instead of the floor.

LONDON: Have you got something wrong with your eyes or something? You can see that the charging cable for my cell phone won't reach the chair.

JACK: And moving the chair is out of the question, obviously.

LONDON: What?

JACK: Nothing.

LONDON: You've got really crap reception in here. Like, one bar . . .

JACK: I'd like you to switch your phone off now so I can ask my questions.

LONDON: I'm not stopping you, am I? Ask away. Are you really a cop? You look too young to be a cop.

JACK: Your name is London, is that correct?

LONDON: 'Correct'. Is that how you talk? You sound like you're doing role-play with someone who gets turned on by accountants.

JACK: I'd appreciate it if you could try to take this seriously. Your name is L-o-n-d-o-n?

LONDON: Yes!

JACK: I have to say, that's an unusual name. Well, maybe not unusual, but interesting. Where's it from?

LONDON: England.

JACK: Yes, I understand that. What I meant was, is there a special reason why you're called that?

LONDON: It's what my parents decided to call me. Have you been smoking something?

JACK: You know what? Let's forget that and just move on.

LONDON: It's not worth getting upset about, is it?

JACK: I'm not upset.

LONDON: Right, because you don't sound at all upset.

JACK: Let's focus on the questions. You work in the bank, is that correct? And you were working at the counter when the perpetrator came in?

LONDON: Perpetrator?

JACK: The bank robber.

LONDON: Yes, that's 'correct'.

JACK: You don't have to do that with your fingers.

LONDON: They're perverted commas. You're writing this down, right, so I want you to use perverted commas when I do that, so anyone reading your notes will get that I'm being ironic. Otherwise anyone reading this is going to think I'm a complete moron!

JACK: They're called inverted commas.

LONDON: Is there an echo in here or something?

JACK: I was just telling you what they're called.

LONDON: I was just telling you what they're called!

JACK: That's not what I sound like.

LONDON: That's not what I sound like!

JACK: I'm going to have to ask you to take this more seriously. Can you tell me about the robbery?

LONDON: Look, it wasn't even a robbery. We're a cashless bank, okay?

JACK: Please, just tell me what happened.

LONDON: Did you put that my name is London? Or have you just put 'witness'? I want you to use my name, in case this ends up online and I get famous.

JACK: This isn't going to end up online.

LONDON: Everything ends up online.

JACK: I'll make sure I use your name.

LONDON: Sick.

JACK: Sorry?

LONDON: 'Sick.' Don't you know what 'sick' means? It means *good*, okay?

JACK: I know what it means. I just didn't hear what you said.

LONDON: I just didn't hear what you saaaid . . .

JACK: How old are you?

LONDON: How old are *you*?

JACK: I'm asking because you seem quite young to be working in a bank.

LONDON: I'm twenty. And I'm, like, only a temp, because no one else wanted to work the day before New Year's Eve. I'm going to study to be a bartender.

JACK: I didn't know you needed to study to do that.

LONDON: It's tougher than being a cop, anyway.

JACK: Of course it is. Can you tell me about the robbery now, please?

LONDON: God, could you be any more annoying? Okay, I'll tell you about the 'robbery' . . .

It was a day completely devoid of weather. During some weeks in winter in the central part of Scandinavia the sky doesn't seem to bother even attempting to impress us, it greets us with the colour of newspaper in a puddle, and dawn leaves behind it a fog as if someone has been setting fire to ghosts. It was, in other words, a bad day for an apartment viewing, because no one wants to live anywhere at all in weather like that. On top of that, it was also the day before New Year's Eve, and what sort of lunatic holds a viewing on a day like that? It was even a bad day for a bank robbery, although, in defence of the weather, that was more the fault of the bank robber.

But if we're being picky, it wasn't by definition even a bank robbery. Which isn't to say that the bank robber didn't fully intend to be a bank robber, because that was very much the intention, it's just that the bank robber failed to pick a bank that contained any cash. Which probably has to be considered one of the main prerequisites for a bank robbery.

But this wasn't necessarily the bank robber's fault. It was society's. Not that society was responsible for the social injustices that led the bank robber on to a path of crime (which society may well in fact be responsible for, but that's completely irrelevant right now), but because in recent years society has turned into a place where nothing is named according to what it is any more. There was a time when a bank was a bank. But now there are evidently 'cashless' banks, banks without any money, which is surely something of a travesty? It's hardly surprising that people get confused and society is going to the dogs when it's full of caffeine-free coffee, gluten-free bread, alcohol-free beer.

So the bank robber who failed to be a bank robber stepped into the bank that was barely a bank, and declared the purpose of the visit fairly clearly with the help of the pistol. But behind the counter sat a twenty-year-old, London, deeply immersed in the sort of social media that dismantles a person's social competence to the extent that when she caught sight of the bank robber she instinctively exclaimed: 'Are you some kind of joke, or what?' (The fact that she didn't phrase her question as 'Is *this* some kind of joke?' but went straight for 'Are *you* a joke?' perhaps says a lot about the younger generation's lack of respect for older bank robbers.) The bank robber shot her a disappointed-dad look, waved the pistol, and pushed over a note which said: 'This is a robbery! Give me 6,500 kronor!'

London's entire face frowned and she snorted: 'Six thousand five hundred? You haven't left off a couple of zeroes? Anyway, this is a cashless bank, and are you really going to try to rob a cashless bank, or what? Are you, like, totally stupid?'

Somewhat taken aback, the bank robber coughed and mumbled something inaudible. London threw her arms out and asked: 'Is that a real pistol? Like, a really real pistol? Because I saw a television show where a guy wasn't found guilty of armed robbery because he didn't use a real pistol!'

By this point in the conversation, the bank robber was starting to feel very old, especially since the twenty-year-old on the other side of the conversation gave the impression that she was around fourteen years old. Which of course she wasn't, but the bank robber was thirty-nine, and had therefore reached an age where there's suddenly very little difference between fourteen and twenty. That's what makes a person feel old.

'*Hello?* Are you going to *answer* me, or what?' London exclaimed impatiently, and obviously it's easy in hindsight to think that this was a somewhat poorly considered thing to shout at a masked bank robber holding a pistol, but if you knew London you'd have known that this wasn't because she was stupid. She was just a miserable person. That was because she didn't have any real friends, not even on social media, and instead spent most of her time getting upset that celebrities she didn't like hadn't had their life together ruined, again. Just before the bank robber came in she had been busy refreshing her browser to find out if two famous actors were going to get divorced or not. She hoped they were, because sometimes it's easier to live with your own anxieties if you know that no one else is happy, either.

The bank robber didn't say anything, though, and had started to feel rather stupid by this point, and was now regretting the whole thing. Robbing a bank had clearly been a breathtakingly stupid idea right from the outset. The bank robber was actually on the point of explaining this to London before apologizing and walking out, and then perhaps everything that happened after that wouldn't have happened at all, but the bank robber didn't get a chance, seeing as London announced instead: 'Look, I'm going to call the cops now!'

That was when the bank robber panicked and ran out of the door.

16

JACK: Is there anything more specific you could tell me about the perpetrator?

LONDON: You mean the bank robber?

JACK: Yes.

LONDON: So why not just say that instead?

JACK: Is there anything more specific you could tell me about the *bank robber*?

LONDON: Like what?

JACK: Do you remember anything about his appearance?

LONDON: God, that's such a superficial question! You've got a really sick binary view of gender, yeah?

JACK: I'm sorry. Can you tell me anything else about 'the person'?

LONDON: You don't have to use perverted commas for that.

JACK: I'm afraid I'm going to have to say that I do. Can you tell me anything about the *bank robber's* appearance? For instance, was the bank robber a short bank robber or a tall bank robber?

LONDON: Look, I don't describe people by their height. That's really excluding. I mean, I'm short, and I know that can give a lot of tall people a complex.

JACK: I'm sorry?

LONDON: Tall people have feelings, too, you know.

JACK: Okay. Fine. Then I can only apologize again. Let me rephrase the question: Did the bank robber look like the sort of bank robber who might have a complex?

LONDON: Why are you rubbing your eyebrows like that? It's really creepy.

JACK: I'm sorry. What was your first impression of the bank robber?

LONDON: Okay. My first 'impression' was that the 'bank robber' seemed to be a complete moron.

JACK: I'll interpret that as suggesting that it's perfectly okay to have a binary attitude to intelligence.

LONDON: What?

JACK: Nothing. On what did you base your assumption that the bank robber was a moron?

LONDON: I was handed a note saying 'Give me six thousand five hundred kronor.' Who the hell would rob a BANK for six and a half thousand? You rob banks to get ten million, something like that. If all you want is six thousand five hundred exactly, there must be some very special reason, mustn't there?

JACK: I have to confess that I hadn't thought of it like that.

LONDON: You should think more, have you ever thought about that?

JACK: I'll do my best. Can I ask you to take a look at this sheet of paper and tell me if you recognize it?

LONDON: This? Looks like a kid's drawing. And what's it supposed to be anyway?

JACK: I think that's a monkey, and a frog and a horse.

LONDON: That's not a horse. That's an elk!

JACK: Do you think? All my colleagues have guessed either a horse or a giraffe.

LONDON: Hang on. I just got a flash in my bud.

JACK: No, stay focused now, London — so you think this is an elk? Hello? Put your phone down and answer the question!

LONDON: *Yes!*

JACK: Sorry?

LONDON: At last! *At last!*

JACK: I don't understand.

LONDON: They *are* getting divorced!

17

The truth? The truth is that the bank robber was an adult. There's nothing more revealing about a bank robber's personality than that. Because the terrible thing about becoming an adult is being forced to realize that absolutely nobody cares about us, we have to deal with everything ourselves now, find out how the whole world works. Work and pay bills, use dental floss and get to meetings on time, stand in line and fill out forms, come to grips with cables and put furniture together, change tyres on the car and charge the phone and switch the coffee machine off and not forget to sign the kids up for swimming lessons. We open our eyes in the morning and life is just waiting to tip a fresh avalanche of 'Don't Forget!'s and 'Remember!'s over us. We don't have time to think or breathe, we just wake up and start digging through the heap, because there will be another one dumped on us tomorrow. We look around occasionally, at our place of work or at parents' meetings or out in the street, and realize with horror that everyone else seems to know exactly what they're doing. We're the only ones who have to pretend. Everyone else can afford stuff and has a handle on other stuff and enough energy to deal with even more stuff. And everyone else's children can swim.

But we weren't ready to become adults. Someone should have stopped us.

The truth? The truth is that just as the bank robber ran out into the street, a police officer happened to be walking past. It would later become apparent that no police officers were yet looking for the bank robber, seeing as the alarm hadn't been raised over the radio, seeing as twenty-year-old London and the staff in the emergency call centre took plenty of time to become mutually offended by one another first. (London reported a bank robbery, which led the call operator to ask

'Where?' which led London to give them the address of the bank, which led the call operator to ask 'Aren't you a cashless bank? Why would anyone want to rob that?' which led London to say 'Exactly,' which led the call operator to ask 'Exactly what?' which led London to snap 'What do you mean "Exactly what"?' which led to the call operator hitting back with 'You were the one who started it!' which led London to yell 'No, *you* were the one who . . . ,' after which the conversation quickly deteriorated.) Later it turned out that the police officer the bank robber saw in the street wasn't actually a police officer but a traffic warden, and if the bank robber hadn't been so stressed and had been paying attention, that would have been obvious and a different escape strategy might have been possible. Which would have made this a much shorter story.

But instead the bank robber rushed through the first available open door, which led to a stairwell, and then there weren't exactly many options except to go up the stairs. On the top floor one of the apartment doors was wide open, so that's where the bank robber went, out of breath and sweating, with the traditional bank robber's ski mask askew so that only one eye could see anything. Only then did the bank robber notice that the hall was full of shoes, and that the apartment was full of people with no shoes on. One of the women in the apartment caught sight of the pistol and started to cry, 'Oh, dear Lord, we're being robbed!' and at the same time the bank robber heard rapid footsteps out in the stairwell and assumed it was a police officer (it wasn't, it was the postman), so in the absence of other alternatives the bank robber shut the door and aimed the pistol in various different directions at random, initially shouting, '*No . . . ! No, this isn't a robbery . . . I just . . . ,*' before quickly thinking better of it and panting, '*Well, maybe it is a robbery! But you're not the victims! It's maybe more like a hostage situation now! And I'm very sorry about that! I'm having quite a complicated day here!*'

The bank robber undeniably had a point. Not that this is in any way a defence of bank robbers, but they can have bad days at work, too. Hand on heart, which of us hasn't wanted to pull a gun after talking to a twenty-year-old?

A few minutes later, the street in front of the building was crawling with journalists and cameras, and after they came the police arrived. The fact that most of the journalists arrived before the police should in no way be interpreted as evidence of their respective professions' competence, but in this instance more as proof that the police had more important things to be getting on with, and that the journalists had more time to read social media, and the unpleasant young woman in the bank that wasn't a bank was evidently able to express herself better on Twitter than over the phone. On social media she announced that she had watched through the large front window of the bank as the robber ran into the building on the other side of the street, whereas the police didn't receive the call until the postman who had seen the bank robber in the stairwell called his wife, who happened to work in a café opposite the police station. She rushed across the road, and only then was the alarm sounded, to the effect that what appeared to be a man armed with what appeared to be a pistol, wearing what appeared to be a ski mask, had rushed into a viewing in one of the apartments and had locked the estate agent and prospective buyers inside. This was how a bank robber failed to rob a bank but instead managed to spark a hostage drama. Life doesn't always turn out the way you expect.

Just as the bank robber closed the door to the apartment, a piece of paper dislodged from a coat pocket fluttered out into the stairwell. It was a child's drawing of a monkey, a frog and an elk.

Not a horse, and definitely not a giraffe. That was important.

Because even if twenty-year-olds can be wrong about a lot of things in life (and those of us who aren't twenty can probably agree that most twenty-year-olds are wrong so often that most of them would have just a one in four chance of answering a yes or no question correctly), this particular twenty-year-old was actually right about one thing: normal bank robbers ask for large amounts and round figures. Anyone can go into a bank and yell: 'Give me ten million or I'll shoot!' But if a person walks in armed and nervous and very specifically asks for exactly six thousand five hundred kronor, there's probably a reason.

Or two.

18

The man on the bridge ten years ago and the bank robber who took people hostage at an apartment viewing aren't connected. They never met each other. The only thing they really have in common is moral hazard. That's a banking term, of course. Someone had to come up with it to describe the way the financial markets work, because the fact that banks are immoral is so obvious to us that simply calling them 'immoral' wasn't enough. We needed a way to describe the fact that it's so unlikely that a bank would ever behave morally that it can only be considered a risk for them even to try. The man on the bridge gave his money to a bank so that they could make 'secure investments', because all investments were secure in those days. Then the man used these secure investments as security against loans, and then he took out new loans to pay off the old ones. 'Everyone does this,' the bank said, and the man thought: 'They're the ones who should know.' Then one day all of a sudden nothing was secure any more. It was called a crisis in the financial markets, a bank crash, even though the only ones who crash are people. The banks are still there, the financial markets have no heart that can be broken, but for the man on the bridge, a whole life's savings had been replaced by a mountain of debt, and no one could explain how that had happened. When the man pointed out that the bank had promised that this was 'entirely risk-free', the bank threw out its arms and said: 'Nothing's entirely risk-free, you should have known what you were getting into, you shouldn't have given us your money.'

So the man went to another bank to borrow money to pay off the debts he now had because the first bank had lost all his savings. He explained to the second bank that he might lose his business otherwise, then his home, and he told them he had two children. The second bank nodded and was very understanding, but a woman who worked there told him: 'You've suffered what we call moral hazard.'

The man didn't understand, so the woman explained that moral hazard is 'when one party in an agreement is protected against the negative consequences of its own actions.' When the man still didn't understand, the woman sighed and said: 'It's when two idiots are sitting on a creaking tree branch, and the one closest to the trunk is holding the saw.' The man was still blinking uncomprehendingly, so the woman raised her eyebrows and explained: 'You're the idiot furthest away from the trunk. The bank's going to saw the branch off to save itself. Because the bank hasn't lost any of its own money here, just yours, because you're the idiot who let them hold the saw.' Then she calmly gathered together the man's papers, handed them back to him, and told him that she wasn't going to authorize a loan.

'But it isn't my fault that they lost all my money!' the man exclaimed.

The woman looked at him coolly and declared: 'Yes, it is. Because you shouldn't have given them your money.'

Ten years later, a bank robber walks into an apartment viewing. The bank robber had never had enough money to hear a woman in a bank talk about moral hazard, but the bank robber had a mother who often said that 'if you want to make God laugh, tell Him your plans,' and sometimes that comes down to the same thing. The bank robber was only seven years old the first time this was said, and that may well be a little early to hear something of that nature, because it pretty much means 'life can go all sorts of different ways, but it will probably go wrong.' Even seven-year-olds understand that. They also understand that if their mum says she doesn't like making plans, and even if she never plans to get drunk, she still ends up getting drunk a little too often for it to be a coincidence. The seven-year-old swore never to start drinking hard liquor and never to become an adult, and managed to keep half that promise.

And moral hazard? The seven-year-old learned about that just before Christmas Eve the same year. When Mum knelt down on the kitchen floor and lurched into a hug that left the seven-year-old's hair peppered with cigarette ash. In a voice shaken by sobs, the seven-year-old's mum said: 'Please don't be upset with me, don't shout at me, it wasn't actually my fault.' The child didn't understand exactly what that meant, but slowly began to realize that whatever it was, it might have some connection to the fact that the child had spent the past month selling Christmas editions of magazines every day after school, and had given all the money to Mum so she could buy food for Christmas. The child looked into the mother's eyes, they were shiny with alcohol and tears, intoxication and self-loathing. She wept as she clung to the child. She whispered: 'You shouldn't have given me the money.' That was the closest the woman ever came to asking her child for forgiveness.

The bank robber often thinks about that to this day. Not about how terrible it was, but about how odd it is that you can't hate your mum. That it still doesn't feel like it was her fault.

They were evicted from their apartment the following February, and the bank robber swore never to become a parent, and, when the bank robber ended up becoming a parent anyway, swore never to become a chaotic parent. The sort who can't cope with being an adult, the sort who can't pay bills and has nowhere to live with their kids.

And God laughed.

The man on the bridge wrote a letter to the woman at the bank who had told him about moral hazard. He wrote down exactly what he wanted her to hear. Then he jumped. The woman at the bank has been carrying that letter in her handbag for ten years. Then she met the bank robber.

19

Jim and Jack were the first police officers to arrive on the scene outside the building. That wasn't so much an indication of their competence as a sign of the size of the town: there just weren't that many police officers around, especially not the day before New Year's Eve.

The journalists were already there, of course. Or maybe they were just locals and curious onlookers, it can be hard to tell these days when everyone films, photographs and documents their whole life as if every individual were their own television channel. They all looked expectantly at Jim and Jack, as if the police ought to know exactly what was going to happen next. They didn't. People simply didn't take other people hostage in this town, and people didn't rob banks here, either, especially now that they'd gone cashless.

'What do you think we should do?' Jack wondered.

'Me? *I* don't know, I really don't, you're the one who usually knows,' Jim replied bluntly.

Jack looked at him despondently.

'I've never been involved in a hostage drama.'

'Me neither, son. But you went on that course, didn't you? That listening thing?'

'*Active listening*,' Jack muttered. Sure enough, he'd been on the course, but precisely what use that might be to him now was hard to imagine.

'Well, didn't that teach you how to talk to hostage takers?' Jim said, nodding encouragingly.

'Sure, but in order to be able to listen, there has to be someone talking. How are we going to contact the bank robber?' Jack said, because they hadn't received any kind of message, no ransom demand. Nothing. Besides, he couldn't help thinking that if that course on active listening was as good as the tutor claimed, then surely Jack ought to have a girlfriend by now.

'I don't know, I really don't,' Jim admitted.

Jack sighed.

'You've been in the police your whole life, Dad, you must have *some* experience of this sort of thing?'

Naturally, Jim did his best to act like he definitely had experience, seeing as dads like teaching their sons things, because the moment we can no longer do that is when they stop being our responsibility and we become theirs. So the father cleared his throat and turned away as he took out his phone. He stood there for a good while, hoping he wasn't going to be asked what he was doing. He was, of course.

'Dad . . . ,' Jack said over his shoulder.

'Mmm,' Jim said.

'Are you seriously googling "what should you do in a hostage situation"?'

'I might be.'

Jack groaned and leaned over with his palms on his knees. He was growling silently to himself because he knew what his bosses, and his bosses' bosses, would say when they called him in the very near future. The worst words Jack knew. 'Perhaps we should call Stockholm and ask for help?' Sure, Jack thought, because how would it look if we actually managed to do something for ourselves in this town? He glanced up at the balcony of the apartment where the bank robber was holed up. Swore under his breath. He just needed a starting point, some way of establishing contact.

'Dad?' he eventually sighed.

'Yes, lad?'

'What does it say on Google?'

Jim read out loud that you have to start by finding out who the hostage taker is. And what he wants.

20

Okay. A bank robber robs a bank. Think about that for a moment.

Obviously, it has nothing to do with you. Just as little as a man jumping off a bridge. Because you're a normal, decent person, so you would never have robbed a bank. There are simply some things that all normal people understand that you must never under any circumstances do. You mustn't tell lies, you mustn't steal, you mustn't kill, and you mustn't throw stones at birds. We all agree on that.

Except maybe swans, because swans can actually be passive-aggressive little bastards. But apart from swans, you mustn't throw stones at birds. And you mustn't tell lies. Unless . . . well, sometimes you have to, of course, like when your children ask: 'Why does it smell like chocolate in here? ARE YOU EATING CHOCOLATE?' But you definitely mustn't steal or kill, we can agree on that.

Well, you mustn't kill people, anyway. And most of the time you mustn't even kill swans, even if they are bastards, but you're allowed to kill animals if they've got horns and are standing in the forest. Or if they're bacon. But you must never kill people.

Well, unless they're Hitler. You're allowed to kill Hitler, if you've got a time machine and an opportunity to do it. Because you must be allowed to kill one person to save several million others and avoid a world war, anyone can understand that. But how many people do you have to save in order to be allowed to kill someone? One million? A hundred and fifty? Two? Just one? None at all? Obviously, you won't have an exact answer to that, because no one does.

Let's take a much simpler example, then: Are you allowed to steal? No, you mustn't steal. We agree on that. Except when you steal someone's heart, because that's romantic. Or if you steal harmonicas from guys who play the harmonica at parties, because that's being public spirited. Or if you steal something small because you really have to. That's probably okay. But does that mean it's okay to steal something a bit bigger? And who decides how much bigger? If you really have to steal, how much do you *have to* have to do it in order for it to be reasonable to steal something really serious? For instance, if you feel that you really have to and that no one will get hurt: Is it okay to rob a bank then?

No, it probably isn't really okay, even then. You're probably right about that. Because you'd never rob a bank, so you haven't got anything in common with this bank robber.

Except fear, possibly. Because maybe you've been really frightened at some time, and so was the bank robber. Possibly because the bank robber had small children and had therefore had a lot of practice being afraid. Perhaps you, too, have children, in which case you'll know that you're frightened the whole time, frightened of not knowing everything and of not having the energy to do everything and of not coping with everything. In the end we actually get so used to the feeling of failure that every time we *don't* disappoint our children it leaves us feeling secretly shocked. It's possible that some children realize this. So every so often they do tiny, tiny things at the most peculiar times, to buoy us up a little. Just enough to stop us from drowning.

So the bank robber left home one morning with that drawing of the frog, the monkey and the elk tucked away in a pocket without realizing it. The girl who had drawn it put it there. The little girl has an older sister, they ought to fight the way sisters are always said to do, but they hardly ever do that. The younger one is allowed to play in the older sister's room without the older one yelling at her. The older one gets to keep the things she cares for most without the younger one breaking them on purpose. Their parents used to whisper, 'We don't deserve them,' when the girls were very small. They were right.

Now, after the divorce, during the weeks when the girls live with one of their parents, they listen to the news in the car in the morning. Their other parent is in the news today, but they don't know that yet, they don't know that one of their parents has become a bank robber.

During the weeks when the girls live with their bank robber parent they go on the bus. They love that. All the way they invent little stories about the strangers in the seats at the front. That man there, he could be a fireman, their parent whispers. And she might be an alien, the youngest daughter says. Then it's the older daughter's turn, and she says *really loudly*: 'That one could be a wanted man who's killed someone and has their head in his backpack, who knows?' Then the women in the seats around them shuffle uncomfortably and the daughters giggle so hard that they almost can't breathe, and their parent has to put on a serious face and pretend that it really isn't funny at all.

They're almost always late to the bus stop, and as they run across the bridge and the bus stops on the other side, the girls always shriek with laughter: 'The elk's coming! The elk's coming!' Because their bank robber parent's legs are very long, out of proportion, and that means you look funny when you run. No one noticed that before the girls appeared, but children notice people's proportions in a different way from adults, possibly because they always see us from below, and that's our worst angle. That's why they make such good bullies, the quick-witted little monsters. They have access to everything that's most vulnerable in us. Even so, they forgive us, the whole time, for almost everything.

And that's the weirdest thing about being someone's parent. Not just a bank robber parent, but any parent: that you are loved in spite of everything that you are. Even astonishingly late in life, people seem incapable of considering that their parents might not be super-smart and really funny and immortal. Perhaps there's a biological reason for that, that up to a certain age a child loves you unconditionally and hopelessly for one single reason: you're theirs. Which is a pretty smart move on biology's part, you have to give it that.

The bank robber parent never uses the girls' real names. That's the sort of thing you never really notice until you belong to someone else, the fact that those of us who give children their names are the least willing to use them. We give those we love nicknames, because love requires a word that belongs to us alone. So the bank robber parent always calls the girls what they used to feel like, kicking in their mother's belly six and eight years ago. One of them always seemed to be jumping about in there, and the other always seemed to be climbing. One frog. One monkey. And an elk that would do anything for them. Even when it's completely stupid. Perhaps you have that in common after all. You probably have someone in your life whom you'd do something stupid for.

But obviously you would still never rob a bank. Of course not.

But perhaps, though, you've been in love? Almost everyone has, after all. And love can make you do quite a lot of ridiculous things. Getting married, for instance. Having children, playing happy families, and having a happy marriage. Or you might think that, anyway. Not happy, perhaps, but plausible. A plausible marriage. Because how happy can anyone really be, all the time? How could there be time for that? Mostly we're just trying to get through the day. You've probably had days like that as well. But when you get through enough of them, one morning you look over your shoulder and realize that you're on your own, the person you were married to turned off somewhere along the way. Maybe you uncover a lie. That's what happened to the bank robber. An infidelity comes to light, and even if no one's actually been unfaithful to you, you can probably appreciate that it's enough to knock a person off balance.

Especially if it wasn't just a fling, but an affair that had been going on for a long time. You haven't only been cheated on, you've also been deceived. It's possible for someone to be unfaithful to you without really thinking about you at all, but an affair requires planning. Perhaps that's what hurts most of all, the millions of tiny clues that you didn't notice. Maybe you'd have been even more crushed if there wasn't even a good explanation. For instance, maybe you could have understood if it was about loneliness or desire, 'You're always at work and we never have any time for each other.' But if the explanation is 'Well, er, if you want me to be really honest, the person I've been unfaithful with is your boss,' then it can be harder to get back up again. Because that means that the reason you've been working so much overtime is also the same reason why you no longer have a marriage. When you get to work on the Monday after the break-up, your boss says: 'Well, er, obviously it's going to be uncomfortable for everyone involved, so . . . perhaps it would be easiest if you no longer worked here.' On Friday you were married and had a job, and on Monday you're homeless and unemployed. What do you do then? Talk to a solicitor? Sue someone?

No.

Because the bank robber was told: 'Don't make a scene now. Don't cause chaos. For the children's sake!' So the bank robber didn't. Didn't want to be that sort of parent, so just moved out of the apartment, left work, eyes closed, jaw clenched. For the children's sake. Perhaps you'd have done the same. Once the frog said she'd heard an adult on the bus say 'love hurts', and the monkey replied that maybe that's why hearts end up jagged when you try to draw them. How do you explain a divorce to them after that? How do you explain about infidelity? How do you avoid turning them into little cynics? Falling in love is magical, after all, romantic, breathtaking . . . but falling in love and love are different. Aren't they? Don't they have to be? Good grief, no one could cope with being newly infatuated, year after year. When you're infatuated you can't think about anything else, you forget about your friends, your work, your lunch. If we were infatuated all the time we'd starve to death. And being in love means being infatuated . . . from time to time. You have to be sensible. The problem is that everything is relative, happiness is based on expectations, and we have the Internet now. A whole world constantly asking us: 'But is *your* life as perfect as this? Well? How about now? Is it as perfect as *this*? If it isn't, change it!'

The truth, of course, is that if people really were as happy as they look on the Internet, they wouldn't spend so much damn time on the Internet, because no one who's having a really good day spends half of it taking pictures of themselves. Anyone can nurture a myth about their life if they have enough manure, so if the grass looks greener on the other side of the fence, that's probably because it's full of shit. Not that that really makes much difference, because now we've learned that every day needs to be special. *Every* day.

Suddenly you find yourselves living alongside each other, not with each other. One of us can go around for a shocking length of time thinking our marriage is good. Or at least no worse than anyone else's. Plausible, anyway. Then it turns out that one of us wants more, just getting through the day isn't enough. One of us worked and went home, worked and went home, worked and went home, trying to be amenable in both places. And then it turns out that the person you were married to and the person you were working for have been extremely amenable to each other the whole time.

'Love one another until death do us part,' isn't that what we said? Isn't that what we promised each other? Or am I remembering wrong? 'Or at least until one of us gets bored.' Maybe that was it?

Now the monkey and the frog and one parent and the boss live in the apartment, and the bank robber parent lives somewhere else. Because the apartment was only in the name of the other parent, and the bank robber parent didn't want to make a fuss. Not cause chaos. But it isn't exactly easy to get a home in this part of town, or any other part of any other town, really, if you haven't got a job or any savings. You don't put your name on the list for public housing when you're married and have children and a life, because it never occurs to you that you might lose all of it in the course of an afternoon. The worst thing a divorce does to a person isn't that it makes all the time you devoted to the relationship feel wasted, but that it steals all the plans you had for the future.

Buying an apartment is completely out of the question, the bank said, because who'd lend money to someone without money? You only lend money to people who don't really need to borrow money. So where are you to live, you might ask. 'You'll have to rent,' the bank said. But in order to rent an apartment in this town when you don't have a job, you have to put down four months' rent as a deposit. A deposit you get back when you move out, for all the good it'll do you then.

Then a letter arrived from a lawyer. It said that the monkey and frog's other parent had decided to apply for sole custody of the children because 'the current situation, in which their other custodian has neither a home nor a job, is untenable. We really must think of the children.' As if there were anything else a parent with no home and no job ever thinks about.

The other parent also sent an email saying: 'You need to pick up your things.' Which means, of course, that you have to pick up the things that the other parent and your old boss, after pinching all the good stuff, have decided are rubbish. They're packed away in the storeroom in the basement, so what do you do? Maybe you go there late one evening, to avoid the shame of bumping into any of the neighbours, and maybe you realize you've got nowhere to take the things. You haven't got anywhere to live, and it's starting to get cold outside, so you stay in the storeroom in the basement.

In another storeroom, belonging to a neighbour who's forgotten to lock up, is a box full of blankets. You borrow them to keep yourself warm. For some reason, beneath the blankets is a toy pistol, so you sleep with that in your hand, thinking that if some crazy burglar breaks in during the night, you can scare them away with it. Then you start to cry, because you realize that you're the crazy burglar.

The next morning you put the blankets back but keep the toy pistol, because you don't know where you're going to sleep that night, and it might come in useful. This goes on for a week. You might not know exactly how it feels, but perhaps you've also had moments when you stare at yourself in the mirror and think: *This wasn't how life was supposed to turn out*. That can terrify a person. So one morning you do something desperate. Well, not *you*, obviously, you'd have done something different, of course. You'd have found out about the law and what your rights were, and you'd have got hold of a lawyer and gone to court. Unless perhaps you wouldn't have done that. Because perhaps you didn't want to make a fuss in front of your daughters, you didn't want to be one of those chaotic parents, so maybe you'd have thought: 'Somehow, if I get the chance, I'll find a way to sort this out without upsetting them.'

So when a small apartment becomes available fairly close to the apartment where the monkey and the frog live, right by the bridge, a sublet from someone already subletting from someone else subletting, at a cost of six thousand five hundred a month, you think: *If I can just manage a month I'll have time to find a job, then they won't be able to take the children away from me, as long as I just have somewhere to live*. So you empty your bank account and sell everything you own and scrape together enough money for a month, and you lie awake thirty nights in a row, wondering how you're going to afford another month. And then suddenly you can't.

You're supposed to go to the authorities in that situation, that's what you're supposed to do. But perhaps you stand outside the door and think about your mum and what the air in there was like when you sat on a wooden bench with a numbered ticket between your fingertips, you remember how much a child can lie for their parents' sake. You can't force your heart to cross the threshold. The stupidest thing people who have everything think about people who have nothing is that it's pride that stops a person from asking for help. That's very rarely the case.

Addicts are good at lying, but never as good as their children. It's their sons and daughters who have to come up with excuses, never too outlandish or incredible, always mundane enough for no one to want to check them. An addict's child's homework never gets eaten by the dog, they just left their backpack at home. Their mum didn't miss parents' evening because she was kidnapped by ninjas, but because she had to work overtime. The child doesn't remember the name of the place she's working, it's only a temporary job. She does her best, Mum does, to support us now that Dad's gone, you know. You soon learn how to phrase things in such a way as to preclude any follow-up questions. You learn that the women in the welfare office can take you away from her if they find out she managed to set fire to your last apartment when she fell asleep with a cigarette in her hand, or if they find out she stole the Christmas ham from the supermarket. So you lie when the security guard comes, you take the ham off her, and confess: 'It was me who took it.' No one calls the police for a child, not when it's Christmas. So they let you go home with your mum, hungry but not alone.

If you had been that sort of child, and then grown up and had children of your own, you would never have subjected them to that. Under no circumstances would they have to learn to become such good liars, you would promise yourself that. So you don't go to the welfare office, because you're scared they'll take the girls away from you. You accept the divorce and don't put up a fight for your apartment or your job, because you don't want the girls to have parents who are at war with each other. You try to sort everything out yourself, and eventually you get a stroke of luck: you manage to find a job, against the odds, not the sort you can live comfortably on, but one you can survive on for a while. That's all you need, a chance. But they tell you your first month's wages are being withheld, meaning that they won't pay you for the first month until you've worked two months, as if the first month weren't the time when you can least afford to go without money.

You go to the bank and ask for a loan so that you can afford to work for no wages, but the bank tells you that isn't possible, because it isn't a permanent job. You could get fired at any time. And then how would they get their money back? Because you haven't got any, have you?! You try to explain that if you had money, you wouldn't need a loan, but the bank can't see the logic in that.

So what do you do? You struggle on. Hope that'll be enough. Then you receive another threatening letter from the lawyer. You don't know what to do, who to turn to, you just don't want to start a fight. You run to the bus in the morning, imagine that the girls can't see how you're feeling, but they do. You can see in their eyes that they want to sell subscriptions to magazines and give you all the money. When you leave them at school you go into an alleyway and sit down on the edge of the pavement and cry because you can't stop thinking: *You shouldn't have loved me.*

All your life you've promised yourself that you'll cope with everything. Not be a chaotic person. Not have to beg for help. But Christmas Eve arrives, and you suffer your way through it in lonely despair, because the girls are going to spend New Year's Day with you. The day before New Year's Eve you put the latest letter from the lawyer who wants to take them away from you in your pocket, next to the letter from your landlord which says that if you don't pay the rent today you're going to be evicted. Right there, right then, it takes next to nothing to knock you off balance. One really bad idea is enough. You find the toy pistol that looks like a real pistol. You make holes in a black woolly hat and pull it down over your face, you go into the bank that wasn't prepared to lend you any money because you didn't have any money, you tell yourself that you're only going to ask for six thousand five hundred kronor for the rent, and that you'll return it as soon as you get paid. *How?* a more ordered mind might be asking, but . . . well . . . perhaps you haven't really thought that far ahead? Perhaps you just think you'll go back, in the same ski mask and with the same pistol, and force them to take the money back? Because all you need is one month. All you need is one single chance to sort everything out.

Later it turns out that that damn toy pistol, the one that looked almost real, looked real because it *was* real. And in a stairwell, a drawing of an elk and a frog and a monkey flutters on the breeze, and in an apartment at the top of the building is a rug soaked in blood.

This wasn't how life was supposed to turn out.

21

It wasn't a bomb.

It was a box of Christmas lights that one of the neighbours had strung up on his balcony. He had actually been thinking of leaving them up over New Year's Day, but then he had a row with his wife, because she thought: 'There are far too many lights, don't you think? And why can't we have ordinary white lights like everyone else? Do we have to have flashing lights, all different colours, so it looks like we've opened a brothel?' He had muttered back: 'What sort of brothels have you been to, if they have flashing lights?' and then she had raised her eyebrows and suddenly demanded to know 'what sort of brothels have *you* been to, seeing as you know exactly what they look like . . . ?' and the row had ended with him going out on to the balcony and pulling the damn lights down. But he couldn't be bothered to carry the box down to the storeroom in the basement, so he left them on the landing outside the door to their apartment. Then he and his wife went off to her parents' to celebrate the New Year and argue about brothels. The box was left outside the door, on the floor below the apartment that ended up being the location for a hostage drama. When the postman at the start of this story came up the stairs and suddenly caught sight of the armed bank robber going into the apartment that was open for viewing, obviously he couldn't get downstairs fast enough and stumbled over the box, accidentally dislodging the wires from the top of it.

It didn't look like a bomb, it really didn't, it looked like an over-turned box of Christmas lights. From a brothel. But in Jim's defence perhaps it looked like it could have been a bomb, especially if you'd mostly only heard about bombs but never actually seen one. Or a brothel. Rather like if you're really frightened of snakes and are sitting on the toilet and feel a slight draught on your backside, and you automatically think, *Snake!* Obviously that's neither logical nor plau-sible, but if phobias were logical and plausible they wouldn't be called phobias. Jim was considerably more frightened of bombs than he was of Christmas lights, and at times like that your brain and eyes can have a bit of a falling-out. That's the point here.

So, the two police officers had been standing down in the street. Jim had looked for advice on Google, and Jack had phoned the owner of the apartment where the hostages were to find out roughly how many people might be in there. The owner turned out to be a mother with a young family in a different town altogether. She said the apartment had been passed down to her and that she hadn't been there in person for a very long time. She didn't have anything to say about the viewing. 'The estate agent's in charge of all that,' she said. Then Jack called the police station and spoke to the woman at the café who was married to the postman who first raised the alarm about the bank robber. Unfor-tunately Jack didn't find out very much more, except for the fact that the bank robber was 'masked and fairly small. Not really small, but normally small! Maybe more normal than small! But what's normal?'

Jack tried to come up with a plan based on this scant information, but didn't get very far because his boss called and – when Jack couldn't immediately present him with a plan – the boss called the boss's boss, and the boss's boss's boss, and all the bosses naturally agreed, predict-ably enough, that it would probably be best if they called Stockholm at once.

All of them apart from Jack, of course, who wanted to deal with something himself for once in his life. He suggested that the bosses should let him and Jim go into the stairwell and up to the apartment to see if they could make contact with the bank robber. The bosses agreed to this, despite their doubts, because Jack was basically the sort of police officer that other police officers trusted. But Jim was standing beside him, and heard as one of the bosses shouted down the line that they should 'take it really damn carefully, and make sure there are no explosives or other crap in the stairwell, because it might not be about the hostages, it could be a terrorist incident! Have you seen anyone carrying any suspicious packages? Anyone with a beard?' Jack wasn't bothered by any of that, because he was young. But Jim was seriously bothered, because he was someone's father.

The lift was out of order, so he and Jack took the stairs, and on the way up they knocked on all the doors to see if any of the neighbours were still in the building. No one was home, because the day before New Year's Eve anyone who had to work was at work, and anyone who didn't have to work had better things to do, and anyone who didn't must have heard the sirens and seen the reporters and police officers from their balconies and gone outside to see what was going on. (Some of them were actually afraid that there was a snake loose in the building, because there'd recently been rumours on the Internet that a snake had been found in a toilet in a block of apartments in the neighbouring town, so that was pretty much the level of probability for hostage dramas in those parts.)

When Jack and Jim reached the floor with the box and the wires, Jim started so hard with fear that he hurt his back (here it should be noted that Jim had recently hurt his back in the same place when he happened to sneeze unexpectedly, but still). He yanked Jack back and hissed: 'BOMB!'

Jack rolled his eyes the way only sons can and said: 'That isn't a bomb.'

'How do you know that?' Jim wondered.

'Bombs don't look like that,' Jack said.

'Maybe that's what whoever made the bomb wants you to think.'

'Dad, pull yourself together, that isn't . . .'

If it had been any other colleague, Jim would probably have let him carry on up the stairs. Maybe that's why some people think it's a bad idea for fathers and sons to work together. Because Jim said instead: 'No, I'm going to call Stockholm.'

Jack never forgave him for that.

* * *

The bosses and the bosses' bosses and whoever was above them in the hierarchy who issued orders immediately issued an order that the two officers should go back down to the street and wait for backup. Obviously it wasn't easy to find backup, even in the big cities, because who the hell robs a bank the day before New Year's Eve? And who the hell takes people hostage at an apartment viewing? 'And who the hell has an apartment viewing the day before . . . ?' as one of the bosses wondered, and they carried on like that for a good while over the radio. Then a specialist negotiator, from Stockholm, called Jack's phone to say that he was going to be taking charge of the entire operation. He was currently in a car, several hours away, but Jack needed to understand very clearly that he was expected merely to 'contain the situation' until the negotiator arrived. The negotiator spoke with an accent that definitely wasn't from Stockholm, but that didn't matter, because if you asked Jim and Jack, being a Stockholmer was more a state of mind than a description of geographic origin. 'Not all idiots are Stockholmers, but all Stockholmers are idiots,' as people often said at the police station. Which was obviously extremely unfair. Because it's possible to stop being an idiot, but you can't stop being a Stockholmer.

After talking to the negotiator Jack was even angrier than he'd been the last time he'd had to speak to a customer service representative at his Internet provider. Jim in turn felt the weight of responsibility for the fact that his son wasn't now going to get the chance to show that he could apprehend the bank robber on his own. All their decisions for the remainder of the day would come to be governed by those feelings.

'Sorry, son, I didn't mean . . . ,' Jim began sheepishly, without knowing how he was going to finish the sentence without admitting that if Jack had been any other man's son, Jim would most likely have agreed that it wasn't a bomb. But you don't take any risks if the son is your own son.

'Not now, Dad!' Jack replied sullenly, because he was talking to their boss's boss on the phone again.

'What do you want me to do?' Jim asked, because he needed to be needed.

'You can start by trying to get hold of people living in the neighbouring apartments, the ones we never reached because of you and your "bomb," so we know that the rest of the building is empty!' Jack snapped.

Jim nodded, crushed. He looked up the phone numbers on Google. First the owner of the apartment on the floor where Jim had seen the bomb. A man replied, said he and his wife were away, and when his wife snapped: 'Who's that?' irritably in the background, the man snapped back: 'It's the brothel!' Jim didn't know what that was supposed to mean, so he asked instead if there was anyone in their apartment. When the man said there wasn't, Jim didn't want to worry him by talking about the bomb, and there was no way the man could possibly have known at that point that if he had just said: 'By the way, that box on the landing contains Christmas lights,' then this whole story would have changed instantly, so the man merely asked instead: 'Was there anything else?' and Jim said: 'No, no, I think that's everything,' then thanked him and hung up.

Then he called the owners of the apartment at the top of the building, the one on the same floor as the apartment where the hostage drama was going on. The owners of that one turned out to be a young couple in their early twenties, they were in the middle of splitting up and had both moved out. 'So the apartment's empty?' Jim asked, relieved. It was, but in two separate conversations Jim still had to listen as two twentysomethings took it for granted that Jim would want to know why they had split up. It turned out that one of them couldn't live with the fact that the other one had such ugly shoes, and the other was turned off by the fact that the first dribbled when he brushed his teeth, and that both of them would rather have a partner who wasn't quite so short. One said that the relationship was doomed because the other liked coriander, so Jim said: 'And you don't?' only to receive the reply: 'I do, but not as much as her!' The other one said they'd started to hate each other after an argument that, as far as Jim could understand, started when they were unable to find a juicer in a colour that reflected them both as individuals but also as a couple. That was when they realized that they couldn't live together another minute longer, and now they hated each other. It struck Jim that today's youngsters had far too much choice, that was the whole problem – if all those modern dating apps had existed when Jim's wife first met him, she would never have ended up becoming his wife. If you're constantly presented with alternatives, you can never make up your mind, Jim thought. How could anyone live with the stress of knowing that while their partner was in the bathroom, they could be swiping right or left and finding their soulmate? A whole generation would end up getting urinary tract infections because they had to keep waiting to pee until the charge on their partner's phone ran out. But obviously Jim said none of this, merely asked one last time: 'So the apartment's empty?'

They each confirmed that it was. All that was left in there was a juicer in the wrong colour. The apartment was going to be put up for sale in the new year, with an estate agency whose name one of them couldn't remember, only that it was 'really corny, kind of dad-joke corny!' The other one confirmed this: 'Whoever named that estate agency has a worse sense of humour than hairdressers! Did you know there's one here called "The Upper Cut"? I mean, like, what?'

Jim hung up then. He thought it was a shame that they'd split up, those two, because they deserved each other.

He went over to Jack and tried to tell him about it, but Jack just said: 'Not now, Dad! Did you get hold of the neighbours?'

Jim nodded.

'Is anyone home?' Jack asked.

Jim shook his head. 'I just wanted to say that . . . ,' he began, but Jack shook his head and resumed his conversation with his boss.

'Not now, Dad!'

So Jim didn't say anything more.

* * *

What then? Well, then everything slid out of control, little by little. The whole hostage drama took several hours, but the negotiator got caught up in traffic and ended up stuck behind the worst multi-vehicle pile-up of the year on the motorway ('Bound to be Stockholmers who set out without proper studded tyres,' Jim declared confidently), so he never arrived. Jim and Jack were left to deal with the situation themselves, which wasn't without its complications, seeing as it took them a long time before they even managed to establish contact with the bank robber (culminating in Jack getting a large bump on his head, which itself is quite a long story). But eventually they managed to get a phone inside the apartment (which is an even longer story), and once the bank robber had released all the hostages and the negotiator made a call to that phone, that was when the pistol shot was heard from inside the apartment.

Several hours later Jack and Jim were still sitting in the police station, interviewing all the witnesses. That didn't help at all, of course, because at least one of them wasn't telling the truth.

22

The truth is that the bank robber went to ridiculous lengths not to point the pistol at anyone inside the apartment, to avoid frightening anyone. But the first person the bank robber *accidentally* happened to aim the pistol at was a woman called Zara. She's somewhere in her fifties, and beautifully dressed in that way that people who have become financially independent on the back of other people's financial dependency often are.

The funny thing is that when the bank robber rushed in, stumbled, and ended up waving the pistol in such a way that Zara found herself staring straight down the barrel of the gun, she didn't even look scared. Another woman in the apartment, on the other hand, let out a shriek of panic: 'Oh, dear Lord, we're being robbed!' Which seemed a little odd, because the bank robber had absolutely no intention that *this* bit should be a robbery. Obviously no one likes being treated in a prejudiced way, and the fact that you just happen to be holding a pistol doesn't automatically make you a robber, and even if you are, you can still be a bank robber without necessarily wanting to rob individuals. So when another woman cried, 'Get your money out, Roger!' to her husband, the bank robber couldn't help feeling rather insulted. Not unreasonably, really. Then a middle-aged man in a checkered shirt who was standing by the window – Roger, evidently – muttered sullenly: 'We haven't got any cash!'

The bank robber was about to protest, but caught sight of the reflection captured in the balcony window. A figure with a masked face armed with a pistol, and the other people in the room. One of them was a very old woman. Another was pregnant. A third looked like she was about to burst into tears. They were all staring at the pistol, eyes wild with fear, no one's wilder than the eyes staring out through the holes in the ski mask in the reflection. Then the bank robber reached a crushing realization: *They're not the captives here. I am.*

The only person who didn't look remotely scared was Zara. That's when they heard the sound of the first police sirens from down in the street.

23

Witness Interview
Date: December 30
Name of witness: Zara

JIM: Hello! My name's Jim!

ZARA: Yes, yes, fine. Get on with it.

JIM: So, I'm here to record your version of what happened. Tell me about it in your own words.

ZARA: Who else's words would I use?

JIM: Well, yes, quite. Just a figure of speech, I suppose. But first I'd like to make you aware that everything you say here is being recorded. And you can have a lawyer present, if you'd like one.

ZARA: Why would I want one?

JIM: I just wanted you to be aware of that. My bosses say that their bosses say it's important that everything's done properly. We're going to be getting a team of special investigators from Stockholm who are going to take over this investigation. My son's very angry about that, he's also a police officer, you see. So I just wanted to let you know that bit about having a lawyer present.

ZARA: Listen, I'll pay for a lawyer if *I* ever threaten anyone with a pistol. Not when I'm the one being threatened.

JIM: I understand. I certainly didn't mean to be impertinent, certainly not. I realize you've had a difficult day, obviously I realize that. You just need to answer all my questions as honestly as you can. Would you like coffee?

ZARA: Is that what you call it? I saw what came out of that machine out there, and I wouldn't drink that if you and I were the last people on the planet and you promised me it was poison.

JIM: I'm not sure if that's more of an insult to me or the coffee.

ZARA: You said you wanted me to answer your questions honestly.

JIM: Yes, I suppose I did, didn't I? Well, can I start by asking why you were in the apartment?

ZARA: What a stupid question. Were you the one standing in the stairwell when we were released?

JIM: Yes, that was me.

ZARA: So you were the first one into the apartment after we left? And you still managed to lose the bank robber?

JIM: I wasn't actually first in. I waited for Jack, my colleague. You probably met him earlier. He was the first man into the apartment.

ZARA: You policemen all look alike, did you know that?

JIM: Jack's my son. Maybe that's why.

ZARA: Jim and Jack?

JIM: Yes. Like Jim Beam and Jack Daniel's.

ZARA: Is that supposed to be funny?

JIM: No, no. My wife's never found that funny, either.

ZARA: So you're married, then? Well done you.

JIM: Yes, perhaps that isn't entirely relevant right now. Can you give me a short explanation of why you were at the viewing of the apartment?

ZARA: It was an apartment viewing. Is that phrase too hard to understand?

JIM: So you were there to look at the apartment?

ZARA: You're about as sharp as a wet box of cornflakes, aren't you?

JIM: Does that mean yes?

ZARA: It means what it means.

JIM: What I mean is, were you planning to *buy* the apartment?

ZARA: Are you an estate agent or a policeman?

JIM: I just mean that it would be easy to assume that

	you might be a little too well-off to be interested in that apartment.
ZARA:	Oh, it would, would it?
JIM:	Well, what I mean is that my colleagues and I might think that. One of them, anyway. My son, I mean. Based on some of the witness statements, I mean. You seem comfortably-off, that's what I mean. And at first glance this apartment doesn't look like the sort of thing that someone like you would want to buy.
ZARA:	Listen, the problem with the middle class is that you think someone can be too rich to buy things. But that's not true. You can only be too poor.
JIM:	Well, perhaps we should move on. By the way, have I spelt your surname right here?
ZARA:	No.
JIM:	No?
ZARA:	But there's a perfectly logical reason why you think it's spelt that way.
JIM:	Oh?
ZARA:	It's because of the simple fact that you're an idiot.
JIM:	I'm sorry. Can you spell it out for me?
ZARA:	I-d-i-o-t.
JIM:	I meant your name?
ZARA:	We'd be here all night, and some of us actually have important jobs to do, so why don't I summarize things for you? A lunatic with a gun held me and a group of poor, less well-off people hostage for half a day, you and your colleagues surrounded the building, and the whole thing was on television, but you still managed to lose the bank robber. Right now you could have prioritized being out there trying to find the aforementioned bank robber, but instead you're sitting here sweating because you've never seen a surname with more than three consonants in it before. Your bosses couldn't make my taxes disappear faster if I'd given them matches.

JIM: I understand that you're upset.

ZARA: That's very clever of you.

JIM: I just meant that you're in shock. I mean, no
          one expects to be threatened with a pistol when
          they go to view an apartment, do they? The papers
          may keep saying that the property market's tough
          these days, but taking hostages is probably going
          a *bit* far. I mean, it says in the papers one day
          that it's a 'buyer's market', then the next that
          it's a 'seller's market', but in the end surely
          it's always just the damn banks' market? Don't you
          think?

ZARA: Is that supposed to be a joke?

JIM: No, no, it's supposed to be small talk. I just
          mean that the way society looks right now, the
          bank robber would have had considerably fewer
          police resources looking for him if he'd actually
          succeeded in robbing that bank than if he, as
          was actually the case, took all of you hostage.
          I mean, everyone hates banks. It's like people
          say: 'Sometimes it's hard to know who the biggest
          crooks are, people who rob banks, or the people
          who run the banks.'

ZARA: Do people say that?

JIM: Yes. I think so. They do, don't they? I just mean,
          I read in the paper yesterday about how much
          those bank bosses earn. They live in houses the
          size of palaces worth fifty million while ordinary
          people can barely manage to make their mortgage
          payments.

ZARA: Can I ask you a question?

JIM: Of course.

ZARA: Why is it that people like you always think
          successful people should be punished for their
          success?

JIM: What?

ZARA: Do you do some sort of advanced conspiracy role-
          play at Police College where you're tricked into

thinking that police officers get the same salary as bank bosses, or were you all just not capable of doing a bit of basic mathematics?

JIM: Yes, well. I mean, no.

ZARA: Or do you just think the world owes you something?

JIM: It's just struck me, I never asked what you do for a living.

ZARA: I run a bank.

24

The truth is that Zara, who appears to be a little more than fifty years old, but exactly how much no one has ever dared ask, was never interested in buying the apartment. Not because she couldn't afford it, of course, she could probably have bought it with the spare change she found between the cushions on the sofa in her own apartment. (Zara regarded coins as disgusting little havens of bacteria which have probably been touched by God knows how many middle-class fingers, and she'd rather have burned her sofa cushions than pick one up, so let's put it like this: she could definitely have bought that apartment for the cost of her sofa.) So she went to the viewing with her nose already wrinkled, wearing diamond earrings large enough to knock out a medium-sized child, if that turned out to be necessary. But not even that, if you looked at her really closely, could hide the lurching grief inside her.

The first thing you have to understand is that Zara has recently been seeing a psychologist, because Zara has the sort of career which, if you do it for long enough, sometimes means you have to seek professional help to get instructions on what you can do with your life beyond having a career. Her first meeting with the psychologist didn't go terribly well. Zara began by picking up a framed photograph from the desk and asking: 'Who's that?'

The psychologist replied: 'My mum.'

Zara asked: 'Do you get on well with her?'

The psychologist replied: 'She passed away recently.'

Zara asked: 'And what was your relationship like before that?'

The psychologist noted that a more normal response would have been to offer condolences on her death, but tried to maintain a neutral expression and said: 'We're not here to talk about me.'

To which Zara replied: 'If I'm going to leave my car with a me-chanic, first I want to know if her own car is a worthless heap of junk.'

The psychologist took a deep breath and said: 'I can understand that. So let me just say that my mum and I had a very good relation-ship. Is that better?'

Zara nodded sceptically and asked: 'Have any of your patients ever committed suicide?'

The psychologist's chest tightened; she replied: 'No.'

Zara shrugged her shoulders and added: 'As far as you're aware.'

That was a fairly cruel thing to say to a psychologist. The psych-ologist, however, recovered quickly enough to say: 'I only completed my training relatively recently. I haven't had that many patients, but I do know they are all still alive. Why are you asking these questions?'

Zara looked at the only picture on the walls of the psychologist's office, pursed her lips thoughtfully, and said, with surprising honesty: 'I want to know if you can help me.'

The psychologist picked up a pen, smiled a practiced smile, and said: 'With what?'

Zara replied that she was having 'trouble sleeping'. She had been prescribed sleeping pills by her doctor, but now her doctor was refus-ing to prescribe more unless she spoke to a psychologist first. 'So here I am,' Zara declared, and tapped her watch, as if she were the one being paid by the hour rather than the reverse.

The psychologist asked: 'Do you think your trouble sleeping is related to your work? You said in your phone call that you run a bank. That sounds like it could be quite a stressful, high-pressure job.'

Zara replied: 'Not really.'

The psychologist sighed and asked: 'What are you hoping to ac-complish during our meetings?'

Zara countered at once with a question of her own: 'Will this be psychiatry or psychology?'

The psychologist asked: 'What do you think the difference is?'

Zara replied: 'You need psychology if you think you're a dolphin. You need psychiatry if you've killed all the dolphins.'

The psychologist looked uncomfortable. The next time they met she wasn't wearing her dolphin brooch.

During their second session Zara asked, somewhat out of the blue: 'How would you explain panic attacks?'

The psychologist lit up the way only psychologists can do at that question: 'They're hard to define. But according to most experts, panic attacks are the experience of –'

Zara interrupted: 'No, I want to know how *you* would explain them!'

The psychologist shuffled uncomfortably on her chair and pondered various different answers. Eventually she said: 'I'd say that a panic attack is when psychological pain becomes so strong that it manifests itself physically. The anxiety becomes so acute that the brain can't . . . well, in the absence of any better words, I'd say that the brain doesn't have sufficient bandwidth to process all the information. The firewall collapses, so to speak. And anxiety overwhelms us.'

'You're not very good at your job,' Zara replied drily.

'In what sense?'

'I already know more about you than you know about me.'

'Really?'

'Your parents worked with computers. Programmers, probably.'

'How . . . how on earth . . . how did you know *that*?'

'Has it been hard to deal with the shame of that? The fact that they did jobs that had a tangible application in the real world, whereas you work with . . .'

Zara fell silent abruptly and seemed to be searching for the right words. So the psychologist, somewhat affronted, filled in: '. . . feelings? I work with feelings.'

'I was going to say "fripperies". But okay, let's say "feelings", if that makes you feel better.'

'My dad's a programmer. My mum was a systems analyst. How did you know?'

Zara groaned as if she were trying to teach a toaster to read.

'Does it matter?'

'Yes!'

Zara groaned at the toaster again.

'When I asked you to explain panic attacks in your own words, not with the definition you learned during your training, you used the words "bandwidth", "process" and "firewall". Words that don't fit easily into ordinary vocabulary usually come from their parents. If they had a good relationship with them.'

The psychologist tried to regain the initiative in the conversation by asking: 'Is this why you're good at your job at the bank? Because you can read people?'

Zara stretched her back like a bored cat.

'Sweetie, you aren't that hard to read. People like you are never as complicated as you'd like to be, especially not if you've been to university. Your generation don't want to study a subject, you just want to study yourselves.'

The psychologist looked ever so slightly offended. Possibly more than ever so slightly.

'We're here to talk about *you*, Zara. What are you hoping to get out of this?'

'Sleeping pills, like I said before. Ideally some that will go with red wine.'

'I can't prescribe sleeping pills. Only your doctor can do that.'

'So what am I doing here, then?' Zara asked.

'You're the best person to answer that,' the psychologist replied.

That was the level on which their relationship began. Things went downhill from there. But it's worth saying at once that it wasn't at all difficult for the psychologist to make a diagnosis of this new patient: Zara was suffering from loneliness. But instead of saying that (the psychologist hadn't burdened herself with more than half a decade's worth of student debt just to learn to say what she thought), the psychologist explained that Zara was exhibiting signs that she was suffering from 'nervous exhaustion'.

Zara didn't look up from the newsfeed on her phone when she replied: 'Yes, well, I'm exhausted because I can't sleep, so just get me some pills!'

The psychologist didn't want to do that. Instead she started to ask questions, with the intention of helping Zara to see her own anxieties in a broader context. One of them was: 'Are you worried about the survival of the planet?'

Zara replied: 'Not really.'

The psychologist smiled warmly.

'Let me put it like this: What do you think the biggest problem with the world is?'

Zara nodded quickly, and replied as if the answer were obvious: 'Poor people.'

The psychologist corrected her in a friendly way: 'You mean . . . *poverty*.'

Zara shrugged. 'Sure. If that feels better for you.'

When they parted, Zara didn't shake hands. On her way out she moved a photograph on the psychologist's bookcase and re-arranged three books. Psychologists aren't supposed to have favourite patients, but if this psychologist had one, it definitely would not have been Zara.

It wasn't until their third session that the psychologist realized how unwell Zara was. It was just after Zara had explained that 'democracy as a system is doomed, because idiots will believe anything as long as the story's good enough.' The psychologist did her best to ignore that, and asked Zara instead about her childhood and work, wondering repeatedly how Zara 'feels'. *How do you feel when that happens? How does talking about this make you feel? How do you feel when you think about how you feel, does that feel difficult?* So in the end Zara did feel something.

They had been talking about something else for a long while, and suddenly Zara seemed to be looking deep inside her, and when she spoke she whispered the words, as if her voice were no longer her own.

'I've got cancer.'

The silence in the room was so extreme that you could hear both women's heartbeats. The fingers falling flat on the notepad, the breathing that grew shallower, lungs filled no more than a third with each breath, terrified of making a noise.

'I'm truly very sorry indeed to hear that,' the psychologist eventually said, her voice trembling, and with carefully practised dignity.

'I'm sorry, too. Depressed, actually,' Zara said, and wiped her eyes.

'What . . . what sort of cancer?' the psychologist asked.

'Does it matter?' Zara whispered.

'No. No, of course not. I'm sorry. That was insensitive of me.'

Zara looked out of the window, not really seeing anything, for so long that the light outside seemed to have time to change. From morning to midday. Then she raised her chin slightly and said: 'You don't have to apologize. It's made-up cancer.'

'S . . . sorry?'

'I haven't got cancer. I was lying. But that's what I was saying: democracy doesn't work!'

And that was when the psychologist realized what a very unwell person Zara was.

'That's a . . . an astonishingly insensitive thing to joke about,' she managed to say.

Zara raised her eyebrows.

'So it would have been better if I had cancer?'

'No! What? Absolutely not, but –'

'Surely it's better to joke about it than to actually have cancer? Or would you rather I had cancer?'

The psychologist's neck flushed red with indignation.

'But . . . no! Of course I don't wish you had cancer!'

Zara clasped her hands together in her lap and said in a grave tone, 'But that's how I'm *feeling*.'

The psychologist had trouble sleeping that night. Zara sometimes has that effect on people. The next time Zara visited her office the psychologist had removed the photograph of her mother from her desk, and during that session Zara actually considered telling the truth about the cause of her sleeping problems. She had a letter in her bag that explained everything, and if she had only shown it then, everything that happened after that might have been different. But instead she just sat for a long time staring at the picture on the wall. It was of a woman looking out across an endless sea, toward the horizon. The psychologist moistened her lips and asked gently: 'What are you thinking when you look at that picture?'

'I'm thinking that if I had to choose just one picture to have on a wall, it wouldn't be that one.'

The psychologist smiled tightly.

'I usually ask my patients what they think about the woman in the picture. Who is she? Is she happy? What do you think?'

Zara's shoulders bounced nonchalantly.

'I don't know what happiness is for her.'

The psychologist said nothing for a while before admitting: 'I've never heard that answer before.'

Zara snorted.

'That's because you ask the question as if there's only one type of happiness. But happiness is like money.'

The psychologist smiled with the superiority that only someone who thinks of themselves as being a very deep person can.

'That sounds superficial.'

Zara groaned like a teenager trying to explain anything to anyone who isn't a teenager.

'I didn't say that money was happiness. I said happiness is *like* money. A made-up value that represents something we can't weigh or measure.'

The psychologist's voice wavered, just for a moment.

'Well . . . yes, maybe. But we can measure and evaluate the cost of depression. And we know that it's very common for people suffering from depression to be afraid of feeling happy. Because even depression can be a sort of secure bubble, it can make you start to think, *If I'm not unhappy, if I'm not angry – who am I then?*'

Zara wrinkled her nose.

'Do you believe that?'

'Yes.'

'That's because people like you always look at people who are wealthier than you are and say: "Yes, they may be richer, but are they *happy*?" As if that was the meaning of life for anyone but a complete idiot, just going around being happy all the time.'

The psychologist noted something down, then asked, still looking down at her notepad: 'What is the meaning, then? In your opinion?'

Zara's reply was the response of a person who's spent many years thinking about this. Someone who has decided it was more important for her to do an important job than live a happy life.

'Having a purpose. A goal. A direction. And do you want to know the truth? The truth is that far more people would rather be rich than happy.'

The psychologist smiled again.

'Says the bank director to the psychologist.'

Zara snorted again.

'Remind me again how much you get paid per hour? Can I come here for free if it makes me happy?'

The psychologist let out a laugh, an involuntary laugh, on the brink of unprofessional. It surprised her so much that she blushed. She made a feeble attempt to pull herself together, and said: 'No. But perhaps I'd let you come here for free if it made *me* happy.'

Then Zara suddenly let out a laugh, not consciously, but as if the sound just slipped out of her. It had been a while since that last happened.

They sat in silence for a long while after that, somewhat awkwardly, until Zara finally nodded toward the woman on the wall.

'What do you think she's doing?'

The psychologist looked at the picture and blinked slowly.

'The same as everyone else. Searching.'

'What for?'

The psychologist's shoulders moved up one inch, then down two.

'For something to cling on to. Something to fight for. Something to look forward to.'

Zara took her eyes from the picture and looked past the psychologist, out of the window.

'What if she's thinking of committing suicide, then?'

The psychologist didn't look away from the picture, just smiled and gave away none of the feelings that were raging inside her. It takes years of training and two parents you love and never want to worry to master that facial expression.

'Why do you think that's what she's thinking?'

'Don't all intelligent people think about that, some time or other?'

At first the psychologist was going to reply with some practised phrase she had learned during her training, but she was well aware that wouldn't help. So she replied honestly instead: 'Yes. Maybe. What do you think stops us?'

Zara leaned forward and moved two pens on the desk so they were lying parallel. Then she said: 'Fear of heights.'

There isn't a person on this planet who could have said there and then with any certainty if she was joking or not. The psychologist considered her next question for a long time.

'Can I ask, Zara – do you have any hobbies?'

'Hobbies?' Zara repeated, but not in an entirely condescending way.

The psychologist elaborated: 'Yes. Are you involved in any charities, for instance?'

Zara shook her head silently. The psychologist thought at first that it was a compliment that she didn't just fire back with an insult, but the look in Zara's eyes made her hesitate, as if the question had toppled and broken something inside her.

'Are you okay? Did I say something wrong?' the psychologist asked anxiously, but Zara had already looked at the time, stood up, and was now walking to the door. The psychologist, who hadn't been a psychologist long enough not to be struck by panic at the thought of losing a patient, found herself saying something quite remarkably unprofessional: 'Don't do anything silly, now!'

Zara stopped at the door, surprised.

'Such as what?'

The psychologist didn't know what to say, so she smiled awkwardly and said: 'Well, don't do anything silly . . . before you've paid my bill.'

Zara let out a sudden laugh. The psychologist joined in. It was harder to identify the extent to which that was also unprofessional.

While Zara was standing in the lift, the psychologist sat in her office staring at the woman in the painting, surrounded by sky. Zara was the first person who had ever suggested that the woman might be thinking of ending her life, no one else had looked at it like that.

The psychologist herself always felt that the woman was gazing off towards the horizon in a way that can only have two explanations: longing or fear. That was why she had painted the picture, as a reminder to herself. It was the sort of subject psychologists love, because you can look at it for ages without noticing the most obvious thing. The fact that the woman is standing on a bridge.

25

JIM: I feel stupid now.

ZARA: I don't suppose that's a new feeling for you.

JIM: If I'd known you ran a bank, obviously I wouldn't
        have said that. Well, I mean, I shouldn't have said
        it anyway. I'm not really sure what to say now.

ZARA: In that case, perhaps I can just leave?

JIM: No, hold on. Look, this is all a bit embarrass-
        ing. My wife has often told me that I should just
        keep my mouth shut. I'll stick to my questions
        from now on, okay?

ZARA: Let's give it a try.

JIM: Can you describe the robber? Anything at all that
        you can remember about him, anything you think
        could be helpful to our investigation.

ZARA: You already seem to know the most important thing.

JIM: And that is?

ZARA: You said 'him', so you evidently know he was a
        man. That explains a lot.

JIM: I have a feeling I'm likely to regret asking
        this, but why?

ZARA: You lot can't even piss without missing the tar-
        get. So obviously things are going to go wrong if
        you get hold of a pistol.

JIM: Can I interpret that as meaning you don't remem-
        ber any details about his appearance?

ZARA: If someone's wearing a mask and pointing a pistol
        at you, a psychologist would probably compare the
        trauma to almost being run down by a truck: you'd
        be unlikely to remember the number on the licence
        plate.

JIM: I have to say, that's a very insightful observation.

ZARA:	That's a relief, because what you think really matters to me. Can I go now?
JIM:	Not yet, I'm afraid. Do you recognize this drawing?
ZARA:	Is that what it is? It looks like someone's knocked over a urine sample.
JIM:	I'll interpret that as a no to the question of whether or not you recognize the picture.
ZARA:	Very clever of you.
JIM:	Where in the apartment were you when the bank robber came in?
ZARA:	By the balcony door.
JIM:	And where were you during the rest of the hostage drama?
ZARA:	What difference does that make?
JIM:	Quite a lot of difference.
ZARA:	I can't imagine why.
JIM:	Look, you're not a suspect. Not yet, anyway.
ZARA:	Sorry?
JIM:	Well, look. What I'm trying to get you to understand is that you need to try to understand that my colleague is convinced that one of the hostages helped the bank robber to escape. And it seems odd that you were there at all, to put it bluntly. To start with, you had no reason to want to buy the apartment. And you don't appear to have been frightened when the bank robber aimed his pistol at you.
ZARA:	So now you suspect that *I* helped the bank robber to escape?
JIM:	No. No, not at all. Look, you're not a suspect at all. Well, not yet, anyway. I mean, you're not a suspect at all! But my colleague thinks it all seems a bit odd.
ZARA:	Really? Do you know what I think your colleague seems like?
JIM:	Can you tell me what happened in the apartment, please? So I can record it? That's my job here.

ZARA: Sure.

JIM: Great. How many prospective buyers were there in the apartment?

ZARA: Define 'prospective buyers'.

JIM: I mean: How many people were there who wanted to buy the apartment?

ZARA: Five.

JIM: Five?

ZARA: Two couples. One woman.

JIM: Plus you and the estate agent. So seven hostages in total?

ZARA: Five plus two is seven, yes. You're very smart.

JIM: But there were eight hostages?

ZARA: You haven't counted the rabbit.

JIM: The rabbit?

ZARA: You heard.

JIM: What rabbit?

ZARA: Do you want me to tell you what happened or not?

JIM: Sorry.

ZARA: Do you seriously think one of the hostages helped the bank robber to escape?

JIM: You don't think so?

ZARA: No.

JIM: Why not?

ZARA: They were all idiots.

JIM: And the bank robber?

ZARA: What about the bank robber?

JIM: Do you think he shot himself intentionally or by accident?

ZARA: What are you talking about?

JIM: We heard a pistol shot from the apartment, after you were released. When we got inside the apartment the floor was covered in blood.

ZARA: Blood? Where?

JIM: On the carpet and floor in the living room.

ZARA: Oh. Nowhere else?

JIM: No.

ZARA: Okay.

JIM: Sorry?

ZARA: Excuse me?

JIM: When you said 'okay', it sounded as if you were about to say something more.

ZARA: Definitely not.

JIM: Sorry. Well, my colleague is convinced it was there in the living room that he shot himself. That was what I was going to say.

ZARA: And you still don't know who the bank robber is?

JIM: No.

ZARA: Listen — if you don't explain soon how on earth you suspect I might be involved in this, you'll end up wishing I *had* called my lawyer.

JIM: No one suspects you of anything! My colleague would just like to know why you were there in the apartment, if you weren't there to buy it?

ZARA: My psychologist told me I needed a hobby.

JIM: Viewing apartments is your hobby?

ZARA: People like you are more interesting than you might imagine.

JIM: People like me?

ZARA: People in your socio-economic bracket. It's interesting seeing how you live. How you manage to bear it. I went to a few viewings, then a few more, it's like heroin. Have you tried heroin? You feel disgusted with yourself, but it's hard to stop.

JIM: You're telling me you've become addicted to viewing apartments owned by people who earn far less than you?

ZARA: Yes. Like when kids catch baby birds in glass jars. The same slightly forbidden attraction.

JIM: You mean insects? People do that with insects.

ZARA: Sure. If that makes you feel better.

JIM: So you were at this apartment viewing because it's your hobby?

ZARA: Is that a real tattoo on your arm?

JIM: Yes.

ZARA: Is it supposed to be an anchor?

JIM: Yes.

ZARA: Did you lose a bet or something?

JIM: What do you mean by that?

ZARA: Was someone threatening your family? Or did you do it voluntarily?

JIM: Voluntarily.

ZARA: Why do people like you hate money so much?

JIM: I'm not even going to comment on that. I'd just like you to tell me, so that we've got it on tape, why the other witnesses say you didn't seem at all afraid when you saw the bank robber's pistol. Did you think it wasn't real?

ZARA: I understood perfectly well that it was real. That's why I wasn't frightened. I was surprised.

JIM: That's an unusual reaction to a pistol.

ZARA: For you, maybe. But I'd been contemplating killing myself for quite a long time, so when I saw the pistol I was surprised.

JIM: I don't know what to say to that. Sorry. You'd been contemplating killing yourself?

ZARA: Yes. So I was surprised when I realized that I didn't want to die. It came as a bit of a shock.

JIM: Did you start seeing your psychologist because of those suicidal thoughts?

ZARA: No. I needed the psychologist because I was having trouble sleeping. Because I used to lie awake thinking that I could have killed myself if only I had enough sleeping pills.

JIM: And it was your psychologist who suggested that
             you needed a hobby?

ZARA: Yes. That was after I told her about my cancer.

JIM: Oh. I'm very sorry to hear that. How sad.

ZARA: Okay, look . . .

26

The next time the psychologist and Zara met, Zara said that she had actually found a hobby. She had started to go to 'viewings of middle-class apartments'. She said it was exciting because a lot of the apartments looked like the people who lived there did the cleaning themselves. The psychologist tried to explain that this wasn't quite what she'd had in mind by 'getting involved in a charity', but Zara retorted that at one of the viewings there had been 'a man who was thinking of renovating it himself, with his own *hands*, the same hands he *eats* with, so don't try to tell me I'm not doing all I can to fraternize with the most unfortunate members of society!' The psychologist had no idea how to even begin to answer that, but Zara noted her arched eyebrows and hanging jaw and snorted: 'Have I upset you now? Christ, it's impossible not to upset people like you the moment you start to say anything at all.'

The psychologist nodded patiently and immediately regretted the question she asked next: 'Can you give me an example of when people like *me* have been upset by you without your meaning it?'

Zara shrugged, then told the story of how she had been called 'prejudiced' when she interviewed a young man for a job at the bank, just because she had looked at him when he entered the room and exclaimed: 'Oh! I would have expected you to apply for a job in the IT department instead, your sort tend to be good with computers!'

Zara spent a long time explaining to the psychologist that it was actually a compliment. Does giving someone a compliment mean you're prejudiced these days, too?

The psychologist tried to find a way to talk about it without actually talking about it, so she said: 'You seem to get caught up in a lot of disagreements, Zara. One technique I'd recommend is to ask yourself three questions before you flare up. One: Are the actions of the person in question intended to harm you personally? Two: Do you possess all the information about the situation? Three: Do you have anything to gain from a conflict?'

Zara tilted her head so far that her neck creaked. She understood all the words, but the way they were put together made as much sense as if they'd been pulled at random from a hat.

'Why would I need help to stop getting into conflicts? Conflicts are good. Only weak people believe in harmony, and as a reward they get to float through life with a feeling of moral superiority while the rest of us get on with other things.'

'Like what?' the psychologist wondered.

'Winning.'

'And that's important?'

'You can't achieve anything if you don't win, sweetie. No one ends up at the head of a boardroom table by accident.'

The psychologist tried to find her way back to her original question, whatever it had been.

'And . . . winners earn a lot of money, which is also important, I assume? What do you do with yours?'

'I buy distance from other people.'

The psychologist had never heard that response before.

'How do you mean?'

'Expensive restaurants have bigger gaps between the tables. First class on aeroplanes has no middle seats. Exclusive hotels have separate entrances for guests staying in suites. The most expensive thing you can buy in the most densely populated places on the planet is distance.'

The psychologist leaned back in her chair. It wasn't hard to find textbook examples of Zara's personality: she avoided eye contact, didn't want to shake hands, was – to put it mildly – empathetically challenged, and had perhaps as a result chosen to work with numbers. And she couldn't help compulsively straightening the photograph on the bookcase every time the psychologist moved it out of position on purpose before each session. It was hard to ask someone like Zara about that sort of thing directly, so the psychologist asked instead: 'Why do you like your job?'

'Because I'm an analyst. Most people who do the same job as me are economists,' Zara replied immediately.

'What's the difference?'

'Economists only approach problems head-on. That's why economists never predict stock market crashes.'

'And you're saying that analysts do?'

'Analysts *expect* crashes. Economists only earn money when things go well for the bank's customers, whereas analysts earn money all the time.'

'Does that make you feel guilty?' the psychologist asked, mostly to see if Zara thought that word was a feeling or something to do with gold plating.

'Is it the croupier's fault if you lose your money at the casino?' Zara asked.

'I'm not sure that's a fair comparison.'

'Why not?'

'Because you use words like "stock market crash", but it's never the stock market or the banks that crash. Only people do that.'

'There's a very logical explanation for why you think that.'

'Really?'

'It's because you think the world owes you something. It doesn't.'

'You still haven't answered my question. I asked why you like your job. All you've done is tell me why you're *good* at it.'

'Only weak people like their jobs.'

'I don't think that's true.'

'That's because you like your job.'

'You say that as if there's something wrong with that.'

'Are you upset now? People like you really do seem to get upset an awful lot, and do you know why?'

'No.'

'Because you're wrong. If you stopped being wrong the whole time you wouldn't be so upset.'

The psychologist looked at the clock on her desk. She still believed that Zara's biggest problem was her loneliness, but perhaps there's a difference between loneliness and friendlessness. But instead of saying that, the psychologist murmured in a tone of resignation: 'Do you know what . . . I think this might be a good place for us to stop.'

Unconcerned, Zara nodded and stood up. She tucked the chair back under the table very precisely. She was half facing away when she said, 'Do you think there are bad people?' It sounded as if she hadn't really meant to let the words out.

The psychologist did her best not to look surprised. She managed to reply: 'Are you asking me as a psychologist, or from a purely philosophical perspective?'

Zara looked like she was talking to a toaster again.

'Did you have a dictionary shoved up your backside as a child, or did you end up like this of your own volition? Just answer the question: Do you think there are bad people?'

The psychologist shuffled on her seat so much that she very nearly turned her pants inside out.

'I'd probably have to say . . . yes. I think there are bad people.'

'Do you think they know it?'

'What do you mean?'

Zara's gaze fell upon the picture of the woman on the bridge.

'In my experience there are plenty of people who are real pigs. Emotionally cold, thoughtless people. But even we don't want to believe that we're bad.'

The psychologist considered her response for a long time before she replied: 'Yes. If I'm being honest, I think that almost all of us have a need to tell ourselves that we're helping to make the world better. Or at least that we're not making it worse. That we're on the right side. That even if . . . I don't know . . . that maybe even our very worst actions serve some sort of higher purpose. Because practically everyone distinguishes between good and bad, so if we breach our own moral code, we have to come up with an excuse for ourselves. I think that's known as neutralizing techniques in criminology. It could be religious or political conviction, or the belief that we had no choice, but we need something to justify our bad deeds. Because I honestly believe that there are very few people who could live with knowing that they are . . . *bad*.'

Zara said nothing, just clutched her far too large handbag a little too tightly and, for just a fraction of a second, looked like she was about to admit something. Her hand was halfway to the letter. She even allowed herself, very fleetingly, to entertain the possibility of confessing that she had lied about her hobby. She hadn't only just started going to apartment viewings, she'd been going to them for ten years. It wasn't a hobby, it was an obsession.

But none of the words slipped out. She closed her bag, the door slid shut behind her, and the room fell silent. The psychologist remained seated at her desk, bemused at how bemused she felt. She tried to make some notes for their next encounter, but found herself instead opening her laptop and looking at the details of apartments for sale. She tried to figure out which of them Zara was thinking of looking at next. Which was obviously impossible, but it could have been simple if only Zara had explained that all the apartments she looked at had to have balconies, and that all the balconies had to have a view that stretched all the way to the bridge.

In the meantime Zara was standing in the lift. Halfway down she pressed the emergency stop button so she could cry in peace. The letter in her handbag was still unopened, Zara had never dared read it, because she knew the psychologist was right. Zara was one of the people who deep down wouldn't be able to live with knowing that about herself.

27

This is a story about a bank robbery, an apartment viewing and a hostage drama. But even more it's a story about idiots. But perhaps not only that.

Ten years ago a man wrote a letter. He posted it to a woman at a bank. Then he dropped his kids off at school, whispered in their ears that he loved them, drove off on his own, and parked his car by the water. He climbed on to the railing of a bridge and jumped. The following week, a teenage girl was standing on the same bridge railing.

Obviously it doesn't really make any difference to you who the girl was. She was just one person out of several billion, and most people never become individuals to us. They're just people. We're just strangers passing each other, your anxieties briefly brushing against mine as the fibres of our coats touch momentarily on a crowded pavement somewhere. We never really know what we do to each other, with each other, for each other. But the teenage girl on the bridge was called Nadia. It was the week after the man had jumped to his death from the railing where she was standing. She knew next to nothing about who he was, but she went to the same school as his children, and everyone was talking about it. That was how she got the idea. No one can really explain, either before or after, what makes a teenager stop wanting to be alive. It just hurts so much at times, being human. Not understanding yourself, not liking the body you're stuck in. Seeing your eyes in the mirror and wondering whose they are, always with the same question: 'What's wrong with me? Why do I feel like this?'

She isn't traumatized, she isn't weighed down by any obvious grief. She's just sad, all the time. An evil little creature that wouldn't have shown up on any X-rays was living in her chest, rushing through her blood and filling her head with whispers, saying she wasn't good enough, that she was weak and ugly and would never be anything but broken. You can get it into your head to do some unbelievably stupid things when you run out of tears, when you can't silence the voices no one else can hear, when you've never been in a room where you felt normal. In the end you get exhausted from always tensing the skin around your ribs, never letting your shoulders sink, brushing along walls all your life with white knuckles, always afraid that someone will notice you, because no one's supposed to do that.

All Nadia knew was that she had never felt like someone who had anything in common with anyone else. She had always been entirely alone in every emotion. She sat in a classroom full of her contemporaries, looking like everything was the same as usual, but inside she was standing in a forest screaming until her heart burst. The trees grew until one day the sunlight could no longer break through the foliage, and the darkness in there became impenetrable.

So she stood on a bridge looking over the railing to the water far below, and knew it would be like hitting concrete when she landed, she wouldn't drown, just die on impact. That thought consoled her, because ever since she was very little she'd been scared of drowning. Not death itself, but the moments before it. The panic and powerlessness. A thoughtless adult had told her that a person who's drowning doesn't look like they're drowning. 'When you're drowning you can't call for help, you can't wave your arms, you just sink. Your family can be standing on the beach waving cheerfully to you, completely unaware that you're dying.'

Nadia had felt like that all her life. She had lived among them. Had sat at the dinner table with her parents, thinking: *Can't you see?* But they didn't see, and she didn't say anything. One day she simply didn't go to school. She tidied her room and made her bed and left home without a coat because she wouldn't be needing one. She spent all day in town, freezing, wandering around as if she wanted the town to see her one last time, and understand what it had done by failing to hear her silent screams. She didn't have any real plan, just a consequence. When sunset came she found herself standing on the railing of the bridge. It was so easy. All she had to do was move one foot, then the other.

It was that teenage boy called Jack who saw her. He couldn't explain why he'd gone back to the bridge, evening after evening, for a week. His parents had forbidden it, of course, but he never listened. He snuck out and ran there as if he were hoping to see the man standing there again, so he could turn back the clock and make everything right this time. When he saw the teenage girl on the railing instead, he didn't know what to shout at her. So he didn't shout anything. He just rushed over and pulled her down with such force that she hit the back of her head on the tarmac and was knocked unconscious.

She woke up in the hospital. Everything had happened so quickly that she had only caught a glimpse of the boy rushing towards her out of the corner of her eye. When the nurses asked what had happened she wasn't even sure of that herself, but the back of her head was bleeding, so she said she'd climbed up on to the railing to take a photograph of the sunset, then fell backwards and hit her head. She was so used to saying what she knew other people wanted to hear, so they wouldn't worry, that she did it without thinking. The nurses still looked worried, suspicious, but she was a good liar. She'd spent her whole life practising. So in the end they said: 'Climbing up on that railing, what a silly thing to do! It's sheer luck you didn't slip off the other side instead!' She nodded, dry-lipped, and said yes. Luck.

She could have gone straight back to the bridge from the hospital, but she didn't. It was impossible to explain why, even to herself, because she would never know for sure what she would have done if that boy hadn't pulled her down. Would she have taken a step forward or back? So every day after that she tried to understand the difference between herself and the man who had jumped. That drove her to choose a profession, a career, a whole life. She became a psychologist. The people who came to her were the ones who were in so much pain that it felt like they were standing on a railing with one foot over the edge, and she sat in her chair opposite them with eyes that said: *I've been here before. I know a better way down.*

Of course sometimes she couldn't help thinking about the reasons why she had wanted to jump, all the things she thought were missing from her reflection. Her loneliness at the dinner table. But she found ways to cope, to tunnel her way out of herself, to climb down. Some people accept that they will never be free of their anxiety, they just learn to carry it. She tried to be one of them. She told herself that was why you should always be nice to other people, even idiots, because you never know how heavy their burden is. Over time she realized that deep down almost everyone asks themselves the same sort of questions: Am I good? Do I make anyone proud? Am I useful to society? Am I good at my job? Generous and considerate? A decent shag? Does anyone want me to be their friend? Have I been a good parent? Am I a good person?

People want to be good. Deep down. Kind. The problem, of course, is that it isn't always possible to be kind to idiots, because they're idiots. That's become a lifelong project for Nadia to grapple with, as it is for all of us.

She never met the boy from the bridge again. Sometimes she honestly believes that she made him up. An angel, maybe. Jack never saw Nadia again, either. He never went back to the bridge. But that was the day his plan to become a police officer became unshakable, when he realized that he could be the difference.

Ten years later Nadia will move back to the town, after training to become a psychologist. She will acquire a patient named Zara. Zara will go to an apartment viewing and get caught up in a hostage drama. Jack and his dad, Jim, will interview all the witnesses. The apartment where it happened has a balcony, from which you can see all the way to the bridge. That's why Zara is there. Ten years ago she found a letter on her doormat, written by a man who jumped. His name was written neatly on the back of the envelope; she remembered their meeting, and even though the newspapers never published the name of the person the police found in the water, the town was too small for her not to know.

Zara still carries the letter around with her in her handbag, every day. She's only been down to the bridge once, the week after he climbed on to the railing; she saw a girl climb up on to the same railing, and a boy who rescued her. Zara didn't even move, she just stood hidden in the darkness, shaking. She was still standing there when the ambulance arrived and took the girl to the hospital. The boy vanished. Zara walked out on to the bridge and found the girl's wallet and ID card with her name on it. Nadia.

Zara has spent ten years following Nadia's life and education and the start of her career in secret, from a distance, because she's never dared approach her. She has spent ten years looking at the bridge, also from a distance, from the balconies of apartments that are for sale. For the same reason. Because she's afraid that if she goes down to the bridge again, maybe someone else will jump, and if she seeks out Nadia and discovers the truth about herself, perhaps it will be Zara who does it. Because Zara is human enough to want to hear what the difference is between that man and Nadia, even though she realizes that she doesn't really want to know. That she bears the guilt. That she's the bad person. Maybe everyone says they'd like to know that about themselves, but no one does really. So Zara still hasn't opened the envelope.

* * *

The whole thing is a complicated, unlikely story. Perhaps that's because what we think stories are about often isn't what they're about at all. This, for instance, might not actually be the story of a bank robbery, or an apartment viewing or a hostage drama. Perhaps it isn't even a story about idiots.

Perhaps this is a story about a bridge.

28

The truth? The truth is that that damn estate agent was a damn poor estate agent, and the apartment viewing was a disaster right from the start. If the prospective buyers couldn't agree about anything else, they could at least agree on that, because nothing unites a group of strangers more effectively than the opportunity to come together and sigh at a hopeless case.

The advertisement, or whatever you want to call it, was a poorly spelt disaster, with pictures so blurred that the photographer seemed to believe that a 'panoramic shot' was something you achieved by throwing your camera across the room. 'The HOUSE TRICKS Estate Agency! HOW'S TRICKS?' it said above the date, and who on earth would get it into their head to hold an apartment viewing the day before New Year's Eve? There were scented candles in the bathroom, and a bowl of limes on the coffee table, a brave effort by someone who seemed to have heard about apartment viewings but had never actually been to one, but the closet was stuffed with clothes, and there was a pair of slippers in the bathroom that looked like they belonged to someone who had spent the past fifty years shuffling around without ever lifting their feet. The bookcase was packed, and not even colour-coordinated, and there were even more books piled up on the windowsills and the kitchen table. The fridge was covered with yellowing drawings produced by the owner's grandchildren. Zara had been to enough viewings by this point to be able to spot an amateur: a viewing should make it look as if no one lives in the apartment, because otherwise only a serial killer would want to move in. A viewing should make it look as if anyone could potentially live there. People don't want to buy a picture, they want to buy a frame. They can handle books in a bookcase, but not on the kitchen table. Perhaps Zara could have gone up to the estate agent and pointed that out, if only the estate agent hadn't been a human being, and if only Zara hadn't hated human beings. Especially when they spoke.

Instead Zara did a circuit of the apartment, trying to look interested, the way she had seen people who actually wanted to buy apartments look. That was quite a challenge for her, seeing as only someone on drugs who collected fingernail clippings could possibly be interested in living in this particular apartment. So when no one was looking in her direction, Zara went out on to the balcony, stood by the railing, and stared off towards the bridge until she started to shake uncontrollably. The same reaction as always, time after time for the past ten years. The letter she had never opened lay in her handbag. She had learned to cry almost without tears now, for practical reasons.

The balcony door was ajar and she could hear voices, not just in her head but from inside the apartment. Two married couples were wandering about, trying to ignore all the rather ugly furniture and instead visualize their own really ugly furniture in its place. The older couple had been married for a long time, but the younger couple seemed to have only got married recently. You can always tell by the way people who love each other argue: the longer they've been together, the fewer words they need to start a fight.

The older couple were called Anna-Lena and Roger. They'd been retired for a few years now, but clearly not long enough for them to have got used to it. They were always stressing about something, but without having anything they truly needed to hurry for. Anna-Lena was a woman with strong feelings, and Roger a man with strong opinions, and if you've ever wondered who writes all those too detailed, one-out-of-five-star reviews of household gadgets (or theatre plays, or tape dispensers or small glass ornaments) on the Internet, it's Anna-Lena and Roger. Sometimes, of course, they hadn't even tried out the gadgets in question, but they weren't the sort of people to let that stop them from writing a scathing review. If you had to try things out and read things and find out the truth about things, then you'd never have time to have an opinion about anything. Anna-Lena was wearing a top in a colour usually only seen on parquet floors, Roger was in jeans and a checkered shirt that had received a sulphurous one-out-of-five-stars review online because it 'had shrunk several inches!' not long after Roger's bathroom scale had received the damning judgement that it was 'calibrated wrong!' Anna-Lena tugged at one of the curtains and said: 'Green curtains? Who on earth has green curtains? Honestly, the things people do these days. But maybe they're colour-blind. Or Irish.' She didn't say this to anyone in particular, she had just fallen into the habit of thinking out loud, seeing as that seemed appropriate for a woman who had grown used to the fact that no one listened to her anyway.

Roger was kicking the skirting boards and muttering: 'This one's loose,' and didn't hear a word of what Anna-Lena said. The skirting board may possibly have been loose because Roger had spent ten minutes kicking it, but for a man like Roger a truth is a truth, regardless of its cause. From time to time Anna-Lena whispered to him about what she thought of the other prospective buyers in the apartment. Sadly Anna-Lena was about as good at whispering as she was at thinking quietly, so it was pretty much the sort of shouted whisper that's the equivalent of a fart in an aeroplane that you think won't be noticed if you let it out a little bit at a time. You never manage to be as discreet as you imagine.

'That woman on the balcony, Roger, what does she want with this apartment? She's obviously too rich to want it, so what's she doing here? And she's still got her shoes on. Everyone knows you take your shoes off at an apartment viewing!' Roger didn't answer. Anna-Lena glared at Zara through the balcony window as if Zara were the one who'd farted. Then Anna-Lena leaned even closer to Roger and whispered: 'And those women in the hall, they really don't look like they could afford to live here! Do they?'

At this Roger stopped kicking the skirting board, turned towards his wife, and looked her deep in the eye. Then he said four little words that he never said to any other woman on the planet. He said: 'For God's sake, darling.'

They never argue any more, unless perhaps they argue all the time. When you've been stuck with each other long enough it can seem like there's no difference between no longer arguing and no longer caring.

'For God's sake, darling, remember to tell everyone you talk to that this place needs *serious renovation*! That way they won't want to put in an offer,' Roger went on.

Anna-Lena looked confused: 'But that's good, isn't it?'

Roger sighed. 'For God's sake, darling. Good for us, yes. Because *we* can do the renovations. But the others – you can tell from miles off that none of them knows a thing about renovation.'

Anna-Lena nodded, wrinkled her nose, and sniffed the air demonstratively. 'There's a definite smell of damp, isn't there? Possibly even mold?' Because Roger had taught her always to ask the estate agent that question, loudly, so that the other prospective buyers would hear and be worried.

Roger closed his eyes in frustration.

'For God's sake, darling, you're supposed to say that to the estate agent, not me.'

Wounded, Anna-Lena nodded, then thought out loud: 'I was just practising.'

Zara could hear them from where she was standing looking out over the railing on the balcony. The same swirling panic inside her, the same nausea, the same quivering fingertips every time she saw the bridge. Maybe she was fooling herself by thinking that one day it would feel better, or perhaps worse, so unbearable that she herself went and jumped. She looked down from the balcony but wasn't sure it was high enough. That's the only thing someone who definitely wants to live and someone who definitely wants to die have in common: if you're going to jump off something, you need to be pretty damn sure of the height. Zara just wasn't sure which of those she was: just because you don't much like life doesn't necessarily mean you want the alternative. So she had spent a decade seeking out and attending these apartment viewings, standing on balconies and staring at the bridge, balancing right in the middle of all that was worst inside her.

She heard new voices from inside the apartment. It was the other couple, the younger pair, Julia and Ro. One of them was a blonde, the other had black hair, and they were squabbling noisily the way you do when you're young and think that every feeling fluttering about in all your hormones is completely unique. Julia was the one who was pregnant, and Ro was the one who was irritated. One was dressed in clothes that looked like she'd made them herself out of capes she'd stolen from murdered magicians, the other as if she sold drugs outside a bowling alley. Ro (that was a nickname, of course, but the sort that had stuck to her for so long that even she used it to introduce herself, which was just one of the many reasons Zara found her irritating) was walking around and holding her phone up towards the ceiling, repeating: 'There's, like, no signal at all in here!' while Julia snapped back: 'Well, that's *terrible*, because then we might actually have to *talk* to each other if we lived here! Stop trying to change the subject the whole time, we need to make a decision about the birds!'

They very rarely agreed about anything, but in Ro's defence she didn't always know that. Fairly often when Ro asked Julia 'Are you upset?' Julia would reply 'NO!' and Ro would shrug, as carefree as a family in an advertisement for cleaning products, which obviously only made Julia even more upset, because it was perfectly obvious that she was upset. But this time even Ro was aware that they were arguing, because they were arguing about the birds. Ro had had birds when she and Julia got together, not as lunch but as pets. 'Is she a pirate?' Julia's mum had asked the first time it was mentioned, but Julia put up with the birds because she was in love and because she couldn't help wondering how long birds could actually live.

A very long time, as it turned out. When Julia eventually realized this and tried to deal with the situation in an adult way by sneaking out of bed one night and letting them out of a window, one of the wretched creatures fell all the way to the street and died. A *bird*! Julia had to invite some of the neighbours' children in for a soda the next day when Ro was at work so she could blame one of them when Ro found the cage open. And the other birds? They were still sitting in the cage. What sort of insult to evolution was it that creatures like that managed to stay alive?

'I'm not going to have them put down, and I don't want to talk about it any more,' Ro said, sounding hurt and looking around the apartment with her hands deep in the pockets of her dress. Her dress had pockets because she appreciated looking nice, but still liked to have somewhere to put her hands.

'Okay, okay. So what do you think of the apartment, then? I think we should take it!' Julia said breathlessly, because the lift was broken and every time Ro said, 'We're pregnant,' to family and friends as if it were a team sport, Julia felt like pouring molten wax in her ears when she was asleep. Not that Julia didn't love Ro, because she did, so much that it was almost unbearable, but they had looked at more than twenty apartments in the past two weeks and Ro always found something wrong with every single one of them. It was as if she didn't actually want to move. But Julia woke up every night in their current apartment to play every pregnant woman's favourite game, 'kick or gas?' and then she couldn't get back to sleep because both Ro and the birds snored, so she was more than ready to move anywhere right now, as long as it had more than one bedroom.

'No signal,' Ro repeated morosely.

'Who cares? Let's take it!' Julia persisted.

'Well, I'm not sure. I need to check the hobby room,' Ro said.

'That's a walk-in closet,' Julia corrected.

'Or a hobby room! I'm just going to get the tape measure!' Ro nodded cheerfully, because one of her most charming and simultaneously most infuriating characteristics was that no matter what they'd just been arguing about, she could be in a wonderful mood in the blink of an eye if she thought about cheese.

'You know perfectly well that you're not going to be allowed to store cheese in my walk-in closet,' Julia declared sternly, seeing as their current apartment had a storeroom in the basement that Julia referred to as the Museum of Abandoned Hobbies. Every third month Ro would become obsessed with something, 1950s dresses or bouillabaisse or antique coffee services or CrossFit or bonsai trees or a podcast about the Second World War, then she would spend three months studying the subject in question with unstinting devotion on Internet forums populated by people who clearly shouldn't be allowed Wi-Fi in whatever padded cell they were locked up in, and then she would suddenly get fed up and immediately find a new obsession. The only hobby that had remained constant since they got together was that Ro collected shoes, and nothing could sum up a person more clearly than the fact that she owned two hundred pairs of shoes, yet always managed to have the wrong ones on when it was raining or snowing.

'No, I don't know that perfectly well! Because I haven't measured it yet, so I don't know if there'd be room for the cheese in there! And my plants also need . . . ,' Ro began, because she had just decided to start growing plants under heat lamps in the hobby room. Which was a walk-in closet. Or a . . .

In the meantime, Anna-Lena was running her hand over a cushion cover and thinking about sharks. She'd been thinking about them a lot recently, because in their marriage, she and Roger had come to resemble sharks. That was a source of silent sorrow for Anna-Lena. She kept rubbing the cushion cover and distracted herself by thinking out loud: 'Is this from IKEA? Yes, it's definitely from IKEA. I recognize it. They do a floral version as well. The floral version's nicer. Honestly, the things people do these days.'

You could have woken Anna-Lena in the middle of the night and asked her to recite the IKEA catalogue. Not that there'd be any reason to, of course, but you could if you wanted to, that's the point. Anna-Lena and Roger have been to every IKEA store in the whole country. Roger has many faults and failings, Anna-Lena knows people think that, but Anna-Lena is always reminded that he loves her in IKEA. When you've been together for a very long time, it's the little things that matter. In a long marriage you don't need words to have a row, but you don't need words to say 'I love you', either. Once when they were at IKEA, very recently, Roger had suggested when they were having lunch in the cafeteria that they each have a piece of cake. Because he understood that it was an important day for Anna-Lena, and because it was important to her, it was important to him as well. Because that's how he loves her.

She went on rubbing the cushion cover that was nicer in the floral pattern and glanced over at the two women in a way Anna-Lena thought was discreet, the pregnant one and her wife. Roger was looking at them as well. He was holding the estate agent prospectus with the layout of the apartment in his hand, and grunted: 'For God's sake, darling, look at this! Why do they have to call the small room "child's room"? It could just as well be a perfectly ordinary damn bedroom!'

Roger didn't like it when there were pregnant women at apartment viewings, because couples expecting a baby always bid too much. He didn't like children's rooms, either. That's why Anna-Lena always asks Roger as many questions as she can think of when they walk through the children's section in IKEA. To help distract him from the incomprehensible grief. Because that's how she loves him.

Ro caught sight of Roger and grinned, as if they weren't really at war with each other.

'Hi! I'm Ro, and that's my wife, Julia, over there. Can I borrow your tape measure? I forgot mine!'

'Absolutely not!' Roger snapped, clutching his tape measure, pocket calculator and notepad so hard that his eyebrows started to twitch.

'Calm down, I only want to –' Ro began.

'We all have to take responsibility for our own actions!' Anna-Lena interrupted sharply.

Ro looked surprised. Surprise made her nervous. Nervousness made her hungry. There wasn't much she could eat in the immediate vicinity so she reached for one of the limes in the bowl on the coffee table. Anna-Lena saw this and exclaimed: 'Dear me, what on earth are you doing? You can't eat those! They're viewing limes!'

Ro let go of the lime and stuffed her hands in the pockets of her dress. She went back to her wife, muttering: 'No. This apartment isn't us, hun. It's nice and all that, but I'm getting bad vibes here. Like we could never be our best selves here, yeah? Remember me saying I'd read about *we-energies* that month when I was thinking of becoming an interior designer? When I learned that we had to sleep facing east? And then forgot if it was your head or your feet that . . . well . . . never mind! I just don't want this apartment. Can't we just go?'

Zara was standing out on the balcony. She gathered the wreckage of her feelings into an expression of derision and went back into the apartment. Just as she walked in, the pregnant woman let out a yelp. At first it sounded like a roar of guttural rage from an animal that's just been kicked, but eventually the words became clearer:

'No! That's enough, Ro! I can take the birds and I can take your awful taste in music and I can take a whole load of other crap, but I'm not leaving here until we've bought this apartment! Even if I have to give birth to our child right here on this carpet!'

The apartment fell completely silent. Everyone was staring at Julia. The only person who wasn't was Zara, because she was standing just inside the balcony door and staring at the bank robber. One second passed, then two, in which Zara was the only person in the room who had realized what was about to happen.

Then Anna-Lena also caught sight of the figure in the ski mask and cried out: 'Oh, dear Lord, we're being robbed!' Everyone's mouths opened at the same time but no words came out. Fear can numb people at the sight of a pistol, switch off everything except the brain's most important signals, silence all background noise. Another second passed, then one more, in which all they heard was their own heartbeats. First the heart stops, then it races. First comes the shock of not understanding what's happening, then comes the shock of realizing *precisely* what's happening. The survival instinct and fear of dying start to fight, making space for some surprisingly irrational thoughts in between. It's not unusual to see a pistol and think: *Did I switch the coffee machine off this morning?* instead of: *What's going to happen to my children?*

But even the bank robber was silent, just as scared as all the others. After a while the shock gradually turned to confusion. Anna-Lena sputtered: 'You are here to *rob* us, aren't you?' The bank robber seemed to be about to protest, but didn't have time before Anna-Lena started to tug at Roger like he were a green curtain, crying: 'Get your money out, Roger!'

Roger squinted sceptically at the bank robber and was evidently engaged in a complicated internal struggle, because on the one hand Roger was very cheap, but on the other he wasn't particularly enamoured with the thought of dying in an apartment with this much potential for renovation. So he pulled his wallet from his back pocket, where men like him always keep their wallets except when they're at the beach, when they keep it in their shoe, but found nothing of use in it. So he turned to the person closest to him, who happened to be Zara, standing over by the balcony door, and asked: 'Have you got any cash on you?'

Zara looked shocked. It was hard to work out if that was because of the pistol or the question.

'Cash? Seriously, do I look like a drug dealer?'

The bank robber's eyes, visible through the repeatedly adjusted holes in the sweaty mask, were darting around the room.

Eventually the bank robber shouted: 'No . . . ! No, this isn't a robbery . . . I just . . . ,' then corrected that statement in a breathless voice: 'Well, maybe it is a robbery! But you're not the victims! It's maybe more like a hostage situation now! And I'm very sorry about that! I'm having quite a complicated day here!'

That's how it all began.

29

Witness Interview
Date: December 30
Name of witness: Anna-Lena

JACK: Hello, my name's Jack.

ANNA-LENA: I don't want to talk to any more policemen.

JACK: I can certainly understand that. I've just got a few brief questions.

ANNA-LENA: If Roger was here he'd have told you that you're all idiots, the whole lot of you, for managing to lose a bank robber who was trapped inside an apartment!

JACK: That's why I need to ask my questions. So that we can find the perpetrator.

ANNA-LENA: I want to go home.

JACK: Believe me, I do understand that, we're just trying to work out what happened inside the apartment. Can you tell me what happened when the perpetrator first came in with the pistol?

ANNA-LENA: That woman, Zara, she had her shoes on. And the other one, Ro, was going to eat one of the limes. You don't do things like that at apartment viewings! There are unwritten rules!

JACK: Sorry?

ANNA-LENA: She was going to eat one of the limes. The viewing limes! You can't eat the viewing limes, because the estate agent put them there as decoration, they're not for eating. I was about to go and find the agent and tell her, to get Ro thrown out, because you just can't behave like that. But at that very moment that lunatic burst through the door waving a pistol.

JACK: I see. And then what happened?

ANNA-LENA: You should talk to Roger. He's got a very good memory.

JACK: Roger's your husband? And you'd gone to look at the apartment together?

ANNA-LENA: Yes. Roger said it would be a good invest-ment. Is this table from IKEA? Yes, it is, isn't it? I recognize it. They do it in ivory as well. That would have gone better with the walls.

JACK: I have to confess that I'm not responsible for the way our interview rooms are fur-nished.

ANNA-LENA: Just because it's an interview room doesn't mean it can't look nice, does it? Seeing as you were already in IKEA. That ivory table is right next to this one in the self-service area. But you still picked this one. Well, everyone makes their own choices.

JACK: I'll see if I can raise it with my boss.

ANNA-LENA: Well, that's up to you.

JACK: When Roger said the apartment was a 'good investment', did that mean that you wouldn't be settling there? You'd just buy it and sell it on later?

ANNA-LENA: Why are you asking that?

JACK: I'm just trying to understand who was in the apartment, and why, so that we can rule out the possibility that any of the hostages was in any way connected to the perpetrator.

ANNA-LENA: Connected?

JACK: We think someone may have helped him.

ANNA-LENA: And you think that could have been me and Roger?

JACK: No, no. We just need to ask a few routine questions, that's all.

ANNA-LENA: So you think it was her, that Zara?

JACK: I haven't said that.

ANNA-LENA: You said you think someone helped the bank robber. That Zara was dodgy, I could see it the moment I set eyes on her, she was obviously too rich to want that apartment. And I heard that pregnant woman tell her wife that Zara looked like 'Cruella de Vil'. I think that's from a film? It sounds dodgy, anyway. Or do you think it was Estelle who helped the bank robber? She's almost ninety, you know. Are you going to start accusing ninety-year-olds of helping criminals now? Is that how modern policing works?

JACK: I'm not accusing anyone.

ANNA-LENA: Roger and I never help anyone else at an apartment viewing, I can promise you that. Roger says that the moment we walk in it's war and we're surrounded by enemies. That's why he always wants me to tell everyone that the apartment needs a lot of work done to it and that the cost of that would be very expensive. As well as the smell of damp. Things like that. Roger's a very good negotiator. We've made some extremely good investments.

JACK: So you've done this before? Bought an apartment only to flip it?

ANNA-LENA: There's no point in an investment if you don't sell, Roger says. So we buy, Roger does the renovations, I sort out the decor, then we sell and buy another apartment.

JACK: That sounds like an unusual thing for two people who are retired to do.

ANNA-LENA: Roger and I like working on projects together.

JACK: Are you okay?

ANNA-LENA: Yes.

JACK: You look like you're crying.

ANNA-LENA: I've had a very trying day!

JACK: Sorry. That was insensitive of me.

ANNA-LENA: I know Roger doesn't always come across as particularly sensitive, but he is. He likes us to have a project in common because he's worried we'd run out of things to talk about otherwise. He doesn't think I'm interesting enough to be with all day unless we've got a project.

JACK: I'm sure that's not true.

ANNA-LENA: What would you know about that?

JACK: I guess I don't know anything at all. Sorry. I'd like to ask a few questions about the other prospective buyers now.

ANNA-LENA: Roger's more sensitive than he seems.

JACK: Okay. Can you tell me anything about the other people at the viewing?

ANNA-LENA: They were looking for a home.

JACK: Sorry?

ANNA-LENA: Roger says there are two types of buyer. Those who are looking for an investment, and those who want a home. The ones who are looking for a home are emotional idiots, they'll pay anything because they think all their problems will just disappear the moment they move in.

JACK: I'm not sure I understand.

ANNA-LENA: Roger and I don't let our feelings get in the way of our investments. But everyone else does. Like those two women at the viewing, the one who was pregnant and the other one.

JACK: Julia and Ro?

ANNA-LENA: Yes!

JACK: You think they were the sort who were 'looking for a home'?

ANNA-LENA: It was obvious. People like that go to viewings thinking that everything would feel better if only they were living there. That they'd wake up in the mornings and not find it hard to breathe. They wouldn't have to look in the bathroom mirror with an invisible weight in their chest. They'd argue less. Maybe touch each other's hands the way they did when they were first married, back when they couldn't help it. That's what they think.

JACK: You'll have to excuse me, but it looks like you're crying again?

Anna-Lena: Don't tell me what I'm doing!

JACK: Okay, okay. But you seem to have put a fair amount of thought into how people behave at apartment viewings, is that fair to say?

Anna-Lena: Roger does most of the thinking. Roger's very intelligent, you know. You need to know your enemy, he says, and all your enemy wants is to get it over with. They just want to move in and have done with it and never have to move again. Roger isn't like that. We saw a documentary about sharks once, Roger's very interested in documentaries, and there's a particular type of shark that dies if it stops moving. It's something to do with the way they absorb oxygen, they can't breathe unless they're moving the whole time. That's how our marriage has ended up.

JACK: Sorry, I'm afraid I don't understand.

Anna-Lena: Do you know what the worst thing about being retired is?

JACK: No.

Anna-Lena: That you get too much time to think. People need a project, so Roger and I became sharks, and if we didn't keep moving, our marriage wouldn't get any oxygen. So we buy and reno-vate and sell, buy and renovate and sell. I did suggest that we try golf instead, but Roger doesn't like golf.

JACK: Sorry to interrupt, but I wonder if we might be getting a little off the point here? You only have to tell me about the hostage situation. Not about you and your husband.

Anna-Lena: But that's the problem.

JACK: What is?

Anna-Lena: I don't think he wants to be my husband any more.

JACK: What makes you say that?

Anna-Lena: Do you know how many IKEA stores there are in Sweden?

JACK: No.

Anna-Lena: Twenty. Do you know how many Roger and I have been to?

JACK: No.

Anna-Lena: All of them. Every single one. We went to the last one fairly recently, and I didn't think Roger had been keeping count, but when we were in the cafeteria having lunch Roger suddenly said we should each have a piece of cake as well. We never have cake in IKEA. We always have lunch, but never cake. And that was when I knew that he'd been keeping count. I know Roger doesn't seem romantic, but sometimes he can be the most romantic man on the planet, you know.

JACK: That certainly sounds romantic.

Anna-Lena: He can seem hard on the surface, but he doesn't hate children.

JACK: What?

Anna-Lena: Everyone thinks he hates children because he gets so angry when estate agents put 'children's room' on the plans. But he only gets angry because he says children push the price up like you wouldn't believe. He doesn't hate children. He loves children. That's why I have to distract him when we're walking through the children's section in IKEA.

JACK: I'm sorry.

ANNA-LENA: Why?

JACK: Sorry, I took that to mean that you couldn't have children. And if that's the case, I'm sorry.

ANNA-LENA: We've got two children!

JACK: I apologize. I misunderstood.

ANNA-LENA: Have you got children?

JACK: No.

ANNA-LENA: Our two are about your age, but they don't want kids of their own. Our son says he'd rather focus on his career, and our daughter says the world's already overpopulated.

JACK: Oh.

ANNA-LENA: Can you imagine what a bad parent you must have been for your children not to want to be parents?

JACK: I've never thought about that.

ANNA-LENA: Roger would have been such a good grandfather, you know. But now he doesn't even want to be my husband.

JACK: I'm sure things will work out between you, no matter what's happened.

ANNA-LENA: You don't know what's happened. You don't know what I've done, it was all my fault. But I just wanted to stop, it's been nothing but one apartment after the other for years now, and in the end I've had enough. I'm looking for a home, too. But I had no right to do what I did to Roger. I should never have paid for that darn rabbit.

It's harder than you might think to take people hostage when they're idiots.

The bank robber hesitated, the ski mask was itching, everyone was staring. The bank robber tried to think of something to say, but was forestalled by Roger holding one hand up and saying: 'We haven't got any cash!'

Anna-Lena was standing just behind him, and immediately repeated over his shoulder: 'We haven't got any *money*, understand?' She rubbed her fingertips together in illustration, because Anna-Lena always seemed to think that Roger spoke a language that only she understood, as if he were a horse and Anna-Lena some kind of equine translator, so she was always trying to interpret what he said to the rest of the world. When they were in a restaurant and Roger asked for the bill, Anna-Lena would always turn to the waiter and mouth the words 'Bill, please' while simultaneously pretending to write on the palm of her hand. Roger would no doubt have found this incredibly irritating if he ever bothered to pay attention to what Anna-Lena did.

'I don't want your money . . . please, just be quiet . . . I'm trying to hear if . . . ,' the bank robber said, listening out towards the door of the apartment in an attempt to figure out if the stairwell was already full of police.

'What are you doing here if you don't want money? If you're going to take us hostage, you might want to be a bit more specific in your demands,' Zara snorted from over by the balcony door, giving the distinct impression that she thought the bank robber was underperforming.

'Can you just give me a minute to think?' the bank robber asked.

Sadly it appeared that the people in this particular apartment weren't at all prepared to grant the bank robber that. You might think that if someone has a pistol, then people would be willing to do exactly as they've been asked, but some people who've never seen a pistol before simply take it for granted that it's so unlikely to happen that even when it *is* happening, they can't quite take it seriously.

Roger had barely ever seen a pistol before, even on television, because Roger prefers documentaries about sharks, so he held his hand up again (the other one this time, to show that he was serious) and demanded to know, loudly and clearly: 'Is this a *robbery* or not? Or is this now some sort of *hostage situation*? Which way do you want it?'

Anna-Lena looked rather uncomfortable when Roger switched hands, because nothing good ever came of Roger gesturing with both hands within the space of a few minutes, so she stage-whispered: 'Might it be better not to be provocative, Roger?'

'For God's sake, darling, surely we have a right to accurate information?' Roger replied, insulted, then turned to the bank robber once more and repeated: 'Is this a robbery or not?'

Anna-Lena stretched to see over his shoulder, and stuck out her thumb and forefinger, then waved them about in illustration while mouthing the words 'Bang?' twice, then adding one helpful 'Robbery?'

The bank robber took several deep breaths, eyes closed, the way you do when the children are fighting in the back of the car and you're getting stressed and lose your temper and shout at them rather more loudly than you intended, and they suddenly get so scared that they shut up altogether, and you end up hating yourself. Because you don't want to be that sort of parent. And the tone you use after that, when you apologize and explain that you love them but that you just have to concentrate on driving for a little while, that was the tone the bank robber used to address everyone in the apartment: 'Can you . . . can I ask you all to just lie down on the floor and be quiet for a little while? So I can just . . . do some thinking?'

No one lay down. Roger refused point-blank, saying: 'Not until we know what's going on!' Zara didn't want to, because: 'Have you seen the state of the floor? This is why everyday people have pets, because it makes literally no difference to them!' Julia demanded to be exempt, because: 'Look, if you sit me in an *armchair* it'll take me twenty minutes to get up, so I'm not going to lie down anywhere.'

For the first time the bank robber noticed that Julia was pregnant. Ro leapt in front of her at once, holding her arms up and grinning disarmingly. 'Please, don't mind my wife, she's just a bit hotheaded, please, don't shoot! We'll do exactly what you say!'

'I'm not bloody hothead –,' Julia protested.

'P-i-s-t-o-l!' Ro hissed. She hadn't looked this scared since the last time she tried to photograph her shoes and accidentally clicked the selfie button instead.

'It doesn't even look real,' Julia pointed out.

'Great. Let's take a chance, then. We're only risking our child's life, after all,' Ro retorted. At that point the bank robber clearly felt that enough was enough, and pointed at Julia.

'I . . . I didn't notice you were pregnant. You can leave. I don't want to hurt anyone, especially not a baby, I just need to think for a moment.'

When he heard this, Roger was struck by an idea, an idea so brilliant that only Roger could have been struck by it.

'Yes! Go on! Off you go!' he exclaimed. Then he marched over to the bank robber and added seriously: 'I mean, you can let them all go, can't you? You really only need one hostage, don't you? That would make things a lot easier.'

Roger poked his chest with his thumb repeatedly to indicate who the hostage should be, then added: 'Plus the estate agent. I can stay, with the estate agent.'

Julia glared suspiciously at him and snapped: 'That would suit you, wouldn't it? So you can make an offer on the apartment after the rest of us have gone!'

'Keep out of this!' Roger demanded.

'Like there's *any* chance we're leaving you alone here with the estate agent!' Julia snapped.

Affronted, Roger shook all the loose skin on the lower half of his face.

'This apartment isn't suitable for you, anyway! This is going to need someone who's good at DIY!'

Julia, far too competitive to let that pass, snapped back: 'My wife's pretty damn good at DIY!'

'What?' Ro said in surprise, unaware that there was another wife apart from her.

Anna-Lena thought out loud: 'Don't shout. Think of the baby.'

Roger nodded aggressively: 'Exactly! Think of the baby!'

Anna-Lena looked happy because he'd heard her, but Julia's eyes darkened.

'I'm not going anywhere until I've bought this apartment, you miserable old goat.'

Ro tugged at her arm anxiously and hissed: 'Why do you always have to argue with everyone?'

Because Ro had seen that look in her eyes before. On their very first date, several years ago, Julia was standing outside a bar smoking while Ro was inside ordering drinks. Two minutes later a security guard came over to Ro, pointed through the window, and asked: 'Are you with her?' Ro nodded, and was immediately thrown out of the bar. Apparently there was a delineated smoking area outside the bar, that was the only place you were allowed to smoke, but Julia had been standing two yards beyond the boundary. When the guard told her to go inside the rectangle, Julia started jumping about on the line, mocking him: 'What about here? Am I okay HERE? How about if I hold my cigarette inside while I'm standing outside? What about here? If the *cigarette's* outside but I blow the smoke *into* the rectangle?' When Julia had a bit of alcohol inside her, she tended to have trouble respecting any sort of authority, which might be thought a bad character trait to reveal on a first date, but when Ro was being thrown out, she asked the security guard how he knew she and Julia were there together, and he replied gruffly: 'When I told her to leave, she pointed at you through the window and said: "That's my girlfriend, I'm not leaving without her!"' That was the first time Ro had ever been anyone's girlfriend. That was the evening she went from being hopelessly infatuated to irrevocably in love.

Later on, it turned out that Julia's personality when she was drunk was exactly the same as Julia's personality when she was pregnant, so the past eight months had been fairly tumultuous – but life is full of surprises.

'Please, Jules?' Ro said tentatively.

Julia hissed back: 'If we leave now, this apartment could well be sold by the time we come back! How many apartments have we looked at? Twenty? You've found something wrong with every single one, and I can't bear it! So I'm damn well going to have this one, and no one's going to come along and say I –'

'P-i-s-t-o-l!' Ro repeated.

'Are you going to be farting a ten-pound monkey out of your uterus any time now, Ro? Well? So shut up!'

'It isn't fair to play the pregnancy card every time we have an argument, Jules, we've talked about that . . . ,' Ro muttered, sticking her hands deep into the pockets of her dress, and then Julia realized that she may have gone a bit too far, because Ro's hands had only delved that deeply into her pockets when the neighbours' kids killed one of her birds.

The bank robber let out a quiet cough and said: 'Excuse me? I don't want to interrupt, but . . . ,' then raised the pistol a little higher so that everyone could see it and remember exactly what was going on here.

Julia folded her arms over her chest and repeated, one last time: 'I'm not going anywhere.'

Ro let out a sigh so deep you could have found oil at the bottom of it, then nodded firmly: 'And I'm not going anywhere without her.'

This would obviously have been a very touching moment if Zara hadn't spoiled it by snorting at Ro: 'No one offered *you* the chance to leave. You're not pregnant.'

Ro dug her hands so far into her pockets that she actually punched holes in them, and mumbled: 'We're actually on this journey together.'

Roger, who had been getting more and more frustrated that no one seemed to be focusing on the most important thing here – that Roger hadn't been given any accurate information – was now pointing at the bank robber with both hands: 'So what are you after, then? Well? Is it the apartment you want?'

Anna-Lena described a square in the air with her hands like a mime artist trying to say 'apartment'. The bank robber groaned in resignation at the pair of them.

'Why would I . . . you can't just . . . are you suggesting that I'm trying to steal the apartment?'

Roger seemed to recognize how ridiculous that sounded when it was said out loud, but seeing as Roger was a man who was never wrong even when he was obviously wrong, he clarified: 'Now look here! It's got huge potential for renovation!'

Anna-Lena stood behind him with an imaginary hammer, waving it in the air by way of illustration.

The bank robber coughed quietly again, and could feel the beginnings of a headache, then said: 'Can't you just . . . lie down? Just for a little while? I wasn't trying . . . I mean, I was going to rob a bank, but I had no intention . . . look, this isn't what I had in mind!'

For various reasons the silence that followed was so complete that the only sound was the bank robber's sobs. That's never a comfortable

combination, someone crying with a pistol in their hand, so none of
the others was entirely sure how to react. Ro nudged Julia and muttered: 'Now see what you've done,' and Julia muttered back: 'It was
you who . . .' Roger turned to Anna-Lena and whispered: 'It really
does have immense potential for renovation,' and Anna-Lena replied quickly: 'Yes, it really does, doesn't it? You're absolutely right!
But . . . isn't that damp I can smell? Mold, even?'

The bank robber was still sobbing. None of the others felt like looking in that direction, because, as already mentioned, it's hard to feel
comfortable with armed expressions of emotion, so in the end it was
Estelle who cautiously padded over. Either she didn't know any better, or she most definitely did. It might seem a little odd that Estelle
hasn't been mentioned very often up till now in this story, not because Estelle is easy to forget about, but because she's very hard to
remember. Estelle has what might be called a transparent personality.
Eighty-seven years old, with a body as gnarled and crooked as a piece
of ginger, she slipped over to the bank robber and asked: 'Are you
all right, dear?' When the bank robber didn't answer, she went on
babbling in a singularly untroubled manner: 'My name's Estelle, I'm
here to take a look at the apartment on behalf of my daughter. My
husband, Knut, is parking the car. It isn't at all easy to find anywhere
to park around here, and I don't suppose it will be any easier now
that the street's full of police cars. Sorry, now I've made you worried.
I didn't mean it was *your* fault that Knut couldn't find anywhere to
park, of course. Are you feeling all right? Would you like a glass of
water?'

The pistol didn't seem to bother Estelle, but on the other hand
she seemed to be such a kind person that if she were murdered she'd
probably have taken it as a compliment that someone had noticed her.
Using a paper handkerchief to dry the tears, the bank robber said quietly: 'Yes, please.'

'We've got limes!' Ro called out, pointing at the bowl on the coffee table, full of at least a couple of dozen. Limes seemed to be such a popular adornment at apartment viewings that it's tempting to think that if estate agents were banned, the surface of the earth would become covered with such a thick layer of limes that only young people with very small knives and an inexplicable fondness for Mexican beer would survive.

Estelle fetched a glass of water, and the bank robber raised the mask slightly so as to be able to drink it.

'Is that better?' Estelle asked.

The bank robber nodded gently and handed the glass back to her.

'I'm . . . I'm very sorry about all this.'

'Oh, don't worry, dear, it doesn't matter,' Estelle said. 'I have to say, I think it was smart of you not to have come here to steal the apartment. Because that wouldn't have been very clever, would it, because the police would have known where to find you straight away! Was it the bank across the street that you were planning to rob? Isn't that one of those cashless banks these days?'

'Yes. Thanks. I noticed that,' the bank robber replied through clenched teeth.

'Smart!' Zara declared.

The bank robber turned towards her, losing control altogether and shouting the way you do when the kids start arguing in the back of the car again: 'I didn't *know*, okay? Anyone can make a *mistake*!'

Roger, whose instinct whenever anyone shouted, regardless of context, was always to shout louder, shouted: *'All I want is information!'*

So the bank robber shouted: *'Just let me think!'*

To which Roger shouted: *'You're not much good at being a bank robber, you know!'*

Whereupon the bank robber waved the pistol and shouted: *'Luckily for you!'*

Ro quickly stepped forward and shouted: *'Okay, everyone stop shouting now! It's not good for the baby!'*

Which of course was perfectly true, babies find shouting unsettling, Ro had read that in the same book that had told her that pregnancy was a shared journey. After this pronouncement she turned to Julia as if she were expecting a medal. Julia rolled her eyes. 'Really, Ro? Someone's pointing a gun at us, and you're worried about a few raised voices?'

In the meantime Estelle gently patted the bank robber's arm and explained: 'Yes, those two are going to have a baby together, you know, even though they're from . . . well, you know.'

She winked at the bank robber as if that were all she needed to say. It didn't seem to have worked, though. So Estelle adjusted her skirt and changed tack: 'Well, I don't see why we have to fall out. Can't we start by introducing ourselves instead? My name is Estelle. You never said what your name is.'

With a tilt of the head and a gesture toward the mask, the bank robber said: 'I . . . look . . . that's not a great question to ask me.'

Estelle nodded apologetically at once, and turned to the others.

'Well, then, perhaps we should assume that our friend here wants to remain anonymous. But you could tell us all your names, couldn't you?' she said, nodding at Roger.

'Roger,' Roger muttered.

'And my name's Anna-Lena!' Anna-Lena said, accustomed to not being asked.

'I'm Ro, and this is my wife, Juli – OW!' Ro said, clutching her shin.

The bank robber looked at them all, then gave a brief nod.

'Okay. Hello.'

'So now we all know each other! Lovely!' Estelle declared, so delighted that she clapped her hands. And for such a slight person she could clap her hands surprisingly hard. Which isn't a great thing to do in a room in which someone is holding a pistol, seeing as everyone thought that the sudden clap was a pistol shot and threw themselves down on the floor.

The bank robber looked at the prone bodies in surprise, then, with a scratch of the head, turned to Estelle and said: 'Thanks. That was very helpful of you.'

Anna-Lena was lying curled up on the carpet by the sofa, and had trouble breathing for half a minute until she realized that was because Roger, when he thought he heard a pistol shot, had thrown himself on top of her.

31

Witness Interview
Date: December 30
Name of witness: Estelle

JIM: I really am very sorry about all this. We'll try to get you home as soon as possible.

ESTELLE: Oh, don't worry — to be honest, this has all been rather exciting. Not much exciting happens most days when you're nearly ninety!

JIM: Of course, yes. Well, my colleague and I would very much like to ask you to look at this drawing. We found it in the stairwell and we think it shows a monkey, a frog and an elk. Do you recognize it?

ESTELLE: No, no, I'm afraid not. Is that really supposed to be an elk?

JIM: I don't know, I really don't. To be honest, I'm not sure it really matters. Would you mind telling me what you were doing at the apartment viewing?

ESTELLE: I was there with my husband, Knut. Well, he wasn't there at the time. He was still parking the car. We were going to look at the apartment for our daughter.

JIM: Did you notice anything particular about the other people there before the bank robber appeared?

ESTELLE: Oh, no. Before then I only really had time to talk to those nice women from . . . you know . . . from Stockholm.

JIM: Which ones were they?

ESTELLE: Oh, you know. 'From Stockholm.'

JIM: You're winking as though I ought to know what that means.

ESTELLE: Ro and Jules. They're having a baby together. Even though they're both from, you know, 'Stockholm'.

JIM: You mean that they're homosexual?

ESTELLE: There's nothing wrong with that.

JIM: I didn't say there was, did I?

ESTELLE: That's absolutely fine these days.

JIM: Of course it is. I haven't suggested otherwise.

ESTELLE: I think it's wonderful, I really do, that people are free to love whoever they like nowadays.

JIM: I'd like to make it absolutely clear that I share that view.

ESTELLE: In my day, it would have been regarded as quite remarkable, you know, getting married and having a baby when you're both, well, you know.

JIM: From Stockholm?

ESTELLE: Yes. But I've actually always rather liked Stockholm, you know. You have to let people live their lives however they want. I mean, that's not to say I've been to Stockholm myself, I haven't, of course not. I'm not, that's to say I've never . . . I'm happily married. To Knut. And I'm very happy with the usual, you know.

JIM: I have no idea what we're talking about any more.

32

When the first police siren was heard from the street, the bank robber ran out on to the balcony and peered over the railing. That was how the first blurry mobile phone pictures of 'the masked gunman' appeared on the Internet. Then even more police officers appeared.

'Shit, shit, shit, shit, shit,' the bank robber repeated quietly, then ran back inside the apartment, where everyone except for Julia was still lying on the floor.

'I can't lie down any longer because I need to go to the toilet! Or do you want me to do it all over the floor?' Julia snapped defensively even though the bank robber showed no sign of saying anything.

'Not that it would make much difference,' Zara said, lifting her face from the parquet floor in disgust.

Ro, who seemed to have a lot of experience in being yelled at despite not actually having said anything, sat up and patted the bank robber's leg consolingly.

'Don't take the fact that Julia's shouting at you personally. She's just a bit sensitive, because the baby's having a disco in her stomach, you know?'

'Personal information, Ro!' Julia roared.

They have a definition for what counts as personal, Julia and Ro, even though Julia is the only one who knows what that definition is.

'I was actually talking to our bank robber. You only told me not to talk to the other prospective buyers,' Ro said defensively.

'But I'm not really a bank —' the bank robber began, but was drowned out by Julia.

'Doesn't make any difference, Ro, stop making friends! I know how this ends, they tell you their life story and then you feel bad when we have to outbid them for the apartment!'

'That happened *once*,' Ro called after her.

'*Three times!*' Julia said, reaching for the bathroom door.

Ro gestured apologetically to the bank robber: 'Julia says I'm the sort of person who refuses to eat fish sticks after seeing the dolphins at the sea life centre.'

The bank robber nodded understandingly. 'My daughters are like that.'

Ro smiled. 'You've got daughters? How old are they?'

The numbers seemed to catch in the bank robber's throat: 'Six and eight.'

Zara cleared her throat and asked: 'Are they going to inherit the family business, then?'

Wounded, the bank robber blinked and looked down at the pistol. 'I've never . . . done this before. I'm . . . I'm not a criminal.'

'I certainly hope not, because you really are shockingly bad at it,' Zara declared.

'Why do you have to be so critical?' Ro snapped at her.

'I'm not critical, I'm giving feedback,' Zara said, by way of offering feedback.

'I can't imagine you'd be that good at robbing people,' Ro said.

'I don't rob people, I rob banks,' the bank robber interjected.

'And how good are you at that, on a scale of one to ten?' Zara asked.

The bank robber looked at her sheepishly. 'A two, maybe.'

'Have you even got a plan for how you're going to get out of here?' Zara asked.

'Stop being so demanding! Criticism doesn't help anyone improve!' Ro said critically.

Zara studied her intently. 'Is this what your personality is like? Are you happy with it?'

'Says *you*,' Ro began, then the bank robber tried to calm things down.

'Can you just . . . please? I haven't got a plan. I need to think. It wasn't supposed to turn out like this.'

'What?' Ro asked.

'Life,' the bank robber sniffed.

Zara took her phone out of her pocket and said: 'Okay, let's call the police and get this sorted out.'

'No! Don't!' the bank robber said.

Zara rolled her eyes.

'What are you scared of? Do you honestly think they don't know you're here? You have to call them and tell them how much ransom you want, at least.'

'You can't call, there's no signal in here,' Ro said.

'Are we in prison already?' Zara wondered, shaking her phone as if that might help.

Ro stuck her hands in her pockets and said, half to herself: 'It's actually not that bad, because I've read that children who grow up not staring at screens are more intelligent. Technology stunts the development of the brain.'

Zara nodded sarcastically.

'Really? Tell me about all the Nobel Prize winners who grew up in Amish communities.'

'I've actually read that there's research that says mobile signals cause cancer,' Ro persisted.

'Yes, but what if it's an emergency? What if you move in here and your baby chokes on a peanut and dies because you can't call an ambulance?' Zara said.

'What are you talking about? Where would the baby get the peanut from in the first place?'

'Maybe someone put some through the mail slot during the night.'

'Are you really this sick?'

'I'm not the one who wants my baby to choke to death —'

They were interrupted by Julia, who was suddenly standing beside them again.

'What are you arguing about now?'

'She started it! I was trying to be friendly, and that's not the same as me not wanting to eat fish sticks!' Ro snapped defensively, pointing at Zara.

Julia groaned, and looked apologetically at Zara.

'Did Ro tell you about the sea life centre? And dolphins aren't even fish.'

'What's that got to do with anything? Anyway, weren't you going to the toilet?'

'It was occupied,' Julia said, shrugging.

The bank robber pulled at the ski mask with one hand, then counted the people in the room. Then stammered: 'Hang on . . . what do you mean, occupied?'

'Occupied!' Julia repeated, as if that were going to help.

The bank robber went and tugged at the bathroom door. It was locked.

And that was how this turned into a story about a rabbit.

33

Witness Interview (Continued)

ESTELLE: I'd like to make it clear that I'm sure Stockholm is perfectly pleasant. If you like Stockholmers. And I can tell you right now that I don't think Knut has any prejudices, either, because once when we were younger I was tidying his office and I found an entire magazine all about Stockholm.

JIM: Great.

ESTELLE: I didn't think so at the time. We actually had quite a row about it, Knut and I.

JIM: I see. So, you were talking to Ro and Julia when the bank robber came in?

ESTELLE: They keep birds. And they argued all the time. But in a cute way. Of course, the other couple were arguing, too, Roger and Anna-Lena, but that was nowhere near as cute.

JIM: What were Roger and Anna-Lena arguing about?

ESTELLE: The rabbit.

JIM: What rabbit?

ESTELLE: Oh, it's quite a long story, if I'm honest. They were arguing about the cost of the apartment, per square foot, you see. Roger was worried that everyone was pushing the price up. He said the housing market was being manipulated by bastard estate agents and bastard bankers and Stockholmers.

JIM: Hold on, was he saying that homosexuals were manipulating the housing market?

ESTELLE: Homosexuals? Why would they be doing that? That's a terrible thing to say! Who'd say a thing like that?

JIM: You said Stockholmers were doing it.

ESTELLE: Yes, but I meant Stockholmers. Not 'Stockholmers'.

JIM: Is there a difference?

ESTELLE: Yes. One's Stockholmers, and the other's 'Stockholmers'.

JIM: Sorry, but I'm confused now. Let me try to write this down in chronological order.

ESTELLE: Take your time, as much time as you need. I'm not in a hurry.

JIM: I'm sorry, but I think perhaps it would be best if we went back to the first question?

ESTELLE: Which one was that?

JIM: Did you notice anything particular about the other prospective buyers?

ESTELLE: Zara looked sad. And Anna-Lena didn't like the green curtains. And Ro was worried the closet wouldn't be big enough. But it's one of those walk-in closets, as they're called these days. I didn't know that until I heard Jules call it that.

JIM: No, hold on, that can't be right. There's no walk-in closet on the plans.

ESTELLE: Maybe it looks smaller on there?

JIM: The plan must be to scale, though, surely?

ESTELLE: Oh, must it?

JIM: On the plans, the closet isn't even two square feet in size. Can I ask how big this walk-in closet is?

ESTELLE: I'm not very good at measurements. But Ro said she wanted to use it as a hobby room. She makes her own cheese, you know. And grows flowers. Well, some sort of plants, anyway. Jules isn't very happy about that. Once Ro tried to make her own champagne and made a mess of Jules's underwear drawer. Ro said that caused 'a hell of a fight'.

JIM: Sorry, but can we try to focus on the size of the closet?

ESTELLE: Jules was insistent that it was a walk-in closet.

JIM: Is it big enough to hide in?

ESTELLE: Who?

JIM: Anyone.

ESTELLE: I suppose so. Is it important?

JIM: No. No, probably not. But my colleague was keen that I should ask all the witnesses about possible hiding places. Would you like some coffee?

ESTELLE: A cup of coffee would certainly be very nice, I wouldn't say no to that at all.

34

The bank robber stared at the bathroom door. Then at all the hostages. Then asked: 'Do you think there's someone in there?'

Zara countered in a way that could have been taken as sarcastic: 'What do you think?'

The bank robber blinked so many times that it looked like Morse code.

'So you *do* think there's someone in there, then?'

'Did your parents by any chance have the same surname before they met?' Zara asked.

Ro took offence on behalf of the bank robber, and snapped: 'Why do you have to be such a cow?'

Julia kicked Ro's shin and hissed: 'Don't get involved, Ro!'

'You're the one who's always saying we're going to teach our child to stand up to bullies! I'm not going to stand here and let her talk to –' Ro protested.

'Talk to who? A bank robber? Is that bullying? Heaven forbid that someone who's threatening us with a gun should feel offended!' Julia said with a groan.

'I'm not –' the bank robber began, but Julia raised a warning finger.

'You know what? You're the one who's caused all this, so you can just shut up.'

Zara, who was looking at the dust on her clothes and couldn't have appeared more disgusted if she'd just climbed out of a pile of manure, noted: 'Good that your kid's got at least *one* mother who isn't a communist.'

Julia spun around towards her: 'And *you* can shut up as well.'

Zara did actually shut up. No one was more surprised by that than Zara herself.

* * *

In the meantime Roger cautiously rose to his feet. He helped Anna-Lena up, she looked him in the eye and he didn't really know where to look, they weren't used to touching each other without turning the lights out first. Anna-Lena blushed, and Roger turned around and started knocking absentmindedly on the walls in an attempt to look busy. He always knocked on the walls at apartment viewings, Anna-Lena wasn't entirely sure why, but he said it was because he needed to know 'if you could drill into them.' That was important to Roger, this business of drilling, and it was just as important to know if the wall was load-bearing. If you remove a load-bearing wall, the ceiling collapses. And apparently you could hear that if you knocked on the wall, at least you could if you were Roger, so he did it every-where at every single viewing, knocking and knocking and knocking. Anna-Lena sometimes used to think that everyone gets a few mo-ments that show who they really are, tiny instances that reveal their entire soul, and Roger's were this knocking. Because sometimes, so fleetingly that no one but Anna-Lena would even notice it, he would stand motionless immediately after a knock, looking at the wall in anticipation. The way a child might. As if he were hoping that one day someone would knock back. Those were Anna-Lena's favourite Roger moments.

Knock knock knock. Knock. Knock. Knock.

He suddenly stopped right in the middle of a knock. Because he was listening to the conversation between Ro and Julia and Zara about the locked bathroom door. A shiver ran down Roger's spine when he real-ized that the most terrible thing of all might be hiding in there: another prospective buyer. He therefore decided to take charge of the situation at once. He marched straight over to the locked bathroom and had just raised his hand to knock when Anna-Lena cried out: 'No!'

Roger turned around in surprise and looked at his wife. She was shaking all over, and was blushing right down to her fingertips.

'Please . . . don't open the door,' she whispered, and Roger had never seen her so frightened, and had absolutely no idea what might be the cause. Zara was standing alongside them, looking from one to the other. Then, predictably, she walked to the bathroom door and knocked on it. After a short pause someone knocked back.

By then tears were running down Anna-Lena's cheeks.

35

Witness Interview
Date: December 30
Name of witness: Roger

JACK: Are you okay?

ROGER: What sort of question is that?

JACK: Your nose looks like it's been bleeding.

ROGER: Yes, well, it does that sometimes, the quack says it's 'stress'. Never mind that, just ask your questions.

JACK: Okay, then. You went to the apartment viewing with your wife, Anna-Lena?

ROGER: How do you know that?

JACK: It's in my notes.

ROGER: Why have you got notes about my wife?

JACK: We're interviewing all the witnesses.

ROGER: You shouldn't have notes about my wife.

JACK: Just stay calm now.

ROGER: I'm perfectly freaking calm.

JACK: In my experience, that's what people who are anything but calm say.

ROGER: I'm not going to answer any questions about my wife!

JACK: No, okay, fine. Can you answer some questions about the perpetrator, then?

ROGER: How can I answer that until you've asked them?

JACK: To start with: Where do you think he's hiding?

ROGER: Who?

JACK: Who do you think?

ROGER: The bank robber?

JACK: No, Waldo.

ROGER: Who's that?

JACK: You don't know who Waldo is? It's the title of an
             old kids' book, *Where's Waldo?*. Forget it, I was
             being sarcastic.

ROGER: I have no reason to read kids' books.

JACK: I'm sorry. Can you tell me where you think the
             perpetrator is hiding?

ROGER: How should I know?

JACK: I hope you'll forgive me pressing you for an
             answer, but we have reason to believe that the
             perpetrator is still in the apartment. I thought
             perhaps you might be able to help, because your
             wife says you do exhaustive research before each
             viewing. And that you check all the measurements
             on the plans.

ROGER: You can't trust estate agents. Some of them
             couldn't even measure a ruler using another ruler.

JACK: That's exactly what I mean. Did you discover any-
             thing special about this particular apartment?

ROGER: Yes. The estate agent is an idiot.

JACK: Why?

ROGER: There were three feet missing from the measure-
             ments, between the walls.

JACK: Really? Between which walls? Can you show me on
             the plan?

ROGER: There. You can hear it if you knock. The gap.

JACK: Why would it be there?

ROGER: Probably because this apartment and the one next
             door used to be one single larger apartment once
             upon a time, when people around here had more
             money and apartments were cheaper. Now the whole
             housing market's being manipulated to screw or-
             dinary people. It's the estate agents' fault. And
             the banks'. And people from Stockholm. Driving
             the prices up and everything. What the hell are
             you rolling your eyes for?

JACK: Sorry. I don't want to get involved. But haven't

	you and your wife bought and sold a number of apartments as speculative investments in recent years? Surely that must push prices up as well?
ROGER:	So now there's something wrong with making a bit of money, too?
JACK:	I didn't say that.
ROGER:	I'm a good negotiator, and that isn't a crime, you know!
JACK:	No, no, of course not.
ROGER:	At least I thought I was a good negotiator.
JACK:	I don't follow you?
ROGER:	I used to be an engineer. Before I retired. Does it say that in your notes?
JACK:	What? No.
ROGER:	So that's not relevant, then? A whole life spent doing a job, and it isn't relevant enough to be included in your notes? Do you know what my colleagues did in those last years?
JACK:	No.
ROGER:	They were faking it. Just like her.
JACK:	Your wife?
ROGER:	No, Waldo.
JACK:	What?
ROGER:	You think people in your generation are the only ones who can be sarcastic, boy?

36

Julia nodded toward the bathroom door, held her hand out towards the bank robber, and demanded: 'Give me the pistol.'

'Abso . . . absolutely not! What are you thinking of doing?' the bank robber stammered, hiding the pistol from view like it was a kitten and someone had just asked the bank robber if anyone had seen a kitten anywhere.

'I'm pregnant and I need to go to the toilet. Give me the pistol so I can shoot the lock out,' Julia repeated.

'No,' the bank robber whimpered.

Julia threw her arms out.

'You'll have to do it yourself, then. Just shoot the lock out.'

'I don't want to.'

Julia's eyes narrowed in an unsettling way.

'What do you mean, you don't want to? You're holding us all hostage and the police are outside and you've got an unknown individual in the bathroom. It could be anyone. You need to have a bit of respect for yourself! How else are you ever going to be a successful bank robber? You can't let people tell you what to do the whole time!'

'But you're telling me what to do —' the bank robber started to say, but Julia interrupted:

'Shoot the lock out, I said!'

For a moment it looked like the bank robber was going to do as she said, but suddenly there was a small click, the door handle slowly swung down, and a voice said from inside the bathroom: 'Don't shoot. Please, don't shoot!'

A man dressed in a rabbit costume emerged. Well, if we're being completely truthful, not a complete costume. It was really just a rabbit's head, because apart from that the man was wearing nothing but underpants and socks. He appeared to be in his fifties and, if we're being diplomatic, had the sort of body that wasn't exactly flattered by the ratio of clothing to skin.

'Don't hurt me, please, I'm just doing my job!' the man whined from inside the rabbit's head in a Stockholm accent as he stuck his hands up. He was evidently a Stockholmer, one of the ones who was born there, not just a 'Stockholmer' in the sense that Jim and Jack used it when they actually meant 'idiot'. (Which of course doesn't mean that the man wasn't an idiot as well, because it's still a free country.) And he certainly wasn't a 'Stockholmer' in the way that Estelle used the word to describe the sort of family unit that there's absolutely nothing wrong with (and if he had been, then obviously there wouldn't have been anything wrong with that at all). He was just a perfectly ordinary Stockholmer, who happened to be saying from inside the rabbit's head: 'Tell them not to shoot me, Anna-Lena!'

Everyone fell silent, no one more so than Roger. He was staring at Anna-Lena, she was staring at the rabbit and crying, her fingers fluttering about her hips as she evaded Roger's surprised stare. She couldn't remember the last time she had seen her husband surprised, that's really not supposed to happen when you've been married so long. You're supposed to have just one thing in your life, one single person you can count on to the extent that you end up taking her for granted. And at this precise moment, Anna-Lena knew all that was ruined for Roger. She whispered in despair: 'Don't hurt him. It's Lennart.'

'Do you *know* this person?' Roger spluttered.

Anna-Lena nodded sadly.

'Yes, but it's not what you think, Roger!'

'Is he . . . is he . . . ?' Roger struggled, before finally managing to utter the impossible words: '. . . another prospective buyer?'

Anna-Lena couldn't bring herself to answer, so Roger spun around and lurched towards the bathroom door with such force that both Julia and Ro (Zara, helpfully, merely jumped out of the way) were obliged

to hold him back with all their strength so that he couldn't get a strangle-
hold on the rabbit.

'Why is my wife crying? Who are you? Are you a prospective
buyer? Answer me this instant!' Roger bellowed.

He didn't get an immediate answer, and that upset Anna-Lena as
well. Roger had always been an important, respected man at work, and
even his bosses had listened to him there. Retirement wasn't something that Roger entered into voluntarily, it was something that had
suddenly afflicted him. The first few months he would drive past the
office, sometimes several times a day, because he was hoping to see
some sign that the people inside couldn't cope without him. He never
saw one. He wasn't at all difficult to replace, so he went home and the
business carried on existing. That realization was a great burden to
Roger, and made him slower.

'*Answer me!*' he demanded of the rabbit, but the rabbit was busy
trying to take its rabbit head off. It had evidently got stuck. Beads of
sweat bounced from hair to hair on his bare back, like a singularly
unappealing pinball game, and his underpants were now also sitting
slightly crookedly.

The bank robber stood mutely alongside and looked on, and Zara
clearly felt it was time for a bit more feedback, so she gave the bank
robber a shove.

'Aren't you going to do something?'

'Like what?' the bank robber wondered.

'Take charge! What sort of hostage taker are you?' Zara demanded.

'I'm not a hostage taker, I'm a bank robber,' the bank robber
whimpered.

'That turned out to be a great choice, didn't it?'

'Please, just stop pushing me.'

'Oh, just shoot the rabbit so we can get things sorted out. So you
earn a bit of respect. You only have to shoot it in the leg.'

'*No, don't shoot!*' the rabbit screamed.

'Stop giving me orders,' the bank robber said.

'He could be a policeman,' Zara suggested.

'I still don't want to . . .'

'Give me the pistol, then.'

'No!'

Unconcerned, Zara turned to the rabbit. 'Who are you? Are you a cop or what? Answer, or we'll shoot.'

'I'm the one doing the shooting here! Well, I'm not, actually!' the bank robber protested.

Zara patted the bank robber condescendingly on the arm.

'Hmm. Of course you are. Of course you are.'

The bank robber stamped the floor in frustration.

'No one's listening to me! You're the worst hostages ever!'

'Please, don't shoot, my head's stuck,' Lennart cried from inside the rabbit's head, then went on: 'Anna-Lena can explain everything, we're . . . I'm . . . I'm with her.'

Suddenly there wasn't enough air for Roger. He turned to Anna-Lena again, so slowly that she couldn't remember him turning to her like that since one day in the early 1990s, when he realized she'd used the wrong VHS tape to record an episode of a soap opera and accidentally recorded over an important documentary about antelopes. Roger couldn't find any words for her betrayal, either then or now. They had always been people of simple words. Anna-Lena may have hoped that would improve when they had children, but the reverse had happened. Parenthood can lead to a sequence of years when the children's feelings suck all the oxygen out of a family, and that can be so emotionally intense that some adults go for years without having an opportunity to tell anyone about their own feelings, and if you don't get a chance for long enough, sometimes you simply forget how to do it.

Roger's love for Anna-Lena was visible in other ways. Little things, like checking the screws and hinges of the little mirrored door on her cabinet in the bathroom every day, so it would always open and close with the least possible resistance. At the time of day when Anna-Lena opened the cabinet she really wasn't ready for any difficulties, Roger knew that. Anna-Lena had become interested in interior design late in life, but she had read in a book that every designer needed an 'anchor' in each new scheme. Something solid and definite that everything else can build upon, spreading out from it in ever-increasing circles. For Anna-Lena, that anchor was her bathroom cabinet. Roger understood that, because he appreciated the value of immovable objects, such as load-bearing walls. You can't make them adapt to you, you simply have to adapt to them. So Roger always unscrewed the bathroom cabinet last of all whenever they moved out of an apartment, and installed it first when they arrived at the new one. That was how he loved her. But now she was standing there, full of surprises, and confessing: 'This is Lennart, and he and I . . . well, we're . . . we have a . . . you weren't ever supposed to find out, darling!'

Silence. Betrayal.

'So the two of you . . . you and . . . the two of you . . . behind my back?' Roger said, with some effort.

'It's not what you think,' Anna-Lena insisted.

'Not at all what you think,' the rabbit assured him.

'It really isn't,' Anna-Lena added.

'Well . . . perhaps it is a little bit, depending on what you're thinking,' the rabbit conceded.

'Be quiet now, Lennart!' Anna-Lena said.

'Then just tell him the truth,' the rabbit suggested.

Anna-Lena breathed in through her nose and closed her eyes.

'Lennart's just a . . . we got in touch on the Internet. It wasn't supposed . . . it just happened, Roger.'

Roger's arms were hanging limply by his sides, lost. In the end he turned to the bank robber, pointed at the rabbit, and whispered: 'How much do you want for shooting him?'

'Can everyone please just stop telling me to shoot people?' the bank robber pleaded.

'We can make it look like an accident,' Roger said.

Anna-Lena took several desperate steps towards Roger, trying to reach his fingertips.

'Please, darling . . . Roger, calm down . . .'

Roger had no intention of calming down. He held one hand out towards the rabbit and swore: 'You're going to die! Do you hear me? You're going to die!'

Panic-stricken, Anna-Lena blurted out the only thing she could think of that would grab his attention: 'Roger, wait! If anyone dies in here, this apartment will be a murder scene and then the price per square foot might go up! People love murder scenes!'

Roger stopped at this, his fists were quivering but he took a deep breath and managed to calm down slightly. The price was always the price, after all. His shoulders sank first, followed by the rest of him, both internally and externally. He looked down at the floor and whispered: 'How long has this been going on? Between you and this . . . this bloody rabbit?'

'A year,' Anna-Lena said.

'A *year*?!'

'Please, Roger, I only did it for your sake.'

Roger's jowls were shaking with despair and confusion, his lips were moving but all his emotions remained trapped inside. The man with the rabbit's head appeared to see an opportunity to explain what was really going on, which he did in a tone that only a middle-aged man with a Stockholm accent as broad as a motorway could do: 'Listen, Rog – you don't mind me calling you Rog? Don't feel bad about this! Women often turn to me, you know, because I'm happy to do the things they might not be able to persuade their husbands to do.'

Roger's face was contorted into one large wrinkle.

'What sort of things? What sort of relationship are the two of you actually having?'

'A business *arrangement*, I'm a professional!' the rabbit corrected.

'Professional? Have you been *paying* to sleep with him, Anna-Lena?' Roger exclaimed.

Anna-Lena's eyes doubled in size.

'Are you mad?' she hissed.

The rabbit stepped closer to Roger to sort out the misunder-
standing.

'No, no, not that sort of professional. I don't sleep with people.
Well, not professionally, anyway. I disrupt viewings, I'm a professional disrupter, here's my card.' The rabbit fished a business card out
of one of his socks. *No Boundaries Lennart Ltd*, it said, the *Ltd* indicat-
ing the seriousness of the business.

Anna-Lena bit the inside of her lip and said: 'Yes, Lennart's been
helping me. Us!'

'What the hell . . . ?' Roger exclaimed.

The rabbit nodded proudly.

'Oh, yes, Rog. Sometimes I'm an alcoholic neighbour, sometimes
I just rent the apartment above the one where the viewing is taking
place and watch an erotic film with the volume turned up really loud.
But this is my most expensive package.' He gestured towards himself,
from his white socks to his underpants, then his bare chest, until he
reached the rabbit's head, which he still hadn't managed to remove.
Then he announced proudly: 'This is "the crapping rabbit", you see.
The premium package. If you order this, I sneak into the apartment
before everyone else and hide in the bathroom. Then when the other
prospective buyers open the door, they catch sight of a naked, adult
man with a rabbit's head sitting on the toilet doing his business. People
never really get over it. You can always get rid of scratched floors and
ugly wallpaper when you move in, can't you? But a crapping rabbit?'
The rabbit tapped the temples of the rabbit's head demonstratively: 'It
gets stuck in here! You wouldn't want to live anywhere you saw that,
would you?!' A thought that all of those present, as they looked at the
rabbit, had nothing but sympathy for.

Anna-Lena reached her hand out to Roger's arm, but he pulled
it away as if she'd burned him. She sniffed: 'Please, Roger, don't
you remember that viewing in the recently renovated turn-of-

the-century building last year, when a drunk neighbour suddenly appeared and started throwing spaghetti bolognese at all the prospective buyers?'

Roger was so insulted that he let out a loud snort.

'Of course I do! We bought that apartment for three hundred and twenty-five thousand below its market value!'

The rabbit nodded happily.

'I don't like to boast, but the alcoholic spaghetti-throwing neighbour is one of my most popular characters.'

Roger stared at Anna-Lena.

'Do you mean to say that . . . but . . . what about all my negotiations with the estate agent? All my *tactics*?'

Anna-Lena couldn't meet his gaze.

'You get so upset when you lose a bid. I just wanted you to . . . win.'

She wasn't telling the whole truth. That she had become the sort of person who just wanted a home. That she wanted to stop now. That she'd like to go to the cinema occasionally and see something made-up instead of yet another documentary on television. That she didn't want to be a shark. She was worried that the betrayal would be too much for Roger.

'How many times?' Roger whispered in a broken voice.

'Three,' Anna-Lena lied.

'Six, actually! I know all the addresses by heart . . . ,' the rabbit corrected.

'Shut up, Lennart!' Anna-Lena sobbed.

Lennart nodded obediently, and started to tug and pull at the rabbit's head again. He spent a long time fully absorbed in that, before declaring: 'I think something loosened a bit just then!'

Roger just stared down at the floor with his toes tightly clenched in his shoes, because Roger was the sort of man who felt emotion in his feet. He started to walk around in a wide semicircle, over to the balcony door, accidentally stubbed his toes against one of the skirting boards, and swore quietly, quietly, quietly, both at the damnable skirting board and the damnable rabbit.

'You stupid . . . stupid . . . you stupid . . . ,' he muttered, as if he were searching for the very worst insult he could think of. Eventually he found it: 'You stupid Stockholmer!' His toes hurt as much as his heart, so he clenched his fists and looked up, then ran back through the apartment so quickly that no one had time to stop him, and knocked the rabbit to the floor. With all his love, at full force, one single blow.

The rabbit fell through the door back on to the bathroom floor. Fortunately the padded rabbit's head absorbed most of the impact from Roger's punch, and the softness of the rest of Lennart's physique (he had roughly the same density as a dumpling) absorbed the rest. When he opened his eyes and looked up at the ceiling, Julia was leaning over him.

'Are you still alive?' she asked.

'The head's stuck again,' he replied.

'Are you hurt?'

'I don't think so.'

'Good. Move, then. I need to pee.'

The rabbit whimpered some sort of apology and crawled out of the bathroom. On the way, he handed Julia a business card, nodded so hard towards her stomach that his rabbit's ears fell over his eyes, and managed to say: 'I do children's parties as well. If you don't like your children.'

Julia closed the door behind him. But she kept the business card. Any normal parent would have done the same.

Anna-Lena was looking at Roger, but he was refusing to look back. Blood was dripping from his nose. Their doctor had told Anna-Lena that it was a reaction to stress after Roger was diagnosed as being burnt-out at work.

'You're bleeding, I'll get some tissue,' she whispered, but Roger wiped his nose on the sleeve of his shirt.

'Dammit, I'm just a bit tired!'

He strode out into the hall, mostly because he wanted to be in a different room, which made him curse the open-plan layout. Anna-Lena wanted to follow him but realized he needed some space, so she turned and walked into the closet, because that was as far from him as she could get. There she sat down on a small stool and went to pieces. She didn't notice the cold air blowing in, as if a window were open. As if there could be an open window in a closet.

The bank robber was standing in the centre of the apartment, surrounded by Stockholmers, both figurative and literal. 'Stockholm' is, after all, an expression more than it is a place, both for men like Roger and for most of the rest of us, just a symbolic word to denote all the irritating people who get in the way of our happiness. People who think they're better than us. Bankers who say no when we apply for a loan, psychologists who ask questions when we only want sleeping pills, old men who steal the apartments we want to renovate, rabbits who steal our wives. Everyone who doesn't see us, doesn't understand us, doesn't care about us. Everyone has Stockholmers in their life, even people from Stockholm have their own Stockholmers, only to them it's 'people who live in New York' or 'politicians in Brussels', or other people from some other place where people seem to think that they're better than the Stockholmers think they are.

Everyone inside the apartment had their own complexes, their own demons and anxieties: Roger was wounded, Anna-Lena wanted to go home, Lennart couldn't get his rabbit head off, Julia was tired, Ro was worried, Zara was in pain, and Estelle . . . well . . . no one really knew what Estelle was yet. Possibly not even Estelle. Sometimes 'Stockholm' can actually be a compliment: a dream of somewhere bigger, where we can become someone else. Something that we long for but don't quite dare to do. Everyone in the apartment was wrestling with their own story.

'Forgive me,' the bank robber suddenly said in the silence that had settled upon them. At first it seemed that no one had heard, but they all did, really. Thanks to the thin walls and that wretched open plan layout, the words even reached all the way into the closet, out into the hall, and through the bathroom door. They may not have had much in common, but they all knew what it was like to make a mistake.

'Sorry,' the bank robber said in a weaker voice, and even if none of them replied, that was how it started: the truth about how the bank robber managed to escape from the apartment. The bank robber needed to say those words, and the people who heard them all needed to be allowed to forgive someone.

'Stockholm' can also be a syndrome, of course.

Witness Interview (Continued)

JACK: Okay, okay. Can we focus on my questions now?

ROGER: That bloody rabbit. It's people like him who are manipulating the market. Bankers and estate agents and bloody rabbits. Manipulating everything. It's all just fake.

JACK: This would be Lennart that you're talking about now? He's on my list of witnesses, but he wasn't wearing the rabbit's head when he came out of the apartment. What do you mean about it all being fake?

ROGER: Everything. The whole world's fake. They were even faking where I used to work.

JACK: I meant at the apartment viewing.

ROGER: Ha, yes, of course I got ill at work but obviously that doesn't matter to you. People are all interchangeable in this bloody consumer society, aren't they?

JACK: No, that's not what I meant at all.

ROGER: Some idiot doctor decided I was 'burnt-out'. I wasn't burnt-out, I was just a bit tired. But suddenly everyone started making a fuss, my boss wanted to talk to me about my 'working environment'. I wanted to work, can you understand that? I'm a man. But for the whole of that last year they just kept making up things for me to do, projects that didn't exist. They didn't have any use for me, they just felt sorry for me. They didn't think I understood, but I understood all right, I'm a man, aren't I? Do you understand?

JACK: Absolutely.

ROGER: A man wants to be looked in the eye and told the truth when he's no longer needed. But they faked it. And now Anna-Lena's doing the same thing. Turns out I was never a good negotiator, that bloody rabbit was doing all the work.

JACK: I understand.

ROGER: I can assure you that you don't, you little bastard.

JACK: I understand that you feel hurt, I mean.

ROGER: Do you know what happened to that business after I left?

JACK: No.

ROGER: Nothing. Absolutely nothing happened. Everything just carried on as normal.

JACK: I'm sorry.

ROGER: I doubt that.

JACK: Could you possibly tell me more about the gap between the walls now? Show me again on the plans. How large a space are we talking about? Big enough for a grown man to stand up in?

ROGER: There. At least a yard. When they turned the old apartment into two separate ones they probably put an extra wall in rather than make the existing one thicker.

JACK: Why?

ROGER: Because they were idiots.

JACK: So they left a space here between them?

ROGER: Yes.

JACK: So you mean I could be dealing with a perpetrator who might have vanished into the wall, even if he didn't exactly fit?

ROGER: That's no laughing matter.

JACK: Wait here.

ROGER: Where are you going now?

JACK: I need to talk to my colleague.

38

Roger spent a long time standing by the front door in the hall, with the fingers of one hand pressed tightly against the bridge of his nose to stop the bleeding, and the other hand on the door handle, ready to leave the apartment. The bank robber came out into the hall and noticed, but didn't have the heart to stop him, so said instead: 'Go if you want to, Roger. I understand.'

Roger hesitated. Tugged a little at the handle as though testing it, but didn't open it. He kicked the skirting board so hard that it came loose.

'Don't tell me what to do!'

'Okay,' the bank robber said, incapable at that moment of pointing out that that was the whole point of being a bank robber.

They didn't find much else to talk about after that, but after a bit of rummaging through various pockets the bank robber managed to pull out a packet of cotton balls, and handed it over with a quiet explanation: 'One of my daughters sometimes gets nosebleeds, so I always have . . .'

Roger accepted the gift dubiously. He inserted a piece of cotton into each nostril. He was still clutching the door, but couldn't persuade his feet to leave the apartment. They didn't have any idea where on earth to go without Anna-Lena.

There was a bench in the hall, so the bank robber sat down at one end of it, and shortly afterwards Roger sat at the other end. The nosebleed had stopped, at last. He wiped himself with his shirt, both under his nose and under his eyes. For a long time they didn't say anything at all, until the bank robber finally said: 'I'm sorry I got you all involved in this. I didn't mean to hurt anyone. I just needed six and a half thousand to pay the rent, that was why I was going to rob the bank, I was going to give the money back as soon as I could. With interest!'

Roger didn't answer. He raised one hand and knocked on the wall behind him. Carefully, almost tenderly, as if he were worried it might break. Knock, knock, knock. He wasn't emotionally equipped to say it like it was, that Anna-Lena was his load-bearing wall. So instead he said: 'Fixed or variable?'

'What?' the bank robber said.

'You said you were going to pay the money back plus interest. Fixed or variable interest?'

'I hadn't thought about that.'

'There's a hell of a difference,' Roger said helpfully.

As if the bank robber didn't already have enough to worry about.

Meanwhile Julia emerged from the bathroom. She glared instinctively at Ro, who was standing in the living room.

'Where's Anna-Lena?'

Ro's face looked as uncomprehending as when she had found out that there was a right and a wrong way to put a plate in the dishwasher.

'I think she went into the closet.'

'Alone?'

'Yes.'

'And you didn't think to go after her to see how she was? She's just been yelled at by that emotionally challenged old fart of a husband even though she does *everything* for his sake, and you didn't even go after her? She could be facing a divorce now, and you left her alone? How could you be so insensitive?'

Ro curled her tongue behind her teeth.

'Just so I . . . don't misunderstand me here. But are we talking about Anna-Lena or are we talking about . . . you? I mean, have I done something else that's upset you, and you're pretending to be upset about this so that I understand that . . .'

'Sometimes you really don't understand *anything*, do you?' Julia muttered, and walked off towards the closet.

'I just mean that sometimes it isn't what you say you're upset about that you're upset about! And I'd just like to know if I'm insensitive because I'm insensitive, or . . . ,' Ro called after her, but Julia responded with the body language she usually reserved for communicating with angry men in German cars. Ro went into the living room, picked a lime from the bowl, and started to eat it out of nervousness, rind and all. But Zara was standing at the window and Ro was a bit scared of her, because all smart people are, so she went out into the hall instead.

There the bank robber and Roger were sitting at either end of a bench. Throughout her marriage, Ro had always been told that she needed to 'understand people's boundaries!' but she hadn't quite understood them yet, so she squidged herself in between them on the bench. 'Squidged' might not be a real word, but that's what Ro's dad calls it. He suffers from inadequate boundary perception as well. And Ro's dad has taught her all she knows, for good and ill.

The bank robber glanced awkwardly at her from one end, Roger glanced irritably at her from the other, both of them now squidged so far that they each had one buttock hanging off the end of the bench.

'Lime?' Ro offered. They shook their heads. Ro looked apologetically at Roger and added: 'Sorry my wife called you an emotionally challenged old fart of a husband earlier.'

'What did she call me?'

'Maybe you didn't hear? In that case it was nothing.'

'What does that mean? What the hell is "emotionally challenged"?'

'Don't take it personally, because most people don't really understand Jules's insults, she just says them in a way that makes people understand that they're not nice. It's quite a talent. And I'm sure that you and Anna-Lena aren't heading for divorce.'

Roger's eyes opened so wide that they ended up bigger than his ears: 'Who said anything about *divorce*?'

The rind of the lime was making Ro cough. Somewhere inside the part of the brain that controls logic and rational thinking, a thousand tiny nerve endings were jumping up and down and shouting *Stop talking now*. Even so, Ro heard herself say: 'No one, no one's said anything about divorce! Look, I'm sure it will all work out. But if it doesn't work out, it's actually really romantic when older couples get divorced. It always makes me happy, because it's so great when pensioners still think they're going to find someone new to fall in love with.'

Roger folded his arms. His mouth barely opened when he said: 'Thanks for that, you're a real tonic. You're like a self-help book, only in reverse.'

The nerve impulses in Ro's brain finally got control of her tongue, so she nodded, swallowed hard, and apologized: 'Sorry. I talk too much. Jules is always saying that. She says I'm so positive that it makes people depressed. That I always think the glass is half full when there's just enough to drown yourself in, and –'

'I can't think how she got that idea,' Roger snorted.

Ro replied dejectedly: 'Well, she used to say that, that I was too positive. Since she got pregnant everything's become so serious, because parents are always serious and I suppose we're trying to fit in. Sometimes I don't think I'm ready for the responsibility – I mean, I think my phone is asking too much of me when it wants me to install an update, and I find myself yelling: "*You're suffocating me.*" You can't shout that at a child. And children have to be updated all the time, because they can kill themselves just crossing the street or eating a peanut! I've mislaid my phone three times already today, I don't know if I'm ready for a human being.'

The bank robber looked up sympathetically: 'How pregnant is she? Julia?'

Ro lit up at once.

'Like, really pregnant! It could happen any day now!'

Roger's eyebrows were twitching badly. Then he said, almost sympathetically: 'Oh. Well, if you *don't* want to buy this apartment, I'd advise you not to risk letting her give birth here. Then it will have sentimental value to her. That would push the price up really badly.'

Perhaps Ro should have been angry, but she actually looked more sad.

'I'll bear that in mind.'

The bank robber let out a sigh at the other end of the bench, then groaned disconsolately. 'Maybe I've done something good today after all. A hostage drama might actually lower the price?'

Roger snorted.

'Quite the reverse. That idiot estate agent will probably add "as seen on TV" in the next advertisement, which would make it even more desirable.'

'Sorry,' the bank robber murmured.

Ro leaned back against the wall, chewing on her lime, rind and all. The bank robber looked on in fascination.

'I've never seen anyone eat a lime like that, the whole thing. Is it nice?'

'Not really,' Ro admitted.

'It's good for preventing scurvy. Sailors used to be given lime on board ships,' Roger said informatively.

'Did you used to be a sailor?' Ro wondered.

'No. But I watch a lot of television,' Roger replied.

Ro nodded thoughtfully, possibly waiting for someone to ask her something, but when no one did she said instead: 'To be honest, I don't want to buy this apartment. Not before my dad's had a look at it and decided if it's okay. He always looks at anything I want to buy to see if it's okay before I take any decisions. He knows all about everything, my dad.'

'When's he coming?' Roger asked suspiciously, taking out a pad and pencil with the name IKEA stamped on it and starting to do calculations according to various different prices per square foot. He had already listed the factors that might raise the price: giving birth, murder (if it was covered on television), Stockholmers. In another list he had written the things that ought to lower the price: damp, mold, need for renovations.

'He's not coming,' Ro said, then went on with more air than actual words: 'He's ill. Dementia. He's in a home now. I hate the way that sounds, in a home, rather than living there. And he wouldn't have liked the home, because everything's broken there, the taps drip and the ventilation makes a noise and the window catches are loose, and no one fixes them. Dad used to be able to fix anything. He always had an answer. I couldn't even buy a carton of eggs with a short best-before date without calling and asking him if they were okay.'

'I'm very sorry to hear that,' the bank robber said.

'Thanks,' Ro whispered. 'But it's okay. Eggs last a lot longer than you think, according to Dad.'

Roger wrote *dementia* in his pad, then felt sad when he realized it didn't make him happy. It didn't really matter who their competitors for the apartment were, Roger still had Anna-Lena. So he put the pad back in his pocket again, and muttered: 'That's true. It's the politicians, manipulating the market so we eat eggs quicker.'

He'd seen that in a documentary on television, broadcast right after one about sharks. Roger wasn't particularly interested in eggs, but sometimes he sat up late in the evening after Anna-Lena had nodded off, because he didn't want to wake her and have her move her head from his shoulder.

Ro rubbed her fingertips together, she's the sort of person who has her emotions there, and said: 'He wouldn't have liked the radiators in the home, either. They're those modern ones that adjust the temperature indoors according to what the temperature is outside, so you can't decide for yourself.'

'Urgh!' Roger exclaimed, because he was the sort of man who thought a man should be able to decide the temperature of his home for himself.

Ro smiled weakly.

'But Dad loves Jules, like you wouldn't believe. He was so proud when I married her, he said she had her head screwed on . . .' Then she suddenly blurted out: 'I'm going to be a terrible parent.'

'No, you're not,' the bank robber said consolingly.

But Ro persisted: 'Yes, I am. I don't know anything about children. I babysat my cousin's kid once, and he didn't want to eat anything and kept saying "it hurts" the whole time. So I told him it only hurt because his wings were about to grow out, because all kids who don't eat their food turn into butterflies.'

'That's sweet.' The bank robber smiled.

'It turned out he had acute appendicitis,' Ro added.

'Oh,' the bank robber said, no longer smiling.

'Like I keep saying, I don't know anything! My dad's going to die, and I'm going to be a parent, and I want to be exactly the same sort of parent he is, and I didn't get around to asking him how to do it. You have to know so much as a parent, you have to know everything, right from the start. And Jules keeps wanting me to make *decisions* the whole time, but I don't even know . . . I can't even decide if I should buy eggs. I'm not going to be able to do this. Jules says I keep finding fault with all the apartments on purpose just because I'm scared of . . . I don't know what. Just scared of something.'

Roger was leaning heavily against the wall, picking under his thumbnail with the IKEA pencil. He understood very well what Ro was scared of: buying an apartment, finding one single fault with it and having to admit that you yourself were the fault. It hadn't been hard for Roger to admit this to himself in recent years, he just couldn't bring himself to admit it out loud because he was so incredibly angry. A man can end up like that as a result of the things old age takes away from him, like the ability to serve a purpose, for instance, or at least the ability to fool the person you love into thinking that you can do that. Anna-Lena had seen through him, he realized that now, she knew he didn't have anything to offer her. Their marriage had become a fake show of admiration with rabbits hidden in the bathroom, and one apartment more or less wouldn't make any difference. So Roger picked at his nail with the IKEA pencil until the point broke, then he let out a brief cough and gave Ro the finest gift he could imagine.

'You should buy this apartment for your wife. There's nothing wrong with it. It could do with a bit of minor renovation, but there's no damp or mold. The kitchen and bathroom are in excellent condition, and the finances of the housing association are in good shape. There are a few loose skirting boards, but that won't take long to put right,' he said.

'I don't know how to fix skirting boards,' Ro whispered.

Roger was silent for a long, long time before — without looking at her — he said three of the hardest words an older man can say to a younger woman:

'You'll manage it.'

39

Jim is getting coffee from the police station staffroom, but doesn't have time to drink it because Jack comes rushing in from his interview with Roger, yelling: 'We have to get back to the apartment! I know where he's hiding! In the wall!'

Jim doesn't honestly know what on earth that's supposed to mean, but he obeys. They leave the station, get in the car, and drive back to the crime scene with high hopes that everything is going to fall into place the moment they walk in, that they'll have missed something obvious that will give them all the answers long before the Stockholmers arrive and try to grab the glory for everything.

They're partly right, of course. They have missed something obvious.

There's a young police officer posted in the lobby to stop journalists and random outsiders from going inside and snooping about. Jack and Jim know him, because the town is too small for them not to, and if people sometimes make jokes about some young police officers not being 'the sharpest knife in the drawer', this young man isn't even in the drawer. He barely notices when Jim and Jack pass him, and they look at each other in annoyance.

'I wouldn't let that one guard a crime scene if it was up to me,' Jack mutters.

'I wouldn't let that one guard my beer while I went to the toilet,' Jim mutters back, without making it quite clear which he thought was more serious. But it's the day before New Year's Eve, and they're too short-staffed to have the luxury of choice.

They split up to search. First Jack uses his knuckles, then his pocket torch to knock on all the walls. Jim tries to look as though he, too, has some good thoughts and ideas, so he lifts the sofa to see if anyone just happens to be hiding underneath it. Then Jim runs out of good thoughts and ideas. There are some pizza boxes on the coffee table, so Jim lifts the lid of one of them to see if there's anything left. Jack's nostrils flare to twice their normal size when he sees this.

'Dad, please tell me you weren't thinking of eating any of that if there's some left? It's been sitting there all day!'

His dad closes the lid indignantly.

'Pizza doesn't go bad.'

'If you're a goat living in a rubbish dump, maybe,' Jack mutters, then goes back to carefully knocking, knocking, knocking at various heights on all the walls, first hopefully, then with increasing desperation, palms feeling across the wallpaper like the very first moments after you accidentally drop a key in a lake. His confident facade starts to crack slightly as an entire day's suppressed dissatisfactions finally slip out of him.

'No, dammit. I was wrong. There's no way he's here.'

He's standing in front of the part of the wall behind which the gap Roger mentioned ought to be. But there's no way into it. If the bank robber is in there, someone must have dismantled part of the wall, then sealed him in, and the wall is far too neatly plastered and painted for that. And there wasn't anywhere near enough time, either. Jack utters a series of expletives combining certain sexual terms with various farmyard animals. His back creaks as he leans against the wall. Jim sees a sense of failure settle on his son's face, shrinking the distance between his ears and shoulders, so Jim summons up all of his sympathy as a father and tries to encourage him by saying: 'What about the closet?'

'Too small,' Jack says curtly.

'Only on the plan. According to that Estelle, it's actually an entire walk-in closet . . .'

'What?'

'That's what she said. Didn't I mention that in my notes from the interview?'

'Why haven't you said anything?' Jack blurts out, already on his way.

'I didn't know it was important,' Jim says defensively.

When Jack sticks his head in the closet to look for a light switch, he hits his forehead on a coat hanger, in exactly the same place where he already has the large bump. It hurts so badly that he lashes out at the hanger with his fist. So now his fist hurts as well. But Jim was right. Behind all the old coats and older suits and boxes full of even older things blocking the front, the closet really is far larger than it appeared on the plan.

40

There was a knock on the closet door.

Knock, knock, knock.

'Come in!' Anna-Lena called out hopefully, then fell apart when she saw it wasn't Roger.

'Can I come in?' Julia asked gently.

'What for?' Anna-Lena said with her face turned away, since she considered crying a more private activity than going to the toilet.

Julia shrugged.

'I'm tired of everyone out there. You seem to feel the same. So maybe we have something in common.'

Anna-Lena had to admit to herself that it had been a long time since she'd had anything in common with anyone apart from Roger, and that it sounded rather nice. So she nodded tentatively from her stool, half hidden by a rail full of old-fashioned men's suits.

'Sorry I'm crying. I know I'm the one who's in the wrong here.'

Julia looked around for somewhere to sit, and decided to pull out a stepladder from the back of the closet and sit on the lowest step of that. Then she said: 'When I got pregnant, the first thing my mum said to me was "Now you'll have to learn to cry in the cupboard, Jules, because children get frightened if you cry in front of them."'

Anna-Lena wiped her tears and stuck her head out from beneath the suits: 'That was the *first* thing your mum said?'

'I was a difficult child, so her sense of humour is rather unusual.' Julia smiled.

Anna-Lena joined in with a weak smile. She nodded warmly towards Julia's stomach.

'Are you doing okay? I mean, you and . . . the little one?'

'Oh, yes, thanks. I'm peeing thirty-five times a day, I hate socks, and I'm starting to think that terrorists who make bomb threats against public transport are all pregnant women who hate the way people smell on buses. Because people really do smell disgusting. Would you believe that an old guy sitting next to me the other day was eating salami? Salami! On the bus! But thanks, the little one and I are doing fine.'

'It's terrible being held hostage when you're pregnant, I mean,' Anna-Lena said gently.

'Oh, it's probably just as bad for you. I've just got more to carry.'

'Are you very scared of the bank robber?'

Julia shook her head slowly.

'No, I'm not, actually. I don't even think that pistol's real, if I'm being honest.'

'Nor me,' Anna-Lena nodded, even though she didn't really have any idea.

'The police will probably be here any minute, if we just stay calm,' Julia promised.

'I hope so.' Anna-Lena nodded.

'The bank robber actually seems more scared than us.'

'Yes, you're probably right about that.'

'How are you doing?'

'I . . . I don't really know. I've hurt Roger badly.'

'Oh, something tells me you've put up with far worse from him over the years, so I doubt you're even yet.'

'You don't know Roger. He's more sensitive than people think. He's just a bit wedded to his principles.'

'Sensitive and principled, you hear that a lot.' Julia nodded, thinking that it was a good description of all the old men who've started wars throughout human history.

'Once a young man with a black beard asked if he could have Roger's parking space in a car park, and Roger waited twenty minutes before he moved the car. Out of principle!'

'Charming,' Julia said.

'You don't know him,' Anna-Lena repeated with a blank look on her face.

'With all due respect, Anna-Lena — if Roger was as sensitive as you say, he'd be the one crying in the closet now.'

'He is sensitive . . . inside. I just can't understand how . . . when he saw Lennart, he immediately assumed we were . . . having an *affair*. How could he think something like that of me?'

Julia was trying to find a comfortable way to sit on the stepladder, and caught a glimpse of her own reflection in the metal. It wasn't flattering.

'If Roger thought you were being unfaithful, then he's the one with the problem, not you.'

Anna-Lena was pressing her hands hard against her thighs to stop her fingers shaking. She stopped blinking.

'You don't know Roger.'

'I knew enough men like him.'

Anna-Lena's chin moved slowly from side to side.

'He waited twenty minutes before he moved the car out of principle. Because on the news that morning there was a man, a politician, who said we ought to stop helping immigrants. That they just come here thinking they can get everything for free, and that a society can't work like that. He swore a lot, and said they're all the same, people like that. And Roger had voted for the party that man belonged to, you see. Roger has very firm ideas about the economy and fuel taxes and things like that, he doesn't like it when Stockholmers turn up and decide how everyone outside Stockholm should live. And he can be very sensitive. Sometimes he expresses himself a bit harshly, I'll admit that, but he has his principles. No one can say he hasn't got principles. And that particular day, after he'd heard that politician say that, we were at a shopping centre, it was just before Christmas so the car park was completely full when we got back to the car. Long, long queues. And that young man with the black beard, he saw us walking back to our car and wound his window down and asked if we were leaving, and if he could have our space if we were.'

By now Julia was ready to get up and turn the walk-in closet into a walk-out closet.

'Do you know what, Anna-Lena? I don't think I want to hear the rest of that story . . .'

Anna-Lena nodded understandingly, this certainly wasn't the first time someone had said that about her stories. But she was so used to thinking out loud now that she finished it anyway.

'There were so many cars there that it took the young man twenty minutes to get to the part of the garage where we were parked. Roger refused to move the car until he got there. He had two little children in the back of the car, I hadn't noticed, but Roger had. When we drove away I told Roger I was proud of him, and he replied that it didn't mean he'd changed his mind about the economy or fuel taxes or Stockholmers. But then he said that he realized that in that young man's eyes, Roger must look just like that politician on television, they were the same age, had the same colour hair, the same dialect and everything. And Roger didn't want the man with the beard to think that meant they were all exactly the same.'

Anna-Lena wiped her nose with the sleeve of one of the suit jackets, and wished it had been Roger's.

It's worth pointing out that Julia was trying to stand up while this anecdote was being related, a manoeuver that took a fair amount of time, so it took just as long for her to slump back into a seated position again. Only then did she open her mouth, and at first the only sound that emerged was a breathless cough, before she burst out laughing.

'That's simultaneously the sweetest and most ridiculous thing I've heard in a very long time, Anna-Lena.'

The tip of the other woman's nose moved up and down in embarrassment.

'We argue a lot about politics, Roger and I, we have very different opinions, but you can always . . . I think you can understand someone without necessarily agreeing with them, if you see what I mean? And

I know people sometimes think Roger's a bit of an idiot, but he isn't always an idiot in the way people assume.'

Julia admitted: 'Ro and I also vote for different parties.'

She thought of adding that Ro was a deluded hippie when it came to politics, and that you don't always discover that sort of thing until a couple of months into a relationship, but decided against it. Because it was actually perfectly possible to love each other despite that.

Anna-Lena wiped her whole face on the jacket sleeve.

'I should never have gone behind Roger's back! He was very good at his job, he should have been one of the bosses, but he never got the chance. And now he gets so upset when he doesn't . . . win. I want him to feel like a winner. So I called that "No Boundaries Lennart", and to start with I told myself it would only be the one time . . . but it gets easier every time you do it. You tell yourself that . . . well, of course, you're young, so it's hard to believe, but . . . the lie gets easier each time. I told myself I was doing it for Roger's sake, but of course it was for my own sake. I've decorated so many apartments to make them look just like a home is supposed to look, so that someone can come to the viewing and think "Oh, this is where I want to live!" I just wish that I could be that person one day. Settling somewhere again. Roger and I haven't lived anywhere properly for such a long time. We've just been . . . passing through.'

'How long have you been together?'

'Since I was nineteen.'

Julia thought about the question for a long time before finally asking: 'How do you do it?'

Anna-Lena replied without thinking at all: 'You love each other until you can't live without each other. And even if you stop loving each other for a little while, you can't . . . you can't live without each other.'

Julia says nothing for several minutes. Her own mum lived on her own, but Ro's parents had been married for forty years. No matter how much Julia loved Ro, that thought occasionally horrified her.

Forty years. How can you love someone that long? Gesturing vaguely towards the walls of the closet, she smiled to Anna-Lena. 'My wife drives me crazy. She wants to make wine and store cheese in here.'

Anna-Lena poked her tear-streaked face out between two pairs of suit trousers made of the same fabric, and replied as if she were revealing an embarrassing secret: 'Sometimes Roger drives me crazy, too. He uses our hairdryer to . . . well, you can guess . . . he sticks it under his towel. That's not how you're supposed to use a hairdryer . . . not there. That makes me want to scream!'

Julia shuddered.

'Urgh! Ro does exactly the same thing. It's so disgusting it makes me feel sick.'

Anna-Lena bit her lip.

'I have to admit that I'd never thought of that. That you might have problems like that. I always assumed it would be easier if you lived with a . . . woman.'

Julia burst out laughing.

'You don't fall in love with a gender, Anna-Lena. You fall in love with an idiot.'

Anna-Lena started laughing as well, much louder than she usually did. Then they looked at each other. Anna-Lena was twice Julia's age, but they had a lot in common just then. Both married to idiots who didn't know the difference between different types of hair. Anna-Lena looked at Julia's stomach and smiled.

'When's it due?'

'Any time now! Do you hear that, you little alien?' Julia replied, half to Anna-Lena and half to her little alien.

Anna-Lena didn't seem to understand the reference, but she closed her eyes and said: 'We have a son and a daughter. They're your age. But they don't want kids of their own. Roger's taken it badly. You might not think it if you meet him like this, if you don't really know him, but he'd be a good grandfather if he got the chance.'

'There's still plenty of time for that, isn't there?' Julia wondered, mostly because if those children were the same age as her, she didn't want to be old enough to be an old mum.

Anna-Lena shook her head sadly.

'No, they've made up their minds. And of course that's their choice, that's . . . that's how it is these days. My daughter says the world is already overpopulated, and she's worried about climate change. I don't know why ordinary anxieties aren't enough. Does anyone really need something new to worry about?'

'Is that why she doesn't want kids?'

'Yes, that's what she says. Unless I've misunderstood. I probably have. But maybe it would be good for the environment if there weren't quite so many people, I don't know. I just wish Roger could feel important again.'

Julia didn't seem to follow the logic.

'Grandchildren would make him feel important?'

Anna-Lena smiled weakly.

'Have you ever held a three-year-old by the hand on the way home from preschool?'

'No.'

'You're never more important than you are then.'

They sit there with nothing more to say, shivering slightly in the draught. Neither of them thinks to wonder where it's coming from.

41

Estelle was moving silently through the hall, her old body was now so light that she would have been an excellent hunter if only she didn't talk so much. She looked indulgently at the bank robber, Ro and Roger in turn on the bench, and when none of them noticed her, she cleared her throat apologetically and asked: 'Can I ask if anyone's hungry? There's food in the freezer, I could throw something together. That's to say, I'm sure there's food. In the kitchen. People usually have food in the kitchen.'

Estelle knew no better way of saying that she cared about people than to ask if they were hungry. The bank robber gave her a sad but appreciative smile.

'Some food would be great, thanks, but I don't want to be any trouble.'

Ro, on the other hand, nodded enthusiastically, for no other reason than that she was so hungry she could eat a lime with the rind still on. 'Maybe we could order pizza?'

The thought delighted her so much that she accidentally elbowed Roger, who seemed to wake up from being deep in thought. He looked up.

'What?'

'Pizza!' Ro repeated.

'Pizza? Now?' Roger snorted and looked at his watch.

The bank robber, who had been struck by another thought, in turn sighed in resignation: 'No. To start with, I haven't actually got enough money to order pizza. I can't even manage to take hostages without them starving to death . . .'

Roger folded his arms and looked at the bank robber, for the first time not judgementally, but more curiously.

'Can I ask what your plan is? How are you thinking of getting out of here?'

The bank robber blinked hard, then admitted without bothering to dress it up: 'I don't know. I didn't think this far. I was just trying . . . I just needed money for the rent, because I'm getting divorced and the lawyer said they'd take my children away otherwise. My girls. Oh, it's a long story, I don't want to bore you with . . . sorry, it's probably best if I give myself up. I get it!'

'If you give yourself up now and go out into the street, the police might kill you,' Ro said, not altogether encouragingly.

'What a thing to say!' Estelle said.

'That's probably true, they see you as armed and dangerous, and people like that tend to get shot on sight,' Roger added informatively.

The ski mask suddenly looked rather moist around the eye holes.

'This isn't even a real pistol.'

'It doesn't look real,' Roger agreed, based on his almost breathtakingly total lack of experience in the subject.

The bank robber whispered: 'I'm an idiot. I'm a failure and an idiot. I haven't got a plan. If they want to shoot me, they might as well. I can't get anything right anyway.'

The bank robber stood up and walked towards the door of the apartment with newfound determination.

It was Ro who went and stood in the way. Partly because the bank robber had talked about having kids, of course, but also because at this point in her life Ro could sympathize with the feeling of getting things wrong the whole time. So she exclaimed: 'Hello? You're just going to give up now, after all this? Can't we at least order pizza? In hostage films the police always provide pizza! Free of charge!'

Estelle folded her hands over her stomach and added: 'I've got nothing against pizza. Do you think they'd send some salad, too?'

Roger grunted without looking up: 'Free? Are you serious?'

'Serious as kidney stones,' Ro swore. 'Hostages *always* get pizza in films! If we can just think of a way of contacting the police, we can order some!'

Roger stared down at the floor for a long, long time. Then he glanced over at the closed door of the closet at the other end of the apartment, trying to sense his wife's presence through it. The skin beneath his eyes kept twitching spasmodically. Then it was as if he'd made up his mind to act, because in Roger's experience nothing good ever came of him thinking things through for too long, so he slapped his hands down firmly on his knees and stood up. He was seizing the initiative. And just doing that made him feel warm inside.

'Okay! I'll organize pizza!'

He marched towards the balcony. Estelle scuttled quickly into the kitchen to find plates. Ro in turn set off towards the closet to ask what sort of pizza Julia wanted. The bank robber was left alone in the hall, clutching the pistol and muttering quietly: 'Worst hostages ever. You're the *worst* hostages ever.'

42

Jack and Jim turn the entire closet upside down without finding any trace of the bank robber. The chest at the back is empty, apart from a collection of mostly empty wine bottles – and what sort of drunk hides wine bottles in a closet? They pull out all the clothes, men's suits and some dresses that seem to have been made before the invention of colour television. But otherwise they find nothing. Jim gets so sweaty while he's searching that he doesn't notice the cold draught in there. It's Jack who stops and sniffs keenly at the air like a bloodhound at a music festival.

'It smells of cigarette smoke in here,' he says, tentatively feeling the bump on his forehead.

'Maybe one of the prospective buyers had a sneaky smoke, that would be understandable in the circumstances,' Jim speculates.

'Okay, but then it ought to smell MORE of smoke. There's no smell of it anywhere else in the apartment, so it's almost as if someone has . . . I don't know, aired the closet somehow?'

'How would that be possible?'

Jack doesn't answer, just moves through the space hunting for the draught he initially thought he had imagined. Suddenly he picks up a stepladder that's lying on the floor, shoves a pile of clothes out of the way, climbs up the steps, and starts hitting the ceiling with the flat of his hand until something gives way.

'There's some sort of old air vent up here!'

Jim doesn't have time to respond before Jack sticks his head through the hole. Jim takes the opportunity to shake the wine bottles he found in the chest, and takes a swig out of one that isn't quite empty. Because wine doesn't go bad, either.

Jack calls from up the ladder: 'There's a narrow passageway up here, above the false ceiling, I think the draught's coming from the attic.'

'A passageway? Big enough to crawl through and get out somewhere else?' Jim wonders.

'God knows, it's very narrow, but someone slim could probably . . . hold on . . .'

'Can you see anything?'

'I'm trying to shine the torch to see where it leads, but there's
something in the way . . . something . . . fluffy.'

'Fluffy?' Jim repeats anxiously, thinking about all the animals Jack
probably wouldn't want to discover dead in a ventilation duct. Jack
doesn't like most animals even when they're alive.

Jack curses, pulls the thing out and tosses it down to Jim. It's a
rabbit's head.

43

Roger glanced over the balcony railing at the police, then took a deep breath and shouted: 'We need supplies!'

'Medical? Are you hurt?' one of the police officers called back. His name was Jim, his hearing wasn't great, and he hadn't experienced many hostage situations before. Or any at all, if we're being strictly correct.

'No! We're hungry!' Roger shouted.

'Angry?' the policeman yelled.

There was another police officer, a younger one, standing next to him. He was trying to shut the older one up so he could hear what Roger was saying, but of course the older one wasn't listening.

'NO! PIZZA!' Roger yelled, but because he had cotton stuffed in both nostrils unfortunately it sounded more like 'pisser'.

'MELISSA? SOMEONE CALLED MELISSA IS INJURED?' the older police officer shouted.

'YOU'RE NOT LISTENING!'

'WHAT?'

'BE QUIET, DAD, SO I CAN HEAR WHAT HE'S SAYING!' the younger officer shouted at the older police officer down in the street, but by then Roger had already left the balcony in frustration. He hadn't actually sworn that much since a group of damn activists had changed the name of his favourite chocolate bars because the old name was regarded as insulting to someone or other. He stomped back inside the apartment and waved his notepad and IKEA pencil in the air.

'We'll make a list and throw it down,' he declared. 'What sort of pizza does everyone want? You first!' he demanded, pointing at the bank robber.

'Me? Oh, I don't really mind. Anything will do,' the bank robber piped up feebly.

'Are you hard of thinking or something? Just make a decision for once! No one's going to respect you otherwise!' Zara exclaimed from the sofa (where she had only sat down after first fetching a towel from the bathroom to put between her and the cushion, because heaven only knew what sort of individuals had sat there before her. They probably had tattoos and goodness only knew what else).

'I can't decide,' the bank robber said, which were probably the truest words the bank robber had uttered all day. When you're a child you long to be an adult and decide everything for yourself, but when you're an adult you realize that's the worst part of it. That you have to have opinions all the time, you have to decide which party to vote for and what wallpaper you like and what your sexual preferences are and which flavour yogurt best reflects your personality. You have to make choices and be chosen by others, every second, the whole time. That was the worst thing about getting divorced, in the bank robber's opinion, the fact that you thought you were done with all that, but now you had to start making decisions about everything again. We already had wallpaper and crockery, the balcony furniture was almost new, and the children were about to start swimming lessons. We had a life together, wasn't that enough? The bank robber had reached a point in life where everything felt . . . complete, at last. Which means that you're in no fit state to be thrown out into the wilderness to find out who you are all over again. The bank robber tried to make sense of all these thoughts, but didn't have time before Zara interrupted again.

'You need to make demands!'

Roger agreed. 'She's actually right. If you don't, the police will get nervous, and that's when they start shooting. I've seen a documentary about it. If you take hostages, you have to tell them what you want so they can start to negotiate.'

The bank robber replied unhappily and honestly: 'I want to go home to my children.'

Roger took this under consideration for a while. Then he said: 'I'll put down a capricciosa for you, everyone likes capricciosa. Next! What sort would you like?'

He was looking at Zara now. She seemed to be in a state of total shock.

'Me? I don't eat pizza.'

When Zara went to a restaurant she always ordered shellfish, and made it very clear that she wanted them served with the shells intact, because then she could be sure than no one in the kitchen had touched the insides. If the restaurant didn't have any shellfish, Zara ordered boiled eggs. She hated berries, but liked bananas and coconuts. Her idea of hell was a never-ending buffet with her stuck in the queue behind someone who had a cold.

'Everyone's having pizza! Besides, it's free!' Roger clarified, with a badly timed sniffle.

Zara wrinkled her nose and the rest of her face followed suit.

'People eat pizza with their hands. The same hands they use to renovate apartments.'

But of course Roger didn't back down, just looked in turn at Zara's handbag, shoes and wristwatch, then scribbled something on his pad.

'I'll say you want whatever the most expensive one is, will that do? Maybe they've got something with truffle, gold leaf and some sort of endangered baby turtle on it, like some ridiculous stuck-up marinara. Next!'

Estelle looked worried about having to decide so quickly, so she exclaimed: 'I'll have the same as Zara.'

Roger peered at her, then wrote 'capricciosa' on his pad.

Then it was Ro's turn, and her face took on an expression that only a mother or a manufacturer of defibrillators could love.

'A kebab pizza with garlic sauce! Extra sauce. And extra kebab. Preferably a bit charred. Hang on, I'll go and see what Jules would like!'

She banged on the closet door.

'*What is it?*' Julia yelled.

'*We're ordering pizza!*' Ro cried.

'*I want a Hawaiian without pineapple and without ham, but with banana and peanuts instead, and tell them not to cook it for too long!*'

Ro took such a deep breath that her back creaked. She leaned closer to the door.

'Can't you have a pizza from the menu just for once, darling? A nice, normal pizza? Why do I always have to call and give them a set of instructions like I'm trying to help a blind person land a plane?'

'*And extra cheese if it's good cheese! Ask if they have good cheese!*'

'*Why can't you just have something off the menu like a normal person?*'

It wasn't entirely clear if Julia had failed to hear what Ro said, or if she was ignoring her, because she yelled back from inside the closet: '*And olives! Not green ones, though!*'

'That isn't a Hawaiian,' Ro muttered very quietly to herself.

'*Of course it is!*'

Roger did his best to note all that down. Then the closet door opened and Julia peered out, then said out of the blue in a friendly voice:

'Anna-Lena says she'll have the same as you, Roger.'

Roger nodded slowly, looking down at his pad. He had to go out into the kitchen so that no one saw him write a new note, because the first one was impossible to write on when it was wet. When he got back to the living room the rabbit raised his hand timidly.

'I'd like a –' the voice said from inside the head.

'Capricciosa!' Roger interrupted, blinking away the tears and giving the rabbit a look that said this wasn't the time to be vegetarian or any other crap like that, so the rabbit just nodded and mumbled: 'I can take the ham off, no problem, that's fine.'

Then Roger looked around for something heavy enough to attach the note to, and eventually found a round object that seemed just the right density. That was how the police came to hear someone shout from the balcony again, and when Jack looked up, a lime hit him on the forehead.

From that distance, that makes one hell of a bump.

44

Jack only manages to slither halfway into the space above the closet. Then Jim has to climb the ladder and pull on both his feet as hard as he can, as if his son were a rat who had crawled into a soda bottle to drink the contents and had become too fat to squeeze out again. When Jack finally comes loose, the two of them fall to the floor, Jim with a crash and Jack with a thud. They lie there sprawled on the closet floor, surrounded by women's underwear from the last century and with the rabbit's head rolling around, sending the dust balls fleeing in fear of their lives. Jack embarks upon another verbal demonstration of his knowledge of farmyard anatomy, before getting to his feet and saying: 'Well, there's a very narrow old ventilation duct up there, but it's sealed at the far end. Cigarette smoke might blow out, but there's no way anyone could get through there. Not a chance.'

Jim looks unhappy, mostly because Jack looks so unhappy. The father remains standing in the closet for a while after his son storms out, to give him time to walk a few circuits of the living room and get the swearing out of his system. When Jim eventually walks out he finds Jack standing in front of the open fireplace, thinking.

'Do you think the bank robber could have got out this way?' Jim wonders.

'Do you think he's Santa Claus or something?' Jack answers, with unnecessary cruelty that he regrets at once. But there's ash at the bottom of the grate, and it's still warm — there's been a fire here fairly recently. When Jack carefully pokes about with his flashlight, he fishes out the remains of a ski mask. He holds it up to the light. Looks at the blood on the floor and the furniture around him, trying to put the pieces of the puzzle together.

* * *

In the meantime Jim wanders about apparently at random, and finds himself in the kitchen, where he opens the fridge (which perhaps indicates that it wasn't entirely random, after all). There's leftover pizza in there, on a china plate, carefully covered with clingfilm. Who would do that, in the middle of a hostage drama? Jim shuts the fridge and returns to the living room. Jack is still standing by the fireplace holding the partially burned ski mask in his hand, his shoulders slumped in resignation.

'No, I can't see how he got out of the apartment, Dad. I've tried looking at it from every possible and impossible angle, but I still don't understand how the hell . . .'

Jack suddenly looks so sad that his dad immediately tries to cheer him up by asking questions.

'What about the blood? How can the bank robber have lost this much blood and still – ?' Jim begins, but is interrupted by a voice from the hall. It's the police officer who's been standing guard.

'Er, that isn't the bank robber's blood,' he blurts out cheerfully, picking something from his teeth.

'What?' Jack asks.

'Schusssschfnurschulle,' the officer says, with almost his entire hand stuck in his mouth, as if the blood were nowhere near as important as the souvenir from his lunch that had got stuck in there. The hand re-emerges with a piece of cashew nut, and the newly liberated mouth laughs and looks remarkably happy.

'Sorry?' Jim says, with rapidly dwindling patience.

The cheerful police officer points at the dried blood on the floor.

'I said: that's stage blood. Look at the way it's drying, real blood doesn't look like that,' he says, holding the piece of cashew nut as if he's unsure whether to throw it away or frame it as a memory of this great personal achievement.

'How do you know that?' Jim asks him.

'I'm a bit of a magician in my spare time. Well, to be more accurate, I'm a bit of a *policeman* in my spare time!'

His expectation that Jim and Jack are going to laugh at that turns out to be an optimistic prognosis, so he coughs rather forlornly and adds: 'I do a few shows, stuff like that. Old people's homes and so on. Sometimes I pretend to cut myself, and then I use stage blood. I'm quite good, actually. If you've got a pack of cards on you, I can . . .'

Jack, who has never looked like he just happened to 'have a pack of cards on him' at any time in his life, points at the blood.

'So you're quite sure this isn't real blood?'

The police officer nods confidently.

Jack and Jim look thoughtfully at each other. Then they each switch their flashlights on, even though the ceiling lights are already on, and start to go through the apartment, inch by inch. Around and around and around. Staring at everything but still seeing nothing. There's a bowl of limes next to the pizza boxes on the table. All the glasses are neatly placed on coasters. There's a marker on the floor to indicate where the police found the bank robber's pistol. Right beside it is a small table with a small lamp on it.

'Dad? The phone we sent in for the perpetrator, where did we find it when we came in?' Jack suddenly asks.

'It was there, on that little table,' Jim says.

'That explains it,' Jack sighs.

'Explains what?'

'We've been thinking about this wrong all along.'

Witness Interview
Date: December 30
Name of witness: 'Jules' and 'Ro'

JACK: Because you're witnesses to such a serious offence as this, I really must insist on being able to speak to you separately rather than both at the same time.

JULES: Why?

JACK: Because that's just the way it is.

JULES: Sorry, but has your body been taken over by a demon that sounds like my mother? What do you mean, 'just the way it is'?

JACK: You're witnesses in a criminal investigation. There are rules.

JULES: Is either of *us* suspected of committing a crime, then?

JACK: No.

JULES: Well, then. Then we'll do this together. You know why?

JACK: No.

JULES: Because that's just the way it is!

JACK: Christ, if there's ever been a more difficult group of witnesses, I have no idea where that could have been.

JULES: Excuse me?

JACK: I didn't say anything.

JULES: Yes you did, I heard you muttering.

JACK: It was nothing. Okay, you win, you can do this together!

RO: Jules is just worried I'll say something stupid if she isn't here.

JULES: Quiet now, darling.

RO: See?

JACK: For God's sake, don't you two ever stop babbling? I said okay! I'll interview you both at the same time! But this isn't how it's supposed to work!

RO: Do you have to be so angry?

JACK: I'm not angry!

RO: Okay.

JULES: Yeah, right.

JACK: I need your real names.

RO: These are our real names.

JACK: They're nicknames, surely?

JULES: Please, can't you just focus on the interview? It doesn't really matter, does it? I need to go to the toilet.

JACK: Okay, okay, sure. Because 'what's your name?' is a really complicated question.

JULES: Stop muttering and just ask your questions.

JACK: Right, I'm just a police officer, so obviously it's perfectly reasonable for *you* to decide what goes on in here.

JULES: What?

JACK: Nothing. I just need to confirm that the two of you were inside the apartment for the entirety of the hostage situation. Were you?

RO: I don't know about 'hostage situation'. That sounds very harsh.

JULES: Please, Ro, pull yourself together now. What do you think we were if we weren't hostages? Accidentally threatened with a pistol?

RO: We were more just an unfortunate consequence of some bad decisions.

JULES: Because someone tripped and happened to slip inside a ski mask?

JACK: Please, can you both just try to focus on my question?

JULES: Which one?

JACK: Were you inside the apartment the whole time?

RO: Jules was in the hobby room for quite a long time.

JULES: It's not a hobby room!

RO: Closet, then. Stop being picky.

JULES: You know perfectly well what it's called.

JACK: You were in the closet? How long for? I mean, how long before you came out of the closet?

JULES: What did you just say?

JACK: I mean, well, no, that's not what I mean.

JULES: Right. So what exactly did you mean, then?

JACK: Nothing. I didn't mean 'come out of the closet' in any way except in relation to the fact that you were physically inside a . . . well, a closet.

JULES: We were in the apartment the whole time.

RO: Why do you sound so angry?

JULES: Maybe it's the *hormones*, Ro? Is *that* what you're trying to say?

RO: No, it really isn't. Well, I certainly didn't actually say that, in which case it doesn't count.

JACK: I appreciate that you've had a difficult day, but I'm just trying to understand where everyone was at various times. For instance, when the pizzas were delivered.

RO: Why's that important?

JACK: That's the last time we know for certain that the perpetrator was in the apartment.

RO: I was sitting on the chaise longue when we had the pizza.

JACK: What's that?

JULES: That bit at the end of the sofa. Kind of like a divan.

RO: No, it isn't — how many times do I have to tell you that it's nothing like a divan? Do you know how you can tell that a chaise longue isn't a divan? Because then it *would be a divan*!

JULES: Give me strength! Are we going to have the same
        argument now as when I didn't know what a commode
        was? Do you know what a commode is?

JACK: Me? It's a type of lizard, isn't it?

JULES: See? I told you.

RO: *It's not a lizard!*

JULES: It's that cabinet in the bathroom, under the
        washbasin, apparently.

JACK: I had no idea.

JULES: No normal person knows that.

RO: Did you both grow up in caves? Seriously? A com-
        mode is a kind of cousin to a vanity. You know
        what one of those is, presumably?

JACK: Yes, I know what a vanity is.

JULES: How can you know that and yet still call a ward-
        robe a walk-in closet?

RO: Because a wardrobe is a word used by someone who
        blogs about juicing and hasn't pooped a solid
        turd for three years, whereas a vanity is a proper
        piece of furniture!

JULES: See what I have to put up with? She was obsessed
        with vanities and commodes for three months last
        year because she was going to be a cabinetmaker.
        Just before she was going to be a yoga instruc-
        tor, and just after she was going to be a hedge
        fund manager.

RO: Why do you always have to exaggerate? I was never
        going to be a hedge fund manager.

JULES: What were you going to be, then?

RO: A day trader.

JULES: What's the difference?

RO: I didn't get around to learning that. That was
        around the time I started to get interested in
        cheese.

JACK: I'd like us to go back to my question.

RO: You look stressed. It's not good to bite your
        tongue like that.

JACK: I'd be less stressed if you just answered the question.

JULES: We sat on the sofa and ate pizza. That's the answer to your question.

JACK: Thank you! And who was in the apartment at that time?

JULES: The two of us. Estelle. Zara. Lennart. Anna-Lena and Roger. The bank robber.

JACK: And the estate agent?

JULES: Of course.

JACK: And where was the estate agent?

JULES: Just then?

JACK: Yes.

JULES: Am I your GPS or something?

JACK: I just want you to verify that everyone else was sitting around the table eating pizza.

JULES: I suppose so.

JACK: You suppose so?

JULES: What's your problem? I'm pregnant and there were people with guns, I had a lot of things to think about, I'm not some preschool teacher counting knapsacks on a bus.

RO: Is this a sweet?

JACK: It's an eraser.

JULES: Stop eating everything!

RO: I was only asking!

JULES: You know she opens the fridge in every apartment we look at? Do you think that's acceptable behaviour?

JACK: I really don't care.

RO: They *want* you to look in the fridge. That's all part of the estate agent's so-called 'home-styling', everyone knows that. Once I found tacos. They still rank in the top three tacos I've ever eaten.

JULES: Hang on, you ate the tacos?

RO: They want you to.

JULES: You ate food you found in some stranger's fridge? Are you kidding?

RO: What's wrong with that? It was chicken. Well, I think it was chicken. Everything tastes like chicken when it's been in the fridge awhile. Apart from turtle. Have I told you about the time I ate turtle?

JULES: What? No! Stop talking now, I'm going to throw up, seriously.

RO: What do you mean, stop talking? You're the one who keeps saying you want us to know everything about each other!

JULES: Well, I've changed my mind. Right now I think we know just the right amount about each other.

RO: Do you think it's weird to eat tacos at a viewing?

JACK: I'd appreciate it if you didn't involve me in this.

JULES: He thinks it's sick.

RO: He didn't say that! You know what is sick? Jules hides sweets and chocolate. What sort of adult does that?

JULES: I hide *expensive* chocolate, sure, because I'm married to a wormhole.

RO: She's lying. One time I discovered she'd bought sugar-free chocolate. Sugar-free! And then she hid that as well, as if I wouldn't even be able to stop myself eating sugar-free chocolate, like some bloody psychopath.

JULES: And then you ate it.

RO: To teach you a lesson. Not because I enjoyed it.

JULES: Okay, I'm ready to answer your questions now!

JACK: Wow. Lucky me.

JULES: Do you want to ask your questions or not?

JACK: Okay. When the perpetrator let you go, and you left the apartment, do you remember who went downstairs with you?

JULES: All the hostages, of course.

JACK: Can you list them, please, in the order you remember them going down the stairs?

JULES: Sure. Me and Ro, Estelle, Lennart, Zara, Anna-
Lena and Roger.

JACK: What about the estate agent?

JULES: Okay, and the estate agent.

JACK: The estate agent must have been with you as well?

JULES: Are we nearly finished here?

RO: I'm hungry.

46

All professions have their technical aspects that outsiders don't understand, tools and implements and complicated terminology. Perhaps the police force has more than most, its language is constantly changing, older officers lose track of it at the same rate that younger officers invent it. So Jim didn't know what the damn thing was called, the telephone thingy. He just knew that there was something special about it that meant you could make calls even though there was hardly any signal, and that Jack was delighted that the station had been given one. Jack was perhaps capable of being more delighted by telephone thingies than Jim thought was strictly reasonable, but it was this phone they had sent in to the bank robber at the end of the hostage drama, so it turned out to be fairly useful after all. It was actually Jim who came up with the idea, which he was not a little proud of. Just after the hostages had been released, the negotiator had called the bank robber on that phone in an attempt to negotiate a peaceful surrender. That was when they heard the shot.

Naturally, Jack has explained the technology in the phone to Jim in great detail, so obviously Jim still calls it 'that special telephone thingy which gets a bloody signal where there isn't a bloody signal'. When they were about to send it in to the bank robber, obviously Jack told Jim to make sure the ringtone was set properly. Which of course it wasn't.

Jack is looking around the apartment.

'Dad, did you make sure the ringtone on that phone was switched on when we sent it in?'

'Yes. Yes. Yes, of course,' Jim replies.

'So . . . no, then?'

'I might have forgotten that. Maybe.'

Jack rubs his whole face with his palms in frustration.

'Could it have been on vibrate?'

'It could have been, yes.'

Jack reaches out and touches the little table where the phone had been lying when they stormed the apartment. It's barely standing up on three legs, a definite challenge to gravity. He looks at the place on the floor where they found the pistol. Then he follows something invisible with his gaze and goes over to the green curtain. The bullet is in the wall.

'The perpetrator didn't shoot himself,' Jack says in a low voice.

Then it dawns on him that the perpetrator wasn't even in the apartment when the shot was fired.

'I don't get it,' Jim says behind him, not angrily like some dads would, but proudly, like only a few dads can. Jim likes hearing his son explain the reasoning behind his conclusions, but there's no satisfaction in Jack's voice when he does so now. 'The phone was on that wobbly table, Dad. The pistol must have been lying next to it. When we called the phone after all the hostages had been released, it started to vibrate, the table shook, and the pistol fell to the floor and fired. We thought the perpetrator shot himself, but he wasn't even here. He was already gone. The blood . . . the stage blood or whatever the hell it is . . . must have been poured out in advance.'

Jim looks at his son for a long time. Then scratches his stubble.

'Do you know something? On the one hand this seems like the smartest crime in the world . . .'

Jack nods, stroking the large lump on his forehead, and finishes his dad's thought for him: '. . . but on the other, it seems to have been carried out by a complete idiot.'

At least one of them is right.

Jack sinks down on to the sofa, and Jim collapses on it as if he's been pushed. Jack picks up his bag, takes out all the notes from the witness interviews, and spreads them out around him without explaining what he's doing. He reads through everything one more time. When he puts the last page down, he bites his way methodically along his tongue, because that's where Jack's stress lives.

'I'm an idiot,' he says.

'Why?' Jim wonders.

'Bloody hell! Bloody, bloody . . . I'm an *idiot*! How many people were in the apartment, Dad?'

'You mean how many prospective buyers?'

'No, I mean in total, how many people were there *in total* in the apartment?'

Jim starts waffling, in the hope that it will make him sound like he understands anything of all this: 'Let's see . . . seven prospective buyers. Or, well . . . there were really only those two, Ro and Jules, and Roger and Anna-Lena, and Estelle, who wasn't really interested in buying the apartment . . .'

'That's five.' Jack nods impatiently.

'Five, yes. That's it, yes. And then there's Zara, we don't really know why she was there. And then there's Lennart, who was there because Anna-Lena had hired him. So that makes . . . one, two, three, four, five . . .'

'Seven people in total!' Jack nods.

'Plus the perpetrator,' Jim adds.

'Exactly. But also . . . plus the estate agent.'

'Plus the estate agent, yes, so that makes nine, then!' Jim says, immediately cheered by his own mathematical prowess.

'Are you sure, Dad?' Jack sighs.

He looks at his dad for a long time, waiting for him to realize, but gets no response. Absolutely none at all. Just two eyes staring at him the way they did many years ago after they'd watched a film together, and Jack had to explain at the end: 'But, Dad, the bald guy was *dead*, that's why only the little kid could see him!' And his dad exclaimed: 'What? Was he a ghost? No, he couldn't have been, because we could see him!'

She laughed at that, Jim's wife and Jack's mum, God, how she laughed. God, how they miss her. She's still the one who makes them more understanding towards each other, even though she's no longer here.

Jim aged badly after she died, became a lesser man, never quite able to breathe back in all the air that had gone out of him. When he sat in the hospital that night, life felt like an icy crevice, and when he lost his grip on the edge and slipped down into the darkness inside him, he whispered angrily to Jack: 'I've tried talking to God, I really have tried, but what sort of God makes a priest this sick? She's never done anything but good for other people, so what sort of God gives an illness like this to *her*?!'

Jack had no answer then, and he has no answer now. He just sat quietly in the waiting room and held his dad until it was impossible to tell whose tears were running down his neck. The following morning they were angry at the sun for rising, and couldn't forgive the world for living on without her.

But when it was time, Jack got to his feet, grown-up and straight-backed, walked through a series of doors, and stopped outside her room. He was a proud young man, certain in his beliefs; he wasn't religious and his mum had never said a single stern word to him about that. She was the sort of priest who got shouted at by everyone, by religious people for not being religious enough, and by everyone else because she was religious at all. She had been to sea with sailors, in the desert with soldiers, in prison with inmates, and in hospitals with sinners and atheists. She liked a drink and could tell dirty jokes, no matter who she was with. If anyone even asked what God would think about that, she always replied: 'I don't think we agree about everything, but I have a feeling He knows I'm doing the best I can. And I think maybe He knows I work for Him, because I try to help people.' If anyone asked her to sum up her view of the world, she always quoted Martin Luther: 'Even if I knew that tomorrow the world would go to pieces,

I would still plant my apple tree.' Her son loved her, but she never managed to get him to believe in God, because although you might be able to drum religion into people, you can't teach *faith*. But that night, all alone at the end of a dimly lit corridor in a hospital where she had held so many dying people by the hand, Jack sank to his knees and asked God not to take his mum away from him.

When God took her anyway, Jack went into her bed, held her hand too hard in his, as if he were hoping she might wake up and tell him off. Then he whispered disconsolately: 'Don't worry, Mum, I'll take care of Dad.'

He called his sister afterwards. She made promise after promise, of course, as usual. She just needed money for the flight. Obviously. Jack sent the money, but she didn't come to the funeral. Naturally, Jim has never once called her an 'addict' or 'junkie', because dads can't do that. He always says his daughter is 'ill', because that makes it feel better. But Jack always calls his sister what she is: a heroin addict. She's seven years older than him, and with that age gap you don't have a big sister when you're little, you have an idol. When she left home he couldn't go with her, and when she tried to find herself he couldn't help, and when she went under he couldn't save her.

It's been just Jack and Jim since then. They send her money every time she calls, every time she pretends she's going to come home, only she just needs help with the airfare, this one last time. And maybe a bit extra to pay a few little debts. Nothing much, she's going to sort it all out, if they could just . . . They know they shouldn't, of course. You always know. Addicts are addicted to their drugs, and their families are addicted to hope. They cling to it. Every time her dad gets a call from a number he doesn't recognize, he always hopes it's her, whereas her younger brother is terrified because he's always convinced this will be the call when someone tells him she's dead. The same questions echo through both of them: What sort of police officers can't even look after their own daughter and sister? What sort of family can't help one of their own to help herself? What sort of god makes a priest ill, and what sort of daughter doesn't show up for the funeral?

When both children were still living at home, when everyone was still tolerably happy, Jack asked his mum one evening how she could bear to sit beside people when they were dying, in their final hours, without being able to save them. His mum kissed the top of his head and said: 'How do you eat an elephant, sweetheart?' He replied the way a child who's heard the same joke a thousand times does: 'One bit at a time, Mum.' She laughed just as loudly, for the thousandth time, the way parents do. Then she held his hand tightly and said: 'We can't change the world, and a lot of the time we can't even change people. No more than one bit at a time. So we do what we can to help whenever we get the chance, sweetheart. We save those we can. We do our best. Then we try to find a way to convince ourselves that that will just have to . . . be enough. So we can live with our failures without drowning.'

Jack couldn't help his sister. He couldn't save the man on the bridge. Those who jump . . . they jump. The rest of us have to get out of bed the following day, priests walk out of the door to do their job, as do police officers. Now Jack is looking at the stage blood on the floor, the bullet hole in the wall, the little side table where the phone was lying, and the large coffee table with the discarded pizza boxes.

He looks at Jim, and his dad holds his hands up and smiles weakly.

'I give up. You're the genius here, son. What have you come up with?'

Jack nods at the pizza boxes. Brushes the hair from the lump on his forehead. Counts out the names again.

'Roger, Anna-Lena, Ro, Jules, Estelle, Zara, Lennart, the bank robber, the estate agent. Nine people.'

'Nine people, yes.'

'But when they dropped that lime on my head, the note only asked for eight pizzas.'

Jim thinks about this so hard that his nostrils quiver.

'Maybe the bank robber doesn't like pizza?'

'Maybe.'

'But that's not what you think?'

'No.'

'Why not?'

Jack stands up, packs the witness statements away in his bag. He bites his tongue.

'Is the estate agent still at the station?'

'She should be, yes.'

'Call and make sure no one lets her go anywhere!'

Jim frowns so hard that you could lose a paper clip in the wrinkles.

'But . . . why, son? What's – ?'

Jack interrupts his dad: 'I don't think there were nine people in this apartment. I think there were eight. There's one person we've just assumed was here the whole time! Bloody hell, Dad, don't you see? The perpetrator didn't hide, and didn't escape, either. She just walked right out into the street in front of us!'

47

The bank robber was sitting alone in the hall. She could hear the voices of the people she'd taken hostage, but they might as well have been in a different time zone. There were eternities between her and everyone else now, between her and the person she had been that morning. She wasn't alone in the apartment, but no one in the world shared her prospects, and that's the greatest loneliness in the world: when no one is walking beside you towards your destination. In a short while, when they all walked out of the apartment, the others would be victims the moment their feet reached the pavement. She would be the criminal. If the police didn't shoot her on sight, she'd end up stuck in prison for . . . she didn't even know how long . . . years? She'd grow old in a cell. She'd never see her daughters learn to swim.

The girls. Oh, the girls. The monkey and the frog who would grow up and have to learn to be good liars. She hoped their dad would have the sense to teach them to do that properly. So that they could lie and say their mum was dead rather than tell the truth. She slowly removed the mask. It no longer served any purpose, she realized that, to think otherwise would be nothing but childish delusion. She was never going to be able to escape the police. Her hair fell around her neck, damp and tangled. She weighed the pistol in her hand, clutching it harder and harder, a little at a time so she barely noticed. Only her whitening knuckles betrayed what was happening, until her forefinger suddenly felt for the trigger. Without any great drama, she asked herself: 'If this had been real, would I have shot myself?'

She didn't have time to finish the thought. Someone's fingers suddenly wrapped around hers. They didn't tear the pistol from her hand, just lowered it. Zara stood there looking at the bank robber, neither sympathetic nor concerned, but without taking her hand off the pistol.

* * *

Ever since the start of the hostage drama, Zara had tried not to think about anything in particular, in fact she always did her best not to think about anything at all — when you're in as much pain as she has been for the past ten years, that's a vital survival skill. But something slipped through her armour when she saw the bank robber sitting there alone with the pistol. A brief memory of those hours in the office with the picture of the woman on the bridge, the psychologist looking at Zara and saying: 'Do you know what, Zara? One of the most human things about anxiety is that we try to cure chaos with chaos. Someone who has got themselves into a catastrophic situation rarely retreats from it, we're far more inclined to carry on even faster. We've created lives where we can watch other people crash into the wall but still hope that somehow we're going to pass straight through it. The closer we get, the more confidently we believe that some unlikely solution is miraculously going to save us, while everyone watching us is just waiting for the crash.'

Zara looked around the office then. There were no fancy certificates hanging on the walls; for some reason it's always the people with the most impressive diplomas who keep them in their desk drawers.

So Zara asked, without any sarcasm, 'Have you learned any theories about why people behave like that, then?'

'Hundreds.' The psychologist smiled.

'Which one do you believe?'

'I believe the one that says that if you do it for long enough, it can become impossible to tell the difference between flying and falling.'

Zara usually fought to keep all thoughts at bay, but that one slipped through. So when she found herself standing in the hall of the apartment, she put her hand around the pistol and said the kindest thing a woman in her position could say to a woman in the bank robber's position. Four words.

'Don't do anything silly.'

The bank robber looked at her, her eyes blank, her chest empty. But she didn't do anything silly. She even gave her a weak smile. It was an unexpected moment for both of them. Zara turned and walked away quickly, almost scared, back to the balcony. She pulled a pair of headphones from her bag, put them on, and closed her eyes.

Shortly after that she ate pizza for the first time in her life. That, too, was unexpected. Capricciosa. She thought it was disgusting.

48

Jack jumps out of the police car while it's still moving. He storms into the police station and runs to the interview room so fast that he hits his already bruised forehead on the door because he can't get it open quickly enough. Jim comes after him, panting, trying to get his son to calm down, but there's no chance of that.

'Hello! How's tricks – ?' the estate agent begins, but Jack cuts her off by roaring:

'*I know who you are now!*'

'I don't underst –' the agent gasps.

'Calm down, Jack, please,' Jim pants from the doorway.

'*It's you!*' Jack yells, showing no sign at all of calming down.

'Me?'

Jack's eyes are glinting with triumph when he leans over the table with his fists clenched in the air and hisses: 'I should have realized right from the start. There was never an estate agent in the apartment. *You're* the bank robber!'

49

Of course it was idiotic of Jack not to realize everything from the start, who the bank robber was, because it seemed so obvious to him in hindsight. Maybe it was his mum's fault. She held the two of them together, him and his dad, but perhaps that sometimes distracted him, and for some reason she had managed to get into his thoughts the whole damn time today. Just as much trouble in death as in life, that woman. Maybe somewhere there was another priest who was more difficult than her, but there could hardly be two. She got into arguments with everyone when she was alive, maybe more with her son than anyone, and that didn't stop after her funeral. Because the people we argue with hardest of all are not the ones who are completely different from us, but the ones who are almost no different at all.

She used to travel abroad sometimes, after disasters when aid organizations needed volunteers, to the constant accompaniment of criticism from all directions both inside and outside the Church. She either shouldn't help at all or ought to be doing it somewhere else. Nothing is easier for people who never do anything themselves than to criticize someone who actually makes an effort. One time she was on the other side of the world and got caught up in a riot and tried to help a bleeding woman get away, and in the chaos she herself got stabbed in the arm. She was taken to the hospital, managed to borrow a phone, and called home. Jim was sitting in front of the news, waiting. He listened patiently, as usual happy and relieved that she was okay. But when Jack realized what had happened, he grabbed the phone and shouted so loudly that the line began to shriek with feedback: 'Why did you have to go there? Why do you have to risk your life? *Why don't you ever think about your family?*

His mum realized, of course, that her son was shouting out of fear and concern, so she replied the way she often did: 'Boats that stay in the harbour are safe, sweetheart, but that's not what boats were built for.'

Jack said something he instantly regretted: 'Do you think God's going to protect you against knives just because you're a priest?'

She may have been sitting in a hospital on the other side of the world, but she could still feel his bottomless terror. So her whispers were half washed away by tears when she replied: 'God doesn't protect people from knives, sweetheart. That's why God gave us other people, so we can protect each other.'

It was impossible to argue with such a stubborn woman. Jack hated how much he admired her sometimes. Jim, in turn, loved her so much he could hardly breathe. But she didn't travel so much after that, and never went so far away again. Then she got sick, and they lost her, and the world lost a bit more of its protection.

So when the hostage drama started, when Jack and Jim were standing out in the street the day before New Year's Eve, outside the apartment block, and had just been told by their bosses to wait for the Stockholmer, the two of them were thinking a lot about her and what she would have done if she'd been there. And when that lime came flying out and hit Jack on the forehead and they realized that the note wrapped around it was an order for pizza, they both concluded that a better opportunity to get in contact with the bank robber was unlikely to arise. So Jack called the negotiator. And, despite the fact that he was a Stockholmer, he agreed that they were right.

'Yes, well, delivering pizzas could be an opening for communication, it certainly could. What about the bomb in the stairwell, though?' he wondered.

'It's not a bomb!' Jack said confidently.

'Would you swear on that?'

'Using whatever swearwords you'd care to choose, and I can tell you that my mum taught me quite a lot of those. This perpetrator isn't dangerous. Just scared.'

'How do you know that?'

'Because if he'd been dangerous, if he'd been aware of what he was doing, then he wouldn't have ordered pizzas for all the hostages by throwing *limes* at us. Let me go in and talk to him, I can . . .' Jack paused. He'd been about to say *I can save everyone.* But he swallowed hard and said instead: 'I can fix this. I can sort this out.'

'Have you spoken to all the neighbours?' the negotiator wondered.

'The rest of the building is empty,' Jack assured him.

The negotiator was still stuck in traffic on the motorway, far too many miles away, not even police cars were able to get through, so in the end he agreed to Jack's plan. But he also demanded that Jack somehow get a phone into the apartment, so that the negotiator himself could call the bank robber and negotiate the release of the hostages. And take the glory when everything turns out okay, Jack thought sullenly.

'I've got a decent phone,' Jack said, because he had the one Jim called the special telephone thingy that got a bloody signal where there wasn't a bloody signal.

'I'll call after they've had the pizzas, it's easier to negotiate when people have eaten,' the negotiator said, as if that were what you learned on negotiation courses these days.

'What do we do if he doesn't open the door when we get there?' Jack wondered.

'Then you leave the pizzas and phone out on the landing.'

'How can we be sure he'll take the phone inside the apartment?' Jack asked.

'Why wouldn't he?'

'Do you think he's made rational, logical decisions so far? He might get stressed and think the phone is some sort of trap.'

That was when Jim suddenly had an idea. Which surprised him as much as anyone.

'We can put it in one of the pizza boxes!' he suggested.

Jim looked at his dad in shock for several seconds. Then he nodded and said into the phone: 'We'll put the phone in one of the pizza boxes.'

'Yes, that's a good idea,' the negotiator agreed.

'It was my dad's,' Jack said proudly.

Jim turned away so his son wouldn't see how embarrassed he was. He looked up local pizzerias on Google, called one of them, and explained the highly unconventional order: eight pizzas and one of the uniforms the delivery guys usually wore. However, Jim made the mistake of saying he was a police officer, and the owner of the pizzeria, who was perfectly capable of reading the local news on social media, was quick-witted enough to say that he gave a discount for bulk orders on pizzas, but charged twice as much for hiring out uniforms. Jim asked angrily if the owner was a character in an English Christmas story from the mid-nineteenth century, and the owner calmly countered by asking if Jim was familiar with the concept of 'supply and demand'. When the pizzas and outfit finally arrived, Jack grabbed at them, but Jim refused to let go.

'What are you playing at? I'm the one going in!' Jack said firmly.

Jim shook his head.

'No. I still think that might be a bomb in the stairwell. So I'm the one going in.'

'Why would *you* go in there if you think it's a bomb? For God's sake, *I'm* going . . . ,' Jack began, but his dad refused to back down.

'You're certain it isn't a bomb, aren't you, son?'

'Yes!'

'Well, then. It doesn't make any difference if I go in.'

'What are you, eleven years old?'

'Are *you*?'

Jack tried desperately to think of a counterargument.

'I can't let you . . .'

Jim was already changing clothes, in the middle of the street even though the temperature was below freezing. They didn't look at each other.

'Your mum would never have forgiven me if I let you go in,' Jim said, looking down at the ground.

'Do you think she would have forgiven me if I let you go in, then? You were her husband,' Jack said, looking down the street.

Jim looked up at the sky.

'But she was your mum.'

There was no arguing with him sometimes, the old bastard.

The police station. The interview room. All the blood has drained from the estate agent's face now. She looks terrified.

'Ba-ba-bank robber? M-m-me? H-h-how c-c-could I . . .'

Jack is marching around the room, waving his arms as if he were conducting an invisible orchestra, incredibly pleased with himself.

'How did I not see this right at the start? You don't *know* anything. Everything you've said about the apartment has been complete gibberish. No *real* estate agent could be this bad at their job!'

The estate agent looks like she's about to start crying.

'I'm doing my best, okay? Do you have any idea how hard it is being an estate agent during a recession?'

Jack fixes his eyes on her.

'But that's *not* what you are, is it? Because you're a bank robber!'

The agent looks in despair over at Jim in the doorway, trying to get some sort of support. But Jim merely looks back at her unhappily. Meanwhile Jack bangs both fists down on the table and glares furiously at the estate agent.

'I should have realized right from the start. When the other witnesses were talking about the hostage drama, they didn't even mention you. Because you were never there. Admit it! We allowed ourselves to be distracted when you asked for those fireworks, and then you walked right out of that apartment, in front of our very eyes. Tell me the truth!'

The truth? It's hardly ever as complicated as we think. We just hope it is, because then we feel smarter if we can work it out in advance. This is a story about a bridge, and idiots, and a hostage drama and an apartment viewing. But it's also a love story. Several, in fact.

The last time Zara saw her psychologist before the hostage drama, she arrived early. She was never late, but it was unusual for her not to walk in at precisely the agreed time.

'Has anything happened?' Nadia wondered.

'What do you mean?' Zara replied contrarily.

'You're not usually early. Is anything wrong?'

'Isn't it your job to work that out?'

Nadia sighed.

'I was only asking.'

'Is that kale?'

Nadia looked down into the plastic tub on her desk. Nodded.

'I'm having lunch.'

Other patients might have taken this as a hint. Not Zara, of course.

'So you're vegan,' she said, without a question mark.

The psychologist coughed, the way you do if your throat takes offence at you being predictable.

'I don't have to be, do I? I mean, I *am* vegan, but surely other people eat kale?'

Zara wrinkled her nose.

'But that was bought in a carryout. So you could have chosen anything. But you chose kale.'

'And only vegans do that?'

'I can only assume that lack of vitamins affects your financial judgement.'

Nadia smiled at that.

'So you look down on me because I'm a vegan, or because I pay for vegan food?'

Nadia swallowed the last bit of both the kale and her self-esteem, closed the lid of the tub, and asked, 'How have you been feeling since we last met, Zara?'

Rather than reply Zara took a small bottle of hand sanitizer from her bag, carefully massaged her fingers with her back to the desk, looked at the bookcase, and declared: 'For a psychologist, you have an awful lot of books that aren't about psychology.'

'And what are the others about, in your opinion?'

'Identity. That's why you're a vegan.'

'It's possible to be vegan for other reasons.'

'Such as?'

'It's good for the environment.'

'Maybe. But I think people like you are vegan because it makes you feel good. It's probably why you've got poor posture, too little calcium.'

Nadia discreetly adjusted her position on her chair, and did her best not to look like she was trying to sit up straighter.

'You pay for your time here, Zara. For someone who criticizes other people's financial choices, you seem remarkably happy to throw away quite a lot of money on talking about . . . me. Do you want to talk about why?'

Zara seemed to consider this seriously, without taking her eyes off the bookcase.

'Maybe next time.'

'That's good to hear.'

'What is?'

'That there's going to be a next time.'

Zara turned around at that and peered at Nadia to see if that was a joke or not. She didn't quite succeed, so turned away again, rubbed more sanitizer into her hands, and looked out of the window behind

Nadia, counting the windows in the building opposite. Then she said: 'You haven't suggested I start taking antidepressants. Most psychologists would have.'

'Have you met many other psychologists?'

'No.'

'So that's your own analysis?'

Zara looked at the picture on the wall.

'I can understand you not wanting to give me sleeping pills, because you're worried I'd kill myself. But surely if that's the case, you should be giving me antidepressants instead?'

Nadia folded two unused paper napkins and tucked them away in her desk drawer. Then nodded.

'You're right. I haven't suggested medication. Because antidepressants are designed to smooth out the highs and lows of your mood, and if used properly they can stop you feeling so sad, but often they stop you feeling as happy.' She held one hand up, her palm horizontal. 'You just end up . . . on a level. And you would expect that patients who take antidepressants mostly miss the highs, wouldn't you? But that isn't actually the case. The majority of people who want to stop medication say they want to be able to cry again. They watch a sad film with someone they love, and they want to be able to . . . feel the same thing.'

'I don't like films,' Zara pointed out.

Nadia laughed out loud.

'No, of course you don't. But I don't think you need fewer feelings, Zara. I think you need to feel more. I don't think you're depressed. I think you're lonely.'

'That sounds like an unprofessional analysis.'

'Maybe.'

'What if I leave here and kill myself.'

'I don't think you'd do that.'

'No?'

'You said a little while ago that there's going to be a next time.'

Zara focused her gaze on Nadia's chin.

'And you trust me?'

'Yes.'

'Why?'

'Because I can see that you don't want to let people get close to you. It makes you feel weak. But I don't think you're afraid of being hurt, I think you're afraid of hurting other people. You're a more empathetic and moral person than you like to admit.'

Zara was deeply, deeply offended by this, and had difficulty working out if that was because Nadia had called her weak, or because she had said she was moral.

'Maybe I just don't think it's worth the effort to talk to people I'm only going to get fed up with.'

'How do you know that if you never try?'

'I'm here, aren't I, and it didn't take me long to get fed up with you!'

'Try to take the question seriously,' Nadia said, which of course was hopeless. Zara bounced away from the subject as usual.

'So why *are* you vegan?'

Nadia groaned wearily.

'Do we really have to talk about *that* again? Okay: I'm vegan because I care about the climate crisis. If everyone was vegan, we could . . .'

Zara interrupted scornfully: 'Stop the ice caps melting?'

Nadia deployed the patience vegans have plenty of time to practise when they spend Christmas with older relatives.

'Not quite, no. But it's part of a larger solution. And the fact that the ice caps are melting is –'

'But do we really need penguins?' Zara asked bluntly.

'I would say that the ice caps are a symptom, not the problem. Like the trouble you have sleeping.'

Zara counted the windows.

'There are frogs threatened with extinction that scientists say would leave us smothered with insects if they disappeared. But penguins?

Who'd be affected if penguins disappeared, except maybe businesses that make padded jackets?'

Nadia lost the thread at that, which may have been Zara's intention.

'You don't make . . . what . . . do you think they make padded jackets out of penguins? They're made of *geese*!'

'So geese aren't as important as penguins? That doesn't sound very vegan.'

'That's not what I said!'

'That's what it sounded like.'

'You're making a habit of this, you know.'

'What?'

'Changing the subject as soon as you get close to talking about real feelings.'

Zara seemed to consider this. Then she said: 'What about bears, then?'

'Sorry?'

'If you get attacked by a bear? Could you kill it then?'

'Why would I be attacked by a bear?'

'Maybe someone kidnaps you and drugs you and you wake up in a cage with a bear, and it's a fight to the death.'

'You're starting to get quite disconcerting now. And I'd like to point out that I've had an awful lot of training in psychology, so I have a *fairly* high threshold for what counts as disconcerting.'

'Stop being so sensitive. Answer the question: Could you kill a bear then, even if you didn't want to eat it? I'm not saying you've got a fork, but if you had a knife?'

Nadia groaned. 'You're doing it again.'

'What?'

Nadia looked at the time. Zara noticed. She counted all the windows twice. Nadia noticed. They looked past each other for a while until Nadia said: 'Let me ask you this, then: Do you think you mock the green movement this way because it's the opposite of the finance industry you work in?'

Zara bit back faster than she herself was expecting, because sometimes you don't know how strongly you feel about something until you're tested: 'The green movement doesn't need any help to look ridiculous! And I'm not defending the finance industry, I'm defending the economic system.'

'What's the difference?'

'One is the symptom. The other is the problem.'

Nadia nodded as if she understood what that meant.

'Surely we created the economic system? It's a construct?'

Zara's reply was surprisingly free from condescension, and almost sounded sympathetic.

'That's the problem. We made it too strong. We forgot how greedy we are. Do you own an apartment?'

'Yes.'

'Have you got a mortgage on it?'

'Hasn't everyone?'

'No. And a mortgage used to be something you were expected to repay. But now that every other middle-income family has a mortgage for an amount they couldn't possibly save up in their lifetimes, then the bank isn't *lending* money any more. It's offering *financing*. And then homes are no longer homes. They're investments.'

'I'm not sure I completely understand what that means.'

'It means that the poor get poorer, the rich get richer, and the real class divide is between those who can borrow money and those who can't. Because no matter how much money anyone earns, they still lie awake at the end of the month worrying about money. Everyone looks at what their neighbours have and wonders, "How can they *afford* that?" because everyone is living beyond their means. So not even really rich people ever feel really rich, because in the end the only thing you can buy is a more expensive version of something you've already got. With borrowed money.'

Nadia looked like a cat who'd just seen someone skating for the first time.

'I heard a man who worked in a casino say that no one gets ruined by losing, they get ruined by trying to win back the money they lost. Is that what you mean? Is that why the stock market and housing market crash?'

Zara shrugged.

'Sure. If that makes it feel better.'

Then the psychologist suddenly, and without quite knowing why, asked a question that knocked the air out of her patient's lungs: 'So do you feel more guilty about the customers you *haven't* lent money to, or the ones you've lent *too much* to?'

Zara looked untroubled, but she was holding on to the arms of the chair so tightly that when she eventually let go her palms were bloodless. She hid it by rubbing them, and evaded eye contact by counting windows. Then she let out a quick snort.

'You know something? If people who worry about animal welfare were really bothered about animal welfare, they wouldn't tell me to eat happy pigs.'

Nadia rolled her eyes. 'I don't see what that's got to do with my question.'

Zara shrugged.

'All this talk about organic farming, adverts for free-range chickens and happy pigs . . . isn't it more unethical of me to eat a happy pig? Surely it's better if I eat a pig that's lived a terrible life than one of those carpe diem pigs with a family and friends? The farmers say happy pigs taste better, so I can only assume that they wait until the pig has just fallen in love, maybe just after it's had kids, when it's at its absolute *happiest*, and then it gets shot in the head and vacuum packed. How ethical is that?'

The psychologist sighed.

'I'll take that to mean that you don't want to talk about your customers and how much they've borrowed.'

Zara dug her fingernails hard into her palms.

'Have you ever thought about how vegans always talk about saving the planet, as if the planet needed you? The planet will survive for billions of years even without human help. The only people we're killing are ourselves.'

It wasn't much of an answer, as usual. Nadia looked at the time, then regretted doing so at once because Zara noticed and got to her feet, as usual. Zara never liked to be asked to leave, and that tends to make you more alert to the way people check the time, and the second time they look you get to your feet. Nadia felt embarrassed and stammered, 'We've got some time left . . . if you'd like . . . I haven't another appointment after this.'

'Well, I've got things to do,' Zara replied.

Nadia composed herself and asked straight out, 'Can you tell me one personal thing about yourself?'

'Sorry?'

Nadia stood up and moved her head in an attempt to catch Zara's eye.

'In all the time we've spent talking to each other, I get the sense that you've never told me anything truly personal about yourself. Anything at all. What's your favourite colour? Do you like art? Have you ever been in love?'

Zara's eyebrows rose as far as they could go.

'Do you think I'd sleep better if I were in love?'

Nadia burst out laughing.

'No. I was just wondering. I know very little about you.'

Of all the moments they shared, this was one of the most remarkable.

Zara stood behind her chair for several minutes. Then she took a deep breath and actually told Nadia something about herself that she had never told anyone: 'I like music. I play . . . music, very loud, as soon as I get home. It helps me gather my thoughts.'

'Only when you get home?'

'I can't play it that loud in the office. It only works if I listen to it at very, very high volume.'

Zara tapped her forehead as she said that, as if to illustrate what it was that didn't work.

'What sort of music?' Nadia asked gently.

'Death metal.'

'Wow.'

'Is that a professional opinion?'

Nadia giggled, which was embarrassing and highly unprofessional – you certainly aren't taught how to giggle on psychology courses.

'It was just so incredibly unexpected. Why death metal?'

'It's so loud that it makes your head silent.'

Zara's knuckles turned white around the handle of her handbag. Nadia noticed, so she pulled a pad of paper from one of her desk drawers, wrote something, and handed Zara a note.

'Is that a prescription for sleeping pills?' Zara asked.

Nadia shook her head.

'It's the name of a good pair of headphones. There's an electronics store down the street. Buy them, then you can listen to music no matter where you are, as soon as things start to feel difficult. Maybe that would help you to get out more? Meet people? Maybe even . . . fall in love.'

Of course the psychologist regretted saying that last bit at once. Zara didn't respond. She tucked the note in her handbag, stared at the letter at the bottom of it, closed it quickly. As she was leaving Nadia called out anxiously, worried that she had gone too far:

'You don't have to fall in love, Zara, that wasn't what I meant! I just meant it might be time to try something new. I just think you should give yourself . . . just give yourself the chance of . . . getting fed up with someone!'

Zara stood in the lift. As the doors closed she thought about loans. The ones we grant and the ones we refuse. Then she pressed the emergency stop button.

52

While the hostage drama was going on, out in the street Jack was try-ing to think of some other way to contact the bank robber rather than let Jim go up with the pizzas. He thought and thought and thought, be-cause young men may be absolutely certain about almost everything nearly all of the time, but even for Jack it would have been easier to be one hundred per cent certain that the bomb wasn't a bomb if he didn't need to send his dad into the stairwell to test the theory.

'Hang on, Dad, I've . . . ,' he began, then raised his phone and said to the negotiator: 'Before we go in with the pizzas, I want to try to get a better idea of what's going on. I can get into the building that's on the other side of the street. I might be able to see into the stairwell windows from there.'

The negotiator sounded sceptical.

'What difference would that make?'

'None, maybe,' Jack admitted. 'But I might be able to tell if it's a bomb or not through the window, and before I send my colleague in I want to know that I've exhausted all options.'

The negotiator put his hand over his phone and talked to someone else, one of the bastard bosses, perhaps. Then he came back and said: 'Yes. Okay, yes.'

He didn't tell Jack that he was impressed that he had called his dad his 'colleague' in such a critical situation, but he was.

So Jack went into the building on the other side of the street. The negotiator stayed on the line, and one and a half floors later he won-dered: 'What . . . what are you doing?'

'I'm going up the stairs,' Jack replied.

'Isn't there a lift?'

'I don't like lifts.'

The negotiator sounded like he was hitting his head with his phone.

'So you're prepared to go into a building containing a bomb and an armed bank robber, but you're scared of lifts?'

Jack hissed back: 'I'm not *scared* of lifts! I'm scared of snakes and cancer. I just don't *like* lifts!'

The negotiator sounded like he was grinning.

'Can't you call in reinforcements?'

'All the staff we have at our disposal are here, the whole lot. They're maintaining the cordon and evacuating the surrounding buildings. I've called in backup, but they're both waiting for their wives.'

'What does that mean?'

'That they've been drinking. Their wives will have to drive them here.'

'Drinking? At this time of day? The day *before* New Year's Eve?' the negotiator wondered.

'I don't know how you do it in Stockholm, but here we take New Year seriously,' Jack replied.

The negotiator laughed.

'Stockholmers don't take anything seriously, you know that. At least, nothing important.'

Jack grinned. He hesitated briefly as he went up a few more steps before asking the question he had been wanting to ask for a while.

'Have you been involved in a hostage drama before?'

The negotiator hesitated before replying.

'Yes. Yes, I have.'

'How did it end?'

'He let the hostages go and came out after we'd spent four hours talking.'

Jack nodded tersely and stopped at the next-to-last floor. He peered out of the landing window through a small pair of binoculars. He could see the wires on the floor of the landing opposite, they were hanging out of a box that someone had written something on with a marker. He wasn't absolutely certain, but from where he was standing it looked very much like the letters C-H-R-I-S-T-M-A-S.

'It isn't a bomb,' he said into his phone.

'What do you think it is, then?'

'Looks like outdoor Christmas lights.'

'Well, then.'

Jack carried on up to the top floor — if the bank robber hadn't closed the blinds, he might be able to see into the apartment.

'How did you get him out?' he asked.

'Who?'

'The hostage taker. Last time.'

'Oh. All the usual, I suppose, a combination of what you get taught. Don't use negatives, avoid *can't* and *won't*. Try to find something you've got in common. Find out what his motivation is.'

'Was that really how you got him out?'

'No, of course not. I was joking.'

'Seriously?'

'Yes, seriously. We talked for four hours and then he suddenly fell silent. And of course that's the first thing we get taught . . .'

'To keep him occupied? Not to let the line go quiet?'

'Exactly. I didn't know what to do, so I took a chance and asked if he wanted to hear a funny story. He said nothing for a minute or so, then he said: "Well? Are you going to tell me or not?" So I told him the one about the two Irish guys in a boat, if you know that one?'

'No,' Jack said.

'Okay, two Irish brothers are out at sea, fishing. A storm blows up, and they lose both oars, they're convinced they're going to drown. Then suddenly one of the brothers spots something in the water, and manages to grab hold of a bottle. They pull the cork out and POOF! A genie appears. He grants them one wish, anything they want. So the two brothers look around at the stormy sea; they're stuck out there with no oars, several miles from shore, and the first brother is thinking about what to ask for when the second brother cheerfully blurts out: "I wish the whole sea was Guinness!" The genie stares at him like he's an idiot, then says, okay, sure, let's go for that. And POOF! The sea turns into Guinness. The genie vanishes. The first brother stares at the second brother and snaps: "You bloody idiot! We had one single wish and you wished the sea was Guinness! Do you have any idea what you've done?" The second brother shakes his head in shame. The first brother throws his arms out and says . . .'

The negotiator left a dramatic pause, but didn't have time to deliver the punchline before Jack cut in from the other end of the line.

'Now we have to piss in the boat!'

The negotiator let out an affronted snort so loud that the phone shook.

'So you had heard it after all?'

'My mum liked funny stories. Is that really what got the hostage taker to give up?'

The line was quiet a little too long.

'Maybe he was worried I was going to tell him another one.'

The negotiator sounded like he wanted to laugh as he was saying this, but didn't quite succeed. Jack couldn't help noticing. He had reached the top floor now, and looked out of the window at the balcony on the other side of the street. He stopped in surprise.

'What the . . . ? That's weird.'

'What?'

'I can see the balcony of the apartment where the hostages are being held. There's a woman standing on it.'

'A woman?'

'Yes. Wearing headphones.'

'Headphones?'

'Yes.'

'What sort of headphones?'

'How many different types are there? What difference does that make?'

The negotiator sighed.

'Okay. Stupid question. How old is she, then?'

'Fifties. Older, maybe.'

'Older than fifty, or older than in her fifties?'

'For God's . . . I don't know! A woman. A perfectly ordinary woman.'

'Okay, okay, calm down. Does she look scared?'

'She looks . . . bored. She definitely doesn't look like she's in any danger, anyway.'

'That sounds like an odd hostage situation.'

'Exactly. And that definitely isn't a bomb in the stairwell. And he tried to rob a cashless bank. I said from the start, we're not dealing with a professional here.'

The negotiator considered this for a few moments.

'Yes, you might well be right.'

He was trying to sound confident, but Jack could hear his doubt. The two men shared a long silence before Jack said, 'Tell me the truth. What happened in that last hostage drama you were involved in?'

The negotiator sighed.

'The man released the hostages. But he shot himself before we managed to get in.'

Those words would follow Jack throughout the day, right next to his skin.

He had started to walk back down the stairs by the time the negotiator cleared his throat.

'Okay, Jack, can I ask *you* a question? Why did you turn down that job in Stockholm?'

Jack considered lying, but couldn't summon up the energy.

'How do you know about that?'

'I talked to one of the bosses before I set off. Asked her who was on the scene locally. She said I should talk to Jack, because he's bloody good. She said she'd offered you a job several times, but that you keep turning it down.'

'I've got a job.'

'Not like the one she's offering.'

Jack snorted defensively.

'Oh, all you Stockholmers think the world revolves around your bloody city.'

The negotiator laughed.

'Listen, I grew up in a village where you had to drive forty minutes if you wanted to buy milk. Back there we used to think your town was metropolitan. To us, you were the Stockholmers.'

'Everyone is someone else's Stockholmer, I guess.'

'So what's your problem, then? Are you worried you wouldn't be able to cope with the job if you took it?'

Jack rubbed his hands on his trousers.

'Are you my psychologist or something?'

'Sounds like you could do with one.'

'Can't we just focus on the job in hand?'

The negotiator hesitated and took a deep breath before asking: 'Does your dad know you've been offered another job?'

Jack was about to swear, but the negotiator never got to hear what, because at that moment Jack looked out of the window in the stairwell and saw that his dad was no longer waiting in the street like he'd been told.

'What the *hell*?!' Jack exclaimed. Then he ended the call and ran.

53

Zara had just stepped out on to the balcony when Jack saw her. That was just after she had told the bank robber out in the hall not to do anything silly, and she needed fresh air, more than ever. If all you saw was the rear view of Zara heading towards the balcony, you'd probably think she was impatient. You needed to see her face to understand that she was feeling fragile. She had surprised herself back there, had lost control, felt things. For anyone else that might perhaps merely have been vaguely uncomfortable, like when you discover you're starting to share the same taste in music as your parents, or biting into something you think is chocolate but turns out to be liver pâté, but for Zara it unleashed a feeling of complete panic. Was she starting to develop a sense of empathy?

She rubbed her hands carefully with sanitizer, counted the windows of the building on the other side of the street over and over again, tried to take deep breaths. She had been in the apartment too long, these people had shrunk her customary distance, and she wasn't used to that. Out on the balcony she pressed herself up against the wall of the building so no one down in the street could see her over the railing. She clamped the headphones over her ears and turned the volume up until the shrieking noise of the music drowned out the shrieking noise inside her head. Until the bass was thudding harder than her heart.

And just there, perhaps she found it. A truce with herself.

She could see winter making itself comfortable across the town. She liked the silence of this time of year, but had never appreciated its smugness. When the snow arrives autumn has already done all the work, taking care of all the leaves and carefully sweeping summer away from people's memories. All winter had to do was roll in with a bit of freezing weather and take all the credit, like a man who's spent twenty minutes next to a barbecue but has never served a full meal in his life.

She didn't hear the balcony door open, but she felt a furry ear on her hair as Lennart stepped out and stood beside her. He tapped gently on one of the earphones.

'What?' she snapped.

'Do you smoke?' Lennart asked, because even though he hadn't managed to remove the rabbit's head, there was a small hole in the snout that he was fairly certain he'd be able to smoke through.

'Certainly not!' Zara said, putting the headphone back over her ear.

Lennart was surprised, even if that wasn't visible through the un-changing ambivalence of the rabbit's head. Zara looked like someone who smoked, not because she liked it so much as to make the air worse for other people. The rabbit tapped on the headphone again and she removed it with the utmost reluctance.

'What are you doing out on the balcony, then?' he wondered.

Zara took a long, hard look at him, starting from his white socks, via his bare legs and his non-elasticated underpants, to his bare torso, where the chest hair had started to go grey.

'Do you really think you're in any position to question other people's life choices?' she asked, but didn't sound anywhere near as annoyed as she had hoped, which was annoying.

He scratched his big, lifeless rabbit's ears and replied: 'I don't smoke, either, not really. Just at parties. And when I'm being held hostage!'

He laughed, she didn't. He fell silent. She put the headphone back on her ear, but of course he tapped on it again immediately.

'Can I stand out here with you for a while? I'm worried Roger might hit me again if I go back in there.'

Zara didn't answer, just put the headphone back in place, and the rabbit tapped on it at once.

'Are you here on safari, then?'

She glared at him in surprise.

'What does that mean?'

'Just an observation. There's always someone like you at every apartment viewing. Someone who doesn't want the apartment, but is just curious. On safari. Test-driving a lifestyle. You get to recognize that sort of thing in my job.'

The look in Zara's eyes was poisonous, but her mouth remained closed. Being seen through isn't pleasant, you tend to pull your clothes a little tighter when it happens, especially if you're usually the one who sees through other people. Her instinct was to say something cruel to put a bit of distance between them, but instead she found herself asking: 'Aren't you cold?'

He shook his head and she had to duck to avoid one of his ears. Then he patted his furry face and chuckled: 'Nope. They say seventy per cent of your body heat gets lost through your head, so seeing as I'm stuck in here, I suppose I'm only losing thirty per cent right now.'

That isn't the sort of thing a man dressed in tight underwear usually boasts about in freezing temperatures, Zara noted. She put the headphones back on again, hoping that would be enough to get rid of him, but even before he tapped on the headphone again she had already guessed that his next sentence was going to start with the word 'I'.

'I'm really an actor. This business of disrupting apartment viewings is only a sideline.'

'How interesting,' Zara said in a tone that only the child of a telesales operator would interpret as an invitation to go on talking.

'Times are tough for people in the cultural sector.' The rabbit nodded.

Zara pulled the headphones down around her neck in resignation and snorted.

'So that's your excuse for exploiting the fact that times are tough for people selling apartments, too? How come you people in the "cultural sector" never think capitalism is any good except when *you're* the ones profiting from it?'

It just slipped out, she didn't really know why. Between his ears she caught a glimpse of the bridge. The ears wavered thoughtfully in the December wind.

'Sorry, but you don't strike me as the sort of person who feels sorry for people trying to sell apartments,' he said.

Zara snorted again, more angrily.

'I don't care about sellers or buyers. But I do care about the fact that you don't seem to appreciate that your "sideline" is manipulating the economic system!'

The rabbit's head was stuck in a rictus grin while Lennart was thinking hard inside it. Then he said what Zara considered to be the stupidest thing that could ever come out of anyone's mouth, rabbit or human: 'What have *I* got to do with the economic system?'

Zara massaged her hands. Counted the windows.

'The market is supposed to be self-regulating, but people like you spoil the balance between supply and demand,' she said wearily.

Of course the rabbit responded at once by saying the most predictable thing possible: 'That's not true. If I wasn't doing this, someone else would. I'm not breaking the law. An apartment is the largest investment most people make, and they want the best price, so I'm just offering a service that –'

'Apartments aren't supposed to be investments,' Zara replied gloomily.

'What are they supposed to be, then?'

'Homes.'

'Are you some sort of communist?' the rabbit chuckled.

Zara felt like punching him on the nose for that, but instead she pointed between his ears and said: 'When the financial crisis hit ten years ago, a man jumped off that bridge because of a property market crash on the other side of the world. Innocent people lost their jobs and the guilty were given bonuses. You know why?'

'Now you're exaggerat –'

'Because people like you don't care about the balance in the system.'

Lennart chuckled superciliously inside the rabbit's head. He still hadn't realized who he'd embarked on a discussion with.

'You need to calm down, the financial crisis was the banks' fault, I don't make the —'

'The rules? Is that what you were about to say? You don't make the rules, you just play the game?' Zara interrupted wearily, seeing as she'd rather drink nitroglycerin and go on a trampoline than have to listen to yet another man lecturing her about financial responsibilities.

'Yes! Well, no! But . . .'

Zara had spent enough of her life in committee rooms with the target market for cufflinks to be able to predict the rest of this guy's monologue, so she decided to save her time and his larynx: 'Let me guess where you're going with this: you don't care about the seller of this apartment, you don't care about Roger and Anna-Lena, either, you only care about yourself. But you're going to try to defend yourself by saying that it isn't possible to cheat the housing market, because the *market* doesn't really exist, it's a *construct*. Just numbers on a computer screen. So *you* don't have any responsibility, do you?'

'No . . . ,' Lennart began, but didn't even manage to take a breath before Zara stormed on.

'Then you'll dredge up some pop-psychological nonsense about money not having any value because that's also a construct. And then we get to the history lesson, where clever old you gets to teach silly, ignorant me about economic theory and how the stock market came about. Maybe you feel like telling me about Hanoi 1902, when the city tried to fight a plague of rats by offering the inhabitants a reward for every rat they killed and whose tail they handed over to the police. And what did that lead to? People started breeding rats! Do you have any idea how many men have told me that story to illustrate how self-ish and untrustworthy ordinary people are? Do you know how many men like you every single woman on the planet meets every day, who think that every thought that pops into your tiny little male brains is a lovely present you can give us?'

Lennart had backed away three steps towards the railing by this point. But Zara had got into her stride now, so all he had time to say was: 'I —' before she snapped: 'You what? You what? *You're* not the greedy one, *everyone else* is? Is that what you were about to say?'

The rabbit shook its ears.

'No. No, I'm sorry. I didn't know anyone had jumped off that bridge. Did you know . . . ?'

Zara's cheeks were throbbing, her throat was bright red beneath the headphones. She was no longer talking to Lennart, but exactly who she was talking to probably wasn't clear even to her, but it felt like she'd been waiting ten years to yell at someone. Anyone at all. Herself most of all. So she roared: 'People like *you* and *me* are the problem, don't you get that? We always defend ourselves by saying we're only offering a service. That we're just one tiny part of the market. That everything is people's own fault. That they're greedy, that they shouldn't have given us their money. And then *we* have the nerve to wonder why stock markets crash and the city is full of rats . . .'

Her eyes were wild with rage, and little clouds of smoke kept puffing breathlessly out of her nostrils. The rabbit didn't reply, those unblinking eyes just looked at her as she tried to get her pulse under control. Then there was a hacking sound from inside the head, and at first Zara thought the old bastard was having a stroke, then realized that this was what Lennart sounded like when he was laughing, really properly, from deep in his stomach. He held his arms out.

'I don't know what you're talking about any more, to be honest. But I give up, you win, you win!'

Zara's eyes narrowed, from fear as much as anger. It was easier to talk to the rabbit than other people, because she didn't have to look Lennart in the eye. She wasn't prepared for what that was going to do to her. She leaned forward and stretched her fingers out on her thighs, bent and straightened them, over and over again. Then she said in a quieter voice: 'I win, do I? Do Anna-Lena and Roger win? He's trying to get rich and she's trying to make him happy, and all they're really doing is postponing an inevitable divorce. But that probably just makes you happy, because then they'll have to buy *two* apartments.'

At that, something happened. Lennart raised his voice for the first time.

'No! That's not enough! Because . . . because . . . I don't believe that!'

'So what do *you* believe, then?' Zara snapped back, and – regardless of whatever it was that had led her to this point – her voice finally broke. She screwed her eyes shut and clenched her fists around the headphones. She had been waiting ten years for someone to ask her that question. So it almost floored her when he said:

'Love.'

Lennart picked up and dropped the word so carelessly, as if it weren't a big deal at all. Zara wasn't prepared for it, and that sort of thing can make a person angry. Lennart's voice became more muffled inside the rabbit's head, hurt now: 'You're talking like I'd be happy if people got divorced. No one can go to two thousand apartment viewings and not realize that there's more love in the world than the opposite.'

Not even Zara had an answer to that. And he still didn't seem to be freezing, the idiot in the rabbit's head, which just made her more annoyed. *Stop talking about love and feel cold, for God's sake, like any normal idiot*, she thought, and prepared to fire back with some devastating remark. But all she heard herself ask was: 'What do you base that on?'

The rabbit's ears quivered.

'All the apartments that aren't for sale.'

Zara's fingers fumbled around her neck. It wasn't an entirely ridiculous answer, which obviously annoyed her. Why couldn't Lennart have the decency to be a complete idiot? An idiot who is also a romantic is almost unbearable, and that 'almost' can drive a woman with headphones mad.

So she remained silent, gazing off towards the bridge. Then she let

out a resigned sigh and pulled two cigarettes out from her bag. She
stuck one in the rabbit's snout and the other in her own mouth. The
rabbit was smart enough not to start going on about her earlier claim
that she *didn't* smoke. She appreciated that. When she gave him the
lighter he managed to singe the fur on his nose and had to pat the
flames out with his hands. She appreciated that as well.

They smoked without any sense of urgency. Then Lennart said,
heavily but with no trace of accusation, as he looked out across the
rooftops: 'You can think what you like about me, but Anna-Lena is
one of the few clients I've got who I . . . can't help rooting for. She
doesn't want to make her husband rich, she just wants to make him
feel needed. Everyone takes it for granted that she's submissive and
oppressed and that she's always had to stand back and make sacrifices
for his career, but do you know what job she used to do?'

'No,' Zara confessed.

'She was a senior analyst for a big American industrial company. I
didn't believe it at first, because she's as scatty as a box of kittens . . . but
you won't find a smarter, better-educated person in this apartment, I can
assure you of that. When their kids were young his career started to take
off, but hers was going even better, so Roger turned down a promotion so
he could spend more time at home with the children, and she could go on
all her business trips. It was only going to be for a few years, but her career
started to go even better while his was treading water, and the more difference there was between their salaries, the harder it was for them to swap
places. When the kids had grown up and Anna-Lena had accomplished all
her goals, she turned to Roger and said "Now it's your turn". But he wasn't
offered any more promotions. He'd got too old. They didn't have any
way of talking about that, because they'd never practised the right words.
So now she's trying to make it up to him by moving all the time and
renovating apartments, all so they have . . . a project in common. Roger
has no kids to look after any more, so he feels worthless. And Anna-Lena
just wants a home. You can say a lot of things about me, but don't you
dare insinuate that I'm not rooting for those two.'

Zara lit another cigarette, mostly so she could keep her eyes busy staring at the glowing tip.

'Did Anna-Lena tell you all that?'

'You'd be surprised what people tell me.'

'No, I wouldn't,' Zara whispered.

She felt like telling him that she needs distance. That she can't stop massaging her hands. That she counts everything in every room because it calms her down. That she likes spreadsheets and turnover forecasts because she likes order. But she also felt like telling him that the economic system she has devoted her life to working in is the world's biggest problem right now, because we made the system too strong. We forgot how greedy we are, but above all we forgot how weak we are. And now it's crushing us.

She felt like saying all this, but by this point in her life she had got used to the fact that people either didn't understand or didn't want to understand. So she stood there in silence. And, deep down, wished she'd stayed silent the whole time.

They each smoked another cigarette. Zara objected to his presence less than she would have expected, and that day had already offered more new experiences than she felt ready to absorb, so her fingers immediately started to trace the edges of the headphones when the rabbit's ears wavered in her direction again. She could tell that he was trying to think of something to ask her, to keep the conversation going. That was what annoyed Zara most about men. Because they could only ever come up with two questions: 'What line of work are you in?' and 'Are you married?'

But this peculiar Lennart plucked up the courage to ask instead: 'What are you listening to?'

Bloody hell, Zara thought. *Why can't you just feel the cold and not be interested in me?* She opened her mouth, there was so much she wanted to say, but all that came out was: 'The bank robber's going to give up soon. The police will come storming in any time now. You should go and put a pair of trousers on.'

The rabbit nodded disappointedly. He left her with her headphones on, music at top volume, counting the windows over and over again. It may not be the sort of love story anyone would write poetry about. But they floored each other there and then.

54

Estelle knocked tentatively on the door to the closet. Julia opened it.

'I just wanted to let you know that the pizzas are on their way, but I was thinking that you must be starving, eating for two, you poor thing. Would you like something to eat while we're waiting? There's food in the freezer. I mean, people almost always have food in the freezer,' Estelle offered.

'No, thanks, that's sweet of you but I'm fine.' Julia smiled. She liked the fact that Estelle was concerned; more people should do that, ask if you're hungry instead of how you're feeling.

'Well, then, I won't disturb you,' Estelle said, and started to close the door.

'Would you like to come in?' Julia asked, but to be honest she said it the way you do when you kind of hope the answer's going to be no.

'I'd love to!' Estelle chirruped, then stepped in and closed the door behind her. She pushed past the stepladder and sat down on the last available seat in the closet: a chest, tucked right at the back. She folded her hands on her lap, smiled warmly, and said: 'Well, this is all rather nice, really, isn't it? I haven't eaten pizza for years. Of course I'd have to admit that this whole business of the bank robbery and hostage taking hasn't been particularly pleasant for any of us, but I can't help thinking that it's quite encouraging that we've got a female bank robber. Don't you think? It's good when us girls show what we're capable of!'

Julia put her thumb on a specific point right between her eyes, pressed hard, and managed to control herself enough to reply: 'Hmm. Threatening us with a pistol, but still . . . Girl power!'

'I don't think it's a real pistol!' Anna-Lena interjected quickly.

Julia closed her eyes so no one would see she was rolling them. Estelle smiled quizzically and asked: 'Well, I didn't mean to come in and interrupt you like this, like some silly old thing. What were you talking about?'

'Marriage,' Anna-Lena sniffed.

'Oh!' Estelle exclaimed, as if her favourite category had just popped up on a television quiz show.

Her enthusiasm softened Julia's attitude slightly, so she asked her: 'Did you say your husband's name is Knut? How long have you been married?'

Estelle counted in her head until she ran out of numbers. 'Knut and I have been married for ever. It's like that when you get old. In the end there simply wasn't ever a time before him.'

Julia had to admit that she liked that answer.

'How do you manage to have such a long marriage?' she asked.

'You fight for it,' Estelle replied honestly.

Julia didn't seem to like that quite as much.

'That doesn't sound very romantic.'

Estelle grinned knowingly.

'You have to listen to each other all the time. But not *all* the time. If you listen to each other *all* the time, there's a risk that you can't forgive each other afterwards.'

Julia ran her fingernails unhappily across her eyebrows.

'Ro and I used to get along fine. We got along so well that it didn't matter that we were good at falling out, too. Sometimes I used to fall out with her on purpose, because we were so good at . . . the other bit. But now, oh, I don't know. I'm just not quite so sure about us any more.'

Estelle toyed with her wedding ring and moistened her lips thoughtfully.

'When we first fell in love, Knut and I reached an agreement about how we were allowed to argue, because Knut said that sooner or later the first flush of infatuation wears off and you end up arguing whether you like it or not. So we came to an agreement, like the Geneva Convention, where the rules of war were agreed. Knut and I promised that no matter how angry we got, we weren't allowed to consciously say things just to hurt each other. We weren't allowed to argue just for the sake of winning. Because, sooner or later, that would end up with one of us winning. And no marriage can survive that.'

'Did it work?' Julia asked.

'I don't know,' Estelle admitted.

'No?'

'We never got past the first flush of infatuation.'

There was no point even trying not to like her just then. Estelle looked around the closet for a while, as if she were trying to remember something, then she stood up and lifted the lid of the chest.

'What are you doing?' Julia wondered.

'Just having a look,' Estelle said apologetically.

Anna-Lena found this upsetting, because Anna-Lena thought there were actually unwritten rules about how much snooping you were allowed to do at apartment viewings.

'You can't do that! You're only allowed to look in cupboards if they're already open! Except for kitchen cupboards. You're allowed to open kitchen cupboards, but only for a few seconds, to see how big they are, but you're not allowed to touch the contents or make any judgements about their lifestyle. There are . . . there are rules! You're allowed to open the dishwasher, but not the washing machine!'

'You might have been to a few toooo many apartment viewings . . . ,' Julia said to her.

'I know,' Anna-Lena sighed.

'There's wine in here!' Estelle exclaimed happily, pulling two bottles out of the chest. 'And a corkscrew!'

'Wine?' Anna-Lena repeated, suddenly delighted, so it was evidently okay to snoop inside chests if you found wine.

'Would you like some?' Estelle offered.

'I'm pregnant,' Julia pointed out.

'Aren't you allowed to drink wine, then?'

'You're not allowed to drink any alcohol at all.'

'But . . . wine?'

Estelle's eyes were wide with benevolent intent. Because wine is only grapes, after all. And children like grapes.

'Wine, too,' Julia said patiently, and thought of how Ro had said 'All the time! I'm drinking for three now!' when the midwife at the antenatal clinic asked a routine question about how much they drank. The midwife didn't realize Ro was joking, and the atmosphere became tense. Julia laughed as she thought about it now. That happens quite a lot when you're married to an idiot.

'Have I done something wrong?' Estelle wondered anxiously, drinking straight from the bottle before passing it to Anna-Lena, who didn't hesitate before taking two long swigs, which seemed highly out of character for Anna-Lena. It was a strange day for all of them.

'No, not at all, I was just thinking about something my wife did.' Julia smiled, and tried to stop laughing, with mixed results.

'Julia's wife is an idiot! Just like Roger!' Anna-Lena explained helpfully to Estelle, and drank another swig, this time larger than the space in her mouth, which prompted a fit of coughing through her nose. Julia leaned forward and patted Anna-Lena on the back. Estelle helpfully took the bottle from her and made it a bit lighter in the meantime. Then she said quietly: 'Knut isn't an idiot. He really isn't. But it's taking him an awfully long time to park the car. I wish he was here, so I . . . well, I just wasn't prepared to be held hostage on my own.'

Julia smiled.

'You're not on your own, you've got us. And this bank robber doesn't seem to want to hurt anyone, so I'm sure everything's going to be all right. But . . . can I ask you something?'

'Of course you can, sweetheart.'

'Did you *know* there was going to be wine in that chest? If you didn't, why did you decide to have a look?'

Estelle blushed. After a long pause, she confessed: 'I usually hide wine in the closet at home. Knut used to think that was silly. I mean, he *thinks* it's silly. But you assume people think the way you do yourself, so I was thinking that if the person living here was worried about people coming and seeing bottles of wine and thinking "Well, this person's an alcoholic," then the closet would be the perfect place to hide the wine.'

Anna-Lena took another two gulps of wine, hiccupped loudly, and added: 'Alcoholics don't have unopened bottles of wine in the house. They have empty wine bottles.'

Estelle nodded at her gratefully, and replied without thinking: 'That's kind of you to say. Knut would have agreed with you.'

The old woman's eyes were glistening, not only from the wine. Julia frowned so hard and so thoughtfully that she got a whole new hairstyle. She leaned forward, put her hand gently on Estelle's arm, and whispered: 'Estelle? Knut isn't parking the car, is he?'

Estelle's thin lips disappeared sadly beneath each other, so the word barely reached past them when she eventually admitted:

'No.'

Witness Interview
Date: December 30
Name of witness: Lennart

JACK: Let me see if I've got this right: you weren't at the viewing as a prospective buyer, but had been hired by Anna-Lena to spoil it?

LENNART: Exactly. No Boundaries Lennart, that's me. Would you like a business card? I do stag parties, too — if the guy getting married has stolen your girl, that sort of thing.

JACK: So that's your job? To ruin apartment viewings?

LENNART: No, I'm an actor. There just aren't many roles around at the moment. But I was in *The Merchant from Venice* at the local theatre.

JACK: Of Venice.

LENNART: No, at the local theatre here!

JACK: I meant that it's called *The Merchant of Venice*. Not *from* Venice. Never mind. Can you tell me anything else about the bank robber?

LENNART: I don't think so. I've told you everything I remember.

JACK: Okay. Well, I'm afraid I'm going to have to ask you to stay a little longer, in case we have any further questions.

LENNART: No problem!

JACK: Oh, yes, one last thing: What do you know about the fireworks?

LENNART: How do you mean?

JACK: The fireworks the perpetrator asked for.

LENNART: What about them?

JACK: Well, when someone takes other people hostage, it

isn't customary for the perpetrator to demand fireworks before letting them go. It's more normal to
demand money.

LENNART: With all due respect, it's more *normal* not to
take anyone hostage in the first place.

JACK: That's as may be, but don't you think fireworks
is an odd demand? That was the last thing the
perpetrator did before you were released.

LENNART: I don't know. It's New Year. And everyone likes
fireworks, don't they?

JACK: Dog owners don't.

LENNART: Ah.

JACK: What do you mean by that?

LENNART: I was just surprised. I thought all police officers liked dogs.

JACK: I didn't say I didn't like dogs!

LENNART: Most people would have said that dogs don't like
fireworks. But you said *dog owners*.

JACK: I'm not particularly fond of animals.

LENNART: Sorry. A peril of the profession. You learn to
read people in my job.

JACK: As an actor?

LENNART: No, the other. Are the others still here at the
station, by the way?

JACK: Who?

LENNART: You know, the others who were in the apartment.

JACK: Are you thinking of anyone in particular?

LENNART: Zara. For instance.

JACK: For instance?

LENNART: There's no need to look like I asked something
improper. I mean, I'm only asking.

JACK: Yes. Zara's still here. Why do you ask?

LENNART: Oh, just wondered. You get curious about people
sometimes, that's all, and she's the first person
in a long time who I haven't been able to read at

all. I tried, but I didn't get her at all. Why are you laughing?

JACK: I'm not laughing.

LENNART: Yes, you are!

JACK: Sorry, I didn't mean to. Something my dad says, that's all.

LENNART: What?

JACK: He says you end up marrying the one you don't understand. Then you spend the rest of your life trying.

56

'Death, death, death,' Estelle thought in the closet. Many years ago she had read that her favourite author used to start telephone conversations with that. 'Death, death, death.' Then, when that was out of the way, they could discuss other things. Otherwise, after a certain age, no phone call ever seemed to be about life, only the other. Estelle could understand that point of view these days. The same author once wrote that 'you have to live your life in such a way that you become friends with death', but Estelle found that harder. She remembered when she used to read bedtime stories to the children, and Peter Pan declaring: 'To die will be an awfully big adventure.' Maybe for the person doing it, Estelle thought, but not for the one who was left behind. All that awaited her were a thousand sunrises where life is a beautiful prison. Her cheeks quivered, reminding her that she had grown old, her skin was so thin now that it moved the whole time in a breeze that nobody else could feel. She had nothing against old age, just loneliness. When she met Knut it wasn't a love story, not the way she had read it could feel, theirs was always more like a story of a child finding the perfect playmate. When Knut touched Estelle, right up to the end, it made her feel like climbing trees and jumping from jetties. Most of all she missed making him laugh so hard he spat his breakfast out. That sort of thing only got more fun with age, especially after he got false teeth.

'Knut's dead,' she said for the first time, and swallowed hard.

Julia was looking down at the floor in irresolute silence. Anna-Lena sat and tried to think of something to say for a while, then leaned towards Estelle and tapped her on the shoulder with the wine bottle instead. Estelle took it and drank two small sips, before handing it back and going on, half to herself: 'But he was very good at parking, Knut. He could parallel park in tiny spaces. So sometimes, when it's most painful, when I see something really funny and think "He'd have laughed so hard his breakfast would have covered the wallpaper" – that's when I fantasize that he's just outside, parking the car. He wasn't perfect, no man is, God knows, but whenever we went anywhere and it was raining, he would always drop me off just outside the door. So I could wait in the warm while he . . . parked the car.'

A silence forced its way between the three women, and gradually emptied their vocabularies until none of them knew what to say at all. *Death, death, death*, Estelle thought.

When Knut was lying in his sickbed those last nights, she asked him: 'Are you scared?' He replied: 'Yes.' Then his fingers ran through her hair and he added: 'But it'll be quite nice to get a bit of peace and quiet. You can put that on the headstone.' Estelle laughed hard at that. When he left her she wept so hard that she couldn't breathe. Her body was never really the same after that, she curled up and never quite unfurled again.

'He was my echo. Everything I do is quieter now,' she said to the other women in the closet.

Anna-Lena sat for a while before she opened her mouth, because, although she was starting to get drunk, she understood that it wouldn't be good form in the circumstances to appear greedy. They were wasted seconds, of course, because when she spoke the thought out loud, neither good intentions nor wild horses could hide the hopefulness in her voice.

'So . . . if your husband isn't parking the car, can I ask if it was true that you're looking at this apartment on behalf of your daughter, or was that . . . ?'

'No, no, my daughter lives in a nice terraced house with her husband and children,' Estelle replied sheepishly.

Just outside Stockholm, in fact, but Estelle didn't say that, because she didn't think this conversation needed to get any more complicated.

'So you're just here . . . looking?' Anna-Lena asked.

'Seriously, Anna-Lena, she's not competing with you and Roger to buy the apartment! Stop being so insensitive!' Julia snapped.

Anna-Lena stared down into the bottle and mumbled: 'I was only asking.'

Estelle patted them both gratefully on the arm, one at a time, and whispered: 'Now don't fall out on my account, dears. I'm too old to be worth that.'

Julia nodded sullenly and put her hand around her stomach. Anna-Lena did the same with the wine bottle.

'How old are your grandchildren?' she asked.

'They're teenagers now,' Estelle said.

'Oh, sorry to hear that,' Anna-Lena said with feeling.

Estelle smiled feebly. If you've lived with teenagers, you know they only exist for themselves, and their parents have their hands full dealing with the various horrors of life. Both the teenagers' and their own. There was no place for Estelle there, she was mostly something of a nuisance. They were pleased that she answered the phone when they called on her birthday, but the rest of the time they assumed time stood still for her. She was a nice ornament that they only took out at Christmas and Midsummer.

'No . . . I'm not here to buy the apartment. I just haven't got anything to do. Sometimes I go to apartment viewings out of curiosity, to listen to people talking, hear what they're dreaming about. People's dreams are always at their grandest when they're looking for somewhere to live. Knut died slowly, you know. He lay in a care home for years, I couldn't start living as if he was dead, but he . . . he wasn't alive. Not really. So my life was on pause, somehow. I took the bus to the care home each day and sat with him. Read books. Out loud at first, then to myself at the end. That's how it goes. But it was something to do. And a person needs that.'

Anna-Lena thought that yes, that was how it was, people needed to have a project.

'Life goes so fast. Working life, anyway,' she thought out loud, and looked very taken aback when she realized that Julia had heard her.

'What did you used to do?' the young woman asked.

Anna-Lena filled her lungs, simultaneously hesitant and proud.

'I was an analyst for an industrial company. Well, I suppose I was the senior analyst, really, but I did my best not to be.'

'Senior analyst?' Julia repeated, instantly ashamed of how that sounded.

Anna-Lena saw the surprise in her eyes, but she was used to it and didn't take offence. Ordinarily she would just have changed the subject, but perhaps the wine had the upper hand on this occasion, because instead she thought out loud, without any hesitation: 'Yes, I was. Not that I wanted that. To be a boss, I mean. The president of the company said that was precisely why he wanted me to do it. He said you don't have to lead by telling other people what to do, you can lead by just letting them do what they're capable of instead. So I tried to be a teacher more than a boss. I know people find it hard to believe of me, but I'm not a bad teacher. When I retired, two of my staff said they hadn't realized I was actually their boss until they heard the speech thanking me for my work. A lot of people would probably have taken that as an insult, but I thought it was . . . nice. If you can do something for someone in such a way that they think they managed it all on their own, then you've done a good job.'

Julia smiled.

'You're full of surprises, Anna-Lena.'

Anna-Lena looked like that was the nicest compliment anyone had ever given her. Then sorrow and grief swept through her eyes again, she closed them quickly and opened them slowly.

'Everyone thinks I've . . . well, when you meet us, people probably think I've always been in Roger's shadow. That really isn't the case. Roger should have had a chance to fulfill his potential. He had great potential. But my job . . . things were going so well for me, better and better, so he turned down promotions so he could drop the kids off at nursery and all that. I got to travel and have my career, always thinking that it would be his turn next year. But that never happened.'

She fell silent. For once, Julia wasn't sure what to say. Estelle looked like she didn't know what to do with her hands, which resulted in her opening the chest and sticking them in there again. They came back out with a box of matches and a packet of cigarettes.

'Goodness,' she exclaimed brightly.

'What sort of person *lives* here, really?' Julia wondered.

'Would anyone like one?' Estelle offered.

'I don't smoke!' Anna-Lena declared immediately.

'Nor me. Or rather, I've given up. Most of the time. Do you smoke?' Estelle wondered, turning to Julia, then added quickly: 'Well, I don't suppose anyone does when they're pregnant. In my day they used to. You used to cut back a bit, of course. But I'm assuming you don't smoke at all?'

'No, not at all,' Julia said patiently.

'Young people today. You're so aware of how you affect your children. I heard a paediatrician say on television that a generation ago, parents used to come to him and say, "Our child's wetting the bed, what's wrong with him?" Now, a generation later, they come to him and say, "Our child's wetting the bed, what's wrong with *us*?" You take the blame for everything.'

Julia leaned back against the wall.

'We probably make all the same mistakes that your generation did. Just different versions of them.'

Estelle rolled the packet between her hands.

'I used to smoke on our balcony, because Knut didn't like the smell when I smoked indoors, and I liked the view. We could see all the way to the bridge. Just like from this apartment, really. I used to be very fond of that. But then . . . well . . . you might remember that a man jumped off that bridge ten years ago? It was in all the papers. And I . . . well, I checked to see what time of day he jumped, and realized it was right after I'd been out on the balcony smoking. Knut called to say something was happening on television and I hurried back inside, leaving the cigarette to burn itself out in the ashtray, and in that time the man had climbed up on to the railing and jumped. I stopped smoking on the balcony after that.'

'Oh, Estelle, it wasn't your fault that someone jumped off a bridge,' Julia said, trying to console her.

'It wasn't the bridge's fault, either,' Anna-Lena added.

'What?'

'It isn't the bridge's fault if someone jumps off it. I remember it well, you know, because Roger found the whole thing very upsetting.'

'Did he know the man who jumped?' Estelle asked.

'Oh, no. But he knew a lot about the bridge. Roger was an engineer, you see, he built bridges. Not that particular bridge, but if you're as interested in bridges, as Roger is, then you end up being interested in all bridges. They talked about that man on television as if it was the bridge's fault. Roger was very upset about that. Bridges exist to bring people closer together, he said.'

Julia couldn't help thinking that was simultaneously a remarkably odd and a rather romantic thing to say. That was probably why – unless it was the fact that she was hungry and exhausted – she suddenly said: 'My fiancée and I were in Australia a few years ago. She wanted to do a bungee jump off a bridge.'

'Your fiancée? You mean Ro?' Estelle nodded.

'No, my previous fiancée.'

It was a long story. All stories are, when it comes down to it, if you tell them from the start. This story, for instance, would have been considerably shorter if it had just been about three women in a closet. But of course it's also about two police officers, and one of them was on his way up the stairs.

What had happened out in the street was that Jack, before he went into the building opposite, had told his dad to wait there. And definitely not to go anywhere. More specifically, not into the building where the hostage drama was taking place. 'Just wait here,' the son said.

But of course the father didn't do that.

He took the pizzas and went up to the apartment, and when he came back down, he had spoken to the bank robber.

Inside the closet, obviously Julia regretted mentioning her former fiancée as soon as she said it, so she added: 'I was engaged when I met Ro. But that's a long story. Forget I mentioned it.'

'We've got plenty of time for long stories,' Estelle assured her, because she'd found another bottle of wine in the chest.

'Your fiancée wanted to jump off a bridge?' Anna-Lena repeated in alarm.

'Yes. A bungee jump. With a rubber rope tied around your feet.'

'That sounds mad.'

Julia's fingertips massaged her temples.

'I didn't like the idea, either. But she was always wanting to do things. *Experience* everything. It was on that trip that I realized I couldn't live with her, because I haven't got the energy to keep experiencing things the whole time. I started longing for everyday life, all the boring stuff, but she hated being bored. So I came back from Australia a week before her, blaming the fact that I had to work. And that was when I kissed Ro for the first time.'

Julia started to giggle as she said that. Partly out of shame, but possibly also because it was the first time in ages that she'd thought about how they fell in love. You tend to forget that when you're in the middle of the life that follows; when you're going to become a parent with someone, it suddenly feels impossible to remember that you ever loved anyone else.

'How did you meet? You and Ro?' Estelle asked, wine staining the corners of her mouth.

'The first time? She came into my shop. I'm a florist, and she wanted some tulips. That was several months before I went to Australia. I didn't think much about it, she was . . . attractive, of course, anyone can see that . . .'

Estelle nodded eagerly: 'Yes, that was the first thing I thought! She really is extremely beautiful! And so exotic!'

Julia sighed. 'Exotic? Because her hair's a different colour to yours and mine?'

Estelle looked unhappy. 'Aren't you allowed to say that any more?'

Julia didn't know how to begin to explain that her wife wasn't a piece of fruit, so instead she took a deep breath and carried on: 'Either way, she was attractive. Very attractive. Even more attractive than she is now. Not that . . . don't tell her that, whatever you do . . . she's still attractive! But I, well, I'd certainly have liked to, you know . . . with her. But I was already taken. But she kept coming back to buy tulips. Several times a week, sometimes. And she made me laugh, out loud, out of nowhere, and you don't meet many people like that. I happened to mention that to my mum, and she said: "You can't live long with the ones who are only beautiful, Jules. But the funny ones, oh, they last a lifetime!" '

'Your mum's a wise woman,' Estelle said.

'Yes.'

'Is she retired?'

'Yes.'

'What did she used to do?'

'She cleaned offices.'

'What did your dad do?'

'He hit women.'

Estelle looked paralyzed, Anna-Lena appalled. Julia looked at the pair of them and thought about her mum, and how the most beautiful thing about her was the fact that she always stared life right in the eye, and no matter what it threw at her, refused to stop being a romantic. That takes the sort of heart that hardly anyone possesses.

'Poor dear child,' Estelle whispered.

'What a bastard,' Anna-Lena muttered.

Julia shrugged, the way children who grew up too soon do, shaking the feelings off.

'We walked out on him. He didn't come looking for us. I didn't even hate him, because Mum didn't let me. After everything he'd done to her, she wouldn't even let me hate him. I always wanted her to meet someone new, someone who was kind and made her laugh, but she always said I was enough . . . But then . . . when I told her about Ro, Mum saw something in me that made me see something in her. That probably sounds . . . I don't know how to explain it. Something she'd experienced once, and given up all hope of, if you get what I mean? And I thought . . . is this how it feels? That thing everyone talks about? The real thing?'

Anna-Lena wiped some wine from her chin.

'So what happened?'

Julia blinked, first quickly, then slowly.

'My fiancée was still in Australia. And Ro came into the shop. I'd spoken to Mum on the phone that morning, and she just laughed when I said I didn't know how Ro felt, or even if she felt anything at all. Mum just said: "Listen, *no one* likes tulips that much, Jules!" I suppose I tried to deny it, but Mum said I was practically being unfaithful already because I was spending so much time thinking about her. She said Ro was my "flower shop". And I cried. So I was standing there in the shop and Ro came in, and I . . . well, I laughed so hard at something she said that I accidentally spat on her face. She was laughing, too. So I guess she plucked up the courage, because I couldn't do it, and asked if I'd like to go for a drink with her. I said yes, but I was so nervous when we got there that I got really drunk. I went outside to smoke, got into a row with a security guard, and wasn't let back in. So I pointed through the window at Ro, who was standing at the bar, and said she was my girlfriend. The guard went in and told her that, and then she came out, and then she was. I called my fiancée and broke off the engagement. She's probably been having loads of fun ever since. And I . . . damn, I love being boring with Ro. Does that sound mad? I love arguing with her about sofas and pets. She's my everyday. The whole . . . world.'

'I like the everyday,' Anna-Lena admitted.

'Your mum was right, the ones who make you laugh last a life-time,' Estelle repeated, thinking of a British author who had written that nothing in the world is so irresistibly contagious as laughter and good humour. Then she thought about an American author who had written that loneliness is like starvation, you don't realize how hungry you are until you begin to eat.

Julia was thinking about how her mum, when she told her she was pregnant, looked first at Julia's stomach, then at Ro's, then asked: 'How did you decide which of you was going to . . . get knocked up?' Julia got annoyed, of course, and replied sarcastically: 'We played rock-paper-scissors, Mum!' Her mum looked at them both again with deadly seriousness and asked: 'So who won?'

That still made Julia laugh. She said to the women in the closet: 'Ro's going to be a brilliant mum. She can make any child laugh, just like my mum, because their sense of humour hasn't developed at all since they were nine.'

'You're going to be a brilliant mum, too,' Estelle assured her.

The bags under Julia's eyes moved softly as she blinked.

'I don't know. Everything feels such a big deal, and other parents all seem so . . . *funny* the whole time. They laugh and joke and everyone says you should play with children, and I don't like playing, I didn't like it even when I was a child. So I'm worried the child's going to be disappointed. Everyone said it would be different when I got pregnant, but I don't actually like all children. I thought that would change, but I meet my friends' children now and I still think they're annoying and have a lousy sense of humour.'

Anna-Lena spoke up, briefly and to the point:

'You don't have to like all children. Just one. And children don't need the world's best parents, just their own parents. To be perfectly honest with you, what they need most of the time is a chauffeur.'

'Thanks for saying that,' Julia replied honestly. 'I'm just worried

my child isn't going to be happy. That it's going to inherit all my anxiety and uncertainty.'

Estelle gently patted Julia's hair.

'Your child's going to be absolutely fine, you'll see. And absolutely
fine can cover any number of peculiarities.'

'That's encouraging.' Julia smiled.

Estelle went on patting her hair softly.

'Are you going to do all you can, Julia? Are you going to protect
the child with your life? Are you going to sing to it and read it stories
and promise that everything will feel better tomorrow?'

'Yes.'

'Are you going to raise it so that it doesn't grow up to be one of
those idiots who don't take their backpack off when they're on public
transport?'

'I'll do what I can,' Julia promised.

Estelle was thinking about another author now, one who almost
a hundred years ago wrote that your children aren't your children,
they're the sons and daughters of life's longing for itself.

'You're going to be fine. You don't have to love being a mother,
not all the time.'

Anna-Lena interjected: 'I didn't like the poo, I really didn't. At
first it was okay, but when children are around a year old they're like
Labradors. Fully grown ones, I mean, not puppies, but –'

'Okay,' Julia nodded, to get her to stop.

'There's something about the consistency at a certain age, it gets
like glue, sticks under your fingernails, and if you rub your face on the
way to work . . .'

'Thanks! That's enough!' Julia assured her, but Anna-Lena
couldn't stop herself.

'The worst thing is when they bring friends home, and suddenly
there's a five-year-old stranger sitting on your toilet demanding to be
cleaned up. I mean, you can put up with your own kids' poo, but other
people's . . .'

'*Thanks!*' Julia said emphatically.

Anna-Lena pursed her lips. Estelle giggled.

'You're going to be a good mum. And you're a good wife,' Estelle added, even though Julia hadn't even mentioned that last anxiety. Julia was holding the palms of her hands around her stomach, and stared down at her fingernails.

'Do you think? Sometimes it feels like all I ever do is nag Ro. Even though I love her.'

Estelle smiled.

'She knows. Believe me. Does she still make you laugh?'

'Yes. God, yes.'

'Then she knows.'

'You have no idea, I mean, wow, she makes me laugh all the time. The first time Ro and I were about to . . . you know . . .' Julia smiled, but stopped when she couldn't think of a word for what she was sure neither of the two older women would actually be horrified to hear.

'What?' Anna-Lena wondered, uncomprehendingly.

Estelle nudged her in the side and winked.

'You know. The first time they were going to *go to Stockholm.*'

'*Oh!*' Anna-Lena exclaimed, and blushed from her head to her feet.

But Julia didn't quite seem to hear. Her eyes lost their footing; there was a joke there somewhere in her memory, one Ro had made in the taxi that first time that Julia had intended to talk about. But instead she found herself stumbling over the words.

'I . . . it's so silly, I'd forgotten this. I'd done some laundry, and there were some white sheets hanging over the bedroom door to dry. And when Ro opened the door and they hit her in the face, she started. She tried not to let it show, but I felt her flinch, so I asked what the matter was, and at first she didn't want to say. Because she didn't want to burden me with anything, not as early as that, she was worried I'd break up with her before we'd even got together. But I kept on nagging, of course, because I'm good at nagging, and in the end we sat up all night and Ro told me about how her family got to Sweden. They fled across the mountains, in the middle of winter, and the children each had to carry a sheet, and if they heard the sound of helicopters they were supposed to lie down in the snow with the sheet over them, so they couldn't be seen. And their parents would run in different directions, so that if the men in the helicopter started firing, they'd fire at the moving targets. And not at . . . and I didn't know what to . . .'

She cracked, like thin ice on a puddle of water, first just some hairline wrinkles around her eyes, then the rest, all at once. The collar of her top turned a darker colour. She was thinking about everything Ro had told her that night, the incomprehensible cruelties that terrible people are capable of inflicting on each other, and the utter insanity of war. Then she thought of how Ro, after all that, had somehow managed to grow up to be the sort of person who made other people laugh. Because her parents had taught her during their flight through the mountains that humour is the soul's last line of defence, and as long as we're laughing we're alive, so bad puns and fart jokes were their way of expressing their defiance against despair. Ro told Julia all this that first night, and after that Julia got to spend all of the world's everydays with her.

Something like that can make you put up with living with birds.

'An affair that started in a flower shop,' Estelle nodded slowly. 'I like that.' She sat silent for several minutes. Then it burst out of her: 'I had an affair once! Knut never knew.'

'Dear Lord!' Anna-Lena exclaimed, now sensing that this was starting to get out of hand after all.

'Yes, it wasn't all that long ago, you know.' Estelle grinned.

'Who was it?' Julia asked.

'A neighbour in our building. He read a lot, like me. Knut never read. He used to say authors were like musicians who never get to the point. But this other man, the neighbour, he always had a book tucked under his arm when we met in the lift. So did I. One day he offered me his book, saying: "I've finished this one, I think you should read it." And so we started to swap books. He read such wonderful things. I don't have the words to describe it, but it was like going on a journey with someone. Where didn't matter. To outer space. It went on for a long time. I started to fold down the corners of pages when there was a bit I really liked, and he started to write little comments in the margins. Just the odd word. "Beautiful". "True". That's the power of literature, you know, it can act like little love letters between people who can only explain their feelings by pointing at other people's. One summer I opened a book and sand trickled out of it, and I knew he'd liked it so much he hadn't been able to put it down. Every now and then I would get a book where some of the pages were crumpled, and I knew he'd been crying. One day I told him that, in the lift, and he replied that I was the only person who knew that about him.'

'And that was when you . . . ,' Julia nodded with a naughty smile.

'Oh, no, no, no . . . ,' Estelle squeaked, and looked like she might have liked to finish the sentence by saying that she might possibly have *wished* it had happened, but of course that didn't change anything. 'We were never, it never, I could never . . .'

'Why not?' Julia asked.

Estelle smiled, proud and full of longing at the same time. It takes a certain age for that, a certain life.

'Because you dance with the person you went to the party with. And I went with Knut.'

'So . . . what happened?' Anna-Lena wondered.

Estelle's breathing didn't show any sign of speeding up, she didn't have many big secrets left. After this one, possibly none at all.

'One day in the lift he gave me a book, and inside it was a key to his apartment. He said he didn't have any family living nearby, and that he wanted someone in the building to have a spare key "in case anything happened". I didn't say anything, and I didn't do anything, but I got the sense that maybe . . . maybe he would have liked it. If something had happened.'

She smiled. So did Julia.

'So in all that time, you never . . . ?'

'No, no, no. We exchanged books. Until he died a few years later. Something to do with his heart. His siblings put the apartment up for sale, but his furniture was still there at the viewing. So I went along, pretending to be interested in buying it. I walked around in his home, ran my hands over his kitchen counter, the hangers in his closet. In the end I found myself standing in front of his bookcase. It's such an odd thing, the way you can know someone so perfectly through what they read. We liked the same voices, in the same way. So I let myself have a few minutes to think about what we could have been for each other, if everything had been different, somewhere else in our lives.'

'And then?' Julia whispered.

Estelle smiled. Defiantly. Happily.

'Then I went home. But I kept the key to his apartment. I never told Knut. It was my affair.'

Silence settled in the closet for a while. In the end Anna-Lena plucked up the courage to say: 'I've never had an affair. But once I changed hairdressers, and I didn't dare walk past the old one for several years.'

It wasn't the strongest anecdote, but she wanted to feel that she was participating. She had never had time for an affair, how on earth does anyone find the time? All that stress, Anna-Lena thought, and a whole new man to deal with. She had spent her life working and rushing home, working and rushing home, and always felt guilty for not being good enough in either place. In those circumstances it's easy to feel sympathy for other people who aren't quite good enough. That's probably why, out of all the people in the apartment who had already had the thought, it was Anna-Lena who was the first to say out loud: 'I think we should try to help the bank robber.'

Julia looked up, and their eyes met with a whole new sense of respect.

'Yes, so do I! I was just thinking that. I don't think any of this was the intention.' Julia nodded.

'I just don't know how we could go about helping her,' Anna-Lena admitted.

'No, the police must have the building surrounded, so I don't think there's any way she can escape, sadly,' Julia sighed.

Estelle drank more wine. She turned the packet of cigarettes over in her hand, because of course you're not allowed to smoke in front of pregnant women, you really aren't, at least not until you're so drunk that you can claim with a clear conscience that you were too drunk to notice that there was one nearby.

'Maybe she could just wear a disguise?' she suddenly said, with just a hint of a slur on the *s* in 'disguise'.

Julia shook her head uncomprehendingly.

'What? Who could wear a disguise?'

'The bank robber,' Estelle said, taking another swig.

'What sort of disguise?'

Estelle shrugged.

'The estate agent.'

'The estate agent?'

Estelle nodded.

'Have you seen any sign of an estate agent in this apartment since the bank robber arrived?'

'No . . . no, now that you come to mention it . . .'

Estelle drank more wine, then nodded again.

'I'm fairly certain that all the police outside will take it for granted that there's an estate agent present at an apartment viewing. So if . . .'

Julia stared at her. Then started to laugh.

'So if the bank robber pretends to give herself up and let all the hostages go, she can pretend to be the estate agent and walk out with the rest of us! Estelle, you're a genius!'

'Thanks,' Estelle said, and peered down into the bottle with one eye closed to see how much was left before she could start smoking.

Julia struggled to her feet as quickly as she could and hurried over to the door to call to Ro and explain the new plan, but just as she was about to open the door there was a knock on it. Not hard, but hard enough to make the three women jump as if a load of puppies and sparklers had been thrown into the closet. Julia opened the door a crack. The rabbit was standing outside looking awkward, insofar as it was possible to tell.

'Sorry, I don't want to disturb you. But I've been told to put some trousers on.'

'Your trousers are in here?' Julia wondered.

The rabbit scratched his neck.

'No, I had them in the bathroom, before the viewing started. But I washed my hands and managed to splash water on them, then I saw the scented candles on the washbasin, and thought I might be able to dry my trousers by warming them up. And then . . . well . . . I managed to set my trousers on fire. So then I had to pour even *more* water over them to put the flames out. So my trousers ended up soaking wet. And then the viewing started and I heard you all out in the apartment, and then the bank robber started shouting, and there wasn't really time . . . well, to cut a long story short, my trousers are still wet. So I was thinking . . .'

The rabbit's head swayed in the direction of the suits hanging in the closet, which he was hoping he might be able to borrow instead. His ears accidentally hit Julia's forehead and she backed away, but the rabbit evidently interpreted this as an invitation to step inside.

'Yes, well, come in, why don't you . . . ,' Julia grunted.

The rabbit looked around with interest.

'Isn't this lovely!' he said.

Anna-Lena disappeared beneath the suits and wiped her eyes. Estelle lit a cigarette, because she didn't think it mattered any more, and when Anna-Lena aimed a disapproving glance in her direction Estelle said defensively: 'Oh, it'll blow out through the air vent!'

The rabbit tilted his head slightly, then he asked: 'What air vent?'

Estelle coughed, it was unclear if that was because of the cigarette or the question: 'I mean . . . there seems to be some sort of ventilation in here, but it was only a guess. There's a breeze from up in the ceiling, though!'

'What are you talking about?' Julia asked.

Estelle coughed again. Then she stopped coughing. But there was still someone coughing, up in the ceiling.

They stared at each other, the rabbit and the three women, a diverse group of individuals, to put it mildly, huddled inside a closet at an apartment viewing that had been disrupted by the arrival of a bank robber. Stranger things had probably happened to people in the town, but not much stranger. Estelle had time to think that if Knut had opened the closet door just then he would have laughed out loud, there would have been breakfast everywhere, and she would have loved that. The coughing up in the ceiling continued, like when you try to stifle it and it just gets worse. A cinema cough.

Julia dragged the stepladder to the back of the closet, Estelle got off the chest, Anna-Lena helped the rabbit up. He pressed his hands against the ceiling until it gave way. There was a hatch, and above it a very cramped little space.

And there sat the estate agent.

59

In the police station Jack has nearly lost his voice with rage by this
point.

'Tell the truth! Why did you ask for fireworks? Where's the *real*
estate agent? Is there even a *real* estate agent?'

The estate agent, whose jacket is still as crumpled as a bulldog's nose
after the hours she had spent in the cramped space above the closet, tries
and tries to explain everything. But if there's one thing modern life and
the Internet have taught us, it's that you should never expect to win
a discussion simply because you're right. The estate agent can't prove
she isn't the bank robber, because the only way she can do that is to
say where the bank robber is right now, and the estate agent genuinely
has no idea about that. Jack in turn refuses to believe that the estate
agent is an estate agent, because if she was, that would mean he's missed
something very obvious, and that in turn would mean that he isn't particularly smart after all, and he simply isn't ready for that.

Jim, who has been sitting silently throughout most of the interview, if
you can actually call it an interview when it's really only consisted of
Jack screaming nonstop, puts his hand on his son's shoulder and says:
'Shall we take a break, son?'

Jack fixes his eyes on him: 'You were fooled, Dad, don't you get
that? You went up with those pizzas and you let her *fool you*!'

Hurt by this, Jim's shoulders slump as he finds himself declared
an idiot.

'Can't we just take a break? Just a short one? A cup of coffee . . . a
glass of water . . . ?'

'Not until I've figured out what really happened!' Jack snarls.

He won't succeed.

60

What actually happened was that when Jack ended the call with the negotiator and ran out of the building on the other side of the street, Jim was just emerging from the building where the hostage drama was taking place. Jack of course was furious that Jim had gone into the building despite being told to stay outside, but Jim did his best to calm him down.

'Take it easy, now, son. Take it easy. That wasn't a bomb in the stairwell, just a box of Christmas lights.'

'*I know! Why did you go into the building before I came back?*'

'Because I knew you'd never let me go if I waited that long. I've spoken to the bank robber.'

'Of course I wouldn't have . . . hang on, what?'

'I said I've spoken to the bank robber.'

Then Jim told him exactly what had happened. Or rather, as exactly as he could. Because it has to be said that telling stories wasn't one of Jim's greatest talents in life. His wife always said he was the sort of person who tells a joke by starting with the punchline and then stopping, yelping, 'No, hang on, something happened before that, darling, what was it that happened before the funny bit?' then trying to start from the beginning again, only to get it wrong again. He never remembers the end of films, so he can watch them any number of times and still be surprised when he finds out who the murderer is. He's not much good at party games or television quiz shows, either: there's one his son and wife both liked, with celebrities in trains who had to guess where they were going by solving various clues, and Jim's wife used to mimic him as he sat there on the sofa frantically suggesting everything from Spanish capitals to African republics to tiny Norwegian fishing villages, all in the same round. 'See! I was right!' he always declared at the end, and Jack always snapped: 'You're not right if you guess EVERYTHING!' And his wife? She just laughed. Jim missed that so much. With him or at him, he didn't care, as long as she laughed.

So Jim took the opportunity to go into the building when Jack wasn't looking, because Jim knew that's what she would have done. He felt very, very foolish when he reached the landing with the box and realized that sometimes Christmas lights were just Christmas lights. But she would have laughed at that. So he kept going.

There were two apartments on the top floor. The hostage drama was taking place in the one on the right, and the one on the left was owned by the young couple who couldn't agree about coriander or juicers, and who Jim had had to phone not long before (and the details of whose separation he now knew more about than any normal person ought to know). Just to be on the safe side, he peered through the mailslot, but there were no lights on, and the mail on the mat suggested that no one had been there for a while. Only then did Jim ring the doorbell of the apartment containing the bank robber and hostages.

There was no answer for a long time, even though he kept ringing the bell. Eventually he realized that the bell wasn't working, and knocked instead. He had to do that several times as well, but eventually the door opened a crack and a man dressed in a suit and ski mask looked out. First at the pizzas, then at Jim.

'I haven't got any cash,' the man in the mask said.

'Don't worry,' Jim said, holding the pizzas out.

The man in the mask squinted suspiciously.

'Are you a cop?'

'No.'

'Yes, you are.'

Jim noted that the man's accent changed several times, as if he couldn't quite make his mind up. And it wasn't possible to determine much about his appearance, not even if he was tall or short, because he never opened the door properly.

'What makes you think I'm a police officer?' Jim asked innocently.

'Because pizza delivery guys don't give pizzas away for free.'

Jim couldn't really see much point in trying to deny it, so he said: 'You're right, I'm a cop. But I'm on my own, and I'm unarmed. Is anyone in there hurt?'

'No. At least no more than they were when they arrived,' the bank robber said.

Jim nodded amiably.

'My colleagues out in the street are starting to get nervous, you see, because you haven't made any demands.'

Taken aback, the man in the ski mask blinked.

'I asked for pizza.'

'I mean . . . demands in order to release the hostages. We just don't want anyone to get hurt.'

The man in the ski mask took the pizza boxes, held up a finger, and said: 'Give me a moment!'

He closed the door and disappeared into the apartment. One minute passed, then another, and just when Jim was thinking about knocking on the door again, it opened a couple of inches. The man looked out and said: 'Fireworks.'

'I don't follow,' Jim said.

'I want fireworks, the sort I can see from the balcony. Then I'll let the hostages go.'

'Seriously?'

'And no cheap rubbish, either, don't try to trick me! Proper fireworks! All different colours, the sort that look like rain, the whole lot.'

'And then you'll release the hostages?'

'Then I'll release the hostages.'

'That's your only demand?'

'Yep.'

* * *

So Jim went back down the stairs, out to Jack in the street, and told him all this.

But it's worth pointing out again that Jim really isn't good at telling stories. He's completely hopeless, in fact. So he may not have remembered everything entirely accurately.

61

Roger was right that time when he looked at the plans and said that the top floor of the building had probably once been one single large apartment. Then, when the lift was installed, the apartment was split in two and sold as two separate apartments, which led to a number of creative solutions, among them the double wall in the living room and the abandoned ventilation duct above the closet. That was left intact, ignored for years, until, like people you think have become superfluous with age, it suddenly made itself known again. Because, in winter, cold air would blow in from the attic of the old building: the insulation up there is poor and the air finds its way down in the form of a draught in the closet. You have to sit right at the back, on a chest full of wine, to notice it. Not a bad place to smoke, of course, if you're that way inclined, but apart from that the vent hasn't served any purpose at all for many years. Not until an estate agent realized that the space was just large enough for a fairly small estate agent to climb up and hide so she didn't get shot by an armed bank robber.

The opening in the ceiling was so tight that she had only just managed to squeeze through, which of course meant it was far too tight for Lennart not to get stuck, so much so that when he tried to pull himself free, the rabbit's head *finally* came loose. He fell backwards from the hatch, off the stepladder, and landed heavily on the floor. Horrified, the estate agent leaned past the rabbit's head and out of the hatch to see if he'd killed himself, whereupon she, too, promptly lost her balance and tumbled through the hole, landing on top of him. Anna-Lena's foot was trapped beneath them and she fell over, too. The stepladder wobbled and in turn fell over, hitting the hatch on the way and swinging it shut with a bang. The rabbit's head remained up there.

* * *

Roger, Ro and the bank robber heard the commotion from out in the apartment and came rushing over to see what was going on. Everyone inside the closet tried to crawl out, and everyone outside tried to figure out which limbs to pull on, not altogether unlike trying to untangle the wiring of the Christmas lights the Christmas after the Christmas when you had a row with your wife about brothels and ended up stuffing the whole lot into the box, thinking: 'I'll sort the whole darn mess out next Christmas!'

When they were all finally back on their feet, they stared in unison at Lennart's underpants, because it had become difficult not to, even if Lennart himself had no idea what was going on until Anna-Lena howled: '*You're bleeding!*'

Lennart, now free of the rabbit's head, leaned over quite a way to see past his stomach, and, sure enough, blood was dripping from his underpants.

'Oh no,' he groaned, then stuck his hand inside his underwear and pulled out a small, leaking bag that looked like the sort of thing you hope your child won't notice when you pass it on the motorway. He ran towards the bathroom, but tripped over the edge of the carpet in the living room and fell headfirst, and the bag of blood flew out of his hands and the contents exploded across the floor.

'What the . . . ?' Roger exclaimed.

Lennart gasped breathlessly: 'Don't worry! It's stage blood! I had a bag of it in my underpants, because sometimes you need that little bit extra in the whole "rabbit on the toilet" routine to really frighten people away.'

'I didn't order *this*!' Anna-Lena was quick to point out.

'No, it's an optional extra,' Lennart confirmed, getting clumsily to his feet.

'Go and put some trousers on,' Julia said sharply.

'Yes, please do,' Anna-Lena pleaded.

Lennart obeyed them and set off towards the closet. When he came back out, Zara had just come in from the balcony. It was the first time she'd seen him with clothes on, without the rabbit's head. It was an improvement, she had to admit to herself. She didn't hate him.

The rest of them were staring at the blood on the carpet and floor, uncertain about what they ought to do now.

'Nice colour, anyway,' Ro said.

'Very modern!' Estelle nodded, because she'd heard on the radio recently that murder was fashionable in popular culture at the moment.

Roger, in the meantime, was naturally feeling an increasing need for information, so he turned to the estate agent and interrogated her: 'Where the hell have you been?'

Embarrassed, the estate agent adjusted her rather too large and very crumpled jacket.

'Well, you see, when the viewing started I was in the closet.'

'What for?' Roger demanded.

'I was nervous. I always am before any big viewing, so I usually shut myself in the bathroom for a couple of minutes to give myself a pep talk. You know, "You can do this! You're a strong, independent estate agent and this apartment *will* be sold, by *you*!" But the bathroom was occupied, so I went into the closet. And then I heard . . .'

She gestured politely but nervously towards the woman standing in the middle of the room with her mask in one hand and the pistol in the other. Estelle intervened helpfully and said: 'Yes, this is the bank robber, but she isn't dangerous! She's just been holding us hostage, but we've been very well looked after. We're going to get pizza!'

The bank robber nodded apologetically to the estate agent and said: 'Sorry. Don't worry, this isn't a real pistol.'

The estate agent smiled in relief and went on: 'Well, I was in the closet, and then I heard someone scream "We're being robbed." And then I suppose I acted on instinct.'

'What do you mean by *on instinct*?' Roger wanted to know.

The estate agent started to brush off her jacket.

'I've actually got several viewings over the next few weeks. The House Tricks Estate Agency has a duty to its clients. So I thought, I can't die. That would have been irresponsible of me. And then I discovered the hatch in the ceiling, so I climbed up there and hid.'

'All this time?' Roger wondered.

The estate agent nodded so hard that her back creaked. 'I hoped I might be able to crawl out of the other end somehow, but I couldn't.' Then she seemed to think of something important and clapped her hands together and exclaimed: 'Well, goodness, look at me standing here chattering away. First and foremost, HOW'S TRICKS? How lovely that so many of you were able to come to this viewing, is there anyone who'd like to make an offer on the apartment straight away?'

The assembled gathering didn't look particularly impressed by the question. So the agent threw her arms out happily.

'Would you like to look around a bit more? No problem! I haven't got any other viewings today!'

Roger's eyebrows sank.

'Why are you even holding a viewing the day before New Year's Eve? I've never experienced that before. And I've attended quite a few viewings, I can tell you.'

The estate agent looked as cheerful as only an estate agent who's recently been released from a confined space can look.

'It was one of the seller's requests, and I didn't mind, because at the House Tricks Estate Agency, *every* day is a working day!'

The others collectively rolled their eyes at this. All except Estelle, who shivered and asked: 'It's cold in here, isn't it?'

'Yes, it is, isn't it? Cooler than Roger had budgeted for!' Ro exclaimed, to lighten the mood, then regretted it at once because Roger's mood didn't seem to have been lightened at all.

Julia, who by now was aching in most parts of her body, and who had run out of patience altogether, elbowed her way past them all and went and closed the balcony door. Then she went over to the open fireplace and started to sort out the wood.

'We might as well light a fire while we wait for the pizzas.'

The bank robber stood in the middle of the room with the pistol in her hand, for all the good that was doing. She looked at the group of hostages, which had now grown by one more person, which the bank robber could only assume would increase the length of her prison sentence proportionately. So she sighed: 'You don't have to wait for the pizzas. You can all go now. I'll give up and let the police do . . . well, whatever they're thinking of doing. You can all go first, I'll wait here, so that no one else gets hurt. I never meant to . . . take anyone hostage. I just needed money for the rent so my ex-husband's lawyer wouldn't take my daughters away from me. It was . . . sorry . . . I'm an idiot, you didn't deserve any of this . . . sorry.'

Tears were streaming down her cheeks, and she was no longer making any attempt to stop them. Maybe it was the fact that she looked so small that got to the others. Or maybe they each in turn found themselves thinking about what they'd actually experienced that day, and what it had meant for them. Suddenly they all started to protest at the same time, talking over each other:

'But you can't just . . . ,' Estelle began.

'You haven't hurt anyone!' Anna-Lena went on.

'There must be some way of solving this.' Julia nodded.

'Perhaps we could find a way out?' Lennart suggested.

'We certainly need a bit of time to gather all the information before you let us go!' Roger declared.

'And the bidding hasn't even started yet,' the estate agent piped up.

'We could just wait for the pizzas, couldn't we?' Ro suggested.

'Yes, let's have something to eat. This has all turned out to be rather pleasant, hasn't it, getting to know each other like this? And that's all thanks to *you*!' Estelle beamed.

'I'm sure the police won't shoot you. Not much, anyway,' Anna-Lena said comfortingly.

'Why don't we all go outside with you? They won't fire if we all leave at the same time!' Julia insisted.

'There must be a way out, if it's possible to sneak into a viewing, then it must be possible to sneak out,' Lennart pointed out.

'Let's all sit down and make a plan!' Roger demanded.

'And make bids on the apartment!' the estate agent added hopefully.

'And eat pizza!' Ro said.

The bank robber looked at each of them in turn for a long time. Then she whispered gratefully: 'Worst hostages ever.'

'Help me lay the table,' Estelle said, taking her by the arm.

The bank robber didn't resist, and went with Estelle into the kitchen. She returned with glasses and plates. Julia carried on sorting out the fire. Zara wrestled with her personality for a while, then handed Julia her lighter without her having asked for it.

Roger was standing beside the fireplace, unsure of how to make himself useful, and said to Julia: 'Do you know how to do that?'

Julia glared at him, and was about to tell him that her mum had taught her how to make a fire, in such a way that Roger couldn't be sure that didn't mean Julia and her mother had set fire to her father. But it had been a long day, they had all heard one another's stories, and that made it harder to dislike one another, so Julia said something incredibly generous instead.

'No. Can you show me how to do it?'

Roger nodded slowly, crouched down, and started to talk to the wood.

'We can . . . I'm assuming we can, unless you . . . we can do it together,' he mumbled.

She swallowed and nodded.

'I'd like that.'

'Thanks,' he said quietly.

Then he showed her how he usually started fires.

'Is it supposed to smoke that much?' Julia wondered.

'There's something wrong with the wood,' Roger grunted.

'Really?'

'There's something wrong with the damn wood, I tell you!'

'Have you opened the damper?'

'Of course I've opened the damn damper!'

Julia opened the damper. Roger muttered under his breath and she started to laugh. He joined in. They weren't looking at each other, but the smoke was stinging their eyes and tears were streaming down their cheeks. Julia glanced at him.

'Your wife's nice,' she said.

'So's yours,' he replied.

They each poked at separate pieces of wood in the fireplace.

'If you and Anna-Lena would really like the apartment, then –' Julia began, but he interrupted her.

'No. No. This is a good apartment for children. You and Ro should buy it.'

'I don't think Ro wants it, she finds fault with everything,' Julia sighed.

Roger poked harder at the fire.

'She's just scared she isn't good enough for you and the baby. You need to tell her that's nonsense. She's worried she won't be able to mend the skirting boards herself, so you'll just have to tell her that no one can fix the damn skirting boards until they've done it once. Everybody has to start somewhere!'

Julia let that sink in. She stared into the fire. Roger did the same. Each of them staring at a different piece of wood, a bit of flame, a lot of smoke.

'Can I say something personal, Roger?' she whispered after a while.

'Hmm.'

'You don't have to prove anything to Anna-Lena. You don't have to prove anything to anyone any more. You're good enough.'

They each poked at the fire. And they both got a hell of a lot of smoke in their eyes. They said nothing more.

There was a knock at the door. Because the policeman outside had finally figured out that the doorbell didn't work.

62

'I'll get it,' the bank robber said.

'No! What if it's the police?!' Ro exclaimed.

'It's probably just the pizzas,' the bank robber guessed.

'Are you mad? The police would never send a pizza delivery guy into a hostage situation! I mean, you're armed and dangerous!' Ro said.

'I'm not dangerous,' the bank robber said, hurt.

'I didn't mean it like that,' Ro said, apologetically.

Roger got to his feet over by the fireplace, which was smoking considerably less now, and pointed at the bank robber with a lump of wood as if it were his hand.

'Ro's right. If you open the door, the police might shoot you. It would be better if I went!'

Julia agreed, albeit a little too readily for Roger's liking. 'Yes! Let Roger go! Who knows? We might manage to come up with a way to help you escape, and then the police will never know that you're a woman. Everyone will just assume that the bank robber's a man!'

'Why?' Roger wondered.

'Because women aren't usually that stupid,' Zara interjected, ever helpful.

The bank robber sighed hesitantly. But Anna-Lena took a tiny, tiny step towards the middle of the room and whispered: 'Please, don't open the door, Roger. What if they shoot?'

Roger got some smoke in his eyes, even though there wasn't any now. He didn't say anything. So Lennart stepped forward and said: 'Oh, let me do it! Give me the mask and I'll pretend to be the hostage taker. I'm an actor, after all — I was in *The Merchant of Venice* at the local theatre.'

'Isn't it *The Merchant* from *Venice*?' Anna-Lena wondered.

'Is it?' Lennart asked.

'Oh, I like that play, there's a lovely line in it. Something about a light!' Estelle declared happily, but she couldn't for the life of her remember what it was.

'God, just stop babbling and *concentrate* for a minute!' Julia snapped, because there had just been another knock on the door.

Lennart nodded and held his hand out to the bank robber. 'Give me the mask and pistol.'

'No, give them here, I'll go!' Roger snapped, with a renewed need for validation.

The two men squared up against each other, as well as they could. Roger would probably have liked to hit Lennart again, all the more so now that the rabbit's head was gone. But perhaps Lennart could see how much Roger was hurting, so before Roger had time to clench his fists, he said: 'Don't be angry with your wife, Roger. Be angry with me.'

Roger still looked angry, but that must have struck home somewhere, making a tiny crack in his anger where the air slowly seeped out of it.

'I . . . ,' he grunted, not looking at Anna-Lena.

'Let me do this,' Lennart asked.

'Please, darling,' Anna-Lena whispered.

Roger looked up, only as far as her chin, and saw it was quivering. And he backed down. It could have been a touching moment, actually, if only he could have stopped himself muttering: 'For what it's worth, I hope they shoot you in the leg, Lennart.'

It was nicer than it sounded.

At that moment Estelle managed to remember the line from the play, so she declared: 'That light we see is burning in my hall. How far that little candle throws his beams! So shines a good deed in a naughty world.'

There was another she remembered now, *such a want-wit sadness makes of me*, but she didn't say that one out loud because she didn't want to spoil the mood. The bank robber looked at the little old lady.

'I'm so sorry, I've only just remembered that you were waiting for your husband – Knut, wasn't it? He was parking the car when I . . . he must be so worried!' she said, distraught with guilt.

Estelle patted the bank robber's arm.

'No, don't worry about that. Knut's already dead.'

The bank robber's face turned white.

'While you've been in here? He *died* while you were here . . . ? Oh, dear Lord . . .'

Estelle shook her head.

'No, no, no. He's been dead awhile. The whole world doesn't revolve around you, dear.'

'I . . . ,' the bank robber managed to say.

Estelle patted her arm.

'I just said Knut was parking the car because I get lonely sometimes. And it feels better to pretend that he's on his way. Especially at this time of year, he always used to like New Year, we used to stand at the kitchen window watching the fireworks. Well . . . we used to stand on the balcony for years . . . but I couldn't bring myself to go out there after something that happened down on the bridge ten years ago. It's a long story. Anyway, Knut and I used to stand in the kitchen watching the fireworks through the window, and . . . oh, you miss such peculiar things. I almost miss that more than anything. Knut loved fireworks, so I suppose I always feel extra lonely at New Year. I'm such a silly old woman.'

Everyone else had fallen silent, listening as she related this. It could have been a touching moment, actually, if Zara hadn't cleared her throat at the other end of the room.

'Everyone thinks Christmas is when most people kill themselves. That's a myth. Far more people commit suicide at New Year.'

* * *

That spoiled the mood. It's hard to deny that it did.

Lennart looked at Roger, Roger looked at the bank robber, the bank robber looked at them all. Then she nodded decisively. When the apartment door was finally opened, Jim the police officer was standing outside. A short while later he went back down to the street and told his son he'd spoken to the bank robber.

63

Jack stomps out of the interview room, exhausted with anger. The estate agent is still sitting in there, terrified, looking on as the younger of the two police officers starts to march up and down the corridor. Then she turns hopefully to the older officer, who is still seated in the room, looking sad. Jim doesn't seem to know what to do with his hands, or any other part of his body, for that matter, so he just passes the glass of water to her. It shakes, even though she's holding it with all ten digits.

'You have to believe me, I swear I'm not the bank robber . . . ,' she pleads.

Jim glances out at the corridor, where his son is walking around hitting the walls with his fists. Then Jim nods to the estate agent, hesitates, nods again, stops himself, then finally puts his hand very briefly on her shoulder and admits: 'I know.'

She looks surprised. He looks ashamed.

When the old policeman – and he's never felt older than he does right now – lifts his hand, he toys with his wedding ring. An old habit, but scant comfort. He's always felt that the hardest thing about death is the grammar. Often he still says the wrong thing, and Jack hardly ever corrects him, sons probably don't have the heart to do that. Jack mentions the ring once every six months or so, saying: 'Dad, isn't it time you took that off?' His dad nods, as if he'd just forgotten about it, tugs it a little as if it fits more tightly than it actually does, and mumbles: 'I will, I will.' He never does.

The hardest thing about death is the grammar, the tense, the fact that she won't be angry when she sees that he's bought a new sofa without consulting her first. She won't *be* anything. She isn't on her way home. She *was*. And she really did get angry that time Jim bought a new sofa without consulting her first, goodness, how angry she was. She could travel halfway around the world to the worst chaos on the planet, but when she came home everything had to be exactly the way it always was or she got upset. Of course that was just one of her many strange little habits and quirks: she put onion flakes on breakfast cereal and poured béarnaise sauce on popcorn, and if you yawned when she was next to you, she would lean forward and stick a finger in your mouth, just to see if she could pull it out again before you closed your mouth. Sometimes she put cornflakes in Jim's shoes, sometimes little bits of boiled egg and anchovies in Jack's pockets, and the looks on their faces when they realized seemed to amuse her more and more each time she did it. That's the kind of thing you miss. That she used to do this, that she used to do that. She *was*, she *is*. She was Jim's wife. Jack's mum is dead.

The grammar. That's the worst thing of all, Jim thinks. So he really wants his son to be able to pull this off, solve the whole thing, save everyone. It just doesn't seem to be working.

He goes out into the corridor. Looks at Jack. They're alone out there, no one can overhear their conversation. The son turns around, despairing.

'It *must* be the estate agent who did it, Dad, it *must* be . . . ,' he manages to say, but the words get weaker and weaker the further into the sentence he gets.

Jim shakes his head, painfully slowly.

'No. It isn't her. The bank robber wasn't in the apartment when you stormed in, son, you're right about that. But she didn't leave with the hostages, either.'

Jack's eyes dart wildly around the corridor. He clenches his fists, looking for something else to hit.

'How do you know that, Dad? How the hell do you know *that*?!' he yells, as if he were yelling at the sea.

Jim blinks as if he were trying to hold back the tide.

'Because I didn't tell you the truth, son.'

And then he does.

64

All the witnesses from the hostage drama were released at the same time. In a way, this story stops as suddenly for them as it began. They gather their things and are shepherded gently out on to the little flight of steps at the back of the police station. When the door closes behind them they look at each other in surprise: the estate agent, Zara, Lennart, Anna-Lena, Roger, Ro, Julia and Estelle.

'What did the police say to you?' Roger immediately asks the others.

'They asked loads of questions, but Jules and I just played dumb!' Ro declared happily.

'How clever of you,' Zara says.

'So none of the police said anything particular to any of you at all when they let you go?' Roger demands to know.

They all shake their heads. The young police officer, Jack, had just gone from room to room, saying no more except that they were free to go, and that he was sorry it had taken such a long time. The only thing he was careful to say was that they wouldn't be leaving via the front entrance of the police station, because there were reporters waiting out there.

So now the little group is gathered at the back of the station, glancing nervously at each other. In the end Anna-Lena asks the question they're all thinking: 'Is she . . . okay? When we left the apartment I saw a police officer standing in the stairwell, that older one, and I thought: *How on earth is she going to get into the other apartment now?*'

'Exactly! When the police told me the pistol was real and that they'd heard a shot from inside the apartment, I thought . . . ugh . . .' The estate agent nods, without wanting to finish the thought.

'Who helped her get out if it wasn't us?' Roger wants to know, eager for correct information.

No one has an answer to that, but Estelle looks down at her phone, reads a text message, and nods slowly. Then she smiles, relieved.

'She says she's okay.'

Anna-Lena smiles at that.

'Say hi from us.'

Estelle says she will.

Behind them, a woman in her twenties emerges from the police station on her own. She's trying to look confident, but her eyes are darting about wildly in search of somewhere to go, and someone to go there with.

'Are you okay, dear?' Estelle wonders.

'What? Why are you asking?' London snaps.

Julia looks at the name badge on London's blouse; she never took it off after she left work for the interview.

'Were you the person working at the counter in the bank that got robbed?'

London nods hesitantly.

'Oh my, were you very frightened?' Estelle wonders.

London nods, not as if she means to, but as if her body is answering for her when her brain doesn't dare.

'Not at the time. Not . . . when it happened. But afterwards. When I . . . you know, when I found out that it might have been a real pistol after all.'

The others on the steps nod understandingly. Ro puts her hands in the dress pockets beneath her coat, inclines her head towards a small café on the other side of the street, and says: 'Do you fancy a coffee?'

London feels like lying and saying that she has places to be, people to see, because it's, like, New Year's Eve tomorrow. But instead she says: 'I don't like coffee.'

'We'll find something else for you,' Ro promises.

That's a nice thing to promise someone, so London nods slowly. Ro becomes the first friend she's had in a long time. Ever, perhaps.

'Wait for me!' Julia says.

'What? Worried I'm going to get *robbed* if I go on my own or something?' Ro grins.

Julia doesn't grin. Ro clears her throat and mumbles: 'Okay, okay, too soon to make jokes about it, I get it, I get it!'

As they cross the street London whispers to her: 'That wasn't a very good joke.'

'Who are you, the joke police, or what?' Ro grunts.

'Darling! If you get shot, I'm going to give your birds away!' Julia calls behind them.

'Now *that* was funny!' London chuckles. She hasn't had anything to laugh at for a long time. Ever, perhaps.

She receives a letter a few days later, written by a bank robber who wants to apologize, which means more to the twenty-year-old than she can admit to anyone for many years. Not until she falls in love, in fact. But that's an entirely different story.

Julia hugs everyone on the steps and is hugged back in turn. When she gets to Estelle, the young woman and the much older one look into each other's eyes for a long time. Estelle says: 'There's a book I'd like to give you. By my favourite poet.'

Julia smiles.

'I was thinking that maybe we could meet up, you and me. Now and then. Maybe we can exchange books in the lift.'

'How do you mean?' Estelle wonders.

Julia turns to the estate agent.

'Will you sort out the paperwork?'

The estate agent nods so enthusiastically that she actually starts to jump off the ground. Roger finds himself grinning as well, suddenly delighted.

'So you and Ro bought the apartment after all? Did you get a good price?'

Julia shakes her head.

'No. Not that apartment. We bought the other one.'

Roger laughs out loud at that. It's been a while since he last did that. That makes Anna-Lena so happy that she has to sit down, in the middle of the steps, in the middle of winter.

65

The truth the truth the truth.

So, Jim came back down to the street and told Jack what had just happened inside the building, after he spoke to the bank robber. But that isn't quite what happened, not really. Not at all, in fact. In part that was because Jim was bad at telling stories, but it was mostly because he was very good at lying.

Because it wasn't Lennart who opened the door when Jim showed up with the pizzas. It was the bank robber, the real bank robber. Both Roger and Lennart had insisted on being allowed to wear the ski mask, but after a long pause she had said no. She had looked at them, her voice gentle with appreciation, then given them a determined nod.

'Obviously I can't set a good example to my daughters and teach them not to do idiotic things now. But I might at least be able to show them how you take responsibility for your actions.'

So when Jim knocked on the door again, she opened it. Without the mask. Her hair was draped over her shoulders, the same colour as Jim's daughter's hair. Sometimes two strangers only need one thing in common to find each other sympathetic. She saw the wedding ring on his finger, old and dented, tarnished silver. He saw hers, thin and discreet, gold, no gemstones. Neither of them had taken them off yet.

'Are you a police officer?' she asked so quickly that Jim lost his train of thought.

'How did you . . . ?'

'I don't think the police would send a real pizza delivery guy if you thought I was armed and dangerous,' she smiled, more like her face actually cracking than cracking into a smile.

'No, no . . . well, yes . . . and yes, I am a police officer.' Jim nodded, holding the pizzas out.

'Thanks,' she said, taking them with one hand as the pistol dangled in the other. Jim couldn't take his eyes off it.

'How are you doing?' he asked, which he may not have done if she'd been wearing a mask.

'I'm not having the best day,' she confessed.

'Is anyone in there hurt?'

She shook her head in horror.

'I'd never . . .'

Jim looked at her, noting her trembling fingers and the bite marks on her lower lip. He couldn't hear anyone crying inside the apartment, there was no one shouting, no one who sounded afraid at all.

'I need you to put the pistol down for a little while,' he said.

The bank robber nodded apologetically. 'Can I give them the pizzas first? They're hungry. It's been a long day for them . . . I . . .'

Jim nodded. She turned around and disappeared for a while, then came back without the boxes and without the pistol. From behind her, someone exclaimed, 'That isn't a Hawaiian!' and someone else laughed: 'You don't know a damn thing about Hawaiians!' *Laughed*. Then came the sound of idle chatter between strangers who were no longer quite that. It's probably hard to say precisely what would be normal in a hostage drama, but this certainly wasn't it. Jim looked intently at the bank robber.

'Can I ask, how did you get caught up in all this?'

The bank robber, now unarmed, took such a deep breath that she doubled in size, then she became smaller than ever.

'I don't know where to start.'

Then Jim did something deeply unprofessional. He reached out his hand and wiped a tear from the bank robber's cheek.

'My wife had a joke she used to like. How do you eat an elephant?'

'I don't know.'

'A bit at a time.'

She smiled.

'My kids would have liked that. They have a terrible sense of humour.'

Jim put his hands in his pockets and sat down heavily on the landing next to the door. The bank robber hesitated for a moment, then sat down with her legs crossed. Jim smiled.

'My wife had a terrible sense of humour as well. She liked laughing and causing trouble. The older she got, the more trouble she was. She always told me I was too nice. That's a terrible thing to be told by a priest, isn't it?'

The bank robber laughed quietly. Then nodded.

'Who did she used to cause trouble with?'

'Everyone. The Church, the parish, politicians, people who believed in God, people who didn't believe in God . . . she made it her job to defend the weakest: the homeless, migrants, even criminals. Because somewhere in the Bible Jesus says something like: "I was hungry and you gave me food, I was homeless and you looked after me, I was sick and you cared for me, I was in prison and you visited me." And then He says something like, what we do for the weakest among us, we also do for Him. And she took everything so *damn* literally, my wife. That's why she kept causing trouble.'

'Has she passed away?'

'Yes.'

'I'm sorry.'

He nodded gratefully. It's so odd, he thought, that still, after all this time, it feels so incomprehensible that she isn't here. That his heart hasn't got used to the fact that no giggling idiot is going to stick her finger in his mouth when he yawns, or pour flour in his pillowcase just as he's about to go to bed. No one to argue with him. Love him. There's no getting used to the grammar of it all. He smiled sadly and said: 'Now your turn.'

'At what?' the bank robber said.

'Telling your story. About how you ended up here.'

'How long a story do you want?'

'As long as you like. One bit at a time.'

Which was a nice thing to say. So the bank robber told him.

'My husband left me. Well, he kicked me out, actually. He'd been having an affair with my boss. They fell in love. They moved in together, in our apartment, because it was only in his name. Everything happened so quickly, and I didn't want to make a fuss or cause . . . chaos. For the children's sake.'

Jim nodded slowly. He looked at her ring and toyed with his own. There's nothing harder to remove.

'Girls or boys?'

'Girls.'

'I've got one of each.'

'I . . . someone needs to . . . I don't want them to . . .'

'Where are they now?'

'With their dad. I was supposed to pick them up tonight. We were going to celebrate New Year together. But now . . . I . . .'

She trailed off. Jim nodded thoughtfully.

'What did you need the money from the bank robbery for?'

The desperation on her face revealed the chaos in her heart as she said: 'To pay the rent. I needed six thousand five hundred. My husband's lawyer was threatening to take the girls away from me if I didn't have anywhere to live.'

Jim held on to the handrail to stop himself collapsing as his heart broke. Empathy is like vertigo. Six thousand five hundred, because she thought she'd lose her children otherwise. Her *children*.

'There are rules, legislation, no one can just take your children away from you simply because . . . ,' he began, then thought better of it and said: 'But *now* they can . . . now you've held up a *bank* and . . .' His voice almost gave out as he whispered: 'You poor child, what have you got yourself mixed up in?'

The woman had to force her tongue to move, her lips to open, as her smallest muscles seemed to have almost given up.

'I . . . I'm an idiot. I know, I know, I know. I didn't want to cause any trouble with my husband, I didn't want to expose the girls to that, I thought I might be able to sort it all out for myself. But all I've done is create chaos. It my fault, it's all my fault. I'm ready to give up now, I'll let all the hostages go, I promise, the pistol's still in there, it isn't even real . . .'

Jim couldn't help thinking that was one hell of a reason to rob a bank: because you're scared of conflict. He tried to see her as a criminal, tried to look at her without seeing his daughter, and failed at both.

'Even if you release the hostages and give up, you'll still end up in prison. Even if the pistol isn't real,' he said mournfully, and of course he'd been a police officer long enough to have seen that it was. He knew she wouldn't stand a chance, no matter how sympathetic any decent person might feel about her situation. You're not allowed to rob banks, you're not allowed to run around with firearms, and we can't let criminals like that go unpunished if we catch them. So Jim concluded there and then that the only way she wouldn't get punished was not to catch her.

He looked around in the stairwell. On the door of the apartment behind the bank robber was an estate agent's sign bearing the text: *For sale! HOUSE TRICKS Estate Agency! HOW'S TRICKS?* Jim stared at it for a while, ransacking his memory.

'That's odd,' he finally said.

'What is?' the bank robber wondered.

'House Tricks Estate Agency. That's a fairly . . . silly name.'

'Maybe.' The bank robber nodded, not having given it much thought before then.

Jim rubbed his nose.

'It might just be a coincidence, but I spoke to the couple who own the neighbouring apartment on the phone a little while ago. They're splitting up. Because one of them likes coriander, and the other also likes coriander, but not quite as much, but apparently that's enough of a reason if you're young and are on the Internet.'

The corners of the bank robber's mouth tried to form a smile.

'No one wants to be bored any more.'

She was thinking that the worst thing of all, the most impossible thing to reconcile herself to emotionally, was the fact that she still loved her husband. Every blood vessel felt like it was exploding every time that realization struck her. That she couldn't stop loving him, not even after everything he'd done, not even then could she stop herself wondering if it had all been her fault. Maybe she wasn't enough fun – maybe it's unreasonable to expect someone to stay with you if you're not fun.

'No, that's just it! Everything has to be like the first flush of infatuation for youngsters, nothing can be mundane, they've got the attention span of a kitten with a glittery rubber ball,' Jim agreed, suddenly excited, and went on: 'So they're separating and selling the apartment. One of them couldn't remember what the estate agent's name was, just that it was a silly name. And you know what? House Tricks Estate Agency – that's a really silly name!'

He pointed at the sign on the door of the apartment where the estate agent was. Then at the door opposite. It was too small a town to have many estate agencies with silly names. It wasn't even big enough to have more than one hairdressing salon called The Upper Cut.

'Sorry, I don't understand the significance,' the bank robber said.

Jim scratched his stubble.

'I was just thinking . . . is the estate agent in there with you?'

The bank robber nodded.

'Yes, she's driving everyone mad. When I went in with the pizzas just now she was making Roger stand near the balcony, then she went and stood at the other end of the apartment, then she threw her keys to him so he could see how far you could throw something because it's all open plan.'

'How did that go?'

'Roger ducked. The window very nearly broke.' The bank robber smiled. It was a friendly smile, Jim thought. Not the sort that wants to hurt anyone. He looked at the sign again.

'I don't know . . . this might be . . . but if it is the same estate agent who's going to sell the neighbouring apartment, then maybe she's got the keys to that one with her, and then . . .'

He couldn't quite bring himself to say it.

'What do you mean?' the bank robber said.

Jim pulled himself together, stood up, and cleared his throat.

'What I mean is that if the estate agent is also selling the next apartment, and if she's got the keys with her, then perhaps you could hide in there. When the other police officers come up here, they won't break open all the doors to the other apartments to look for you, not right away, at least.'

'Why not?'

Jim shrugged. 'Because we're not that good. Everyone will be concentrating on getting the hostages out first, and if you tell them to close the door behind them, then everyone will assume that the bank robber . . . you . . . are still in the apartment. *This* apartment. Then, once we've smashed the door in and discovered you're not there, we can't just smash the other doors in willy-nilly, that would cause a huge stink. Bureaucracy, you know. We'll have to take the hostages to the station first and get witness statements from them and, I don't know . . . you might be able to come up with a way of getting out. And you know what? If anyone were to find you in the other apartment, you can always pretend you live there! We've been assuming that the bank robber is a man right from the start.'

The bank robber was still wide-eyed and uncomprehending.

'Why?' she asked again.

'Because women don't normally do . . . this sort of thing,' Jim said, as diplomatically as he could.

She shook her head.

'No, I mean, *why*? Why are you doing this for me? You're a

police officer! I mean, you're not supposed to do this sort of thing for me!'

Jim nodded feebly. He rubbed his hands on his trousers, then his wrists across his brow.

'My wife used to quote some guy who said . . . what was it? He said that even if he knew that the world was going to hell tomorrow, he'd plant an apple tree today.'

'That's lovely,' the bank robber whispered.

Jim nodded. He wiped the back of his hand over his eyes.

'I don't want to . . . catch you. I know you've made a big mistake here, but . . . that sort of thing happens.'

'Thank you.'

'You need to go in and ask the estate agent if she's got the keys to the other apartment. Because it won't be long before my son loses patience and comes storming in here, and then . . .'

The bank robber blinked several times.

'Sorry? Your son?'

'He's a police officer, too. He'll be the first one through the door.'

The bank robber felt her throat tighten and her voice faltered.

'He sounds brave.'

'He had a brave mum. She would have robbed banks for his sake, if she'd had to. I didn't even believe in God when we met. She was beautiful, I wasn't. She could dance, I could barely stay on my feet. Back when we first met, the way we thought about our work was probably all we had in common. The fact that we save those we can.'

'I don't know if I deserve to be saved,' the bank robber whispered.

Jim just nodded, looked her in the eye, an honest, decent man about to do something that went against the principles of a profession he's belonged to all his adult life.

'Come and find me in ten years' time and tell me if I was wrong.'

He turned to go. She hesitated, swallowed hard, then called: 'Wait!'

'Yes?'

'Can I . . . Is it too late to make a demand in exchange for releasing the hostages?'

'What the hell . . . ?'

He raised his eyebrows, then frowned, at first taken aback, then almost annoyed. The bank robber was trying to make her mind up.

'Fireworks,' she eventually said. 'There's an old lady in here who always used to watch the fireworks with her husband. He's dead now. I've been holding her hostage all day. I'd like to give her some fireworks.'

Jim grinned. Nodded.

Then he went downstairs and lied to his son.

66

The bank robber went back inside the apartment. There was blood on the floor, but the fire was crackling in the hearth. Ro was sitting on the sofa eating pizza and making Julia laugh. Roger and the estate agent were arguing about the measurements on the plan, not because Roger was thinking about buying the apartment any more, but because 'it's pretty damn important that you're given the correct information'. Zara and Lennart were standing by the window. Zara was eating a slice of pizza, and Lennart was having fun watching the expression of disgust on her face. It didn't look as if she liked him, it really didn't, but she didn't seem to hate him, either. He in turn seemed to think she was wonderful.

Anna-Lena was standing on her own, holding a plate in one hand, but the pizza on it was untouched and going cold. Naturally it was Julia who spotted her and got up from the sofa. She went over and asked: 'Are you okay, Anna-Lena?'

Anna-Lena looked over at Roger. They still hadn't talked since the rabbit emerged from the bathroom.

'Yes,' she lied.

Julia took hold of her arm, encouragingly rather than to comfort her.

'I don't exactly know what you think you've done wrong, but the fact that you hired Lennart all those times so that Roger would feel like a winner is one of the daftest, weirdest, most romantic things I've ever heard!'

Anna-Lena prodded the pizza on her plate tentatively.

'Roger should have had a chance at being promoted. I always thought, next year it'll be his turn. But time goes faster than you think, all those years all at once. Sometimes I think that when you live together for a very long time, and have children together, life is a bit like climbing trees. Up and down, up and down, you try to cope with everything, be good, you climb and climb and climb, and you hardly ever see each other along the way. You don't notice that when you're young, but everything changes when you have children, and sometimes it feels like you hardly ever see the person you married any more. You're parents and teammates, first and foremost, and being married slips down the list of priorities. But you . . . well, you keep climbing trees, and see each other along the way. I always thought that was just the way it is, life, the way it has to be. We just had to get through everything, I thought. And I kept telling myself that the important thing was that we kept climbing the same tree. Because then I thought that sooner or later . . . and this sounds so pretentious . . . but I thought that sooner or later we'd end up on the same branch. And then we could sit there holding hands and looking at the view. That's what I thought we'd be doing when we got old. But time goes quicker than you think. And it never did get to be Roger's turn.'

Julia was still holding her arm. Less in encouragement, more to comfort her.

'My mum always says I should never apologize for myself. Never say sorry for being good at something.'

Anna-Lena took a dubious bite of her pizza, then said with her mouth full: 'Wise mum.'

They stood there in silence.

And then there was a loud bang.

Once. Twice. A few seconds later came the whistling and explosions, so many and so close together that you couldn't count them. Lennart was standing closest to the window, so he was the one who exclaimed: 'Look! Fireworks!'

Jim had sent a young officer from the station to buy them. He was setting them off from down by the bridge. Lennart, Zara, Julia, Ro, Anna-Lena, Roger and the estate agent went out on to the balcony. They stood there watching in amazement. They weren't pathetic little bangers, either, they were the real thing, different colours, the sort that look like rain, the whole deal. Because, as luck would have it, Jim liked fireworks, too.

The bank robber and Estelle watched them from the kitchen window, arm in arm.

'Knut would have liked this,' Estelle nodded.

'I hope you like it, too,' the bank robber managed to say.

'Very much, you sweet child, very much indeed. Thank you!'

'I'm so sorry for everything I've done to you all,' the bank robber sniffed.

Estelle pouted her lips unhappily.

'Perhaps we could explain everything to the police? Tell them it was all a mistake?'

'No, I don't think so.'

'Perhaps you could escape somehow? Hide somewhere?'

Estelle smelled of wine. Her pupils were ever so slightly unfocused. The bank robber was about to reply, then realized that the less Estelle knew, the better. Then the old woman wouldn't have to lie for the bank robber's sake when she was questioned by the police. So she said: 'No, I don't think that would work.'

Estelle held her hand. There wasn't much else she could do. The fireworks were beautiful, Knut would have loved them.

When they were finished the bank robber went into the living room, and the others all came back in from the balcony. The bank robber tried to signal discreetly that she wanted to talk to the estate agent, but sadly that was impossible given that the estate agent was busy arguing with Roger about the price Julia and Ro ought to pay for the apartment if they bought it.

'Okay, then! *Okay!*' the estate agent finally snapped. 'I can go a bit lower, but *only* because I have to put the other apartment up for sale in two weeks' time, and I don't want that competing with this one!'

Roger, Julia and Ro all tilted their heads in such a way that they bumped into one another.

'Which . . . other apartment?' Roger asked.

The estate agent harrumphed, annoyed with herself for having let that slip out.

'The apartment opposite, on the other side of the lift. I haven't even put it up on my website yet, because if you sell two apartments at the same time, you get less for both, all good estate agents know that. The other apartment looks just the same as this one, only with a slightly smaller closet, but for some reason it has excellent mobile reception and that seems to be ridiculously important for people these days. The couple who own it are splitting up, they had a terrible row in my office, they've removed all the furniture from the apartment, the only thing left in there is a juicer. And I can quite see why neither of them would want it, because it's a truly *terrible* colour . . .'

The estate agent went on babbling for a long time, but no one was really listening any more. Roger and Julia looked at each other, then at the bank robber, then at the estate agent.

'Hang on, you're saying you're going to be selling the neighbouring apartment as well? The one on the other side of the lift? And . . . there's no one living there at the moment?' Julia asked, just to be sure.

The estate agent stopped babbling and started to nod instead. Julia looked at the bank robber, and of course they were both thinking exactly the same thing, a possible solution to all this.

'Have you got the keys to the other apartment?' Julia asked with a hopeful smile, convinced that this would be a perfect end to the whole thing.

Unfortunately the estate agent looked back at Julia as if that were a ridiculous question. 'Why would I? I'm not even going to start trying to sell it for another two weeks, and do you think I carry people's keys around just for the fun of it? What sort of estate agent do you take me for?'

Roger sighed. Julia sighed, more deeply. The bank robber wasn't even breathing, just tumbling headlong into the hopelessness inside her.

'I had an affair once!' Estelle said cheerfully from the other end of the apartment, because she'd found another bottle of wine in the kitchen.

'Not now, Estelle,' Julia said, but the old woman was insistent. She was slightly drunk, that can't be denied, because the closet had already provided quite a lot of wine for an elderly lady.

'I had an *affair* once!' she repeated, with her eyes fixed on the bank robber's, and the bank robber suddenly felt nervous about the possible details that might slip out in a story that started like that. Estelle waved the wine bottle and went on: 'He loved books, and so did I, but my husband didn't. Knut liked music. I suppose music's all right, but it's not the *same*, is it?'

The bank robber shook her head politely.

'No. I like books, too.'

'I thought as much from looking at you! As if you understand that people need fairy tales as well, not just narrative. I've liked you from the moment you came in here, you know. You messed things up a bit, with the pistol and all that, but who hasn't messed things up at one time or another? All interesting people have done something really stupid at least once! For instance, I had an affair, behind Knut's back, with a man who loved books, just like me. Whenever I read anything now I think of the pair of them, because he gave me a key, and I never told Knut that I kept it.'

'Please, Estelle, we're trying to . . . ,' Julia said, but Estelle ignored her. She ran one hand along the bookcase. One of the last times she met her neighbour in the lift he gave her a very thick book, written by a man. He had underlined one sentence, several hundred pages in: *We are asleep until we fall in love*. Estelle gave him a book in exchange, one written by a woman, so it didn't need hundreds of pages to say things. Close to the start Estelle had underlined: *Love is wanting you to exist.*

Her fingers traced the spines of the books on the shelf, as if she were dreaming, not as if she were looking. A book fell out from the middle of a row, not as if it had done so on purpose, but simply because her fingernails happened to touch its spine. It landed on the floor and fell open a few pages in. The key that fell out bounced off the pages, then landed on the parquet floor with a tinkling sound.

Estelle's chest was rising and falling breathlessly and her voice may have been slurred but her eyes were crystal clear when she said: 'When Knut fell ill we signed the apartment over to our daughter. I thought she might want to move in here with her children, but that was obviously a silly idea. They didn't want to live here. They've got their own lives, in a place of their own. Since then there's only been me here, and . . . well, you can see . . . it's too big for me. This isn't a sensible apartment for a single person. So in the end my daughter said we ought to sell it and buy something smaller for me, something easier to look after, she said. So I called several different estate agents and obviously they all said that it wasn't usual to hold a viewing so close to New Year, but I wanted . . . well, I thought it would be nice to have a bit of company at this time of year. So I went out before the estate agent arrived, then I came back up once the viewing had started and pretended to be a prospective buyer. Because I didn't want to sell the apartment without knowing who was going to be buying it. This isn't just an apartment, it's my home, I don't want to hand it over to someone who's just going to be passing through, to make money from it. I want someone who's going to love living here, like I have. Maybe that's hard for a young person to understand.'

That wasn't true. There wasn't a single person in the apartment who didn't understand perfectly. But the estate agent cleared her throat.

'So . . . when your daughter commissioned me, I wasn't the first person she'd called?'

'Oh, no, she called *all* the other estate agents before she felt obliged to ring you. But just look how it's all turned out!' Estelle smiled.

The estate agent brushed the dust off her jacket and her ego.

'So this is the key to . . . ,' the bank robber began, staring at it but still not quite able to believe it.

Estelle nodded.

'My affair. He lived in the neighbouring apartment, on the other side of the lift. That's where he died. I was standing in front of the bookcase when the apartment was put up for sale, and I wondered what would have happened if I'd met him first, before Knut. You can let yourself do that when you get old, go for a little stroll in your imagination. A young couple bought the apartment. They never changed the lock.'

Julia cleared her throat, rather taken aback.

'How . . . sorry, Estelle, but how do you know that?'

Estelle gave her an embarrassed little smile.

'Every so often I . . . well, I've never actually *opened* the door, of course, I'm not a criminal, but I . . . sometimes I check to see if the key still fits. It does. It doesn't surprise me that they're splitting up, that young couple, it really doesn't, because I often used to hear them arguing when I was smoking in the closet. The walls are rather thin in there. You get to hear all sorts of things. Some of it would shock even Stockholmers, I can tell you.'

The bank robber put the book back on the shelf. Clutched the key tightly. Then she turned to the others and whispered: 'I don't know what to say.'

'Don't say anything at all. Go and hide in the other apartment until this is all over. Then you can go home to your daughters,' Estelle said.

The key was dancing in the bank robber's palm when she un-clenched her fist, she couldn't hold it still.

'I haven't got a home to go back to. I can't pay the rent. And I can't ask any of you to lie for my sake when you talk to the police. They're going to ask who I am and if you know where I'm hiding, and I don't want you to lie for me!'

'Of course we're going to lie for you,' Ro exclaimed.

'Don't worry about us,' Julia cajoled.

'We don't actually have to lie, any of us,' Roger said. 'We just need to play dumb.'

'Yes, well, there's no problem, then, is there? Because *that's* hardly going to be a challenge for any of you!' Zara declared. For once, it wasn't actually meant as an insult, it just sounded like it.

Anna-Lena nodded thoughtfully at the bank robber.

'Roger's right. We just have to play dumb. We can say you never took the mask off, so we can't give a description.'

The bank robber tried to protest. They didn't give her a chance. Then there was a knock at the door, and Roger went into the hall and peered through the spyhole, and saw Jim standing outside. That was when Roger realized what the real problem was.

'Damn. That policeman's out in the stairwell, how are you going to get past him into the other apartment without him seeing you? We didn't think of that!' he exclaimed.

'Perhaps we could distract him?' Julia suggested.

'I could squirt lime juice in his eyes!' Ro nodded.

'Perhaps we could just try reasoning with him?' Estelle said hopefully.

'Unless we all run out at once so he gets confused!' Anna-Lena said, thinking out loud.

'Naked! People always get more confused when you're naked!' Lennart informed them, in his capacity as an expert.

Zara was standing next to him, and he was probably expecting her to tell him he was a damn idiot, but instead she said: 'Perhaps we could bribe him. The policeman. Most men can be bought.'

Lennart of course noticed that she could have said 'most *people*', she didn't have to say 'most *men*', but he couldn't help thinking it was a nice gesture on her part to try to be part of the group.

The bank robber stood in front of them for a long while with the key in her hand, on the brink of telling them about Jim, but instead she said thoughtfully: 'No. If I tell you how I'm going to escape, you'd have to lie when the police question you. But if you just walk out of here now and go downstairs, you can tell the truth: when you closed the door behind you, I was still in here. You don't know what happened to me after that.'

They looked like they wanted to protest (all except Zara), but eventually nodded in response (even Zara). Estelle put some cling-film over the remains of the pizza and put it in the fridge. She wrote her phone number on a scrap of paper, put it in the bank robber's pocket, and whispered: 'Send me a text when you're safe, otherwise I'll worry.' The bank robber promised. Then all the hostages walked out of the apartment. Roger went last, and carefully closed the door behind him until he heard the latch click. Jim directed them to walk down the stairs, where Jack was waiting to escort them into the police cars that would drive them to the station to be questioned.

Jim was left alone in the stairwell for a while, and waited until Jack came up the stairs.

'Is the bank robber still in there now? Are you *sure*, Dad?' Jack asked.

'One hundred per cent,' Jim said.

'Good! The negotiator's going to call the phone in there shortly and try to get him to come out voluntarily. Otherwise we'll have to break the door in.'

Jim nodded. Jack looked around, then crouched down by the lift and picked up a piece of paper.

'What's this?'

'Looks like a drawing?' Jim said.

Jack put it in his pocket. Looked at the time. The negotiator made the call.

It had been tucked inside one of the pizza boxes, the special telephone thingy. It was Ro who had found it. She was very hungry, so she just thought it was odd to find a phone in a pizza box, put it down, and decided to eat first before bothering to think about it. And by the time she'd finished eating she'd forgotten all about it. There was so much else going on, the fireworks and all the rest of it, and perhaps you had to know Ro to understand just how absentminded she could be. But perhaps it's enough to know that once she'd finished her own pizza, she opened all the other boxes and ate the crusts the others had left. At that point Roger turned to her and said she needn't worry, he was sure she was going to be a good parent now, because good parents eat other people's crusts out of other people's boxes just like that. Hearing that meant so much to Ro that she burst into tears.

So the phone was left on the little three-legged table beside the sofa, as unsteady as a spider on an ice cube. When all the hostages had gone, the bank robber put her pistol down next to the phone, after wiping it carefully first, of course, because Roger had seen a documentary about how the police find fingerprints at crime scenes. She also threw her ski mask on the fire, because Roger had said the cops might be able to get DNA and all sorts of other stuff off it otherwise.

Then the bank robber went out through the door. Jim was standing alone on the landing. They glanced at each other quickly, she gratefully, he full of stress. She showed him the key. He breathed out.

'Hurry up,' he said.

'I just want to say . . . I haven't told anyone you're doing this for me. I didn't want anyone to have to lie for me when they were questioned,' she said.

'Good,' he nodded.

She tried in vain to blink away the dampness in her eyes, because of course she knew she was actually asking someone to lie for her, more than he had ever lied for anyone. But Jim wouldn't let her apologize, just pushed her past the lift door and whispered: 'Good luck!'

She went inside the neighbouring apartment and locked the door behind her. Jim was left standing on his own in the stairwell for a minute, which gave him time to think of his wife and hope she was proud of him. Or at least not really angry. With all the hostages safely on their way to the station, Jack came running up the stairs. Then the negotiator made the call. And the pistol hit the floor.

67

Back at the police station, Jim has told Jack the truth, the whole truth. His son wants to be angry, he wishes he had the time, but because he's a good son he's busy trying to come up with a plan instead. Once they've let the witnesses leave through the back door of the police station, he sets off towards the main entrance at the front.

'You don't have to do this, son, I can go,' Jim says disconsolately. He stops himself from saying: *Sorry I lied to you, but deep down you know I did the right thing.*

Jack shakes his head firmly.

'No, Dad. Stay here.'

He stops himself from saying: *You've caused enough problems.* Then he walks out on to the steps at the front of the building and tells the waiting reporters everything they need to know. That Jack himself has been responsible for the whole of the police response, and that they have lost the perpetrator. That no one knows where he is now.

Some of the journalists start shouting accusing questions about 'police incompetence', others merely smirk as they take notes, ready to slaughter Jack in articles and blog posts a few hours from now. The shame and failure are Jack's alone, he carries them on his own, so that no one else gets blamed. Inside the station, his dad sits with his face in his hands.

The detectives from Stockholm arrive early the next morning, New Year's Eve. They read through all the witness statements, talk to Jack and Jim, check all the evidence. And then the Stockholmers snort, in voices more self-important than adverts for washing-up liquid, that they really don't have the resources to do more than that. No one was hurt during the hostage drama, nothing was stolen in the robbery, so there aren't really any victims here. The Stockholmers need to focus their resources where they're really needed. Besides, it's New Year's Eve, and who wants to celebrate in a town as small as this?

They're going to be in a hurry to get home, and Jack and Jim will watch them drive off. The journalists will already have disappeared by then, on their way to the next big story. There's always another celebrity who might be on the point of getting divorced.

'You're a good police officer, son,' Jim will say, looking down at the ground. He'll want to add *but an even better person*, but won't be able to bring himself to say it.

'You're not always such a damn good police officer, Dad.' Jack will grin up at the clouds. He'll want to add *but I've learned everything else from you*, but the words won't quite come out.

They'll go home. Watch television. Have a beer together.

That's enough.

68

On the steps at the back of the police station Estelle hugs each of them in turn. (Except Zara, of course, who blocks her with her handbag and jumps out of the way when she tries.)

'I have to say, if you have to be held hostage, then there's no better company to be in than all of you.' Estelle smiles at them all. Even Zara.

'Would you like to come and have coffee with us?' Julia asks.

'No, no, I need to get home.' Estelle smiles, then she suddenly becomes serious and turns to the estate agent: 'I really am very sorry I changed my mind and didn't let you sell the apartment after all. But it's . . . home.'

The estate agent shrugs.

'I think that's rather lovely, actually. People always think estate agents just want to sell, sell, sell, but there's something . . . I don't quite know how to say it . . .'

Lennart fills in with the words she can't find: 'There's something romantic about the thought of all the apartments that aren't for sale.'

The estate agent nods. Estelle takes several deep, happy breaths. She's going to be neighbours with Julia and Ro, in the apartment on the other side of the landing, and she and Julia will be able to swap books in the lift. The first one Estelle is going to give her is by her favourite poet. She'll fold down the corner of one page, underline some of the finest words she knows.

Nothing must happen to you
No, what am I saying
Everything must happen to you
And it must be wonderful

Julia will give Estelle a completely different type of literature in exchange. A guidebook about Stockholm.

Ro will lose her dad, she'll visit him every week, he's still on earth but already belongs to heaven. Ro's mum will find the strength to cope with the loss because another man will show her that life goes on. Julia will give birth to him with her hand clasped so tightly around Ro's fingers that the nurses have to give both mothers painkillers, one before the birth, the other after.

Ro will sleep beside him, perfectly still, on white sheets, without feeling afraid. Because she would have crossed mountains for his sake, would have done anything. Robbed banks, if necessary. They're going to be good parents, Ro and Julia. Good enough, anyway.

Julia will still hide sweets, and Ro will be allowed to keep her birds. The monkey and the frog will love them, visit them every day, and even when Julia offers them lots of money, they won't leave the cage open. Julia and Ro will argue, then make up, and all you have to do is make sure you're better at the latter than the former. So they will shout loudly and laugh even louder, and when they make up, the walls will shake and Estelle will feel embarrassed in her closet. Their love will continue to be a flower shop.

Outside the police station Zara skips quickly down the steps to the street, afraid that someone else might try to hug her. Lennart hurries after her.

'Would you like to share a taxi?' he asks, as if that weren't the very definition of anarchy.

Zara looks like she's never shared a taxi in her life, or anything else for a very long time. But after a long pause she mutters, 'If we do, you can sit in the front. And we're not going in a car with lots of crap dangling from the rearview mirror. That's an evolutionary dead end.'

* * *

Anna-Lena is still sitting on the steps. Roger sits down beside her with an effort, just close enough that they're almost touching. Anna-Lena stretches out her fingers towards his. She wants to say sorry. So does he. It's a harder word than you might think, when you've been climbing trees for so long.

She looks up at the sky, dark now, December is merciless. But she knows that IKEA is still open. A light out there, somewhere.

'We could go and look at that countertop you were talking about,' she whispers.

She crumbles when he shakes his head. Roger says nothing for a long time. He keeps changing his mind.

'I thought perhaps we could do something else,' he eventually mumbles.

'What do you mean?'

'The cinema. Maybe. If you'd like that.'

It's a good thing Anna-Lena is already sitting down, because otherwise she would have had to.

They go and see something made up. Because people need stories, too, sometimes. In the darkness of the auditorium they hold hands. For Anna-Lena it feels like coming home, and for Roger, like being good enough.

Estelle hurries back to her apartment. On the way she calls her daughter and tells her not to worry, either about the hostage drama or the fact that her mum lives alone in that large apartment. Because she doesn't any more. Estelle will have to give up smoking, because the young woman who's going to be renting a room in the apartment won't even let her smoke in the closet.

If we're being pedantic, the young woman actually rents the whole apartment from Estelle's daughter, and then Estelle rents a room from her for the same amount: six thousand five hundred. On the door of the fridge hangs a crumpled drawing of a monkey and a frog and an elk. Estelle stole it from the interview room when Jim was getting coffee. Each morning, every other week, the monkey and the frog will eat breakfast with their mum in Estelle's kitchen. For many years, on the last night of the year, they will watch fireworks together from the window. Then, eventually, a night will come which will be Estelle's last night without Knut, and everyone else's last night with Estelle.

At her funeral Ro will suggest an inscription for her headstone: 'Here lies Estelle. She certainly liked her wine!' Julia will kick Ro on the shin, but not hard. Their son will hold each of them by the hand as they walk away. Julia keeps the old woman's books for the rest of her life, the wine bottles, too. When the monkey and the frog grow into teenagers, they smoke in secret in the closet.

Somewhere, in some sort of heaven, Estelle will be listening to music with one man and talking about literature with another. She's earned that.

Oh, yes. In the basement storage area of an apartment block not far from there, where a mother of two little girls who became a bank robber once slept, alone and frightened, there's still a box of blankets there the day after the hostage drama. Somewhere else entirely a bank doesn't get robbed the day after New Year, because the person who hid their pistol down there under the blankets turns the whole storage area upside down, shouting and swearing because it's gone. Because what sort of callous bastard would steal a person's *pistol*?

Idiots.

69

The windowsill outside the office is weighed down by snow. The psychologist is talking to her dad on the phone. 'Darling Nadia, my little bird,' he says in the language of his homeland, because 'bird' is a more beautiful word there. 'I love you, too, Dad,' Nadia says patiently. He never used to talk to her like that, but late in life even computer programmers become poets. Nadia assures him over and over that she'll drive carefully when she sets off to visit him the following day, but he'd still prefer to come and fetch her. Dads are dads and daughters are daughters, and not even psychologists can quite come to terms with that.

Nadia hangs up. There's a knock on the door, like when someone who doesn't want to touch the door taps on it with the end of an umbrella. Zara is standing outside. She's holding a letter in her hand.

'Hello? Sorry, I thought . . . have we got an appointment booked for now?' Nadia wonders, fumbling first for her diary, then for her mobile to see what time it is.

'No, I just . . . ,' Zara replies quietly. A gentle tremble of the metal spokes of the umbrella gives her away. Nadia spots it.

'Come in, come in,' she says anxiously.

The skin under Zara's eyes is full of tiny cracks, worn down by everything it's had to hold back, finally on the brink of bursting. She looks at the picture of the woman on the bridge for several minutes before she asks Nadia: 'Do you like your job?'

'Yes,' Nadia nods, unsettled.

'Are you happy?'

Nadia wants to reach out and touch her, but refrains.

'Yes, I'm happy, Zara. Not all the time, but I've learned that you don't have to be happy all the time. But I'm happy . . . enough. Is that what you came here to ask?'

Zara looks past her.

'You asked me once why I like my job, and I said it was because I was good at it. But I unexpectedly found myself with some time to think recently, and I think I liked my job because I believed in it.'

'How do you mean?' the psychologist asks, in her professional voice, despite the fact that she feels like saying, unprofessionally, that she's really pleased to see Zara. That she's been thinking about her a lot. And has been worrying about what she might do.

Zara reaches out her hand, as close to the picture as possible without actually touching the woman.

'I believe in the place of banks in society. I believe in order. I've never had any objection to the fact that our customers and the media and politicians all hate us, that's our purpose. Banks need to be the ballast in the system. They make it slow, bureaucratic, difficult to manoeuver. To stop the world lurching about too much. People need bureaucracy, to give them time to think before they do something stupid.'

She falls silent. The psychologist sits down quietly on her chair.

'Forgive me for speculating, Zara, but . . . it sounds like something's changed. In you.'

Zara looks her straight in the eye then, for the first time.

'The housing market is going to crash again. Maybe not tomorrow, but it's going to crash again. We know that. Yet we still lend money. When people lose everything, we tell them it was their responsibility, that those are the rules of the game, that it was their own fault they were so greedy. But of course that isn't true. Most people aren't greedy, most people are just . . . like you said when we were talking about the picture: they're just looking for something to cling on to. Something to fight for. They want somewhere to live, somewhere to raise their children, live their lives.'

'Has anything happened to you since we last met?' the psychologist asks.

Zara gives her a troubled smile. Because how do you answer that?

So instead she answers a question that's never been asked: 'Everything's become lighter, easier, Nadia. The banks aren't ballast any more. One hundred years ago practically everyone who worked in a bank understood how the bank made money. Now there are at most three people in each bank who really understand where it all comes from.'

'And you're questioning your place there now, because you no longer think you understand?' the psychologist guesses.

Zara's chin moves sadly from side to side.

'No. I've handed in my notice. Because I realized that I was one of the three.'

'What are you going to do from now on?'

'I don't know.'

The psychologist finally has something important to say. Something she didn't learn at college but knows that everyone needs to hear, every so often.

'Not knowing is a good place to start.'

Zara doesn't say anything more. She massages her hands, counts windows. The desk is narrow, the two women probably wouldn't have felt comfortable sitting so close to each other if it hadn't been there between them. Sometimes we don't need distance, just barriers. Zara's movements are wary, Nadia's cautious. Only after a long time has passed does the psychologist venture to speak again.

'Do you remember asking me, one of the first times we met, if I could explain what panic attacks were? I don't think I ever gave you a good answer.'

'Have you got a better one now?' Zara asks.

The psychologist shakes her head. Zara can't help smiling. Then Nadia says, as herself, in her own words rather than those of her psychology training or anyone else: 'But you know what, Zara? I've learned that it helps to talk about it. Unfortunately I think most people would still get more sympathy from their colleagues and bosses at work if they show up looking rough one morning and say "I'm hung-over" than if they say "I'm suffering from anxiety". But I think we pass people in the street every day who feel the same as you and I, many of them just don't know what it is. Men and women going around for months having trouble breathing and seeing doctor after doctor because they think there's something wrong with their lungs. All because it's so damn difficult to admit that something else is . . . broken. That it's an ache in our soul, invisible lead weights in our blood, an indescribable pressure in our chest. Our brains are lying to us, telling us we're going to die. But there's nothing wrong with our lungs, Zara. We're not going to die, you and I.'

The words drift around between them, dancing invisibly on their retinas before the silence takes them. *We're not going to die. We're not going to die. We're not going to die, you and I.*

'Yet!' Zara eventually points out, and the psychologist bursts out laughing.

'Do you know what, Zara? Maybe you could get a new job writing mottos for fortune cookies?' She smiles.

'The only note a cake-eater needs to find is "this is why you're fat" . . . ,' Zara replies. Then she laughs, too, but the quivering tip of her nose gives her away. Her gaze darts first through the window, then it sneaks back to glance at Nadia's hands, then her neck, then her chin, never quite up to her eyes, but almost. The silence that follows is the longest they've shared. Zara closes her eyes, presses her lips together, and the skin beneath her eyes finally gives way. Her terror forms itself into fragile drops and sets off towards the edge of the desk.

Very slowly she lets the envelope slip out of her hand. The psychologist picks it up hesitantly. Zara wants to whisper that it was because of the letter that she came here, that very first time, when exactly ten years had passed since the man jumped. That she needs someone to read out loud what he wrote to her, and then, when her chest has caught fire, stop her from jumping herself.

She wants to whisper the whole thing, about the bridge and about

Nadia, and how Zara watched as the boy came running over and saved her. And how she has spent every single day since then thinking about the difference between people. But all she manages to say is: 'Nadia . . . you . . . I . . .'

Nadia feels like embracing the older woman on the other side of the desk, hugging her, but she doesn't dare. So instead, while Zara keeps her eyes closed, the psychologist gently slips her little finger beneath the back of the envelope and opens it. She pulls out a ten-year-old handwritten note. Four words.

70

The bridge is covered with ice, sparkling beneath the last few valiant stars as dawn heaves its way over the horizon. The town is breathing deeply around it, still asleep, swaddled in eiderdowns and dreams and tiny feet belonging to hearts our own can't beat without.

Zara is standing by the railing. She leans forward, looks over the edge. It almost looks, just for a single, solitary moment, as if she's going to jump. But if anyone had seen her, had known the whole of her story and everything that had happened in the past few days . . . well, then of course it would have been obvious that she wasn't going to do that. No one goes through all this just to end a story that way. She isn't the sort who jumps.

And then?

Then she lets go.

The drop is further than you realize, even if you've just been standing up there. It takes longer than you think to hit the surface. A gentle scraping sound, wind seizing hold of paper, the fluttering and crumpling as the letter drifts out across the water. The fingertips that have held that envelope ten thousand times since they first picked it up from the doormat give up their struggle and let the letter sail off towards its own eternity.

The man who sent it to her ten years ago wrote down everything he thought she needed to know. It was the last thing he ever told anyone. Only four words in length, no more than that. The four biggest little words one person, anyone at all, can say to another:

It wasn't your fault.

By the time the letter hits the water Zara is already walking away, towards the far side of the bridge. There's a car parked there, waiting for her. Lennart is sitting inside it. Their eyes meet when she opens the door. He lets her put the music on as loud as she wants. She's planning to do her absolute utmost to get tired of him.

71

They say that a person's personality is the sum of their experiences. But that isn't true, at least not entirely, because if our past was all that defined us, we'd never be able to put up with ourselves. We need to be allowed to convince ourselves that we're more than the mistakes we made yesterday. That we are all of our next choices, too, all of our tomorrows.

The girl always thought that the weirdest thing was that she could never be angry with her mum. The glass surrounding that feeling was impossible to break. After the funeral she did the cleaning, pulling empty gin bottles from all the hiding places she never had the heart to tell her mum she already knew about. Perhaps that's the last lifeline an addicted parent clings to, the idea that their child probably doesn't know. As if the chaos could possibly be hidden. *It can't even be buried*, the daughter thought, *it just gets handed down*.

Once her mum slurred in her ear: 'Personality is just the sum of our experiences. Don't let anyone tell you otherwise. So don't you worry, my little princess, you won't get your heart broken because you come from a broken home. You won't grow up to be a romantic, because children from broken homes don't believe in everlasting love.' She fell asleep on her daughter's shoulder on the sofa, and her daughter covered her with a blanket and wiped the spilled gin from the floor. 'You're wrong, Mum,' she whispered in the darkness, and she was right. No one robs a bank for their children's sake unless they're a romantic.

Because the girl grew up and had girls of her own. One monkey, one frog. She tried to be a good mum, even though she didn't have an instruction manual. A good wife, a good employee, a good person. She was terrified of failing every second of every day, but she did genuinely believe that everything was going well for a while. Fairly well, anyway. She relaxed, she wasn't prepared, so infidelity and divorce hit her hard in the back of the head. Life knocked her flat. That happens to most of us at some point. Maybe you, too.

A few weeks ago, on the way home from school, the elk and the monkey and the frog all got off the bus as usual and started to walk across the bridge. Halfway across the girls stopped, their mum didn't notice at first, and when she looked back they were ten yards behind her. The monkey and the frog had bought a padlock, they'd seen people attaching them to the railings of bridges in other towns on the Internet. 'If you do that, you lock the love in for ever and then you never stop loving each other!'

Their mum felt crushed, because she thought the girls were worried she was going to stop loving them after the divorce. That everything was going to be different now, that she'd stop being theirs. It took ten minutes of sobbing and confused explanations before the monkey and the frog patiently cupped their mum's cheeks in their hands and whispered: 'We're not worried about losing you, Mum. We just want you to know that you're never going to lose us.'

The lock clicked as they fixed it in place. The monkey threw the key over the railing and it spun down towards the water, and all three of them cried. 'For ever,' the mum whispered. 'For ever,' the girls repeated. As they were walking away the youngest daughter admitted that when she first saw that thing about the padlocks online, she thought they were doing it because they were worried someone might steal the bridge. Then she wondered if they might be worried that someone was going to steal the padlock. Her big sister had to explain it to her, but managed to do so without making her little sister feel stupid. Their mum couldn't help thinking that she and their dad had at least got something right, because the girls were capable of admitting when they were wrong, and of forgiving others when they got things wrong.

They had pizza that evening, the girls' favourite. When they'd fallen asleep on their mattresses on the floor of the little apartment that cost six thousand five hundred a month, and which she at that particular moment had no idea how she was going to pay the next month's rent on, the mum sat up on her own in the darkness. It wasn't long to Christmas, then it would be New Year, she knew how much the girls were looking forward to the fireworks. It was tearing her apart that they still trusted her, unaware of how many things she'd failed at. When dawn came she packed their backpacks, and a notebook fell out of her eldest daughter's. She was about to put it back, but it fell open at a page that began with the words: 'The Princess with Two Kingdoms'. At first the mum felt annoyed, because she had spent their whole lives trying to persuade her daughters not to want to be princesses – she hoped they'd want to be warriors. And because the girls loved their mum, of course they did as she wanted, or at least pretended to, then did the exact opposite, because it's the duty of children not to pay the slightest bit of attention to their parents. The eldest daughter had been told to write a fairy tale of her own for school, so she wrote 'The Princess with Two Kingdoms'. It was about a princess who lived in a big, beautiful castle, and one night the princess found a hole in the floor under her bed, and down inside the hole was a secret magical world full of strange, fantastical creatures, dragons and trolls and other things her daughter must have thought up herself. Things so fantastical that the imagination and flight from reality that lay behind them crushed the mother, because all she kept thinking was: *How terrible must your real life feel to require this much . . . escape?* All the creatures were happy, they lived in peace, and there was no pain in their little world. But the princess in the story soon uncovered a terrible truth: that the magical realm she had found, where all her new friends lived, was actually located between two castles in two different kingdoms. One of them was ruled by a king, the other by a queen, and they were fighting a horrible war against each other. They sent their armies to fight and fire terrible weapons, but the walls of both kingdoms were too tall and strong to give way, and in the end the girl realized that the war wasn't going to destroy either of them. It would just ruin and kill everything that lay between them. And that was when she learned the truth: that the king and queen were her parents. She was their princess, and the entire war was about her, they were each trying to beat the other with the sole aim of winning her back. When the mum read the last words of the story, her daughters were just starting to wake up on their mattresses, and everything that was worth anything inside her shattered. The story ended with the princess saying goodbye to all her new friends and setting off, alone. She disappeared into the darkness one night and never came back again. Because she knew that if she disappeared, there would be nothing left to fight over. That way she would be able to save both kingdoms and the realm in between.

When her daughters had got up, the mum had breakfast with them, trying to act as if nothing were wrong. She dropped them off at school, then walked all the way back, out on to the bridge, and stood there in the middle of it, holding on to the padlock as tightly as she could.

She didn't fight her ex-husband for her old home, she didn't argue with her former boss about her job, she didn't clash with their lawyer, didn't fire any weapons, didn't cause chaos. For the sake of the children. She did all she could to prevent any of the adults' mistakes from affecting them. That doesn't explain why she tried to rob a bank. It doesn't excuse it. But maybe you've had the occasional really bad idea, too. Maybe you deserved a second chance. Maybe you're not alone in that.

On the morning of the day before New Year's Eve she left home with a pistol. That same evening, right now, she is walking back. A few hours after the hostage drama that the town will be talking about for many, many years to come, the mum picks up her daughters and asks: 'Have you had a nice time at Dad's?'

'Yes, Mum! How about you?' the youngest daughter asks.

The mum smiles, thinks for a moment, then shrugs: 'Oh, you

know . . . nothing much has happened. Everything's been the same as usual.'

But as they cross the bridge the mum puts one hand gently on her eldest daughter's shoulder and whispers quickly into her ear: 'You're my princess, and my warrior, you can be both at the same time – promise me that you'll never forget that. I know I'm not always such a great mum, but the fact that your dad and I are getting divorced isn't you . . . you must never think, even for a single second that this is . . . *your* . . .' The eldest daughter nods, blinking away tears. The younger calls to them to hurry up and they run after her, their mum wipes her face and asks if they'd like pizza for supper, and the younger one cries out: 'Do bears poop in the woods, or what?!'

Just after they fall asleep that night, in their mum's new home in the apartment of a kind and just-crazy-enough old lady called Estelle, the eldest daughter takes hold of her mum's hand and whispers: 'You're a good mum, Mum. Don't worry so much. It's okay.'

And there they find it, at last: peace for the realm between the two kingdoms. All the magical, wonderful, made-up creatures can sleep safe and sound. Monkeys, frogs, elks, old ladies, everyone.

72

The new year arrives, which of course never means as much as you hope unless you happen to sell calendars. One day becomes another, now becomes then. Winter spreads out across the town like a relative with slightly too much self-confidence, the building on the other side of the road from the bank changes colour in line with the temperature. It doesn't look like much, of course, a grey building under its temporary white covering in a place where no one seems to choose to live but merely tolerates being stored. In a few years, no doubt one of the locals will point to the door and tell some smug visitor from one of the big cities: 'There was a hostage drama in there once.' The visitor will peer at the building and snort: 'In there? Yeah, right!' Because things like that don't happen in a town like this, everyone knows that.

It's a few days after New Year, and a woman is coming out of the door. She's laughing, her two daughters are with her, and they've just said something that's made them all laugh so hard that their noses are dripping amid the swirling snowflakes. They walk to the bin and dispose of a pizza box, then the woman suddenly looks up and stops mid-stride. One of her daughters starts to climb up her while the other one bounces up and down.

It's getting late, the sky is January-black and the falling snow is obscuring visibility, but she sees the police car on the other side of the street. Inside it are an older and a younger police officer. She stares at them, her daughters haven't noticed her terror yet. All she can think is: *Not in front of the girls*. This takes a matter of seconds, but she manages to live two lifetimes. Theirs.

Then the police car rolls slowly towards her.

Past her.

It drives on, turns right, disappears.

'I'd understand if you want to bring her in,' Jim says quietly in the passenger seat, worried that his son's changed his mind.

'No, I just wanted to see her, so there were two of us in this,' his son says behind the wheel.

'Two of us in what?'

'Letting her go.'

They don't say any more about her. Either the woman outside the building or the one they both miss. Jim saved a bank robber and deceived his son, and Jack might perhaps never quite be able to forgive him for that, but it's possible for them both to move on together despite that.

They drive through their town for several minutes until the father eventually says, without looking at his son: 'I know you've been offered a job in Stockholm.'

Jack looks at him in surprise.

'How the hell did you hear that?'

'I'm not stupid, you know. Not all the time, anyway. Sometimes I just seem stupid.'

Jack smiles shamefacedly.

'I know, Dad.'

'You ought to take it. The job.'

Jack signals, turns, takes plenty of time to come up with a reply.

'Take a job in Stockholm? Do you know how much it costs to live there?'

His dad taps the plastic door of the glove compartment sadly with his wedding ring.

'Don't stay here for my sake, son.'

'I'm not,' Jack lies.

Because he knows that if his mum had been there, she'd have

said, 'You know what, son? There are worse reasons to stay somewhere.'

'Our shift's over,' Jim notes.

'Would you like coffee?' Jack asks.

'Now? It's a bit late,' his dad yawns.

'Let's stop and get coffee,' Jack insists.

'What for?'

'I thought we could pick my car up from the station and go for a
drive.'

'Where to?'

Jack makes his answer sound obvious.

'To see my sister.'

At that, Jim's eyes lose their focus on his son and slide off towards
the road.

'What? Now?'

'Yes.'

'Why . . . why now?'

'It'll soon be her birthday. It'll soon be your birthday. There are
only eleven months to go before Christmas. Does it make any damn
difference why? I just thought she might like to come home.'

Jim has to stay focused on the road, the white line running along
the middle of it, to keep his voice under control.

'That's at least a twenty-four-hour drive, though?'

Jack rolls his eyes.

'What the hell, Dad? I said we'd stop for coffee!'

So that's what they do. They drive all night and all the following day.
Knock on her door. Maybe she'll go home with them, maybe she
won't. Maybe she's ready to find a better way down, maybe she now
knows the difference between how it feels to fly and how it feels to fall,
maybe she doesn't. That sort of thing's impossible to control, just like
love. Because perhaps it's true what they say, that up to a certain age
a child loves you unconditionally and uncontrollably for one simple

reason: you're theirs. Your parents and siblings can love you for the rest of your life, too, for precisely the same reason.

The truth. There isn't any. All we've managed to find out about the boundaries of the universe is that it hasn't got any, and all we know about God is that we don't know anything. So the only thing a mum who was a priest demanded of her family was simple: that we do our best. We plant an apple tree today, even if we know the world is going to be destroyed tomorrow.

We save those we can.

73

Spring arrives. It always finds us, in the end. The wind sweeps winter away, the trees rustle and birds start making a fuss, and nature suddenly crashes through with a deafening roar where the snow has swallowed every echo for months.

Jack gets out of a lift, bewildered and curious. He's clutching a letter in his hand. It landed on his doormat one morning, without a stamp. Inside was a note with this address on it, as well as the floor of the building and office number. Beneath that was a photograph of the bridge and another envelope, sealed, with another name written on it.

Zara saw Jack at the police station and recognized him, in spite of the years that had passed. And because she's been living those same moments over and over again since then, she realized that he's been doing the same.

Jack finds the right office, knocks on the door. Ten years have passed since a man jumped, almost exactly the same amount of time since a young woman didn't. She opens the door without knowing who he is, but his heart turns to confetti the moment he sees her, because he hasn't forgotten. He hasn't seen her since she was standing on the railing of the bridge, but he would still have recognized her, even in darkness.

'I . . . I . . . ,' Jack stammers.

'Hello? Are you looking for someone?' Nadia wonders, friendly but bemused.

He has to reach out for the doorframe, and her fingertips brush his. They don't yet know how they're capable of affecting each other. He hands her the large envelope, with his name written untidily on the front, and inside are the photograph of the bridge and the address of her office. Beneath those are the smaller envelope with *For Nadia* written on the outside. Inside is a small note, on which Zara had written, in considerably neater handwriting, nine simple words.

You saved yourself. He just happened to be there.

When Nadia loses her balance, just for a moment, Jack catches hold of her arm. Their eyes dance around each other. She clings tightly, tightly, tightly to those nine words, but barely manages to formulate any of her own: 'It was you . . . on the bridge, when I . . . was that you?'

He nods mutely. She fumbles for more words.

'I don't know what to . . . just give me a moment. I need to . . . I need to compose myself.'

She walks to her desk and sinks on to the chair. She's spent ten years wondering who he was, and now she has no idea what to say. Where to start. Jack walks cautiously into the office after her, sees the photograph on the bookcase, the one Zara always adjusted when she was there. It's a picture of Nadia and a group of children, at a big summer camp six months before. Nadia and the children are laughing and joking, and they're all wearing matching T-shirts bearing the name of the charitable organization that funded the camp. It collects money to work with children like the ones in the picture, all of whom have lost a family member to suicide. It helps to know that you're not alone when you've been left behind. You can't carry the guilt and the shame and the unbearable silence on your own, and you shouldn't have to, that's why Nadia goes to the summer camp each year. To listen a lot, talk a little and laugh as much as possible.

She doesn't know it yet, but the charity has just received a donation to its bank account. From a woman with headphones who has resigned from her job, given away her fortune and crossed a bridge. They'll be able to hold those summer camps for many years to come.

* * *

Jack and Nadia sit on either side of the narrow desk, looking at each other. He smiles weakly, and after a while she does the same, simultaneously terrified and full of laughter. One day, in ten years' time, perhaps they'll tell someone that was how it felt. The first time.

74

The truth? The truth about all this? The truth is that this was a story about many different things, but most of all about idiots. Because we're doing the best we can, we really are. We're trying to be grown up and love each other and understand how the hell you're supposed to insert USB leads. We're looking for something to cling on to, something to fight for, something to look forward to. We're doing all we can to teach our children how to swim. We have all of this in common, yet most of us remain strangers, we never know what we do to each other, how your life is affected by mine.

Perhaps we hurried past each other in a crowd today, and neither of us noticed, and the fibres of your coat brushed against mine for a single moment and then we were gone. I don't know who you are.

But when you get home this evening, when this day is over and the night takes us, allow yourself a deep breath. Because we made it through this day as well.

There'll be another one along tomorrow.

AUTHOR'S THANKS

J. Very few people have had the effect on my life that you have. The kindest, strangest, funniest, messiest, most complicated friend I've ever had. Almost twenty years have passed now, and I still think about you almost every day. I'm so sorry you couldn't bear it any longer. I hate myself for not being able to save you.

Neda. Twelve years together, ten years married, two children, and a million rows about wet towels on the floor and feelings we're still trying to find words for. I don't know how you've managed to juggle two careers, yours and mine, but without you I wouldn't be standing here now. I know I drive you crazy, but I'm crazy about you. Ducks fly together.

The monkey and the frog. I'm trying to be a good dad. I really am. But when you jumped in the car and asked, 'What's that smell? Are you eating sweets?' I lied. Sorry.

Niklas Natt och Dag. I don't know how many years we've been sharing an office. Eight? Nine? I can honestly say I've never known a genius, but you are the closest I've come. I've never had a brother, either.

Riad Haddouche, Junes Jaddid and **Erik Edlund.** I don't say it as often as I should. But I hope you know.

Mum and **Dad, my sister** and **Paul. Houshang, Parham** and **Meri.**

Vanja Vinter. Stubborn as hell since 2013, and the only person who's worked with me throughout almost all my career. Editor, proofreader, extra pair of eyes, a whirlwind, and a really good friend for all of my stories. Thank you for always giving one hundred per cent.

The Salomonsson Agency. Most of all, of course, my agent **Tor Jonasson**, who doesn't always understand what the hell I'm playing at but always defends me just as doggedly. **Marie Gyllenhammar**, who has been like an extra member of the family when the machinery and circus spin too fast and I'm trying to find myself. **Cecilia Imberg**, who acted as an extra proofreader and linguistic adviser towards the end of this project. (In those instances where we disagreed about grammar, obviously you were right, but sometimes I make mistakes just for the hell of it.)

Bokförlaget Forum, my publishers in Sweden. In particular **John Häggblom, Maria Burlin, Adam Dahlin** and **Sara Lindegren.**

Alex Schulman, who, when I was trying to make this book work, reminded me how it can feel when a text completely floors you. **Christoffer Carlsson**, who read and corrected and laughed. I owe you a beer. Maybe two. **Marcus Leifby**, my absolute first choice when I need to drink coffee and talk about Division 2 ice hockey and Vietnam War documentaries for six hours on a Tuesday.

All the publishers in other countries who publish my books, from Scandinavia to South Korea. In particular, I'd like to thank **Peter Borland, Libby McGuire, Kevin Hanson, Ariele Fredman, Rita Silva** and everyone else who has stubbornly continued to have faith in me over at Atria Books/Simon & Schuster in the USA and Canada, and **Judith Curr**, who helped me to get there. You've become my second-home market.

Everyone who has translated my books, in particular **Neil Smith**. My cover designer, **Nils Olsson**. My favourite bookseller, **Johan Zillén**.

The psychologists and therapists who have worked with me in recent years. In particular, **Bengt**, who helped me get to grips with my panic attacks.

You. For reading this. Thank you for your time.

Finally: the authors Estelle refers to at various points in this story. In order of appearance, they are: Astrid Lindgren (page 248), J. M. Barrie (page 248), Charles Dickens (page 258), Joyce Carol Oates (page 258), Kahlil Gibran (page 259), William Shakespeare (page 281), Leo Tolstoy (page 304) and Bodil Malmsten (pages 305 and 313). If any of them has been misquoted, the fault is mine alone, or possibly my translator's, but certainly not Estelle's.